The Secret Kiss of Darkness

The Secret Kiss of Darkness

Christina Courtenay

W F HOWES LTD

ESSEX COUNTY COUNCIL LIBRARIES

This large print edition published in 2014 by
W F Howes Ltd
Unit 4, Rearsby Business Park, Gaddesby Lane,
Rearsby, Leicester LE7 4YH

1 3 5 7 9 10 8 6 4 2

First published in the United Kingdom in 2014
by Choc Lit Limited

A CIP catalogue record for this book is available
from the British Library

ISBN 978 1 47125 992 0

Typeset by Palimpsest Book Production Limited,
Falkirk, Stirlingshire

Printed and bound in Great Britain
by TJ International Ltd, Padstow, Cornwall

MIX
Paper from
responsible sources
FSC® C013056
www.fsc.org

To my three lovely aunts –
Görel Larsson, Christina Jelmhag and
Barbara Andrews.
With lots of love.

AUTHOR'S NOTE

The characters in this novel are all fictitious, except for the artists Thomas Gainsborough and his nephew Gainsborough Dupont. They really did tour the West Country on at least two occasions, although obviously they never painted any portraits such as the ones in my book.

I have tried to keep the character of Thomas Gainsborough the same as the way he is described in biographies of him, and some of the things he says are apparently more or less his exact sentiments. While reading about him, I got the feeling he would have relished stumbling upon an intrigue and secret such as Jago and Eliza's, and he seemed a very likeable man. I hope I have done him justice.

PROLOGUE

He'd sworn he would wait an eternity for her if he had to, on the assumption that the waiting would eventually be rewarded. But years, centuries passed with no end in sight and he was beginning to despair. To doubt. Would they ever be reunited?

He drifted in and out of the darkness that held him captive, sometimes conscious of things going on around him, sometimes just listening. He learned how the world was changing, evolving into a more tolerant society than the one he'd lived in. It gave him hope, but also made him sad. If only things had been like that in his day.

The scent of honeysuckle and roses unexpectedly jolted him out of the shadows and he looked at the woman standing before him, staring with rapt attention. It wasn't *her*, his lost love, but there were similarities and that perfume teased at his nostrils, bringing bittersweet memories. He felt hope well up inside him once more, stronger this time. Perhaps it was a sign? *Yes*. It had to be.

She walked away, but she would be back, he was sure of it. He smiled as he returned to the secret kiss of darkness.

CHAPTER 1

London 2013

*W*hat on earth am I doing here? I must have been out of my mind to come . . .

Kayla Sinclair fidgeted in her seat, a prey to conflicting emotions. A part of her wanted desperately to stay in the auction room at Sotheby's in New Bond Street, but the rational half knew it was wrong. She really shouldn't be here.

It was surprisingly noisy. Prospective buyers murmured amongst themselves and staff spoke quietly to telephone bidders, creating a constant background buzz. Kayla barely registered this, however, as the sound of her own heart hammering in her ears blocked out everything else. She took a deep breath and tried to concentrate on the auctioneer's next words. He had a loud voice, deep and carrying, which penetrated even Kayla's temporarily deficient hearing.

'And now we come to Lot number three hundred and four,' he announced, but the rest of his sentence was drowned by the sudden rush of blood inside Kayla's head. Two men wearing dark blue aprons brought in a large painting and, with some manoeuvring, managed to hold it upright between them, standing to the right of the podium.

Kayla looked down at her lap where the numbered paddle for bidding rested on top of the sale catalogue. Why had she bothered to obtain one? 'I'm not buying anything. I am definitely not buying anything,' she chanted silently to herself and took another deep breath. The noise inside her head subsided and she registered the fact that the auctioneer had begun to take bids.

'Starting now at five thousand pounds. Do I have five thousand?' He scanned the crowd for signs of raised paddles.

Kayla felt her body grow cold.

'I have five thousand five hundred on my right, six thousand the lady near the aisle . . .'

She began to shake, but almost as if it had a will of its own, her right hand raised itself and her bid was acknowledged.

'Seven thousand, the blonde lady at the back.'

Oh hell, that's me. Kayla closed her eyes, not wanting to believe what she'd just done.

'Ah, seven thousand five hundred, do I have eight thousand?'

Kayla grabbed her right hand with the left and held on to it in a childish effort to restrain it. She mustn't buy this painting. It would be sheer madness. For one thing, it was too large and for another . . . no, it just wouldn't do. Perhaps if she tried to concentrate on something else it would take her mind off the proceedings? She turned to study the people around her, looking everywhere except directly at the painting. That way lay danger.

She had never been to an auction before and had had a vague idea that only very rich people went to such events, but the audience was an unexpected mixture. There were ladies in Chanel outfits, dripping with jewellery, and men in expensive tailored suits, but Kayla could also see quite a few rather scruffy individuals. One man in particular looked as if he couldn't afford his next meal, never mind thousands of pounds worth of art, but just then he raised his hand to make a bid.

'Ten thousand the gentleman to my left, ten thousand five hundred, anyone?'

Resolutely ignoring the auctioneer, Kayla continued to look around the room. As she wasn't very tall she had to crane her neck to see the gleaming mahogany podium at the front. To her right a row of desks, manned by staff taking telephone bids, were equally shiny, and she found the whole set-up intimidating. Its occupants looked down on the bidders and Kayla felt like a lesser mortal. She shouldn't have come. She really didn't belong here. But she'd had no choice. Had she?

'Do I have twelve thousand?'

Twelve thousand! That was a huge amount of money. But it was worth every penny. She glanced at the painting, then made another effort to look around the room instead. An enormous skylight let in the pale spring sunshine, aiding the artificial lighting which illuminated the artwork that was hung around the walls. She wondered why none of them appealed to her. The only one she wanted was the one being sold at the moment. Her right hand came up, with the left one still holding on to it, as if someone was pulling an invisible string.

No, this was ridiculous. But she couldn't stop it.

'Ah, twelve thousand the blonde lady at the back, twelve thousand five hundred? Do I have twelve thousand five hundred?' The voice droned on, and Kayla concentrated desperately on the huge board near the ceiling, which showed the present bid in pounds sterling as well as in several other currencies. The amounts changed and the conversions followed automatically. She saw that the bidding was now up to sixteen thousand pounds, but seemed to have slowed down. *Sixteen thousand pounds.* That was definitely more than she could afford, which was just as well, she told herself, and tried to suppress the disappointment welling up inside her.

'I have sixteen thousand pounds,' the auctioneer informed them, and lifted his gavel.

The mounting excitement in the audience was almost tangible as a hush fell on the room. Was this to be the final price? Everyone seemed to hold their collective breath, including Kayla.

She quickly raised her hand again. Surely she could afford an extra thousand pounds somehow? *I'll buy a cheaper wedding dress.*

'Right, sixteen thousand five hundred, with the

blonde lady at the back.' The man lowered the gavel and scanned the room for any further bids. 'And seventeen thousand, the gentleman on my right. Seventeen thousand five hundred anyone? Yes, I have seventeen thousand five hundred, ladies and gentlemen.' He paused once more.

The heavy catalogue fell out of Kayla's suddenly numb fingers, but with a supreme effort she managed to raise her hand yet again. As the auctioneer nodded, a lead weight sank into her stomach.

'Eighteen thousand. I have eighteen thousand, lady at the back.' No one moved and Kayla continued to hold her breath. Would anyone make a last minute bid? The tension was unbearable. She wanted to scream, 'Please, somebody, outbid me! I promise I'll leave straight away. Someone, do something!'

No one moved so much as a finger.

'All done then at eighteen thousand. Selling at . . .' the man waited a few moments more, '. . . eighteen thousand pounds.' The gavel descended with a crack, which made Kayla jump even though she saw it coming. Her heart was beating so hard she thought it might leave her ribcage any minute. Feeling very self-conscious she held up her paddle. 'To bidder number five hundred and sixteen.'

Kayla closed her eyes and breathed rapidly, panic assailing her from all directions. *Oh God, what have I done?* How was she going to explain this? How was she going to pay for it?

Eighteen thousand pounds. That was at least three thousand more than she could afford. There was no going back, however, her bid had been acknowledged. In a daze she stood up and made her way to the desk in the next room to make her payment. She wondered if she'd be arrested or something if she suddenly changed her mind and said she didn't want the painting after all? The thought made her want to giggle hysterically and she made a heroic effort to pull herself together.

'Number five hundred and sixteen, is it? Right, that'll be eighteen thousand pounds then, please.' The woman's brisk and businesslike tone kick-started Kayla's frozen brain. She recovered sufficiently to haul out her cheque book from her handbag and write out the amount with trembling fingers.

'Your cheque will take approximately three days to clear and we'll keep the painting at our ware-house until then before delivering it to you. Thank you very much. I hope you enjoy your purchase.'

The hysterical laughter bubbled up inside Kayla once more and she swallowed hard to keep it down. Enjoy her purchase? Yes, the way some people enjoyed drugs perhaps – illicitly, guiltily. But it was done and the time for regrets had passed. With an outward calm she was far from feeling, she discussed delivery times and terms before leaving the building.

CHAPTER 2

Devon 1781

The path leading up to Marcombe Hall from the coast was steep but Jago Kerswell took it in his stride. Two casks of brandy roped together were slung over his powerful shoulders, bumping his chest and back at every step, but even with this extra load he carried on as if he was out for a Sunday stroll. The darkness was almost absolute, as the sliver of a moon had disappeared behind thick clouds, and he could see only vague outlines of trees and bushes along the path. The deep shadows had cloaked the nefarious activity he and his fellow smugglers had been engaged upon this night and all had gone well. Jago was pleased.

With the surefootedness of an animal with night vision, he continued up the steep incline. He knew these paths like the back of his hand and had no need to see where he was going. He could have done it blindfolded. As he neared the edge of the gardens of the Hall, he calculated rapidly how much profit would be made from tonight's run.

A grin of satisfaction tugged at the corners of his mouth. Even after Sir John had received his cut for turning a blind eye – the two casks Jago was carrying – Jago's men and their families would live well for a while, once the contraband had been sold in London. Some of the goods were even now making their way towards Lambeth, while the rest would await their turn in various hiding places. He almost chuckled out loud. If the good Reverend Mountford knew what the bottom of his pulpit contained he would have an apoplexy.

Still lost in thought, Jago turned the corner of a hedge and was almost knocked off balance as a small white shape hurtled into him with tremendous speed. He gasped and came to an abrupt halt.

'Oh, ow!' From the sound of the voice he deduced it was a female, and her forehead had connected violently with the cask hanging in front of him. She ricocheted back to land on her backside with a thud. Jago heard her moan softly.

'Damnation woman! What are you doing out in the middle of the night? Have you no sense?' Jago hissed. Anger warred with compassion as he hefted the casks over his head and set them down onto the ground next to her. He stretched out a hand, encountered an arm and pulled her upright. 'Are you badly hurt? Let me see, please.' Since he couldn't actually see anything, he reached out and found her forehead. Gently, belying his angry words, he pried loose her hands, and his questing

10

fingers felt a large protrusion. She sucked in her breath and jerked her head away.

'It . . . it's nothing, sir,' she stammered, trying to back away from him. He gripped her right shoulder with one hand to prevent her from leaving.

'My lady,' he began, for indeed it could be none other than the lady of Marcombe Hall herself, as she was the only woman in the neighbourhood who spoke with such cultured accents. 'I don't know what possessed you to go wandering about the gardens in the middle of the night, but I would suggest you return to the house immediately. And find something to put on that egg you're now sporting on your forehead. A piece of raw meat might do the trick. Even so, I fear you'll have some explaining to do tomorrow.'

She shook his hand off impatiently and succeeded only because he let her. 'Thank you for your advice, sir, but I am going for a walk along the cliffs.' Her voice was trembling, but sounded haughty and defiant, with an almost desperate undertone.

'A walk? Now? In nothing but your shift? Really, my lady, I don't think—'

'I'm not concerned with what you think, my good man, and besides I am wearing a perfectly respectable gown. Well, I've brought my shawl anyway, and who's to tell in the dark? Now, why don't you return to your own business before you are caught and leave me to get on with mine.' She turned away from him, but stopped as he spoke again.

'You know what I'm doing?'

'Certainly I do. You're a smuggler. Why else would you be carrying brandy kegs about your person in the middle of the night?'

'We prefer to think of ourselves as free-traders, my lady.' He chuckled briefly, amused by her bravado. 'Be that as it may, have you given any thought to the fact that I might not be the only one about this night? Free-traders operate in groups and most of them are a rough lot. There's no saying what they might do if they catch sight of a lone female wandering about the cliffs in her night clothes.'

She let out a mirthless little laugh. 'I am past caring,' she replied airily. 'I can't stay in that house another minute. Anyway,' she muttered, 'they can do no worse than John, I suppose.' She started to walk away once more, passing him with a swish of soft material that brushed against his breeches, but he caught up with her within seconds, and turned her around abruptly by means of a vice-like grip on her arm.

'What exactly has my sainted brother done now?' he growled. 'Is he beating you?'

'Your brother? What has he to do with anything?' She struggled to free herself again, but her puny efforts went unheeded as this time he held fast.

'Your husband, my lady, is my half-brother. Perhaps he forgot to mention that?'

She stilled instantly. 'Half-brother? But . . . but what . . . how? I don't understand. You are a smuggler and John is . . . well, he is . . .'

It was his turn to laugh. 'I beg your pardon, my lady, I shouldn't have mentioned it. I am but a bastard. Sir John's father sired me after his wife had died, but of course your husband has never acknowledged the relationship openly. I thought he might at least have told his own wife, but obviously I was wrong. You had better not refer to it.'

The thin moon came out briefly and he saw that she stood rooted to the spot, peering into the darkness as if seeking enlightenment. Finally she said, 'You're telling the truth?'

'Why should I lie about being a bastard? Ask anyone hereabouts, they'll tell you exactly what happened. It wasn't a secret at the time.' He let go of her arm and made her an exaggerated bow, although as the moon had disappeared once more she probably couldn't see him. 'Jago Kerswell, at your service, my lady. I'm the proprietor of the King's Head Inn down in the village. Feel free to make enquiries about me.'

'No, no, I believe you. Indeed, why should you lie?'

'As you say. Now tell me, please, Lady . . . what's your name?'

'Elizabeth. Eliza to my family.'

'Very well, Lady Eliza . . .'

'No, no, Mr Kerswell, you can't call me that.

13

I'm not a lady in my own right. I'm Lady Marcombe only by virtue of my husband being a "Sir".'

'And I'm a free-trader, Lady Eliza, I don't concern myself with such niceties. Now where was I? Oh, yes, tell me what my dear brother has been up to. Is he cruel to you? Is that why nobody ever sees you out and about? You are ashamed of the bruises?'

There was no immediate reply but he heard her draw in a sharp breath as if he'd hit upon an uncomfortable truth.

'Lady Eliza?' he prompted, his voice stern, but kind.

'I . . . that is, I would prefer not to speak of such things to a stranger.'

'Stranger? But have we not just established I'm family?' He hoped she could hear that he was smiling, but thinking about the topic of discussion he grew serious once more. 'Now, come, my dear lady, tell me what made you dash into the night in such a fashion? I really can't permit my sister-in-law to wander about alone.'

To his utter dismay the lady didn't answer him, but burst into tears. Absolute floods of tears at that, and Jago began to wish he'd kept his mouth shut for once. If there was one thing he had no idea how to cope with, it was a woman crying.

'Oh hell! Begging your pardon, but . . .' He ran a hand distractedly through his hair, which was dishevelled enough from the sea breeze already and coming loose from its queue. This was not turning out to be such a perfect night after all. He had exulted too soon. Well, there was only one thing he could possibly do under the circumstances.

With a sigh, he put his arms around Lady Eliza and pulled her close, rocking her like a child and whispering soothing words. The sobs racked her small body for a considerable time, but he did nothing to stop them. He knew it was cleansing, she had to let the anguish out. Only then could he find its cause. And find it he must.

CHAPTER 3

'Where on earth have you been? I was going to take you out for lunch today since it's the only day I'm free this week.' The impatient voice of her boss, Mike Russell, greeted Kayla as she entered the office and she stared at him in surprise.

'Oh, I'm sorry, you should have said.' She managed to answer him in a fairly calm and reasonable tone, despite the fact that she was still shaking from her recent ordeal. 'But today was the auction, remember? I did tell you I was going. That's why I took the morning off.'

'Oh, the auction. Damn, I'd forgotten. Sorry.' He frowned and raked long fingers through his fair hair, making it stand on end, then bent to kiss her when no one else was looking. Mike wasn't just her boss, he was her fiancé as well, but ever since he'd been made a partner in the law firm they both worked for, he had become self-conscious about open displays of affection.

'We really must be seen to act professionally at all times now I'm a senior member of staff,' he'd told Kayla, and although she privately thought that surely it didn't matter since everyone knew they were a couple anyway, she had reluctantly gone along with this. Today, however, it irritated her, but she didn't say anything. It wasn't Mike's fault she was a trembling wreck after all.

Kayla hung up her coat on a hanger behind the door and shook out her shoulder-length hair before sinking down onto the seat behind her desk. To occupy her still shaking hands, she sorted through the day's workload, while taking deep breaths to calm her erratic heartbeat.

'Which tape do you want me to do first? This one?' she asked. There were two piles of files, each with a small audio cassette perched on top, and she pointed to the nearest one.

'What? Oh, it doesn't matter. Either. They've both got to be finished before this evening.' He still seemed a bit irritated and Kayla knew he hated to have his plans disrupted, but honestly, he hadn't mentioned anything about lunch. Or had he? A flash of guilt shot through her. She had been rather preoccupied these last two weeks . . .

It was all Auntie Emily's fault. She had died just before Christmas and left all her nephews and nieces a legacy of fifteen thousand pounds each. Kayla's portion had arrived in her bank account only two weeks previously, and she had by then decided what she wanted to do with the money.

'I think I'll buy myself a painting or an antique. Something which will increase in value, but at the same time be decorative,' she'd told Mike. Even though it was her money to do with as she wished, she thought it best to at least discuss the matter with him. After all, everything they had would soon be owned jointly once they were married.

'Are you sure?' he asked. 'Don't you think it would be better to invest it in shares or something? It takes years before you can sell an antique and make a profit, but with shares you would receive regular dividends.'

Deep down Kayla knew he was right. It would be a more practical option, but something inside her rebelled against the idea. It seemed mercenary and clinical and she was sure Auntie Emily had meant for her to enjoy her legacy by indulging herself in one way or another.

'No, I want something I can see. Something to remind me of Auntie Em,' she insisted.

'Well, I suppose I can't stop you. It's your money after all.' Mike's displeasure had been clear, but for once Kayla ignored him. It *was* her money and she intended to spend it her way.

Her mind made up, Kayla had gone to visit Sotheby's, the famous auction house, which was only a few streets away from the solicitor's office in Mayfair where she and Mike worked. She'd passed the building almost every day on her way to work, but had never entered it before. As she approached this ancient establishment for the first time, it was with a slight feeling of trepidation.

Just inside the double doors was a small, dark

foyer, where a uniformed doorman greeted her. She smiled at him hesitantly and continued straight on into the main reception area, which was spacious and bright. There was a large desk in the middle of one wall and Kayla almost tiptoed over, feeling seriously out of place.

'Excuse me, but do you have a calendar of upcoming auctions, please?' she asked the lady on duty.

'Yes, of course, madam.' She was handed a little leaflet and sat down on a red leather sofa to have a look at it.

It seemed there would be a sale of British paintings within the next two weeks, and Kayla thought it best to buy the catalogue. She almost fainted when she was told the price, but didn't have the nerve to tell the lady she thought it too expensive, so she paid quickly and left.

Most of the paintings listed in the catalogue were way above her means, but Kayla went back to have a look the next day anyway. As she mounted the U-shaped staircase, which led upstairs to the viewing galleries on the first floor, the excitement took hold and she started to enjoy herself. She walked slowly round the rooms, stopping from time to time in front of a particularly lovely piece of art. There were some pretty landscapes, but nothing that really caught her fancy and none of them gave her that instant urge to buy.

Until she entered the last room.

*   *   *

'Kayla? Kayla, hello, anyone in there?' Mike's voice brought her back to the present with a jolt.

'What? Sorry, I was thinking about something.'

'I *said* did you buy anything then?' He was frowning slightly and drumming his fingers on her desk while waiting for her reply. It was a habit she was used to, as he wasn't the most patient of men, but today Kayla had to restrain the urge to smack them into silence. *God, what's the matter with me?* She took another deep breath to calm herself. It was unlike her to be so irritable, especially with Mike.

'Yes, as a matter of fact I did. I bought a painting.' She felt a guilty blush spread over her cheeks as she remembered exactly how much she had paid for it, but Mike didn't notice.

'Great,' he said, as if her answer hadn't really interested him much, and returned to their previous topic of conversation. 'So, can we have dinner instead? I've hardly seen you all week. I'm sure there must be a thousand things we should be discussing with regard to the wedding. It's not long now.'

'Yes, I know. Five weeks and three days.' She smiled up at him and he shook his head at her. Kayla's count down amused him. She was sure he was just as impatient for their big day to arrive, although she knew he only wanted it out of the way since the whole process was disrupting his orderly life and the endless planning that was necessary drove him crazy. She swallowed a sigh.

Mike wasn't much of a romantic, but then all males probably thought of weddings as a palaver so he wasn't unique.

Unusually, though, a sense of panic shot through Kayla as the words echoed round her brain. Five weeks and three days? That wasn't very long at all. Before this business with the painting, her pre-wedding nerves had been growing steadily as she counted down the days, but she knew it was normal. Today, however, she wondered for the first time why she'd been in such a rush. There was no particular reason why they'd had to marry so quickly. No, what was she thinking? They'd wanted to get married as soon as possible. She shook herself mentally and concentrated on the man in front of her, who was looking at her with raised brows, obviously waiting for a reply again.

'Uhm, I have a bit of a headache today and it looks like you've left me plenty to do here. I might have to work late,' she prevaricated. 'And tomorrow I've promised to go out with Maddie and you've got that dinner at the—'

'Oh, yes. Well, I'd hoped to spend some time with you tonight, but maybe I'll go for a pint with the guys upstairs instead then. You haven't forgotten the party on Saturday, though?'

Kayla almost laughed. 'No, of course not.' As if she could possibly have forgotten about the party his parents were holding in their honour. A gathering of the Russell clan to inspect the latest addition to see if she would pass muster, she thought with an inward grimace. She'd been worrying for weeks about what to wear, but suddenly it didn't seem to matter.

She gave him a placating smile and took hold of his hand, which was still hovering above her desk, giving it a squeeze. 'I'm sorry, Mike. I would have loved to go out tonight, but soon we'll be together every evening, won't we? Once the wedding is over and done with and I've moved into your flat, we'll have plenty of time for ourselves.'

'Yes, you're right.' He bent over the desk to give her another quick kiss, after first looking around again. Kayla felt another twinge of annoyance. What did it matter if anyone saw them? They'd soon be man and wife.

'I'd better get on with this.' She put on the audio headphones and inserted the first tape into the machine, effectively ending the conversation, but Mike hadn't quite finished and tapped her on the shoulder. Reluctantly she freed her ears.

'Yes?'

'Don't forget to do that Local Authority search for the Peterson's house and send it off with the right payment. I promised them it would be done today.'

'It's on my list of things to do.' Kayla gritted her teeth against another sudden wave of irritation as Mike disappeared into his office. She had been a legal secretary for seven years and knew as well as he did what needed to be done, but since his promotion he seemed to feel the need to reinforce his role as the boss from time to time. Sometimes, just sometimes, he annoyed the hell out of her. Another small doubt entered her mind, shattering her former confidence. Was she doing the right thing in marrying him?

'Oh, for heaven's sake, don't be silly,' she muttered. 'Of course you are.'

Kayla dismissed her doubts as pre-wedding jitters, switched on the tape and started to type. Mike's voice droned on, dictating the same kind of letters she had typed a hundred times before, so she continued on automatic and let her thoughts return to her recent purchase. She wondered how soon Sotheby's would deliver it. Within the next few days, perhaps? A quiver of excitement snaked up her back.

The endless letters on the computer screen in front of her blurred and instead her thoughts returned to the first time she saw her painting in all its glory.

CHAPTER 4

Eliza felt fragile in his embrace, but so soft and womanly. Although small in stature, she had a luscious figure, and he was acutely aware of her full breasts pressing against his chest. Jago tried not to hold her quite so close, but she clung to him as if he was the only thing in the world that could save her. He tried to think of other things, but the longer he held her, the more he wanted her. It was impossible to stop his body's reaction to her.

She smelled divine, like honeysuckle and roses combined. Not just her person, but her hair and her skin, too. Jago breathed in deeply, storing her unique scent in his memory. He was sure he'd never forget this night for as long as he lived.

He knew what she looked like. He'd seen her once or twice peering out through the window of the carriage as it passed through the village. She had wispy ash-blonde hair and hazel-green eyes fringed with thick, dark lashes, set in an enchanting little elfin face. There was no doubt that it had been her beauty which had captivated his half-brother, for she had no dowry to speak of, or so

Jago had heard tell. And now she was in his arms, her lovely hair hanging loose over her shoulders, caressing the back of his hands as it was blown about by the breeze from the sea.

When the sobs turned into sniffles, he turned her face up to his with a large calloused hand and lowered his mouth to hers. He kissed her as gently as he knew how. A secret kiss in the darkness that no one would ever know about. He was well aware he shouldn't have done it, but the urge to kiss her was too strong to resist. In her weakened state she didn't fight him, but neither did she kiss him back. He had the strange feeling she had no idea how, indeed had never been kissed properly before, but that couldn't be? Or could it?

'Eliza,' he said quietly. 'Tell me what troubles you. Perhaps I can help you.'

'No. No one can help me,' she whispered back in a voice as bleak as the sea in winter. She held on to him and he breathed in her fragrance again, then fought to control his desire so he could concentrate on her words. 'Marriage is for life. I swore to love, honour and obey, and although I struggle with the first two, I have no choice about the third.'

'I see.' So she didn't love her husband. Well, that wasn't unusual. Most marriages were made for convenience, at least for women of her kind. But there was something else here that wasn't right. 'What is it John wishes you to do? In what way do you have to obey him?'

'He wants me to give him a child. An heir. And I can't. The Lord knows we have tried for two years now. Continuously.' Her voice caught on a sob again, and he quickly kissed her once more to stop another flood of tears. It had the desired effect and this time she responded timidly, her lips moving softly, almost questioningly, under his.

'Do you . . . er, does he not give you pleasure in the process?' he asked, stroking her hair absently.

'Pleasure? I don't understand.' She twisted in his arms as if to try to see his face, but the darkness was almost impenetrable.

'No, perhaps you don't.' He sighed and let go of her. His arms felt empty. 'There should be pleasure in the marriage bed, Lady Eliza, whether there are any children or not, but you were right. In this I can't help you. My brother is a fool.' After a short pause, he added, 'Look, I was serious about the other men. They wouldn't hesitate to attack you and, believe me, it would be worse than anything John could do. Please, go home now and forget we ever had this conversation. It should never have happened.' With a supreme effort he turned away from her and bent to pick up the kegs of brandy. It was one of the hardest things he'd ever had to do.

'Mr Kerswell? Jago?' He heard the hesitation in her voice and held his breath, waiting for her next words, wondering if she had understood him. 'Could you show me?' She put a small hand tentatively on his muscular forearm. He felt her touch burn him like a branding iron and drew a deep steadying breath. He let go of the rope binding the kegs together.

'I beg your pardon, my lady?' He emphasised her title to make her realise the folly of what he thought she was suggesting.

She stood her ground. 'Just once? Could you show me that pleasure? Perhaps it would make it more bearable next time.' Her voice was pitched so low he almost doubted his hearing, but both her hands were feeling their way up the length of his arms now, driving him almost insane with desire.

This was utter madness. He knew it was a plea born out of desperation. John had driven her to the brink with his selfish behaviour. She was obviously not in her right mind and it was Jago's duty to protect her from herself. He clenched his fists. When her searching fingers reached his face and traced its outline it took all his willpower not to drag her into his arms and show her then and there, but he couldn't. He must not.

He seized her by her slight shoulders and shook her roughly. 'Have you taken leave of your senses, woman? Do you know what you're asking?'

She giggled, a slightly hysterical little sound which ended on a sob. 'Yes, I believe I do, but if you don't want me . . .'

Not want her? She was tempting him beyond reason. 'Why me?' he ground out from between gritted teeth. 'You don't even know what I look

27

like.' He knew he was clutching at straws, but his mind refused to function properly when the mere scent of her was tantalising him, distracting him.

'Does it matter? I know that you're an honourable man or you would have used me already. You are also kind and compassionate and honest. What more do I need? I sleep with a man who is none of those things every night.'

He struggled with himself for perhaps another ten seconds, but it was no use. He knew she had won the battle even before it began. There was no way on earth he could resist her invitation, even though he knew he should. He was only human.

'Very well, Eliza, it will be as you wish. I am honoured that you trust me.' He took her tiny soft hand into his and laced his fingers with hers. 'Let us go to the summer house and I will show you the meaning of making love. But only this once. It must never happen again. Do you hear me?'

'Yes, Jago Kerswell, I hear you.' The words were meek, but in her voice he heard excitement and hope.

'Come then.'

Kayla had almost decided to give up on that particular auction when, out of curiosity, she wandered into the final room which seemed to contain only portraits of various sizes. And there in the corner she found it.

The painting she had to have.

A tall, dark man looked down at her almost defiantly, with his arms crossed over a powerful chest and one foot nonchalantly perched on a rock. As she stared into his eyes Kayla found herself unable to turn away. His gaze kept her rooted to the spot, utterly mesmerised, and a strange languor crept into her body as if he had somehow sapped her of all willpower. She wanted nothing more than to stand there and stare at him for the rest of the day. The noises around her faded into the background and nothing existed in that moment except the two of them.

Of an intense, piercing blue colour those eyes seemed to penetrate into her very soul as they gazed into hers in silent challenge, holding her spellbound. She noticed that they'd been painted in such a way that whenever she moved her head, even slightly, the eyes followed her. It was as if he were standing in front of her, watching her. Kayla shivered. It was uncanny. With difficulty she blinked and moved back a few paces to better study the rest of the portrait. She was quite sure it hadn't been included in the catalogue, because she would have noticed it immediately.

She simply had to have him.

She peered at the card on the wall next to the frame. *'Portrait of a Gentleman. English School, late eighteenth century.'* Incredibly the estimated sale price was a mere £10,000, which was much lower than most of the other portraits on sale. Even if the bidding went higher she should be able to

29

afford him. For a long time Kayla stood staring at him, then rational thinking reared its head.

'Where on earth are you going to hang a painting that size?' the little voice inside her asked reasonably. It was a full-length, life-size portrait with quite a lot of background, making it over seven feet tall and at least five feet wide. Impossible. She and Mike were going to share his two bedroom flat in Battersea after they were married and, although it was quite spacious, there wouldn't be anywhere suitable to hang a picture of this magnitude. Besides, Mike's taste ran more to modern art than eighteenth century portraits. She knew even a pretty landscape would probably be relegated to their bedroom.

Mike! Good grief . . . He would think she'd gone mad if she bought this. Kayla took herself severely to task and, after a last regretful glance at the man, she forced herself to leave the gallery.

The following two days, however, had seen her return again and again to gaze at the portrait. She spent her lunch hour there, all thoughts of food forgotten, and popped in on her way home from work. The unknown man occupied her every waking thought and even invaded her dreams at night. She started to wake up each morning feeling bereft, as if something vital was missing. She forgot about Mike, relegated all thoughts about her forthcoming wedding to the back of her mind and performed her duties at work like a zombie. And she couldn't keep away from the auction rooms.

There was a woman on duty at a small desk in one of the viewing galleries and Kayla asked her for more information about the painting.

'Lot three hundred and four did you say?' The woman was very friendly and keyed in the number on her computer to find the necessary data. 'Oh yes, I remember this one, a late addition to the sale. He's that dark-haired man in a red velvet coat, right? Isn't he just divine?' She giggled conspiratorially. Kayla grinned back. The man wasn't classically handsome, but he was definitely attractive. There was something arresting about him, some indefinable quality which drew the eye. His obvious self-confidence perhaps, the 'bad boy' glint in his eyes, or the way he looked as if he could read her innermost thoughts.

'Yes,' Kayla replied. 'That's the one. Can you tell me anything more about the actual painting, though? The artist, its provenance, that sort of thing?'

'Not much, I'm afraid. There was a bit of a to-do about it, I remember. Our experts thought at first it might have been by Gainsborough, or possibly his nephew. But although it looks like his style, it's a bit sloppy in places as if the artist was trying to finish it quickly. There's no signature. We have dated it to around 1780 because of the man's clothing, but there were no other clues to his identity. In fact, it says here the background is "a rather hazy seascape with dark cliffs", which could be anywhere. And the only other items that could be distinguished were some barrels and a pistol. Perhaps the man was a retired soldier turned vintner? I'm sorry, but your guess is as good as mine.'

'I see. Well, thank you very much.'

'Not at all. Good luck in the sale.' The woman smiled broadly and Kayla turned away, blushing like a schoolgirl caught having a crush on the current sixth form heart-throb.

As she headed back to the far gallery, a thought struck her – she *did* have a crush on the man in the painting, in the same way she'd swooned over pop stars during her teens. Just looking at him made her heart beat faster and her legs turn to mush. It was like being hopelessly, passionately in love with the man you wanted to marry.

Like Mike?

She stopped in front of the painting yet again and gazed at that enigmatic face. No, what she felt for Mike didn't even come close to the crazy sensations that washed over her every time she came here. So what on earth did that say about her? About her relationship with her fiancé?

What the hell is wrong with me?

Kayla swallowed hard and closed her eyes. She and Mike would be fine. This was a temporary aberration. Like all crushes it would run its course and she'd return to normal life and her future with her husband-to-be. Her love for him was more ordinary perhaps, down-to-earth, but at least he was real. The man in the painting could never be anything other than a fantasy. Everyone had fantasies, didn't they?

She knew it was crazy, but she just couldn't let anyone else buy him. Although she had tried to stay away from the actual auction, it hadn't worked. And now he belonged to her.

'So there you have it, a full confession of my recent crimes,' Kayla said with a sigh the following evening and took a sip of her drink. She looked at her best friend, Maddie, and waited for the verdict, but for once, uncharacteristically, Maddie remained silent for a long time.

They were seated in a small booth in one of the new wine bars near Maddie's office and thankfully the music hadn't yet been turned up to the level where conversation became impossible. Kayla had poured out the tale of the painting without leaving anything out. She and Maddie had been inseparable since they'd first met on a course for legal secretaries and they didn't have any secrets from each other. If anyone could understand her feelings, it would be Maddie, so her friend's continued silence unnerved Kayla slightly.

'Well?' she prodded anxiously, watching Maddie twirl a long coppery curl around her middle finger.

'I don't really know what to tell you,' Maddie finally said, 'except, I think you're in big trouble.'

'I've figured that out for myself, thank you very much.' Kayla laughed. 'The question is, how do

I go about softening the blow? I've got to tell Mike, obviously, but I don't really know how.'

'You're absolutely sure you want to keep this monstrosity? I mean, you don't even know who this guy is, so it's not like he's an ancestor or anything.' Maddie was frowning, deep in thought. 'Although, that's an idea. Perhaps you should claim that he is? Didn't you have some uncle down in Devon or something who was drawing up your family tree? Blame him.'

'The man in the picture is not a monstrosity. Just wait till you see him. He's incredible! The artist who painted him must have been a genius. Every time I look at him I think he's about to step out of the frame and talk to me. I swear, I thought he winked at me the other day.'

'Well, that's a great help,' Maddie muttered sarcastically.

'No, seriously, I'm not taking him back. I'm keeping him no matter what.' Kayla was adamant, but as she said the words she wasn't entirely sure whether she was trying to convince Maddie or herself. 'Besides, I've nearly bankrupted myself to buy him. I can't back down now.'

'How much overdrawn are you?'

'Not overdrawn exactly, but I had to use up all my savings, as well as the money from Auntie Em, so I'll have to borrow money from my mother to pay for the wedding dress. And if Mike wants a contribution towards the honeymoon, well, that could be a bit tricky.'

'Oh, Kayla.' Maddie shook her head. 'You realise you might be jeopardising your wedding here? What's Mike going to say when he finds out you've spent every penny you have? And on a painting of a handsome bloke?'

'Not handsome exactly, but . . . I don't know.' Kayla hung her head. 'Actually, I was going to ask you something.' She hesitated before plunging on. 'The thing is, yesterday Mike was being really irritating and suddenly I had this feeling that maybe I'm making a huge mistake. How well do I know him really? We've kind of rushed into things, haven't we? I mean, we've only been engaged for a short time and hadn't been going out all that long either when Mike proposed. It seemed like it was meant to be, but now I'm not so sure. What do you—'

'Hang on a minute.' Maddie held up a hand to stop Kayla in mid-flow. 'It's not because of this painting business, is it?'

'No, it has nothing to do with that at all.' Even as she said the words, Kayla knew she was lying. It had everything to do with the mystery man. He'd made her realise that perhaps there was something missing from her real life romance. Something vital. She looked away and thankfully Maddie didn't argue the point.

'Well, you know everyone always gets nervous before their wedding. It's entirely normal. You have to expect it.'

Kayla shook her head. 'I know, but right now I suddenly feel I need more time to think about it.

It happened so quickly – the proposal and all that, I mean – and I was swept up in the preparations before I knew what was going on. Perhaps we should have had a longer engagement, but everyone kept saying there was no point in waiting, and somehow I just went along with it.'

'Oh, stop worrying. You've been going out with the guy for what . . . a year? And you haven't wanted to leave him once in that time. Okay, so maybe Mike isn't the demonstrative kind, but he did propose without you having to prompt him. That's got to mean something, right?' Maddie flashed her a grin to show she was joking. 'Seriously, I'm sure you'll be fine. Everyone has their off days and I bet he's getting a bit jittery himself, you know.'

'Yes, I suppose, although Mike doesn't really get nervous about things. That's what makes him such a good lawyer.'

'This is different, personal. You don't get married every day. It's bound to affect him.'

'Maybe, but then there's this party on Saturday. You know I don't get on too well with his mother and if the rest of his relatives are the same, it's going to be absolute hell.'

'Well, you're not marrying them or her, you're marrying Mike. And you love him, don't you?' Kayla nodded slowly, annoyed with herself for hesitating even a fraction of a second. 'Right, so stop worrying and help me come up with some cunning plan about this painting of yours instead. Perhaps it will be okay if you introduce the idea to Mike gently and promise not to hang it in his flat? Oh, and tell him it'll be worth loads of money within a few years.'

Kayla hesitated. 'You think that'll do the trick? I suppose it's worth a try, although he's bound to see through it.'

'Rubbish. Just bat your eyelashes at him and smile sweetly and he'll forget everything else. Anyway, you're going to keep your flat after the wedding, aren't you?'

'Yes, I was going to rent it out. It'll give us an additional income which might come in handy if I should become pregnant or something.' Maddie gave her a searching look and she hurried to add, 'Not that I'm planning on starting a family any time soon.' Thankfully Maddie let it pass, even though she knew how much Kayla loved kids.

'Well, then, just leave the picture there as part of the furnishings.'

'I guess I could.' Kayla giggled. 'I'll have to sneak in whenever the tenant is away to look at him for a while, though. Oh, Maddie, just wait till you see him, he really is—'

'For goodness sake, woman, just listen to yourself!' Maddie rolled her eyes. 'I'm not sure you deserve my help, but here's what I think you should do . . .'

As Maddie outlined her plan, Kayla had to concentrate really hard. All her brain wanted to do was think about the man in the painting and even when she briefly closed her eyes, his features were all she could see. She took a sip of wine and fixed her eyes on Maddie. *Enough already*, she told herself sternly. She had to get a grip.

CHAPTER 5

Of course once was not enough. It would never have been enough, and Jago had known it before he even uttered the words. One night with Eliza had sealed his fate, binding him to her forever.

He stayed away from her of course. How could he do otherwise? It wasn't as if he could walk up to the Hall and demand to speak to the mistress. He was a lowly innkeeper, a bastard at that, and she was a lady. It simply wasn't done. But she found a way to overcome this barrier.

A week after their first meeting, on the afternoon of the day Sir John left for a prolonged visit to London, she entered the taproom of the King's Head. Her midnight-blue riding habit with its mannish jacket suited her to perfection, and she wore a jaunty black hat, set at a slight angle, with a couple of ostrich feathers adding height. She passed several startled customers and sat down at one of the tables. Her groom, a young, nervous-looking man, hovered behind her until she told him to be seated. He looked as though he would have liked to protest, but was too much in awe of her ladyship to remonstrate with her.

A serving girl approached her respectfully and bobbed a curtsey. 'My lady? What can I get ye, ma'am?'

'Ale for my groom and a mug of your best cider for me, if you please.'

'Right away, m'lady.'

Eliza looked around her with interest, her beautiful eyes seemingly taking in every detail of the establishment. She smiled at the other customers, who were regarding her with a mixture of awe and consternation, and nodded at them. Their mouths fell open in astonishment. This was the first time the new Lady Marcombe had ever ventured out of her eyrie and into the village, and they didn't know what to make of her. Not to mention the fact that no one had thought to see her set foot in a common inn with only her groom in attendance.

Jago watched from behind the counter and deemed it time to intervene. He took the tray of drinks from the serving maid and carried them to the table himself, bowing low to her ladyship.

'Lady Marcombe, you honour us with your presence.' He straightened up and gave her a warning look as he set the drinks down on the table. She gazed back innocently, and then he noticed her eyes open wide in startled admiration when she caught sight of his eyes. He knew their clear blue colour was a marked contrast to his otherwise dark looks, and he was aware, without being vain, that women found the combination attractive. They'd told him so. Eliza continued to study his face and smiled again. Perhaps she liked what she saw? A frisson snaked down his back. It shouldn't matter to him, but it did. Lord help him, it did. He wanted her to like how he looked, not just what he could make her feel.

'Allow me to introduce myself. I am Jago Kerswell, owner of this inn.' He bowed again.

'I'm pleased to make your acquaintance, Mr Kerswell. Would you care to have a mug of cider with me and tell me a bit more about the inn and the village? I fear I have been very remiss in not visiting before and I would like to make amends.'

It was a highly irregular request, as he was sure she was well aware, but coming from her it sounded innocent enough. She had courage, he had to give her that. He knew what she'd really come for, but at least she had brought a chaperone of sorts and she'd acted as prudently as possible under the circumstances. Just as well, for he felt sure this incident would be reported back to Sir John upon his return. It must never happen again.

'Certainly, my lady. I would be honoured.' He pulled up a stool on the other side of the table, as far away from her as possible.

For the next half-hour he sat with her and told her all about the village and any amusing anecdotes he could think of, and all the while he revelled in her smiles. At such close quarters and in daylight she was exquisite, like one of the porcelain dolls he'd seen in a shop window in Exeter once. She played the gracious lady to the hilt for the benefit of their audience, with just the right note of condescension in her voice, but he knew it was all an act. It wasn't the real Eliza, because he had already met her.

Finally, when she obviously realised she couldn't possibly stay any longer, she nodded to the groom and said, 'Hobbs, would you be so kind as to ready my mare for me, please?' The tone was imperious, brooking no argument, even if the groom had been so inclined.

'Yes, of course, my lady.' The young man, who'd remained silent during the entire visit, jumped up to do her bidding, and Jago was alone with her at last, out of earshot of the other customers.

'Meet me tonight,' she whispered so quietly only he could hear her. 'Please, Jago?'

He nodded, stood up and bowed to her again. 'It has been a great pleasure to have you here, my lady. I hope you will come again soon.'

'Thank you, Mr Kerswell. Your cider is excellent.' She swept out of the door without a backward glance. And Jago knew that although she would never again visit the inn, he would see a lot more of her from now on.

The party was as dreadful as only large family gatherings could be.

'You're late,' Mike hissed, as Kayla arrived with her parents, 'and what the hell are you wearing?'

'It's a new dress and I thought it was rather nice, thank you very much. I was sure you'd like it.' Kayla pushed past him into the house, trying to swallow her annoyance and disappointment. They were only five minutes late, and that was because her father had insisted on taking what he called a short cut, which of course turned out to be no such thing.

'I do, I mean, it's great, but . . . my parents.' Mike looked flustered, then added unwisely, 'Well, for God's sake don't sit down whatever you do!'

Kayla ignored this comment and helped her mother find somewhere to hang her coat. Choosing what to wear for the party had been way down on her list of priorities that morning. So far Sotheby's hadn't rung to tell her when the painting would be delivered and Kayla was almost frantic with worry. What if there wasn't enough money in her account and her cheque had bounced? She'd been so sure there would be sufficient funds, but she could have miscalculated. Or what if the painting had been lost or stolen on the way to the warehouse?

'Stop it,' Kayla had told herself sternly while she tried to concentrate on her choice of clothing. She hesitated between a rather conventional little black dress, which she knew became her well, but which his parents had seen before, and a new one in lilac, which was a bit on the short side but came

43

with a pretty little matching cardigan. She finally chose the lilac one. Although she wasn't very tall, she had quite long legs and they were one of her best features. She didn't see why she shouldn't show them off. Besides, the Russells may as well get used to the way she looked, she reasoned, and if they didn't like it, too bad.

'Shouldn't you have worn something a fraction longer?' was her mother's first question when she arrived with Kayla's father to pick up their daughter.

'Oh, Mum, don't fuss. This is a perfectly respectable dress.'

'That's debatable, I suppose.'

'Well, short is all the rage at the moment.'

Her mother smiled as Kayla bristled. 'Seriously, dear, there may be staid old aunts and uncles present.'

'They're not marrying me,' Kayla said, echoing Maddie's comforting words. 'Anyway, there's no time to change now.'

Overhearing Mike's comment when they arrived, her mother gave Kayla a meaningful glance, which made Kayla even more determined to disregard them. The awful truth was that she didn't care what the Russells thought and it bothered her. She ought to care. She should want to impress Mike's relations, but at the moment all she could think about was the man in the painting. When would he arrive?

Giving herself a mental shake, Kayla went to

do her duty by Mike's relatives, tugging surreptitiously at the hem of her dress every so often. She made her way around the room, answering every banal and unoriginal question with a polite smile.

Yes, she was very nervous about the ceremony.

Yes, she was a very lucky girl.

Yes, she was looking forward to the honeymoon and no, she wasn't in the family way already.

This last question was asked with a wink and a nudge by an elderly uncle, and Kayla quickly removed herself from his vicinity. As soon as she could decently manage it without offending anyone, she poured herself a glass of wine and then skulked in a corner for a while, observing the assembled company.

Her parents were chatting to Mike's parents. Kayla noticed they were all icily polite to each other, but there was no real friendliness and everything they said appeared to be some sort of competition.

'Well, of course, dear Mike is aiming to be a QC and he's doing awfully well at that firm where they work.'

'Yes, but our oldest daughter's husband is a heart specialist and he's seeing patients in Harley Street several days a week now. So lucrative, you know. I really don't know who can afford to go there these days.'

'You should see our latest grandson, he's so clever! And his sister . . .'

Kayla had a vision of endless Christmases and birthdays spent listening to the same kind of thing and she turned away in horror, looking for more congenial company. Unfortunately, it wasn't to be.

'Darling, there you are. Come, you must meet Aunt Phyllis, she has been so looking forward to seeing you.' Mike was at her elbow, steering her away from a girl of her own age who had looked like a promising candidate for decent conversation. 'And for heaven's sake, try to pull your dress down a bit when you talk to her,' he whispered between his teeth. Kayla scowled at him, since that was precisely what she'd been doing already.

There followed another seemingly endless parade of aunts, uncles, cousins and grandparents and Kayla smiled until her jaw ached. When she couldn't stand it any longer she fled to the bath-room, where she stayed, daydreaming about the blue-eyed man in the portrait, until the banging on the door became too irate to ignore.

It was the party from hell, just as she'd been afraid it would be. And when Kayla finally arrived home, having developed a monumental headache, it was to find a message on her answerphone saying that Sotheby's had called to arrange delivery of her painting, but since she wasn't at home they would call some other day. She swore and threw a cushion at the wall.

The wind from the sea caressed her hair and tore at her skirts, but Kayla hardly noticed. She closed her eyes and leaned her back against the solid chest behind her as two strong arms came up to hold her in a tight embrace. He leaned his chin on her shoulder, putting his cheek next to hers and she felt the stubble rasping her delicate skin. She shivered with delight.

'I wish we could stay like this forever,' she whispered with a sigh, and turned in his arms.

He smiled and drew his thumb gently along her cheekbone. 'Me too.'

Her arms came up to circle his neck, and the gesture pushed her breasts up so they brushed against him. She trembled once more, rocked by a desire stronger than any she had ever felt before. There was no need for words after that. She gazed into his heavenly eyes as his mouth descended on hers, not wanting to miss the slightest look from him. When he kissed her, she knew she would be oblivious to the world around her, and she ignored the fact that she couldn't have him, forgot everything but the feel of him. She never wanted to let go . . .

Kayla woke up abruptly with tears of frustration running down her cheeks and her heart beating rapidly. The dream had been so real. She had felt his arms around her, his lips on hers, and tasted the salt in the air. Her body was tense with unfulfilled desire. She wanted the man in the portrait and she wanted him now.

'Damn it!' She sat up and picked up her pillow, shaking it roughly and ramming it down onto the bed again. Perhaps Maddie had been right after all.

She should return the painting before it was too late, before it ruined everything. The weeks leading up to her wedding were supposed to be some of the happiest times of her life. She should be immersing herself in the preparations, becoming caught up in the excitement, but all she had done was to dream of making love with a man who didn't exist. A man she had absolutely no chance of ever meeting because he'd been dead for hundreds of years, if indeed he had even existed in the first place.

It wasn't right. It had to stop.

'All right, I'll sell him.' She nodded to herself, pleased to have come to a decision. But a little voice inside her whispered that it was too late, all too late. She wanted him too much. More than she'd ever wanted Mike.

Was it fair to her fiancé to marry him, feeling like this? She was beginning to have serious doubts.

At last he arrived and he was every bit as wonderful as he'd been in the showroom. Perhaps more so because now he was definitely hers.

For a short while, she reminded herself.

Kayla sat on her sofa and gazed at the large portrait which was standing on the floor, leaning against the fireplace. She had no idea how she would hang him on the wall or if it would even fit. The painting must weigh a ton. She thought vaguely that she should have asked Sotheby's for advice, but right now she didn't care. He was fine where he was.

It was his burgundy-red jacket – or coat as it was probably called in those days – which had first caught her eye. Threadbare and worn in places, it was definitely not the sort of thing an aristocrat would have worn unless he was slumming it around his estate, although from the man's arrogant stance you could be forgiven for thinking him a 'Sir' at the very least. Despite the obvious scruffiness of the material, however, the artist had managed to give the illusion of soft, worn velvet. It looked so perfect that Kayla wanted to touch it, to trail her fingers along the sleeve and feel its smoothness. *And the hard muscle underneath.* Without thinking she stretched out a hand towards the canvas, but pulled it back at the last moment. She shook her head, which felt as if it was stuffed full of cotton wool. How was it possible to create such an image with only a few strokes of a brush and some paint?

She tried to study the man with detachment, but her eyes drank him in, etching his face into her brain forever. He had strong, rough-hewn features which appeared to have been weathered by the elements since his complexion was very dark. The artist hadn't done anything to embellish his looks, but had painted the real man, exactly as he must have seen him. This included tiny crow's feet radiating from the corners of his eyes and deep laughter lines on either side of his mouth. A shining, blue-black ponytail fell over one shoulder, adding to the overall obscurity of the portrait. The man stared at Kayla with a half-smile playing about his mouth, as if he knew something she didn't and was amused by her confusion.

'Why are you looking at me like that?' she whispered, then closed her eyes to break the spell. He had to go. There was nothing else for it. But until she could arrange for Sotheby's to take the painting back he would have to stay where he was. 'I'm sorry, but I've got to leave you now. Mike's taking me out to dinner.' She sighed. 'Hell, now I'm talking to a painting! I must be going mad.'

The thought sent a chill through her, but she shook it off. She was just a bit emotional at the moment, which wasn't to be wondered at.

'I'll be fine,' she muttered, then glanced at the portrait one last time. 'And you're not staying.'

But the man's smile seemed to mock her and she had to force herself to turn her back on him.

CHAPTER 6

The summer house was too close to Marcombe Hall and Jago didn't want to run the risk of being caught. Not that he was scared of his half-brother, who was much smaller than he was and weak besides. Jago doubted John had ever taken any exercise in his life and, from what he had observed, the man was far too keen on his food. No, it was for Eliza he was afraid. He knew that if they were caught, Eliza would be the one to suffer, and that he couldn't allow.

They went sailing along the coast instead and had brought a huge picnic so they could stay out all day. To Jago, the south Devon coastline was as familiar as his own home and there were plenty of secluded coves where they could spend their day undisturbed. A blanket on the soft sand made the perfect mattress for love-making, and he delighted in showing Eliza everything she'd been missing out on. She learned fast.

'Oh, Jago, I'm so glad I ran into you that night,' she whispered one afternoon. 'I was contemplating something terrible, something I shouldn't have, but you saved me. Gave me a purpose in life once more. Thank you.' She leaned over to stroke his rough cheek with her soft fingers. He caught them with one hand and nibbled playfully on the ends.

'I suppose it was meant to be. The Lord works in mysterious ways, they say, and this is certainly beyond my ken.'

Eliza hung her head. 'Yes, but do you really think this was the Lord's work? I mean, we're committing one of the cardinal sins, aren't we? Or I am, at any rate.'

He gathered her close. 'Hush, my love, it can't be that great a sin and from what I hear it's a very common thing in London, especially in the noble families. Everyone marries for duty and then finds love elsewhere. Besides, your husband doesn't deserve you, in my opinion, if he can't treat you as he ought.'

She gave a shaky laugh. 'I do hope you're right, but if not, well, I'm willing to take the risk of eternal damnation. For you I would risk anything.'

'As would I for you, my love.'

The restaurant Mike had chosen was of the small, but expensive variety with intimate tables in little corners behind huge pot plants. It boasted an impressive seafood menu, which he knew Kayla liked, and she smiled warmly at him, feeling guilty for neglecting him all week. *And for spending hours gazing at another man,* the little voice inside her head added. She ignored it. What harm could it do after all? He would soon be gone and out of her life. It was Mike she loved and Mike she was marrying. It meant nothing more than Mike's blatant admiration for a certain busty actress on television. It was a fantasy. A daydream.

Kayla put all thoughts of the man in the painting out of her mind and concentrated on Mike and reality. 'This is a lovely place,' she told him and he looked pleased at her praise, as he prided himself on his excellent taste when it came to restaurants.

'Yes, isn't it? Only just opened a couple of weeks ago.' He studied the menu gravely, as if the choice of food was a matter of the greatest importance. 'Derek and I had lunch here last week and I would recommend the oysters, followed by Dover sole Walewska or the lobster in Mornay sauce.'

Kayla wasn't too keen on oysters. To her mind they tasted only of seawater with lemon added to it and she really couldn't see the attraction, but she decided to humour him for once. She didn't precisely hate them either and if it would help to keep Mike in a good mood, then so much the better.

'All right, oysters it is, then and, uhm . . . the Walewska, please.'

Mike beamed at her and ordered the same, plus an expensive white wine, which tasted fresh and fruity, just the way Kayla liked it. They had a very nice meal, during which they discussed various aspects of the upcoming wedding in perfect harmony. But over dessert, Kayla decided to broach a subject that she'd been mulling over for some time.

'Mike, I've been thinking. I would like to switch jobs with one of the other secretaries after we're married. Working together can't be very good for our relationship in the long run, so I thought I'd speak to Human Resources about it soon and ask for a transfer. What do you . . .?' She trailed off as she saw the expression of incredulity on his face.

'What on earth are you talking about? I swear you're becoming more difficult to understand every day. This wedding stuff must be really getting to you.' He was growing red in the face and Kayla braced herself for an explosion. She didn't have long to wait. 'Do you mean to say I'm a bad boss? Is that it? And there was I thinking we'd always had a good working relationship. Well, what do I know?'

'No, Mike, calm down. That's not what I meant at all. You're getting the wrong end of the stick.' Kayla tried to explain. 'We *have* worked well together. Extremely well, in fact. It's just that when we're married we are supposed to be partners, equals, but in the office you're always the boss. It doesn't feel right to have to follow your orders all day long and—'

Mike cut her off, shaking his head in disbelief. 'No, I'm not having this. How will it look if my own wife doesn't want to work for me? Huh? For Christ's sake, Kayla, use your brain.'

'Really, Mike, there's no need to be like that.' Kayla was clenching her fists in her lap and glaring at him. 'I *am* using my brain and there's absolutely nothing wrong with it. It's every bit as good as yours. Only you don't seem to be able to listen to other people's arguments once you've made up your mind about something.'

'Hah! That's rich coming from you. Who was it that wouldn't listen to *my* arguments about buying a stupid painting with your aunt's legacy?'

'Oh, here we go. I knew we'd come back to that again sooner or later.' Kayla rolled her eyes and sighed, even though he did actually have a point there.

'Well, you won that round, but you're not winning this one. Either you stay on as my secretary or you'll have to go and work in another practice. It would be too embarrassing otherwise.'

'I've been there longer than you have. By two years, in fact. So you can move, if it bothers you so much!'

'That's beside the point. And I'm a partner now, I can't just up and leave.'

'And I can? Because I'm *only* a secretary?' Kayla was trying her best to keep her temper in check, but Mike was going too far.

'Well, it is rather different, you must agree.'

Kayla stood up. 'I'm going to the ladies' room.' She was shaking now with both anger and frustration. Why couldn't Mike understand what she meant? Or was it that he just didn't want to?

When she returned he'd obviously realised that he had overdone things. He held out his hand until she reluctantly placed hers on the palm. 'I'm sorry. Maybe you're right and it's something we need to think about, but perhaps not straight away? It really would look bad, you know, if you abandon me the minute we've tied the knot.'

Kayla didn't agree but his olive branch was too large to ignore so she nodded. 'Yes, okay, maybe we can talk about it in a couple of months or so. I guess it's not that urgent.'

He brought her hand to his mouth and kissed her knuckles. 'That's my girl.'

And then he changed the topic of conversation as if the argument had never happened.

Kayla let him as she didn't want to spoil the evening further. By the time the coffee was served, however, she was beginning to feel distinctly queasy. Mike frowned at her, obviously noticing that something was wrong.

'What's the matter? You've gone all pale. Did you eat too much? Maybe having clotted cream was overkill? You should have had ice cream with your strawberries.'

'No, no, I didn't eat that much, and in fact I left half the cream. I just don't feel very well, Mike. Do you think those oysters were off?'

'No way. Mine were perfect. If they'd been off you would've smelled them a mile away. You must be sickening for something. Come on, I'll take you home.'

Kayla hardly noticed as he took care of the bill and propelled her out to a taxi. She was grateful for his arm round her waist, steering her in the right direction, and merely concentrated on breathing deeply so as not to be sick. She didn't want to disgrace herself in public.

Mike insisted on accompanying her into the flat, by which time she had started to shake uncontrollably. He guided her over towards the sofa. Halfway there, however, he stopped dead in his tracks and his mouth fell open as he stared at the enormous painting facing them.

'What the hell? Kayla, is that what you bought at the auction the other day? I don't believe it.' Mike couldn't seem to take his eyes off the man in the portrait. He stared at the fierce blue eyes, apparently as mesmerised as Kayla herself had been, but instead of being impressed by it he looked distinctly uncomfortable. The painting was life-size after all and its subject had been a big man, maybe six foot two or three. He certainly dwarfed Mike, who unconsciously ran a finger around the inside of his collar as if it suddenly felt too tight.

'Yes, isn't he gorgeous?' Kayla tried to joke, but followed this with a groan while she clutched her stomach and sank onto the sofa. 'I just had to buy him as there's a possibility he's a distant relation of mine. Remember Uncle David's family tree? I'm pretty sure he's on there somewhere.' She hated having to lie like this, but she didn't think the truth would go down too well right now, if ever. And who knew, it could be true, couldn't it? Stranger things had happened.

Mike's eyes were still glued to the painting and he didn't seem to be listening.

Kayla swore inwardly. This wasn't quite the way she had envisaged breaking the news to him. They were supposed to be spending the weekend at his flat, and she had planned to bring up the subject when he was in a particularly good mood. Now it was too late, but at the moment she really couldn't care less. She had other more important matters on her mind. Such as rotten oysters. Just the thought of them made her shudder. She swallowed hard as bile rose in her throat.

'Gorgeous? What do you mean?' Mike turned to look at her through narrowed eyes. 'Are you telling me you find the man in the picture attractive? Is that why you bought it? You fancy him?'

'No, of course not, Mike. I was kidding. Sorry, bad joke.'

'You told me you were buying something for investment. Something that would give you a return on your money if you sold it in a few years' time. You never said anything about portraits of good-looking men. Don't think for a minute you can hang this on the walls of my flat.' Mike's own boyish good looks were marred by a petulant expression worse than any Kayla had ever seen before.

'I wasn't going to. It's staying here when I rent my flat out.'

'Damn right it is!'

'Anyway, don't you mean *our* flat?' Kayla asked sarcastically, clutching a cushion to her aching belly. 'Really, Mike, don't be silly. I think it'll be worth loads in a couple of years, that's why I bought it. Or I might be able to sell it to Uncle David if we can prove the connection.' She crossed her fingers underneath the cushion. After all, there was no need to tell Mike exactly what effect the painting had on her. Nor that she had already decided to return it. And surely a person had a right to her own private dreams even after marriage? Or was that forbidden?

'I just don't believe this.' Mike was shaking his head, glaring at the picture. 'You know what? This is going back where it came from. I'm not letting you squander your money like that. How much did you pay for it anyway?'

'That's none of your business, Mike.'

'Oh, really? I suppose that means it was much too expensive. So you expect me to pay for the honeymoon on my own, do you?' He threw up his hands in a theatrical gesture. 'This is just great. We'll be starting married life in debt at this rate. As if I don't have enough problems.'

'What problems? And I didn't say it was that expensive.' Another white lie, so she continued to keep her fingers crossed.

Mike ignored her interruption. 'Well, there's only one thing for it,' he announced.

'What?' A wave of nausea rolled over Kayla and she winced.

'You can take it right back to Sotheby's and buy something else instead. Some little still life or landscape or something that *we* can have on the walls of *our* flat, and perhaps pass on to *our* children one day.' His way of imitating her sarcasm in such a childish fashion was really getting on Kayla's nerves. Besides, she was starting to feel extremely ill and she didn't need this hassle right now. It was too much. Rebellion stirred inside her. She clenched her jaw and prepared for battle.

'I'm *not* taking the painting back, Mike, and that's final. I like it and I bought it with my own money. I'll keep it somewhere other than in our home if you hate it so much, but I'm not selling it. Ever!' She wanted to shout, but kept her voice at a steely low pitch instead, which always had more effect on Mike.

'I see.' The expression on Mike's face was getting uglier by the minute. 'So you're telling me my views don't count? You'd rather own a portrait of a man who's been dead for hundreds of years than listen to the man you supposedly love?'

'Don't be ridiculous. This is a totally stupid argument and I really don't feel well enough for this right now. Can't we talk about it tomorrow, please?'

'No. I want you to promise that you'll get rid of *him*,' he pointed over his shoulder, 'or you can forget about our marriage. I will not take second place to anyone in my wife's affections.'

'Oh, for heaven's sake, he's dead!' Kayla groaned again, the spasms of pain in her abdomen were coming more frequently now, and she was overwhelmed by bouts of nausea. She wished Mike would just go away. 'And you have a *Playboy* calendar in your kitchen,' she added.

'That's different. And I was going to take it down when you moved in anyway.'

'Well, I never said a word about it. Besides, I was only joking about him being gorgeous. I mean, look at him, he's not exactly Brad Pitt.'

'Uh-hmm. So why did you buy it then?'

Kayla made a vague gesture with her hands and Mike clenched his fists.

'I mean it, Kay, take him back. Damn it all, a man's got to be master of his own house.'

'Fine, if that's how you feel, why don't you go back to *your* house and find some other stupid female to lord it over. I'm not marrying anyone who can't see me as an equal in a partnership. This isn't the Middle Ages, you know.' She tugged violently at her engagement ring and yanked it off her finger before throwing it at him. 'And take this with you when you go.' He caught it deftly out of pure reflex. 'I never liked it anyway. It's too damn big and gets stuck everywhere. I'll collect my things when I'm feeling better. Goodbye.'

Without waiting for an answer she rushed off to the bathroom to be violently sick, and barely heard the front door slamming shut. She was too

61

ill to care that she'd just thrown away all her dreams out of sheer stubbornness. Too ill to care that months of planning had been for nothing. And it was all because of a pair of irresistible blue eyes.

Or was it?

CHAPTER 7

'Tell me more about yourself.' Eliza reached out and trailed her fingers along Jago's cheekbone, staring at him almost with reverence. He turned and kissed her hand, awed by the feelings that rose up inside him.

'Why? What do you wish to know? I'm just a simple innkeeper.' He shrugged, trying to make light of her words.

'Have you always lived here? And who was your mother? She must have been very dark.' She smiled. 'You're what my nanny would have called swarthy, with your tanned skin and this, which I love.' Eliza's fingernails grazed the black stubble along his jaw, making him shiver with pleasure. 'But your eyes, they must be from your father, am I right?'

Jago nodded. 'Yes, they are the only feature of his I've inherited. My mother Lenora was a Gypsy, you know, and bequeathed me her exotic colouring. I'm told she was beautiful, enticing and full of life. A temptation to any man, but particularly to someone like Sir Philip.'

'Why do you say that?'

'He'd just lost his wife, he was lonely and needed

to be swept out of his grief. My mother didn't ask much of him, or so I've been told, but she cheered him with her zest for life. They both knew it wasn't a lasting relationship, but they each got what they wanted out of it.'

'You?' Eliza smiled teasingly and Jago chuckled.

'No, I doubt that I was part of the plan. Whether I'd arrived or not, Lenora would have continued her carefree life, moving around with her band of Gypsies, had she not died giving birth to me. I would've been raised with the other children, as indeed I was at first by my grandmother, but then Sir Philip found out about me. He was a nice man. He had me educated and even left me some money in his will. Enough for me to buy the inn and a decent boat.' He spread his hands. 'There you have it, my life story.'

'So you've never wanted to go roaming with your kin?' Eliza put her head to one side. 'I've heard tell anyone with Gypsy blood feels the pull of such a life irresistible.'

Jago grinned. 'Oh, I've done some roaming over the years – leaving the inn in the capable hands of a friend – but not often. My mother's blood only surfaces in me occasionally.'

Eliza sighed. 'It sounds so romantic, such freedom. I wish . . .'

'What do you wish, my love?' He tangled his fingers in her lovely blonde hair and pulled her close so that he could smell the flowery fragrance that was uniquely hers – honeysuckle and roses.

He inhaled deeply and stored it in his memory yet again.

'Nothing, except to be with you.'

'You are, sweeting, you are.'

But he knew they were both wondering the same thing. For how much longer?

Kayla's South Kensington flat consisted of just one large room, with a sleeping platform constructed in one corner on which she had placed a plump, comfortable futon. The Victorian house had such high ceilings that there would have been plenty of room for two floors, and the small platform didn't detract from the sense of spaciousness in any way. The ceiling was ornately plastered with a border of fruit and small animals, and normally Kayla loved to lie in her bed and look at it from all angles. Tonight, however, her legs felt like boiled vermicelli and she was too weak to climb up the ladder. Instead she collapsed onto the sofa with another moan.

'Oh God, I feel awful,' she muttered. She started to tremble and soon she was shivering violently while her stomach continued to cramp as if it wanted to expel every last ounce of food inside her. *Well, you have, so leave me in peace*, Kayla thought grumpily. She pulled a plaid blanket down from the back of the sofa and covered herself, but it was no use. The shivers wouldn't stop. Teeth chattering, she finally reached for the phone and dialled her parents' number. 'Mum?'

'Kayla, dear. What's the matter? I was just getting ready for bed.'

'I'm s-sorry, Mum, but I-I'm afraid I'm i-ill. F-food poisoning, I think. Bad oysters. D-do you think I should c-call the doctor?' Kayla's mother was a nurse, the oracle to whom all her children turned whenever they had any questions of a medical nature and she was invariably right in whatever measures she suggested.

'Have you been sick? Do you have a temperature?' she asked in what Kayla thought of as her professional voice.

'Y-yes. There's nothing left inside me, I can g-guarantee it. And I'm pretty sure I have a bit of a temperature. Maybe more than a bit, actually. I'm shaking like a leaf.'

'Well, wait a while longer, dear. If the temperature goes up even more, then perhaps you should call the doctor. You might need antibiotics; some cases of food poisoning can be nasty. But if you feel a bit better in about half an hour or so, then it should pass. Your body has rid itself of whatever it was, now it has to calm down again. I'll call in a while to check on you, shall I?'

'Okay. Th-thanks, Mum.'

Kayla lay back down and concentrated on relaxing her body, breathing deeply to weather the continued spasms of pain in her stomach. The shivering slowly subsided and an unnatural heat began to spread over her instead.

'Yes, definitely a temperature,' she said to herself

and closed her eyes. She was so tired, so very tired. If only she could sleep for a while, then maybe she'd wake up to find it had all been a bad dream.

'I dare say you'll be as right as rain by tomorrow,' a voice said bracingly, and Kayla jumped and swivelled her head round to see who was talking to her. There was no one in the room. She struggled into a sitting position with some difficulty.

'Who's there? Who said that?' She could hear the panic in her voice and tried to control it. This definitely had to be the worst possible time to be confronted by an intruder. She was too weak to stand up, let alone defend herself. What use were karate lessons if you were unable to even lift your arm?

'Have no fear, no one is going to hurt you, I promise.' The voice – deep, dark and smooth – made her heart do a somersault. It sounded familiar. She cast another frantic look around the room, but there really was no one there. Tears of frustration gathered in her eyes, and one rolled down her cheek as she lay back down and flung one arm across her face.

'Oh great, I'm hallucinating now. I'd better call the doctor after all.'

'No, you're not. Look at your new purchase,' the voice commanded, and her eyes flew to the portrait. The dark man was smiling and she could have sworn he winked at her. Then he raised one hand. Kayla stared for a few moments before a strange buzzing noise began in her ears and the world started to disappear into a dizzying vortex of darkness.

The last thing she heard was the smooth voice exclaiming impatiently, 'Hell and the devil confound it! This is not the time for a swoon, woman. I need to speak to you.'

Kayla opened her eyes and let her gaze roam around the room. She felt extremely lightheaded and it took her a while to focus on the familiar objects around her. She tried taking deep breaths and blinked several times to clear her vision. All was quiet, nothing moved and the man in the painting smiled his enigmatic smile as before without wiggling so much as a finger. She had dreamed the whole thing.

A sense of disappointment washed over her and then she laughed at herself. 'Of course you dreamed it, you idiot,' she muttered. 'Paintings don't talk, for heaven's sake.'

She crawled off the sofa and managed to fetch a glass of soda water from the little kitchenette that was hidden in an alcove at the back of the big room. She sipped the fizzy liquid slowly, not sure whether her stomach would allow her to keep anything down yet. To her relief, there were only a few rumbling protests, nothing more, but her head pounded like the very devil, so she made a second foray to find some aspirin as well.

'I wish I hadn't bought you,' Kayla said, and

glared at the painting. 'I feel so confused and it's all your fault. I thought I knew where I was going with my life, had it all planned out, and now I'm back to square one. What am I going to do? And what about the wedding? Oh hell, it's all booked and everything.'

He didn't reply and she lay down and closed her eyes. 'Huh, you don't have any answers, do you? But then, neither do I, I suppose. We're a fine pair, aren't we?'

With a deep sigh she settled down to sleep some more and let her mind drift wherever it wanted to. It returned to the man's face, again and again, and even with her eyes closed she could see him clearly. She was too tired to do anything about it so she allowed her thoughts free rein and felt herself drifting off.

'I'm sorry, but I really didn't mean to frighten you to death.'

The deep voice startled Kayla again and made her turn too quickly to look at the painting, causing a renewed attack of dizziness. The man in the portrait smiled apologetically and shrugged. 'Please, don't swoon again, I beg of you. I thought you modern women were made of sterner stuff and you don't even have the excuse of a tight bodice.'

Utter silence reigned for a few seconds. Kayla hadn't realised that she had been holding her breath until she heard the wheezing sound her throat made when she finally drew some air into her lungs. She stared at the now so-familiar face and jumped about a foot off the sofa when he started to talk again.

'You see? I'm not dangerous.' He smiled again, showing even white teeth in a piratical grin, obviously pleased with the effect he was having on his audience.

Kayla registered the fact that he spoke with a slight burr. West Country if she wasn't mistaken. She'd been to Devon and Cornwall for a holiday once and remembered the accent. She finally found her tongue. 'But . . . but . . . how is this possible? I mean . . . I'm dreaming, right?'

'Are you?' He became serious again. 'Perhaps, perhaps not. Does it matter? I need to speak to you because there is something I would like you to do for me.'

'Do for you?' she echoed, feeling foolish in the extreme. She was talking to a painting, for God's sake. She shook her head. Next she'd be talking to the walls or the plants on the window ledge. Was she really that ill?

'Yes, something I can't do myself. Being stuck in a painting rather restricts a man's options, don't you know?' The rest of his body was moving now and he gesticulated with his hands as he spoke. Kayla watched in fascination as he seemed to come to life before her. In her trance-like state she forgot to be frightened. She must be very ill indeed, she decided, but what did it matter? This was what she'd been dreaming of all week – to actually meet this man in the flesh – and now her dream was coming true. Or was it?

'So will you do it?'

'Huh, do what?' Kayla blinked and returned to reality, if that was what this was. She shook her head, then immediately regretted it since the vertigo returned with a vengeance. Putting up her hands, she held her head still and closed her eyes. 'No, I don't believe this. Please, just leave me alone. I'm too ill to cope with this. You've already ruined everything.'

'I would dispute that.'

'Really? Guess you weren't listening earlier then.' She croaked out a laugh. 'What am I saying? Of course you weren't, you're a *painting*.'

His expression turned stern. 'This is becoming a little wearisome. I simply wish to ask you to do me a small favour, nothing more. Please?'

'No, stop! I need a rest. I'm obviously extremely ill.' She turned her back on him and huddled under the blanket once more.

'Very well, as you wish.' The voice behind her sounded rather huffy, as if he was insulted. 'We will discuss the matter at a more suitable time.'

'Yes, yes, and pigs will fly, no doubt.' Kayla closed her eyes and savoured the peace for a while. When she couldn't resist the temptation any longer, however, she peeked over her shoulder at the portrait, but there was no movement. It was just strokes of paint on a canvas, nothing more.

'As I thought,' she muttered. 'Well, what did you expect, woman?'

She sighed and settled down.

Kayla dozed fitfully and was jerked out of a bad dream by the shrill ringing of the phone. She answered before she was fully awake.

'Hello?'

'Darling, are you feeling any better?'

Her mother's voice sounded strangely incongruous to Kayla, still lost in her fantasy world, but she shook her head slightly and closed her eyes.

'Yes, Mum, although I've been having the weirdest dreams. Maybe even hallucinations.'

'That's quite normal, dear. It's the temperature affecting you, I'm sure. Is Mike there to look after you?'

Kayla hesitated. If she told her mother the engagement was off, there would be endless questions and she didn't feel well enough to cope with those at the moment. Time enough to break that piece of news to her in the morning. So she opted for a small white lie. 'Er, he's just gone out to get a few things, you know, aspirin and stuff.'

'Well, you're in good hands then. I'll call you in the morning to make sure you're on the mend, okay? Goodnight.'

Kayla put the receiver back and lay down on the sofa again. She glanced over her shoulder at the man in the painting. His blue gaze seemed to mock her, but remained fixed. 'Damn you,' she muttered and punched the cushions into a more comfortable shape before settling down with her back towards him. Sleep was the only thing that could cure her. That and the aspirin.

'*To die, to sleep. No more, and by a sleep to say we end the heart-ache and the thousand natural shocks that flesh is heir to, 'tis a consummation devoutly to be wish'd. To die, to sleep. To sleep, perchance to dream, ay, there's the rub . . .*'

The voice quoting Shakespeare seemed to echo round the room and once again Kayla turned to look at its owner. He looked very satisfied with himself and she frowned.

'Communicating with someone is a wondrous thing, whether in a dream or in a wakeful state. I told you, it makes no difference. All you have to do is help me, whether you believe I can talk to you or not,' he said.

'Oh, for heaven's sake, this is ridiculous! You can't be talking to me. I mean, it's just not possible.' Kayla felt confused and disorientated. She was an intelligent, rational woman and she knew paintings were not able to speak. Yet he persisted in tormenting her. Although she had been sick many times before, nothing like this had ever happened to her in the past.

'Well, this could be a dream, or it could be reality. It's up to your brain to decide. I don't care either way. But you must help me, for there's no one else. I had quite lost hope until I smelled your fragrance and realised you must have been chosen for the task.'

'My fragrance? You mean my perfume? What on earth has that got to do with anything?' Kayla had recently been given a gift voucher for an old-fashioned perfume shop in Jermyn Street; one that had been there since the eighteenth century apparently, and had bought herself a lovely floral scent. It was very girly and sweet, but she loved it.

'Mmm, honeysuckle and roses,' he said, sighing as if the thought of that perfume meant something to him.

'That doesn't make sense. Seriously, you've got me really worried now.' Kayla put her face in her hands and rubbed hard at her eyes. This hallucinating business was scaring the living daylights out of her. Was she becoming unhinged? Could breaking up with your fiancé really have such a dramatic effect or was it just the bad oysters?

'I can see you're not quite ready yet.' He sighed again, although with apparent exasperation this time. 'So I would suggest you sleep for a while longer and try to overcome your prejudices. Then we will speak again.'

'Prejudices?' Her head shot up. 'You think I'm—'

'Well, can you deny it? You don't wish to believe that I'm speaking to you because you have never heard of such a thing, and therefore your brain refuses to accept what it is seeing. That is being prejudiced, surely?'

'No. I mean, I'm asleep. I'm not really seeing anything. My brain is making this up, so I don't have to accept it. When I wake in the morning you'll be a painting again and . . . oh, really, this is too much. I feel so ill,' Kayla wailed and lay back down on the sofa and turned her back on him again. She really couldn't cope with this right now.

'You're sure you don't want to hear what I have to say?'

'No, I don't.'

'Not even a little bit intrigued?' His voice sounded teasing and Kayla was almost tempted to turn around and smile at him. Then she remembered her mind was making it up, presumably to make her stay in this dream world a bit longer.

'I just want oblivion,' she told him. 'You know, deep sleep, the kind where people like you can't reach me. Then I'll be better in the morning.'

'Very well, as you wish. Sweet dreams,' was the last thing she heard before the deep, dreamless sleep claimed her at last.

CHAPTER 8

The weather wasn't always co-operative and Jago was often left standing in the pouring rain for hours, waiting to no avail. He knew deep down that Eliza couldn't pretend to go for a walk in such weather, but he didn't want to leave just in case she found some other way of escaping the house. It never happened though and one evening, when frustration was gnawing at his insides particularly badly, he decided drastic measures were called for. He hadn't seen Eliza for over a week, despite the fact that John was away, and he was sure he'd soon go mad with wanting.

It was not to be borne.

Although he normally preferred to stay as far away from Marcombe Hall as possible, that hadn't always been the case. He had often ventured into the gardens and grounds as a boy, curious about his half-brother's existence and because, despite paying to have Jago educated, Sir Philip never allowed his illegitimate son to visit his home. And it wasn't until he was an adult that Sir Philip told his other son about Jago, or so Jago understood. The two boys had never been officially introduced.

On one such secret visit, Jago had been skulking in a shrubbery and eventually fell asleep, bored with spying on a boy who did nothing other than play with a hoop. When he woke, darkness had fallen and he knew he'd be in trouble with the curate in whose house he was lodged at the time. He was about to set off for home, but as he stood up to leave he noticed movement over by the house. A man emerged, seemingly from nowhere. Jago stood still and just stared.

It was his father, appearing as if he'd come through the very walls of the house. When he set off down a path, Jago waited a moment, then crept closer to peer at the stonework. Eventually he found a door, cleverly concealed so as to blend in with the stones around it, but if you knew where to look, it wasn't hard to find. Jago was elated and determined to go inside at the earliest opportunity, and soon after entered his father's house several times, roaming through the rooms on silent feet. Eventually though, he got bored with having to hide in the shadows. If the man didn't want him there openly, Jago decided he'd prefer to stay away altogether. He hadn't set foot inside the Hall since.

Now, however, he perceived that door might have another use.

He made his way into the gardens, making sure no one was around to notice his approach. Fortunately the rain kept everyone indoors and he reached the house unseen. He wondered if anyone else knew about the secret door. It seemed not, since the wall had recently been painted white and looked pristine and untouched. Perhaps Sir Philip had never had a chance to tell his other son about it? He had died rather suddenly. Jago quite liked the thought that he might be the only person in the world with this knowledge.

He felt his way along the stone façade until his fingers encountered a little hole that contained the catch he remembered. The door didn't budge. Jago guessed the door had been locked for obvious reasons, but he wasn't about to let that stop him.

He took out the dagger he carried in his boot and inserted it between the door and the frame until it rested on the locking mechanism. Then he picked up a rock from the ground and struck the top of the dagger repeatedly until he heard the lock give way. As he'd thought, the lock was old and rusty from the salty draughts of the nearby sea. And although he'd probably ruined his knife blade, he didn't care.

Inside the door was a steep staircase, which he knew led to one of the bedrooms. The last time he'd been here, it had been empty, but as he put his ear to the wall that contained an inner hidden door, he heard movement.

Damnation.

But luck was with him. A voice he knew and loved spoke and Jago felt a grin tugging at his mouth.

'You may go now, Harriet. I won't need you again until morning.'

Eliza. Jago waited until he heard the sound of a door closing, then quietly opened the secret door.

Eliza was sitting on a stool in front of a dressing table, looking ethereally beautiful with her long hair, newly brushed, hanging down her back. It looked like a silvery waterfall, shining in the light from a nearby candle. Her face, reflected in the oval mirror, had a sad, faraway look, but as he stepped up behind her, this changed to one of incredulity, then utter joy.

'Jago? Is it really you? Or am I dreaming already? How did you get in here?'

She turned and he pulled her up and into his arms, covering her mouth with his for an answer. She felt so right, so perfect in his embrace, as if she'd been made for him and him alone. How could he have stayed away?

'You shouldn't have come, my love. It's too dangerous,' she breathed, but at the same time she melted into him, her flimsy shift and wrap no barrier to his questing fingers.

'For you, I'll brave any danger,' he whispered back, and he knew it was the truth.

She was all that mattered.

By Monday morning Kayla was well enough to go to work and she left her flat after a last glance at the man in the painting. He hadn't spoken to her again and although she wished it could be otherwise, she knew it had just been a dream. After all, talking paintings were an impossibility and she almost laughed out loud at the conversation her fertile mind had invented between them.

'Talk about vivid imagination,' she muttered to herself. If she told Maddie about this she felt sure her friend would take her to see a doctor at the very least, not to mention a shrink. And she had to admit it was crazy to be so obsessed by a long-dead man in a portrait that she'd had imaginary conversations with him. Definitely not healthy. She decided to blame the food poisoning.

'Bloody oysters.' She shuddered at the thought. Never again would she so much as look at one, that was for sure.

She'd expected things to be awkward at the office, but she found to her relief that Mike had gone on an unexpected business trip.

'Didn't you know?' the receptionist asked, obviously scenting an interesting piece of gossip.

'Yes, of course I did. I'd just forgotten. Had such dreadful food poisoning over the weekend my brain's not in gear.' She tried to laugh it off, but she knew it wouldn't be long before everyone in the office would find out about the broken engagement. Kayla's heart sank. She'd better go and see the Human Resources manager straight away and hand in her notice. There was no way she could stay here now.

By the time Kayla reached her flat that evening, she was exhausted from having to pretend that all was well. The Human Resources manager had promised to keep the news to himself for the moment, but Kayla almost wished she'd had the courage to just tell everyone. It would have been easier than acting unnaturally cheerful all day. A mammoth headache was building behind her eyes as she came through the door. Needing to vent her anger and frustration on someone or something, she marched over to the painting.

'This is all your fault!' she hissed, knuckling away the tears that started to trickle down her cheeks. 'I hope you're pleased now. God, to think if I'd never set eyes on you, I would still be happily engaged. I'd be getting married in a few weeks' time. I'd be having children, well at some point anyway.' She slumped onto the floor and covered her face with her hands. 'What a mess. What a God-awful mess.'

She didn't know how long she sat there, but when the supply of tears had at last run dry, she stood up slowly and climbed up the ladder to lie down on her bed. There was no point in preparing any food, she couldn't face eating at the moment, and watching television or reading held no appeal either. She just wanted to close her eyes and shut out the pain. To forget the entire day and pretend it had never happened.

She yawned and waited for oblivion.

Late in the evening Kayla's stomach decided it wanted sustenance after all, so she climbed down to make herself a cheese sandwich. She'd only just sat down on the sofa and taken the first bite when she heard the now familiar voice.

'You don't really believe it was my fault, do you?'

Kayla raised her eyes to stare at a swarthy face that wasn't smiling any more, but had compassion clearly written all over it. It was dark in the room, as she'd turned off the light in the kitchenette, but a streetlight outside her window illuminated everything and she could see him clearly. He seemed so real and Kayla felt that if she'd gone over to him and reached out a hand, she could have touched him and felt his warmth. She didn't dare because she was sure it would shatter the hallucination and she desperately wanted to cling to it. In silence she waited for him to say something else.

'He wasn't the right man for you, my dear,' he said gently. 'You'll do much better without him. He didn't appreciate you as a man should appreciate the woman he marries. You were never soul mates. Believe me, I should know.'

'You're talking again.' Kayla blinked several times, because he was moving again as well, almost fidgeting. This time she knew she was awake and had no temperature. She was stone cold sober and the sandwich in her hand surely proved that this was all real. She took a bite just to make sure and chewed slowly.

She couldn't stop looking at him. He smiled and

her breath caught in her throat. It was the kind of smile that could win over even the staunchest opponent, the smile of a man who knew he could charm anyone if he wanted to, and she felt herself begin to relax. If only he would continue smiling at her this way, she'd be quite happy to just sit there and look at him, she decided. Why hadn't the artist painted him like that instead of trying for the *Mona Lisa* approach?

'Yes, I'm speaking to you. You don't appear to want for sense and I thought you might be ready to listen at last. Are you?'

'I-I don't know. This isn't real, is it? If I'm dreaming I have all the time in the world.'

He sighed. 'I told you, it doesn't matter. Somehow we are communicating and you will remember my words either way. It is up to you to decide how it happened, if you must.'

'Really?'

'Yes. Trust me, please?'

'Okay. I'm listening. What is it that's so important?' Kayla leaned forward so she could look him in the eyes. They were fringed with thick, black lashes and gleamed like dark sapphires in the faint glow from the streetlight. His gaze soothed her, made her feel protected and safe. She relaxed back against the sofa behind her.

'I need your help,' he said. 'Fate seems to have chosen you to be my assistant in this matter and I have no idea why, so don't ask. We have to accept it is so. Now I will tell you some facts about

83

myself. You will memorise my words, and when you're feeling better you can check the truth of what I say for yourself. Simple, isn't it?' He spread out his hands.

'Sounds easy enough, but . . .'

'But what?'

'I, er, nothing.' She still couldn't take her eyes off him. He was magnificent in his dark red coat which shimmered in the dim light. He seemed awfully big, his six foot two or three frame powerful, but he didn't scare her. On the contrary, she found it almost impossible to quash the impulse to go up to him and touch him. He smiled again, as if he could read her thoughts, and she felt her cheeks heat up. Looking down at her sandwich, she picked little bits of cheese off in order to keep her hands occupied. 'Fire away.'

'I beg your pardon?'

'I mean, continue, tell me about yourself.' Kayla's heart was beating painfully against her ribcage. The excitement was almost unbearable. Finally she would find out who he was.

'Very well.' He looked towards the window, his expression serious and pensive, and began. 'My name is Jago Kerswell. I lived in the village of Marcombe on the coast of Devon. I was born in the year 1754, the bastard son of a Gypsy woman called Lenora.' Kayla looked up swiftly. That would explain his looks, she thought. 'My father was Sir Philip Marcombe, of Marcombe Hall, but you'll not find any evidence of that anywhere so you'll have to take my word for it. He was a good man and did his duty by me, but of course he couldn't acknowledge me openly.' He paused for a moment to let the words sink in. When she looked up once more he continued. 'Sir Philip's legitimate son, John, my half-brother, married twice, the second time to a Miss Elizabeth Wesley. They were not happy together.' He paused again and gazed into the distance, as if his thoughts were far from the present.

'And . . .?' Kayla prompted.

'I'll not bore you with the details, but Eliza and I fell in love and we met whenever Sir John was away, which fortunately for us was quite frequently. In the summer of 1781 we often went for excursions along the coast. There are many secluded coves and inlets where one can be private.' He winked at her mischievously and she felt a smile spread over her features. 'However, one afternoon we found, to our dismay, that we were not alone. An artist and his assistant had set up their easels on the beach, and we fell into conversation with them. They were painting seascapes, but when the older man caught sight of Eliza, he was seized with the urge to paint her instead. She was very beautiful, you see, and she reminded him of a mermaid or some such creature, he said.' He waited once more for Kayla to take it all in. 'Are you with me?'

'Yes, I think I can remember all that.' In fact she was drinking his words in, every last one clear in her mind, but she hoped the story would soon come to an end so she could be sure she didn't forget any part of it.

'Eliza agreed to pose for him on the condition the man would do a portrait of me as well, which she would pay him for, and so it came to pass. You see before you the, in my opinion, rather shoddy result. He wasn't really interested in painting me. It was only Eliza who had fired his enthusiasm.'

'But who was the artist? There's no signature and nobody knew at the auction house where I bought you.' Kayla still couldn't believe she was having this conversation, but she didn't want to question it just yet. She was enjoying the fantasy and for now it was enough that the man was talking to her.

Jago. Even his name was wonderful.

Jago chuckled. 'His name was Thomas Gainsborough, but as this painting was done in secret we agreed he wouldn't sign it. It is meant as a companion piece for the one of Eliza, which is properly signed, but of course the two could never hang together while Sir John was alive. They were eventually displayed side by side in the first floor gallery at Marcombe Hall, but at some point the one of me was sold. I'm not sure why or when. Now, however, it wouldn't matter to anyone if we were together and that is where you come in. I want you to find Eliza's portrait and hang mine next to it.'

Kayla's mouth had fallen open and she stared at him. 'Thomas Gainsborough! You're joking, right?'

'No, I am perfectly serious.'

Kayla flopped back on the sofa and covered her eyes with one hand. 'Now I know for sure I'm dreaming again. Gainsborough. Right. Couldn't my brain come up with anything more original?'

'I don't understand. What is wrong with Mr Gainsborough? I take it you have heard of him?' Kayla glanced at Jago, but he looked genuinely confused.

'Of course I have. Do you have any idea how valuable you . . . I mean your portrait, would be if it was a Gainsborough? I paid eighteen thousand pounds for it, but if it was a real Gainsborough it would be worth at least a hundred thousand, if not more.'

'The devil you say! As much as that? Well, surely that is good for you? You'll make a huge profit.'

'Yes, of course I wish it was authentic, but there's no way to prove it. The experts tried already. You just said it yourself, the painting isn't signed. I can't very well walk into Sotheby's and say "Excuse me, sir, but the man in the portrait I bought last week told me in a dream that he was painted by Gainsborough, so can you sell it for me at the going rate please?" They'd put me in an asylum for sure.'

Jago laughed and Kayla shivered at the sound of it. His laughter was doing strange things to her and it was also infectious. She joined in, shaking her head. 'You know, Jago, this is just about the craziest dream I've ever had, but it's wonderful and I don't want to wake up.'

'Unfortunately we all have to wake up to reality some time,' he said cryptically. 'Now, as for the authenticity of my claim, all you have to do is find the portrait of Eliza, and you can prove this one was painted by the same hand. There are certain details that are similar, one in particular. A true connoisseur would find them and believe you. In fact, anyone should be able to spot the clue Mr Gainsborough left as long as Eliza's portrait is still intact.'

Kayla peered at him sceptically. 'Really? How convenient. My brain surprises even me sometimes.'

'Please will you do it? Will you help me?'

Kayla hesitated. 'To find the other portrait? All right, I don't want to argue with you when I'm having such a nice dream so I'll say yes, if only to keep you talking for a while longer. But tell me, why does it matter? I mean, I thought people in love met up in the afterlife or something.'

'That is another long story, but suffice it to say our portraits need to hang side by side for us to be together. Just trust me on this.'

'And where should I look? Have you any idea where she could be?'

'Why not start at Marcombe Hall? If her descendants are still there the portrait should be as well.

That is, if the house is still standing, of course. I'm not precisely sure what year it is now or how long I have waited.'

'I suppose that would be the logical place to start.'

'Good. That's settled then. Now, go back to sleep so you can wake up refreshed and ready to begin in the morning.'

'But . . . oh, very well. I do have a terrible head-ache as a matter of fact and I probably need to rest, if I'm not already asleep that is.' She knew she sounded grumpy, but she couldn't help it. She didn't want the dream to end, she was enjoying herself too much.

'Goodnight, then.' His voice was a mere whisper, a verbal caress.

She turned to glare at him, but suddenly he wasn't moving any more. She climbed up to her bed and when she leaned over the balustrade to peer at the painting he was still motionless. Only his eyes looked even vaguely alive. Had she dreamed it all? Was she still dreaming? She would have to find out in the morning.

CHAPTER 9

Walking along the coast, deep in conversation, they hadn't noticed the two artists until they were almost upon them, and by then it was too late to avoid a meeting. Jago swiftly let go of Eliza's hand, but he was fairly certain that at least one of the men had noticed.

'Good morning, sirs,' he said politely. 'A pleasant day, is it not?'

'Indeed, my good man. Nature smiles upon us today,' replied the older man. 'I am Thomas Gainsborough of London, here on a tour of the West Country with my nephew, Mr Gainsborough Dupont.' He bowed, and the younger man did likewise before hurriedly returning to his work.

'Pleased to meet you, Mr Gainsborough. I am Jago Kerswell, owner of the King's Head Inn in the village of Marcombe over beyond those cliffs, and this is Lady Eliza.' There was no need to inform the man of her full name, Jago thought. Let him draw his own conclusions.

'Charmed, my lady, to be sure.' Mr Gainsborough's eyes had lit up at the sight of Eliza, and he bent over her hand to kiss it with a graceful flourish, while Jago studied him covertly.

The artist had heavy brows over big, brown eyes, a large Roman nose and full lips. His hair, greying now although it looked as though it had been brown once, was drawn back into a queue tied with a plain black ribbon. His coat was of good quality cloth, but simple in colour and cut, and he seemed exceedingly affable and in good spirits. Jago decided he liked the look of the man.

'But why am I wasting my time painting seascapes, when there are such lovely ladies as yourself to portray? A veritable sea sprite,' Mr Gainsborough was saying, and Eliza smiled at him uncertainly. Jago guessed she was discomposed by this sudden meeting and fearful that her husband would learn of their trysts. By the twinkle in his eyes, Jago didn't think Mr Gainsborough would be the bearer of such tales, however. He looked to be relishing the little secret he had stumbled upon.

'I'm sure your seascapes are wonderful, Mr Gainsborough,' Eliza replied. 'May I have a look?'

'Certainly, my lady, though this one is far from finished.'

'Oh, but it's beautiful! You have a rare talent, sir,' Eliza exclaimed, then inspected the work of the younger man. 'And you too, Mr Dupont. You are obviously both masters of your craft. How I wish I could draw even a little, it must be such a pleasure.'

Mr Dupont flushed at the praise and his uncle beamed at Eliza. 'It's nothing, a mere sketch. Now if I were to paint you, my lady, then you would truly see a lovely picture.' He turned to Jago. 'Where did you say your inn was, sir?'

'Just along the coast here at Marcombe, about half a mile perhaps as the crow flies.'

'Splendid. We may see you later then as we shall require a room for the night.'

'But uncle, I thought we were supposed to go to—'

'We have no firm schedule.' Mr Gainsborough fixed his nephew with a glare and the younger man wisely held his tongue. 'Would you have a room for tonight, Mr Kerswell?'

'Certainly. I shall see to it that one is made ready for you. I hope you don't require luxury, however? It is but a small establishment, although I can vouch for the cleanliness and the first-rate cooking.'

'Excellent. I cannot abide gentlemen who think themselves too good to stay at a simple country inn. Indeed, what could be cosier? We shall see you later then.'

Jago couldn't help but notice the man's final glance at Eliza and very much hoped he was only appraising her in his capacity as a painter and nothing else. She was beautiful enough to tempt any man, but she was his. He'd make sure Mr Gainsborough found that out sooner rather than later if he was staying in these parts.

★　★　★

The sound of rain splashing onto the windowpanes woke Kayla the following day, and she sat up and stretched. All the crying she had done last night had left her feeling exhausted and her eyes stung. No doubt they would be puffy and swollen, but she didn't care. She didn't plan on seeing anyone that day anyway, so what did it matter how she looked? She'd already decided to call in sick as she couldn't face going to the office, even if Mike was still away.

She threw back the cover and climbed down to the sitting room, glancing at the man in the painting. Jago. She said his name out loud, savouring the sound of it, and the strange dream of the night before flooded into her memory, clear in every last detail. He had been so alive, so real. Oh, why hadn't she touched him when she had the chance? But he had distracted her with his strange tale. An authentic Gainsborough indeed. She shook her head at herself. What would her brain come up with next? But at least she now had a name for him and whether it was his real one or not didn't matter. Jago suited him to perfection.

She stumbled to the bathroom to freshen up and emerged some time later feeling half-way human again. She sipped at a strong cup of tea, liberally laced with sugar to restore some of her strength. The thought of any other kind of sustenance didn't appeal to her yet, so she just sat on the sofa and stared at Jago Kerswell.

'If only you were real and actually needed my help. I think I would have done anything for you if I had lived during your lifetime,' she whispered, but of course he didn't answer. Idly, she picked up a pad and scribbled down the things he'd said in her dream. She remembered them all and they sounded like true facts from a real person's life. Was she going crazy? Had her mind produced this incredible story, complete with names and dates? It seemed impossible, but the human brain was a strange thing.

'Maybe I knew you in a previous life?' She knew there were people who claimed to have memories from long ago, sometimes remembered during hypnotic sessions. Perhaps it was possible for the brain to bring them to the surface without the help of hypnosis in certain cases? That would certainly explain the vividness of her dream and the wealth of information she had scribbled on her pad. 'I suppose it wouldn't hurt to check it out,' she muttered, feeling extremely stupid for even contemplating such a thing. But if she didn't, how would she ever know? It would just nag at the back of her mind, giving her no peace. The only question was where to start. She hadn't the faintest idea.

Then, unexpectedly, inspiration struck.

'Yes, of course!' She reached for the phone and dialled Maddie's number. It rang for a long time before a sleepy voice answered.

'Yes?'

'Maddie? It's me, Kayla. I need your help.'

'Kayla?' Maddie cleared her throat loudly and

Kayla heard a crashing sound. 'It's only six o'clock and I think I just broke my alarm clock, damn it.'

'Is it? Sorry, didn't check the time. I'm a bit distracted this morning.'

'I'd say. Please tell me it's not the bloody painting again? Look, you're really starting to worry me. Honestly, you've got to stop mooning over him or else your marriage is going to be very short-lived.'

Kayla cut the lecture off. 'Maddie, listen. I'll explain it all later, but I need to ask you something. Weren't you talking about someone you knew who was researching their family tree a while back?'

'Genealogy you mean? What's that got to do with anything? You want to help your uncle?'

'No, but didn't you say you had a friend who did it as a hobby?'

'Yeah, sure. It was Jessie, one of the girls in the office where I'm temping at the moment. But why?'

'Well, could you ask her how you go about finding out where someone was born?'

She heard Maddie sigh and answer the question in the voice of someone who is resigned to dealing with a lunatic. 'Even I know that. You go to the Record Office for the district in which you were born and look through the parish registers. If you were baptised, that is.' There was a pause before she added, 'Why? You need a new passport? You're not thinking of fleeing the country are you? Weddings aren't that bad, honest. You will survive.'

'No, no, it's not for me. I need information on, uhm, someone who lived in seventeen hundred something.'

'Well, why don't you ask your uncle then?'

'He'd want to know why I needed to know about this particular person when I've never shown much interest in his research before. It has to be someone who doesn't know me or my family.'

'In that case, I think Jessie's probably the person to speak to. She's definitely into all that kind of stuff. I'll ask her to give you a call, okay?'

'Great, thanks. Do you think she could be persuaded to take me on a research expedition?'

'Are you feeling all right?' Maddie sounded suspicious.

'Yes, yes, I'm fine. Well, sort of anyway, but . . .' Kayla took a quick sip of tea. 'I would really appreciate it if she could take me next week. Or even this week. Soon anyway.'

'Look, if it's that important to you I'll call her today. Although perhaps a bit later since most people are asleep at this time of day, you know,' Maddie added in a dark voice.

Kayla ignored this jibe. 'Would you? Oh, thanks, Maddie. I'd really appreciate it.'

'What are friends for? Not that you deserve it after waking me from my much needed beauty sleep. God, my head feels like it's going to split open any second. I knew I shouldn't have had that fourth drink, but Jamie would keep insisting.'

'Oh, Maddie, I'm sorry. Wait, who's Jamie? He's

not there with you, is he? Aargh, I didn't think about that.'

'No, no, he's just a friend. Never mind that. Why do you want to know all this stuff about genealogy anyway? Are you researching your ancestors so you can prove to your mother-in-law you're good enough for her son?' Maddie giggled. 'If she hasn't figured that out by now, I don't think a pedigree will do the trick. Or hang on, are you trying to prove you're related to the guy in the portrait for real? I was only kidding, you know.'

'Not exactly. I'll explain later,' Kayla hedged.

'Okay. I'll stop by this evening and you can tell me if Jessie has rung you back. You're not seeing Mike tonight?' she added as an afterthought.

'Er, no.' Kayla knew she couldn't hope to avoid the issue any longer so she might as well confess everything and get it over with. 'I'm afraid Mike and I broke up on Friday.'

As Maddie shrieked 'What?' in a voice of disbelief, Kayla realised that she hadn't given the row with Mike any thought this morning. She'd been too intent on Jago and her strange dream and the break-up seemed almost unimportant. 'Broke up? But you can't. I mean, why?' Maddie's shrill tone made Kayla wince and hold the receiver away from her ear. She knew her friend was justified, however, so she didn't protest. 'Come on, Kayla, you're not serious? You're getting married in less than a month. I'm your maid of honour, remember? I've got the dress and everything.'

'I'm sorry, Maddie, but there isn't going to be a wedding. You're excused from your duties. I'll tell you all about it tonight, I promise.'

'Right, well you'd better. I'm going to want to know everything,' Maddie said darkly. 'Do you hear me? Every last detail.'

'Yes, everything, I swear.' Kayla resigned herself to a lengthy session of soul-searching that evening, even though it was the last thing she wanted. 'But please, can you call Jessie for me now? I need her help.'

With a sinking feeling she hung up and contemplated the next phone call she had to make. Somehow she had to tell her parents the wedding was off.

It wasn't something she was looking forward to.

'So how did your mum take it?' Maddie was comfortably ensconced on the sofa with a takeaway sandwich packet open on her lap, eating rapidly. Although tall and slim she had a very healthy appetite, which at the moment Kayla envied her.

Kayla toyed with her own sandwich. The wrapping had advertised it as 'an authentic American BLT', but it didn't look very appetising; the lettuce was limp, the tomatoes soggy and the bacon chewy. The bread tasted like sawdust, at least in Kayla's opinion. She wrinkled her nose at it and recoiled from the strong smell of Brie cheese coming from Maddie's corner. Instead she tried to concentrate on the question.

'Quite well, actually, considering how happy she's been that her youngest daughter was finally tying the knot. You know she's revelled in all the planning and organising, it's her forte, but I could tell she was upset and . . .' Her voice tailed off forlornly.

'I know. Guilt trip, right? Don't let it bother you. All mums are like that, I think. Mine despairs of me ever making it down the aisle.' Maddie chewed on another mouthful before turning a searching glance onto her friend. 'You're absolutely sure there's no possibility of a reconciliation with Mike?'

'No, none whatsoever.' Kayla had no doubts about that. The thought of marrying Mike, which only a few weeks ago had filled her with such happiness, was now completely unappealing. 'I think I was marrying him for the wrong reasons, you know. I was in love with the idea of getting married, not him. It was a sort of fantasy thing I suppose and everyone more or less expected it once he proposed. I mean, why wait once you've agreed to marry? But now I know Mike is not the right man and probably never was, to be honest.'

'Well, as long as you're sure. I don't want you pining away or anything.' Maddie glanced at the sandwich on Kayla's lap that had hardly been touched.

Kayla smiled and made an effort to take a bite. 'No chance of that. Let's forget the whole thing, okay? I'm sorry about your dress and everything, but I'm sure you'll find another use for it. Maybe you'll bump into your Mr Right soon and we can swap dresses.'

'Not bloody likely. Besides, that would be quite a sight, wouldn't it?' They both dissolved into laughter as Kayla was several inches shorter than her friend and with a much curvier figure, at least up top.

'Well maybe some other friend of yours will need a maid of honour. Please, let's change the subject.'

'All right, tell me instead about this sudden urge of yours to delve into your family history. I've been dying of curiosity all day, you know.'

'I'm not sure I should. You'll never believe me, Maddie.'

'Try me.'

So Kayla told her all about her strange dreams and Maddie completely forgot about her dinner and sat with the half-eaten sandwich dangling from her fingers during the entire story. When Kayla finished, Maddie snapped her mouth shut and looked at the painting. She whistled softly. 'Wow! You really are hooked on this guy, aren't you?'

'I'm afraid so. It's almost like when I was a teenager and was crushing on some unattainable pop star. Do you know what I mean? It's hard to explain, but, oh, Maddie, I've got to find out. What if I didn't make it up? Do you think it's likely? I mean, how could I possibly know anything about anyone called Jago Kerswell who lived over two hundred years ago? I've only ever been to

Devon for a holiday once and I was just a kid. Why would my mind come up with such a story? It seems crazy.'

'I don't know. It does seem weird. Maybe you read it somewhere. Or perhaps you knew him in another life. You've heard of people who think they've lived before, haven't you?'

'Yes, I thought of that myself, but this is different somehow.'

'Hmm. Did Jessie ring you?'

'Yes, she's going to take me researching on Monday. She had taken a day off work for that purpose anyway, so I'll call in sick again. I can't face Mike in any case. Just the thought of having to go to the office and act as if nothing has happened gives me a headache.'

'I can understand that. Well, I guess you'll just have to wait and see what you find on Monday then. How very strange. Are you going to finish that sandwich? Cause if not, I'll have it.'

Kayla laughed and handed it over. Only Maddie would talk about reincarnation in one breath and food in the next, but it was good to have someone to share her thoughts with. And she had no doubt Maddie would help her keep her feet on the ground.

Together they would get to the bottom of all this.

'Do you think he'll tell anyone about seeing us together?' Eliza fiddled with the buttons on the front of Jago's coat, while staring up into his eyes with a troubled expression.

They had stopped at the summer house, the scene of their first meeting, and just the thought of that encounter made Jago's heart beat faster. His life had changed that night and there was no going back. Whatever happened, he would love Eliza forever, but how could they be together without this constant fear of discovery? He couldn't bear the thought that it might all have to come to an end if John found out what had been going on. But he felt sure Mr Gainsborough wouldn't be the one to tell tales.

'No, love, he won't. Why would he? And who is he going to tell? He doesn't know anyone hereabouts. Besides, he seemed like a nice man.'

'I can't help worrying.' Eliza's hands were splayed across his chest now and Jago covered them with his own, stroking his thumbs over the softness of her skin.

'Leave him to me. If need be, I'll have a chat to him, man to man. But I honestly don't think he'll bring us any trouble. We still need to be vigilant though, as ever.'

He glanced out at their surroundings. The summer house was set near the cliff top with a path leading down to a little used cove nearby. It was only for the occasional outing in summer and hardly anyone walked this way as it was on Marcombe land. But there was always the possibility that someone would, so how long could they keep their meetings secret?

It was surely only a question of time before they were found out.

Monday couldn't come fast enough for Kayla and the hours crawled by for the rest of the week. Jessie had told her to meet her outside Farringdon tube station at ten o'clock. Kayla was so eager she arrived half an hour too early and ended up pacing up and down the pavement for what seemed like ages. Promptly at ten a fairly nondescript, brown-haired girl with glasses came up to her and asked if she was Kayla.

'Yes, how did you know? I forgot to tell you what I looked like, so I was worried you wouldn't find me.'

'Actually, I think we met at a drinks party or something, but it was quite a while ago. I don't go out much.'

Kayla couldn't help but wonder why. Although Jessie wore no make-up and had put her hair up into an untidy knot at the back of her head, she wasn't unattractive and didn't seem shy. The violet-blue eyes behind the spectacles were large and intelligent. Perhaps she just didn't like social-ising or preferred other pastimes, Kayla thought. Either way it was none of her business.

'Oh, yes, that's right. Now you mention it I remember Maddie introducing us. Anyway, thanks ever so much for taking the time to show me what to do today,' Kayla replied. 'I'm a complete novice at this, so I wouldn't have had a clue how to even start.'

'That's okay. As I said on the phone, I was going anyway. Come on, it's this way.'

Jessie set off down the street. 'We're going to the Society of Genealogists. It's not too far from here. They have loads of information there, but if we don't find what you're looking for we can try somewhere else later. It might mean having to go to the National Archives at Kew, but it's not a big deal. Can be done. There's also a whole load of stuff online if you're willing to pay to see it.'

'Great. Thank you.'

The Society of Genealogists was much smaller than Kayla had expected, but all the available space was crammed with genealogical information of every kind. There was a library, a bookshop and a large room full of microfilms and fiche. They left their jackets in a locker downstairs and headed for the library. Kayla felt as if she had entered a whole new world. She had never been interested in her family tree and hadn't realised there were such places as the SoG, as Jessie called it.

'Right, what are we looking for then?' Jessie asked.

'This is the information I've been given, but I'm not sure my, uhm, informant got it right so I'd like to verify these facts if possible.' Kayla held out the piece of paper on which she had written down the things Jago had told her in her dream. Now that she was actually here she suddenly felt very stupid. Surely it must have been a figment of her imagination? After all, how could it not have been? And what would Jessie say when none of it was found to be true and no one of that name had ever existed?

'Jago Kerswell, born 1754 at Marcombe in Devon,' Jessie read out loud. 'Okay, let's see if there are any indexes here for the parish of Marcombe.' The library had an entire shelf full of books relating to the county of Devonshire, and Jessie was soon browsing while Kayla waited nearby. She chewed on a fingernail and looked around in awe at all the other people in the room who seemed very busy with their research. She felt like a fraud, but Jessie's next words calmed her down slightly. 'You mustn't expect too much, you know. Sometimes the records of a certain place haven't survived and even if they have, they might be fragmentary. So don't be too upset if we don't find anything today.'

'All right.'

'Oh, look, here's something.' Jessie took a book off the shelf and started to leaf through it. 'Hmm, well, it says here that Marcombe is a tiny little place by the coast and there is a family of the same name who held the manor for a long time, but there's no index to the parish registers.'

Kayla almost blurted out, 'So it exists then!', but managed to bite back the words. She didn't want Jessie to think her completely mad. She was extremely relieved to find there was at least a place of that name in Devon though, but she supposed she could have heard it somewhere and still made the rest of the story up. 'Er, so then what do we do?' she asked.

'We'll have to go downstairs and see if they have the actual register on microfilm. Then it's just a case of trawling through it. Let's go.' Jessie replaced the book and set off towards the stairs, looking over her shoulder with a smile. 'You'll have to excuse me if I get a bit carried away. It's the thrill of the chase, so to speak. I just love it.'

'You do this a lot?'

'Oh, yes. I'm doing a one-name study on my mother's surname which is Delessay and I've been working on it for years. My grandmother got me started with one of those stories about how the family had been rich and owned lots of land which they were subsequently cheated out of. I was curious to find out if it was true and pretty soon I was hooked on genealogy. It's really addictive, you know.'

'And was it true, the story?'

Jessie laughed. 'No, at least not back to the seventeenth century, which is as far as I've got. I think it was wishful thinking on Grandma's part, but then she was never happy with anything she had. I've found farmers, blacksmiths and innkeepers, but the majority of my ancestors were agricultural labourers who couldn't even read or write. None of them owned much land, if any.'

'What did your granny say when you told her?'

'Luckily she died before I got very far, so I didn't have to disillusion her.' Jessie smiled again. 'I doubt if she'd have believed me anyway. She was the sort of person who would say it was a misprint if you showed her proof of something in a book.' They both laughed.

'I know the type. My dad's a bit like that.'

Kayla found the microfilm room fascinating. There were lots of other eager genealogists – whether amateur or professional she didn't know – who were glued to the lit-up screens of the microfilm readers, quietly browsing through reel after reel of genealogical documents. She observed them and admired their patience, while Jessie left her to look for the Marcombe parish registers.

'I've got it.' Jessie returned, triumphantly brandishing a small plastic box. 'That was lucky because they don't have copies of all the registers here. Saves you going all the way to Exeter or waiting weeks for the film to arrive at the Mormon centre.'

'What have they got to do with anything?'

'They have a great research centre and they'll order in microfilms for you but, as I said, we won't need to go there.'

Kayla wasn't really listening to this explanation, however, but watched intently as Jessie extracted the film from the box and threaded it deftly onto the two reel-holders.

'I can see you've done that before. It would have taken me ages to figure out which way it was supposed to go.'

'Ah, yes, practice makes perfect, right? Okay, here goes.' Jessie wound the film forward. It contained a number of different villages, since they were quite small and consequently didn't have too many records, and soon Jessie found the right one. 'Here's Marcombe, look.'

Kayla peered at the screen and the barely decipherable and decidedly spindly handwriting on the faded documents. 'How on earth can you read that? Looks like Greek to me.'

'Oh, you get used to it, although some are worse than others. I hate when they're really faint. Anyway, let's see, sixteen hundreds, seventeen, seventeen fifty-one, two, three and . . . four. Right, here it is.'

Kayla's eyes were now glued to the screen and she held her breath. This was it. The moment of truth. Now that they had actually found it she was suddenly not sure she wanted to know. If her brain had invented the whole story she would feel like a complete idiot, but on the other hand, if it turned out to be true, wouldn't that be even more scary? It was too late for regrets, however. Jessie gave a whoop of delight, then clapped a hand over her mouth.

'Oops, sorry, we're supposed to be quiet in here. But look, Kayla, there it is.' She pointed to a line of old-fashioned writing on the screen and read out, '*Baptisms, 1754. Jago Kerswell, son of Lenora Kerswell, a Traveller. Baseborn. June 24th.*'

'Wow, I don't believe it,' Kayla whispered and

let out a shaky breath. And she didn't. Somehow she'd counted on the fact that it was all something her mind had dreamed up. But there it was, in black and white, right in front of her eyes. It was for real. She swallowed hard and added, 'So he was right.'

'Who?'

'What? Oh, just one of my relatives. Uhm, can we look for the rest of the things I wrote down?'

'Sure, let me see. "*Sir John Marcombe*", you want to find his christening? You haven't written down a date.'

'I know, but it should be around the same time, perhaps slightly before or after.'

'Let's check from 1740 onwards and see what we find. We'll write down any Marcombes and then puzzle out their relationships later.'

They found the christening of '*John Marcombe, son of Sir Philip, gent. and his wife Martha, Lady Marcombe*' in 1750, then the baptism of another baby called Margaret roughly a year later. A week after the christening, both baby Margaret and Martha, Lady Marcombe, were buried, presumably together.

'Oh, how sad,' Kayla said. 'So Sir Philip was left all alone with a one-year-old son, poor man.'

'Yes, Lady Marcombe probably died of puerperal fever. A lot of the midwives didn't know the meaning of hygiene in those days.'

'How awful. We're so lucky nowadays, aren't we?'

They continued their search and the parish

registers revealed that Sir Philip had died in 1774 and a year later, in 1775, his son, Sir John, married a Miss Mary Ashford.

'They don't seem to have had any kids though,' Jessie commented when they found no children of that union. 'And look, this Lady Marcombe is recorded in the burial register in 1778 having apparently succumbed to a fever of some sort, and barely a year later Sir John, widower, remarries a Miss Elizabeth Anne Wesley.'

'Yes, you're right.' Kayla could hardly believe her eyes. Everything Jago had said was true. Every last thing. *Damn! How can that be?*

'Let's see if they had any children then,' Jessie muttered, scrolling the film slowly forward, not noticing that Kayla had gone very quiet. 'Nothing in 1780 . . . nor '81, strange. I usually find babies within the first two years of marriage. Oh, hang on, look.'

Kayla peered at the screen and read, *'Baptised, April 30th, 1782, Wesley John son of Sir John Marcombe, Bt. (born March 23rd).* No mention of his wife. I wonder why?'

'Their names weren't always written down, it was the father who was important. Oh, and look, there's a page missing here so we don't know if mother and child survived. I hate when that happens!'

There appeared to be no other children either before or after this date, although they checked the baptismal register up to and including the year

1810, by which time the son called Wesley John was married and had children of his own.

'So does that help you?' Jessie asked.

'Yes, it was exactly what I needed. I don't know how to thank you enough, you've been great.'

'Don't worry about it, I enjoyed myself. Seriously, it's always satisfying when you find what you're looking for and believe me, that's not usually the case. You see what I mean now about the thrill of the chase?' Jessie's violet-blue eyes were shining with excitement.

Kayla nodded, but thought to herself that Jessie had no idea of the added spice involved in this particular chase.

CHAPTER 10

As Jago soon discovered, Mr Gainsborough was an easy enough man to please. Plenty of good wine and a willing serving wench and the man was happiness personified. Long after his nephew had retired, Mr Gainsborough entertained Jago's other customers with his witty comments, animated conversation and musical abilities. Having caught sight of a fiddle, he played a number of tunes, and the taproom was a lively, happy place that evening.

Jago found the time to sit with his guest for a while.

'Ah, Mr Kerswell. This is a very snug little inn you have here. Very nice indeed.'

'Thank you kindly. Most gentlemen find it beneath their expectations.' Jago grinned to show he didn't care about such men or their opinions.

'Bah! Gentlemen. There is only one good thing about them – their purse. Do you know,' Mr Gainsborough leaned closer to whisper confidentially in the manner of someone who has drunk slightly more than is advisable, 'if it were not for the fact that I must needs earn some money and my wife won't stop her infernal nagging, I wouldn't paint another portrait. Not ever.'

'You paint a lot of them then, Mr Gainsborough?'

'Oh, yes. The wretched face business is what keeps the wolf from my door. If I had a choice, I would spend all my time painting landscapes. To me, there is nothing more wonderful than such tranquil, rural scenes – it's what life is all about.'

'I agree, sir.'

'Mind you, there are the occasional faces which are worth capturing in paint. Take the lady we met with this morning, for instance. Now that is what real grace and beauty looks like. I would like to do a portrait of her, indeed I would.'

'Why don't you stay for a few days then, at my expense of course, and paint the lady? I'm sure she would be agreeable.' And I would love to have a likeness of her, Jago added silently to himself. 'No doubt she'll pay you well for your efforts too. Her husband is well to do. In fact, I'm sure she could persuade him to buy some of your landscapes and seascapes too.'

'Excellent idea, dear fellow. I shall tell my nephew in the morning.' Mr Gainsborough's decision made with admirable speed, he continued with the evening's entertainment.

Eliza proved uncommonly stubborn, however, and refused to have her portrait done unless Mr Gainsborough promised to do one of Jago as well. He grudgingly agreed and set up his easel near the cove where they had first met.

'Why do you wish to paint me here, Mr Gainsborough? Would it not be more convenient indoors?' Eliza asked him.

'No, dear lady. You see, your colouring blends in perfectly with the natural environment here and that is how I wish to capture you.'

The artist chalked in the rough position of the face on his canvas, then he released it from the stretcher and pulled it over by strings fastened temporarily at the back until he came to the edge of the canvas. He placed his easel right up against Eliza's head and she glanced at him in confusion.

'I need to see your features at close quarters, my lady,' he explained. 'It will make for a better likeness, I assure you.'

'Very well.' Never having sat for her portrait before, Eliza didn't argue. She was wearing a simple moss-green gown, of which Mr Gainsborough had heartily approved, and he insisted on her hair hanging loose.

'Wonderful. Your ash-blonde hair, hazel eyes and green gown blend in with the rocks, moss and lichen perfectly. This will be a superb composition, I promise you.'

Jago, keeping watch from a respectful distance, felt sure the man was right. Besides, any picture with Eliza in it was bound to be delightful.

'You actually found it? All of it?' Maddie's voice on the phone sounded incredulous, which was exactly how Kayla herself felt.

114

'Yes, down to the last detail. It was amazing, truly amazing.'

'And you thought you dreamed it all?'

'I did dream it, I swear to you. I can't possibly have talked to a man in a painting. But how do you explain all the facts we found?'

'It's weird. Really spooky, actually. It's sending shivers down my spine. Maybe he's haunting you and it's not the painting you're talking to but a spirit.'

'It's a possibility I suppose. I hadn't thought of that. A ghost.' Kayla drew in a deep breath. She had always been slightly afraid of the supernatural and never wanted to hear ghost stories as a child.

Maddie was quiet for a while before asking, 'So what are you going to do now?'

'I don't know. I guess I'll have to find out if this Marcombe Hall is still owned by Sir John's descendants, and then maybe pay them a visit. What do you think? Does that sound crazy to you?'

'Actually, I think this is the most exciting thing I've ever heard. And the most incredible.'

They both started laughing in a slightly hysterical way, which let out some of the tension and made it all seem more bearable somehow. Kayla felt that maybe everything was going to be all right after all. If Maddie believed her and was on her side, she could face anything. She had proved beyond doubt her mind wasn't playing tricks on her. Now she had to continue the search. What else could she do? It was too intriguing not to.

'When will you go?' Maddie asked.

'Who knows? I'm afraid I have to sort out my own life first before I can even think of doing anything about this. I'm going to have to find a new job as I can't possibly work in the same office as Mike now, it would be unbearable. Even if I switch with one of the other girls, I'd still have to see him all the time. Can you imagine how embarrassing that would be?'

'Yes, not a good thing, that's for sure. You'd better tell them as soon as possible.'

'I've handed in my notice already. I figured the sooner, the better.'

'You can always do temp work like me until you find another permanent job. It pays the rent and it's very flexible.'

'Yes. It's a great shame though. I really liked it there, but I'm sure they understand.'

'Oh, I wish I could go to Devon with you, but I have a really good assignment at the moment and I had to agree to stay for at least a month or they wouldn't give it to me.' Maddie sounded wistful. 'That's the only problem with temping, you have to take what you can get.'

'Hey, slow down will you. I'm not even sure I'll be going to Devon. The Marcombe family might have moved away ages ago. We're talking over two hundred years here. Or the house might have crumbled and fallen into the sea or whatever. I'll have to find out.'

'Well, either way you'll be going somewhere, and it sounds a lot more exciting than working.'

Kayla smiled. 'You're right. I think I'm actually going to enjoy this search.' She glanced at the portrait of Jago and could have sworn he winked at her. 'Wretched man,' she whispered, after she had hung up the phone, but she couldn't help but smile at him.

It was all surprisingly easy in the end and Kayla almost started to believe in the fate that Jago had talked about in her dream.

Because old Mr Martin, the head of Human Resources, liked her and sympathised with her dilemma, he'd agreed to let her work for two weeks in a different department and then take the rest of the time as unpaid holiday.

'Of course we'll miss you,' he told her kindly, 'but I can quite see that it would be impossible for you to stay on. I have no doubt you will easily find another position, but I will write you a glowing reference just in case it's needed.' Kayla was extremely grateful and almost burst into tears.

She bumped into Mike a few times during the next few days and she could tell he had expected her to apologise for her 'hasty' words. Since no such apology was forthcoming, he made a great show of asking one of the other secretaries out to lunch and buying her a bouquet of flowers the next day. Red roses, naturally. Kayla ignored him and a few days later he left some carrier bags on her desk, which contained items of clothing and a few other bits and pieces she had left at his flat. Kayla reciprocated with a bin bag full of his possessions and sent him an internal e-mail to say thank you, but received no reply. And that, it seemed, was that.

'Isn't it strange how relationships can be over so abruptly?' she said to Maddie on the phone that evening. 'A year is quite a long time, really, and all I have to show for it are three plastic carrier bags of stuff.'

'Yes, but look on the bright side – at least he didn't chuck them in the bin. And think of the wisdom you've gained,' Maddie added in a theatrical voice. Kayla giggled. You could always count on Maddie to cheer you up.

'The only thing I've learned is that I should stay the hell away from auctions,' she retorted and glanced over at Jago, who was doing his *Mona Lisa* impression yet again.

The following Saturday, Kayla made her way to the central Kensington library, near the Town Hall, to search for further information. She lived within walking distance of the huge, Victorian red-brick building, so it was familiar to her. Books were as necessary to her as breathing and she went to the library on a regular basis since her flat was too small for her to buy more than her absolute favourites, but this time she wasn't looking for reading matter.

She was directed to the second floor, and there in the Reference Library she found what she was looking for – the enormously fat volume of the current issue of *Debrett's Peerage & Baronetage*. She took it to a reading table and sat down to find the right page. The names were all in alphabetical order, so it didn't take her long.

'Bingo!' she exclaimed without thinking, and was given several dirty looks from other readers. She blushed and shrugged her shoulders in silent apology, then stared at the page in front of her. There it was in black and white:

MARCOMBE (E) 1740, of Marcombe Hall, Marcombe, Devon

Sir Wesley John, 7th Baronet, born 1977, elder son of Sir John Philip, m. 2002 Caroline Marie Campbell, d. of Henry Andrew Campbell, and has issue.

Daughter Living. Eleanor Elizabeth Marie b. 2005

Brother Living. Alexander Philip b. 1980

So there was still a descendant of Sir John living at Marcombe Hall. 'Excellent,' Kayla whispered and made a note of this information before returning the book to its shelf.

Next, she had a look in the telephone directory for Devon South East and noted down the phone number listed under 'Marcombe, W.J.'. There was no mention of his title, but since there were only a few other Marcombes, all with different initials, and the address was Marcombe Hall, she assumed he had to be the right one. Now all she had to do was find the courage to call and ask if he had any paintings by Gainsborough, and if so, whether she could come and have a look at them.

Before she left the library, she borrowed three books about Thomas Gainsborough, just in case there might be any further clues in them. Although she still doubted Jago's story about the famous artist, it would be best to be properly prepared for any eventuality, she thought.

Her mobile rang as Kayla walked in through the door of her flat and she hurried to answer. 'Hello?'

'Kayla, it's Maddie. I was just wondering if you feel like going out tonight? There's a group of us going to a really nice pub we've just discovered. It's down by the river.'

'Thanks, but no thanks. I'm going to spend the evening with Jago.'

'You're kidding, right?'

'No.' Kayla giggled. 'I'm perfectly serious.'

'Is he talking to you again? If he is, I'm coming over straight away. I want to speak to him too. It's not fair that you should have all the fun.'

'No, no, you're not missing out on anything. And he doesn't talk to me when I'm awake, only in my dreams. I think. I just meant I'm doing some research that has to do with him, so I really don't have time to go out.'

'Hmm.' Maddie didn't sound convinced. 'Well, if I really can't tempt you?'

'Nope, sorry. I'm not really in the mood anyway after all that's happened. I'm sure you understand.'

'Of course. I'm sorry, I should have thought about that. Maybe I'll see you tomorrow?'

'All right. Come over for lunch or something.'

Kayla fixed a quick supper of scrambled eggs on toast, and settled down on the sofa with a glass of wine and one of the Gainsborough biographies. Outside the incessant noise of traffic, sirens and humanity that made up the everyday sounds of London continued as always, but Kayla's flat was quiet and she was able to concentrate on her reading. She soon became absorbed in the details of Gainsborough's life and found that he'd been a fascinating man. When she read about some of the things he was alleged to have said, or the somewhat bawdy notes he added to some of his letters, a chuckle escaped her. Time flew by and when she looked up at last, it was past midnight. She drained the last of her wine, which was now lukewarm.

'Please, won't you tell me what is so amusing?'

Kayla choked on the drink and the heavy book fell to the floor with a thump. Between coughs she looked up at the enigmatically smiling face of Jago and gave him an angry glare. He wasn't moving, but she had recognised his voice. It was the voice she heard in her dreams. There was no mistaking it.

'Damn it, Jago, you could have waited until I had swallowed my wine,' she grumbled. The coughing fit over at last, she bent to retrieve the book. 'I think I need to see a doctor, I really do. Or maybe I've had too much wine, though I could have sworn it was only the one glass.'

'I apologise.' She could hear his voice clearly, although it sounded as if it was coming from a long way off. 'I shall try to be more careful in future.'

A cold sensation swirled around her stomach and it had nothing to do with the wine she'd drunk. It was pure fear, its icy tentacles spreading through her veins. She stared at the painting. He really was talking to her and she didn't think she was asleep this time. 'Are you a ghost?' she whispered. 'Is that how you talk to me?'

'Perhaps,' came the reply. 'I am certainly dead, but whether I'm a ghost or not, I have no idea.' He didn't sound too bothered about either condition.

Kayla closed her eyes. If she allowed herself to think about what was happening, she would faint. It scared the hell out of her. Talking to a ghost or a painting, both were equally frightening prospects, and yet that was apparently what she was doing. She pinched herself viciously to make sure she wasn't dreaming this time and watched the red mark spread on her arm.

'Try not to think about it,' he advised, as if he could read her mind. 'Now please tell me what was amusing you. I'm rather lonely over here and could do with a diversion.'

'I'm not sure I should be talking to you at all. If anyone heard me they'd lock me up for sure. Besides, I'm absolutely terrified.'

'Of me? You needn't be. I can't hurt you.'

'No, not of you exactly, but of what's happening.'

'But you told your friend you were going to spend the evening with me. I heard you distinctly. She didn't seem to mind. Was it that lovely red-head who was here the other day?'

'Jago! Are you eavesdropping on all my conversations and spying on me?' The thought gave her goosebumps, but some of her fear drained away and was replaced with righteous indignation.

'Well, not all of them.'

'Are you alive all the time? I mean, not alive precisely, but . . . you know, conscious or whatever?' Kayla sighed. 'I can't believe I'm even asking this,' she muttered before looking up at him again. He still wasn't moving a muscle.

'It's difficult to describe.' Jago hesitated. 'I suppose you could say I exist. I can hear some things, I can see others, although by no means everything. Sometimes I find myself in darkness. When that happens, I have no concept of time passing by and I hear nothing. I can only think.' He paused for a moment. 'There appears to be something which prevents me from speaking to anyone other than you. I expect it is part of the spell.'

'Spell? What spell? God, I don't believe this – ghosts, spells, whatever next?'

'I can't go into any details at the moment. Suffice it to say that what is taking place between us right now is courtesy of a spell, which is why I need you to find Eliza for me. When you do, and when I am reunited with her, the spell will be broken.'

'And you won't be able to talk to me any more?'

'That I can't tell you. It might be possible, but we will have to see when the time comes.'

'Great, I can't wait.' Kayla was silent for a while before continuing. 'It's strange, you know, but now that we've been talking for a while I don't feel quite so scared. I feel more sort of numb. It's like I have conversations with dead people all the time.' Kayla blinked. It was true, the frozen fingers inside her had eased off and she felt almost frighteningly calm. She wondered vaguely why she wasn't panicking and running for the door – anything, except sitting there talking to a disembodied voice.

'I believe that is part of the magic. If you were too frightened of me you wouldn't be able to help me. Now if you like me, on the other hand, then you will do your best. Therefore, the spell makes you like me, I think.'

Like him! If only he knew. 'Like' was not the word she would use to describe how she felt when she gazed at him. It was far too tame. 'Obsessed' or 'love-struck' would be nearer the mark. But maybe that was part of the spell too. Spell? She shook her head. She really didn't believe in such things, nor in ghosts, but what was she supposed to think now?

'So why aren't you moving this time? Or did I dream that part?'

'No, but sometimes I have less energy and it's too much of an effort. Just speaking to you is hard work. I'm sorry, I can't explain it. Now please, Kayla, entertain me. What were you reading?'

'Hmm? Oh, I'm reading about Thomas Gainsborough. He must have been quite a character. Honestly, the things he's supposed to have said.'

It was Jago's turn to chuckle. 'That's nothing. You should have seen him in action, but truly, I don't think I should sully a lady's ears with such tales. Read to me from the book, please, and I will tell you if it rings true.'

Kayla did as she was told and they laughed together. After a while, however, Jago's voice began to sound tired and he said he had to go.

'Go where?'

'Back to my resting place, wherever it is. As I said, speaking to you for any length of time tires me. Forgive me.'

'No, that's all right. I understand, I think.' She hesitated before asking, 'Jago? Will you speak to me again?'

'Certainly I will. If you wish it, that is.'

Kayla smiled. 'Yes, I actually think I do.' She clapped a hand to her forehead. 'I really am going mad, aren't I?'

'No, you're not, I promise you. Have faith and all will be well. Goodnight, my dear.' The voice faded away and silence reigned. There were only the usual sounds of traffic from the street outside and the distant rumbling of the underground. Kayla stared at Jago's portrait for a long time before returning to her book. After trying unsuccessfully to concentrate, however, she gave up and went to bed, only to dream of a swarthy pirate with Jago's features who didn't speak to her, but did other things she liked even better.

CHAPTER 11

Jago was just coming up the stairs from the cellar of the inn with a keg of ale on his shoulder, when the door to the taproom was flung open so hard it slammed into the wall. It was late afternoon, the day after Mr Gainsborough and his nephew had finally departed. Only two customers sat nursing a tankard each by the fire, but they both looked up at the same time as Jago. Their mouths gaped when they saw who came striding in.

Sir John Marcombe.

Jago drew in a steadying breath and pretended he hadn't noticed anything out of the ordinary. With slow and deliberate movements, he placed the keg behind the counter and tried not to show how hard his heart was thumping. Had John found out, he wondered. Was that why he had a face on him like a stormy thundercloud? Well, he couldn't prove anything, or could he? Had Gainsborough talked after all? Jago swallowed hard.

'You there.' John slapped his riding gloves down onto the counter next to Jago. 'I hear you're the man in charge.'

127

'I own this inn, yes,' Jago replied warily and decided not to add, 'as you well know'.

'No, I don't mean this miserable hovel.' John lowered his voice, although only slightly. 'The free-trading, you fool.'

Jago felt relief flood through him when he realised John hadn't come about Eliza. Then he registered what he had said and raised his eyebrows, seriously annoyed at being addressed like that by his half-brother. He decided to let it go for now.

'What of it?' he said non-committally. Did John really think Jago was stupid enough to admit to any such thing in public?

'You owe me a lock, that's what.' John scowled at him. 'I'll not have anyone enter my property without permission and if I have a lock put in anywhere, it's there for a purpose.'

'A lock?' It took Jago a moment to remember that behind the secret door he'd opened there were also stairs leading down to the Marcombe Hall cellars. As far as he knew, no one ever put Sir John's share down there, but perhaps they had done so in the past? And he'd thought he was the only one who knew about the hidden entrance – obviously that was not the case. At least if John thought that was the reason for breaking the lock, it was better than the truth. And now he knew that John – and possibly others – were aware of the secret door after all, he'd be more careful.

'Yes, I'm warning you, anyone found in my

cellars will be handed over to the magistrate, brandy or no brandy,' John said. 'Is that clear?'

'I'm sure everyone hereabouts will know about it before nightfall,' Jago replied with a small nod towards their audience. The two men by the fire turned away when John fixed them with a glare, but Jago was sure they weren't deaf.

'Good. And if anyone tampers with the lock again, I'll hold you responsible. Now you owe me three shillings for the old one.'

'The hell I do.' Jago stared his half-brother straight in the eyes, his gaze not wavering for a second. Eliza was one thing, he was guilty as charged if John ever found out about that, but he'd be damned if he'd kowtow to him over any other matter.

John was the first to lower his eyes, red colour flooding his cheeks at what he obviously took for insolence. 'Well, tell the free-traders they owe me an extra keg of brandy then. Someone's responsible and I will have compensation.'

Jago just continued to glare at John. There was no way he'd admit to knowing any free-traders or having any connections with them and this fact finally seemed to penetrate John's fury.

He turned on his heel and left without another word.

During the following week Kayla had several conversations with Jago and each time it happened she became less incredulous and more accepting of the situation. She stopped doubting her own sanity – or at least caring about the fact that she might be going crazy – and began to take it for granted that he would reply whenever she addressed a comment to him. More often than not, he did.

She even found that their talks helped her through the difficult time she was having at the office where, because it was a small firm, she was forced to see Mike every day. Although she managed to avoid having to speak to him directly, it was still an awkward situation. When she came home depressed after the leaving party some of her workmates threw for her in her last week, Jago tried to comfort her, even though she sensed he didn't quite understand why she was upset.

'It was time for you to move on, Kayla. And you can still see those people from time to time, surely? They're not going anywhere.'

'Yes, I know it would have been impossible to stay and of course I can still see them. I'm turning into a real Moaning Minnie, aren't I? I'm sorry, I'm not usually like this. It's all just been a bit too much lately.'

'Think of it this way, you may be entering a new and exciting phase of your life. There are endless possibilities,' Jago said.

'Yes, the phase where I'm committed to a lunatic asylum for talking to paintings.' But she couldn't help laughing and felt better after that.

Her mother made things worse by calling almost

every day to try and persuade Kayla to change her mind. No one in her family seemed to want to believe the wedding was cancelled for good.

'But darling, surely it was just a tiff? Everyone has them. It's wedding nerves, that's all.'

'No, Mum.' Kayla sighed. She was so sick of hearing about wedding nerves. Surely if she'd been marrying the right person there wouldn't have been any and no doubts either? 'I'm not going to change my mind, Mum. I'm sorry, but I mean it. There won't be a wedding, okay?'

'But Kayla . . .' Her mother thought she was being hasty, but Kayla knew better now. Marrying Mike would have been a disaster, she could see that with hindsight. She could only be grateful to Jago for coming between them, even if he hadn't done it on purpose. In the end, her mother had to admit defeat and reluctantly cancelled all the arrangements.

'You do realise I'll have to send all the wedding gifts back? It wouldn't be right to keep them.'

'Of course I know that.' Kayla gritted her teeth. Why on earth would she want to keep them now anyway?

When the two weeks were finally up, Kayla left the office for the last time with mixed feelings. She knew Jago was right, and she could visit her former workmates at any time, but she was quite sure she wouldn't be going back for a long while, if ever.

With nothing to do, other than to try and find another job, Kayla had no excuse for putting off her call to Sir Wesley Marcombe. She waited until the Monday morning, then gathered her courage and dialled the number quickly before she could change her mind. A woman's voice answered.

'Marcombe Hall, good morning.'

'Could I speak to Sir Wesley, please?'

'I'm sorry, he's not in at the moment. I'm his secretary, can I help you?'

'Well, yes, perhaps you can.' Kayla hesitated, then quickly made up a story about being an art student wanting to study paintings by Gainsborough. 'I've been told Sir Wesley might have one in his possession and I was wondering if I could come and have a look at it?'

'I don't see why not. There are loads of paintings here, just gathering dust if you ask me. Let me see . . .' The secretary made a rustling noise as if she was leafing through a diary. 'How about Wednesday afternoon at four o'clock? I think Sir Wesley is free then and I'm sure he'd be delighted to show you around.'

'Wednesday. So soon? Er, yes, that should be fine. Thank you so much.'

Kayla hung up and leaned back against the wall, taking deep breaths. Things were moving too fast and her heart beat a rapid tattoo of panic. She didn't like lying, it made her feel very uncomfortable and she was usually betrayed by a blush staining her cheeks whenever she tried it. What if

Sir Wesley caught her out? He might think her an art thief or worse.

'Don't be silly,' she told herself. 'You're only going to have a quick look at the painting, then you'll be on your way. Besides, why would Sir Wesley care who you are anyway?'

Kayla set off for the West Country early on the Wednesday morning, having said a reluctant goodbye to Jago. It almost felt like parting from an old friend and the thought made her smile.

'I promise I'll come back and tell you what I find as soon as I can, but please don't hold out too much hope. After all, over two hundred years have passed and there's no guarantee Eliza's painting even exists any more,' she told him.

'I know, but somehow I feel that I would know if it had been destroyed. I should have passed on to somewhere else, if you see what I mean. There would've been no reason for me to remain in this limbo if my link to her was gone. Am I making sense?' For the first time he'd seemed vulnerable to Kayla, no longer the self-assured rogue she had become used to talking to. This, more than anything, strengthened her resolve to help him if she could.

'Yes, I understand, Jago. I'll do my best. Look after my flat and scare away any burglars, won't you? Most people run a mile if they see or hear a ghost or anything paranormal. Don't know why I didn't.'

'You may be certain I will. And Kayla?'

'Yes?'

'Thank you. I appreciate your efforts on my behalf, no matter what the outcome may be.'

Kayla had discussed her journey with Maddie. 'I think I'll make it easy for myself and take the M4 to Bristol and then the M5 down to Exeter,' she told her friend. 'If I stay on the motorway I can't get lost, can I? Perhaps I'll even make a little detour and stop for lunch at Bath, it's such a lovely place.'

'What about after Exeter?' Their heads were bent over the road map and Maddie peered at it, following the route Kayla's finger travelled.

'I'll have to try and follow the signs to Totnes and then on towards the coast. It shouldn't be too difficult.'

'Hmm. Maybe I should come with you? You know what you're like when it comes to following directions. If you change your appointment and wait until next week I might be able to take a couple of days off.'

'Come on, I'm not that bad. I don't think it's very far from Exeter and I can always stop and ask the way. It should be a piece of cake.'

'If you say so.' Maddie looked very sceptical and shook her head, but that only made Kayla even more determined to manage by herself.

It had sounded like a nice, relaxing journey, a bit of a holiday after all the recent upheavals in her life, but Kayla later acknowledged she should have known better. Nothing was ever that simple, especially not for her.

Everything went well to begin with and she drove into Bath just before lunchtime as planned. She even had time for a quick stroll around the busy streets before treating herself to an early lunch at the Pump Room. The spring sunshine flooded the large airy restaurant and Kayla felt as if she was eating in the lap of luxury. A pianist playing classical pieces softly in the background added to the atmosphere. She allowed herself to daydream for a while of how it would have been to promenade round the room in Jago's day, taking the waters and greeting friends and acquaintances. Ladies in beautiful dresses, the men in long coats and cascading cravats, although perhaps none as attractive as Jago. Even so, it was a pleasant fantasy. Refreshed and relaxed Kayla continued her journey.

Later that afternoon, however, she had to acknowledge that Maddie's misgivings had been well founded. Mike's words to her during their last holiday together came back to taunt her.

'Honestly, the clichéd description "couldn't find your way out of a paper bag" fits you perfectly, Kayla.' They'd been driving around the sun-drenched landscape of Mallorca at the time, searching for some caves which the tourist brochures had promised were spectacular and easy to find. Instead they'd ended up somewhere in the middle of the island and that was when Mike decided he had better do the navigating. 'You drive,' he'd said with a sigh, and Kayla had taken her place at the steering wheel without a word.

'I can't believe I've done it again,' she wailed now, trying to suppress the rising panic. She was completely lost in the Devon landscape and pulled up by the side of the road. In sheer frustration she hit the steering wheel with the flat of her hands. 'Damn it all to hell!'

There had been quite a lot of traffic around Exeter and in the confusion she had missed her turning at the southern end of the motorway, which meant she had to retrace part of her route. This took quite a while due to some roadworks on her side of the carriageway. After that she'd been fine as far as Totnes, but then something had gone seriously wrong.

The roads became smaller and narrower the further she went. There were tall hedges on either side, completely obscuring the view, with the consequence that she lost what little sense of direction she possessed in the first place. Down towards the coast the roads were almost not worthy of the name. In fact, they were nothing more than a single track and not a wide one at that. Each time she met an oncoming vehicle, Kayla had to either reverse to a slightly wider meeting point, or squeeze her little Peugeot as far into the nearest hedge as possible.

'Oh God, the scratches,' she murmured, but tried not to think about the damage she must be causing the car's paintwork.

After several miles of these tiny, winding lanes, Kayla slowed the car to a crawl and tried to look around, but there was nothing to see. She had passed the occasional farm and small village, but they were few and far between and she couldn't locate them on the map.

'Argh, I'm going to be so late,' she moaned now, glancing at her watch. She was pretty sure she hadn't seen a road sign for quite some time, and she also had a sneaking suspicion that she'd already passed this particular turning before. It looked awfully familiar. Well, there was nothing for it but to continue.

'Should I go right or left, or maybe straight on?'

She gazed forlornly at the crumpled map, but couldn't make head nor tail of it. There was no one to ask either, not a living soul for miles, apart from the occasional flock of sheep.

As she finally decided to turn left a few raindrops spattered the windscreen, and these quickly turned into a complete deluge. It became impossible to see more than a few yards along the road and the windscreen wipers had to work overtime, squeaking in outraged protest.

'Great, this is all I need,' Kayla muttered, clamping her teeth together in frustration. And now was definitely not the best time to find out that the blade of the windscreen wiper on the driver's side of the car needed to be changed. Why hadn't she noticed that before?

She checked her watch once more. It was only half past four in the afternoon, but it was so dark that she had to turn on the headlights. The wind picked up and she could feel the little car being buffeted again and again by a particularly strong gust. Every time she passed under a tree, torrents of rain slapped onto the car's roof, making her jump, and Kayla had to slow right down in order to navigate safely around the sharp bends. To add insult to injury, patches of mist began to appear and she started to despair in earnest.

'For heaven's sake, does this road never end?' she exclaimed. Her eyes stung from concentrating so hard and she felt exhausted. It had been a very long day, and unfortunately it wasn't over yet.

Time became a blur and Kayla wondered if this nightmare journey would continue for all eternity. Then the road suddenly turned abruptly to the right and she thought she might be driving along the coast at last. She could just make out what seemed to be a sheer drop on her left and when she opened the window a cautious inch, the salty smell of the sea came wafting into the car. Ten minutes later the road wound its way inland again and Kayla caught sight of a light up ahead.

Oh, thank God, at least I can ask for directions.

The light turned out to be the porch lamp of a small house standing next to a massive pair of wrought iron gates, its posts guarded by two fierce looking eagles carved in stone. Kayla drew up in front of them and stopped the car. Grabbing her handbag and car keys she made a dash for a smaller gate, which led to the house, and shivering from the cold wind, she rang the doorbell.

The owner of the house took his sweet time. Kayla was almost jumping up and down by the time a man in his mid-fifties with a weather-beaten face opened the door a crack at last and peered at her suspiciously. 'Yes, can I help you?' His West Country burr was much stronger than Jago's, but even the familiarity of this didn't calm Kayla.

'I'm very sorry to bother you but I'm afraid I'm completely lost. Could you possibly tell me where I am and how to get to the nearest town?' She held out her creased map and gave him a look that she hoped would have melted a heart of stone. The rain was pouring down her face and her jacket was soaked already. She prayed the man could help her.

He narrowed his eyes for a fraction of a second, then apparently decided she was trustworthy. He opened the door wide. 'You'd best come in then,' he said grudgingly.

'Thank you.' Kayla stepped inside and shut the door behind her. She was careful not to go any further than the doormat in case she dripped water on the gleaming floor tiles. To her right Kayla caught a glimpse of a cosy living room and a huge, shaggy dog came padding out from there to see who had come to visit. He didn't bark and after a perfunctory sniff at her sodden shoes he went back to the comfort of the fire without so much as a wag of his tail.

The man took the by now extremely soggy map from her and asked, 'So where is it you wish to go then, miss?'

'Well, I was on my way to Marcombe Hall which is supposed to be somewhere near the village of Marcombe, but I lost my way and I'm afraid I've missed my appointment now. I suppose the best thing to do is go to the nearest town and find a hotel room, and I can call from there and see if I can rearrange my visit for tomorrow.'

The man looked up sharply. 'Marcombe Hall, did you say?' He gave a short crack of laughter. 'No need to go any further then. This here is the gatehouse for the Hall.'

'You're joking! Well, what a coincidence.' Kayla couldn't believe her luck had finally turned. 'Thank you, I'm so sorry to have troubled you then.' As she turned to go there was a sudden screech of tyres and the sound of a car horn hooting impatiently outside.

'Oh, that'll be the master,' the man said. 'Erm, you didn't by any chance park your car in front of the gate, did you?'

'What? Oh, yes. I suppose I'd better move it.'

'Too late, I reckon.'

'No! You don't mean . . .?' Kayla rushed out into the downpour and ran towards her little car, but thankfully it seemed to be in one piece. It was spot-lit by the headlights of a moss-green Land Rover which had pulled up behind it and it looked as though the second car had only just managed to stop. There was a mere inch between its bumper and Kayla's. A man was bent over the front fender of the larger car, presumably making sure he hadn't hit her car, and as he straightened out, the breath lodged in her throat. She couldn't see much of his face, since he had a baseball cap pulled down over his eyes, but she could tell he wasn't best pleased, his mouth an uncompromising line.

'What the hell do you mean by parking in front of my gate with your lights switched off like that?' he hissed at her. 'Have you no sense, woman? I could have totalled your little Peugeot. In fact, you're damn lucky I didn't.'

Kayla's first reaction was that she wanted to sink into a small dark hole somewhere and never come out again, but then something inside her snapped. It had been a long day, she was extremely tired, and she'd had enough. She faced him with her arms crossed defensively over her chest.

'Well, how was I supposed to know someone was going to come along just now? I only stopped for five minutes in this godforsaken place to ask for directions, and I haven't met anyone for miles,' she shot back angrily. 'Hours, in fact.' She glanced at the minute space between the Land Rover and the rear of her Peugeot. She had been very lucky, but she wasn't in the mood to be grateful. 'This really is the last straw,' she muttered.

The older man had come out to join them and he patted her arm consolingly. 'Could've been worse, eh? And at least you're where you wanted to be.'

'I've changed my mind. Can you please tell me how to get to the nearest town? I don't think I'll bother staying here after all.' She threw an angry glare in the other man's direction.

'But I thought you said you had an appointment. With the master, was it?'

'It doesn't matter.' Kayla gritted her teeth. All she wanted now was to get as far away from here as possible and forget this day had ever happened. Jago would have to find another champion. She'd had it with his quest.

'You had an appointment with me?' The younger man had obviously calmed down since he sounded less angry. Rain was pouring down his face, obscuring most of his features, but Kayla could hear the puzzlement in his voice.

'Yes, if you're Sir Wesley Marcombe.'

'I am, but I don't recall making any appointments for this afternoon,' he said, almost to himself. 'I wouldn't have gone out if I had.'

'You didn't exactly. I spoke to your secretary and she assured me you would be delighted to see me at four o'clock today. So much for that. And unfortunately, I couldn't find the way here.' Kayla emphasised the word 'delighted' sarcastically, and she thought she saw Sir Wesley's jaw tighten.

'Well, that explains it. Emma is probably the

most useless secretary I've ever had the misfortune to employ and I would guess she forgot to tell me.' He glanced at his watch. 'You'd better come up to the house though. You won't get far in that at the moment.' He nodded in the direction of her car.

'What do you mean? It's not broken.' Kayla started to circle the little car in order to make sure there wasn't any damage after all, a fresh wave of anxiety washing over her.

'No, but it's not exactly the biggest car in the world and when it rains like this around here some of the roads get flooded. You might get stuck in the middle of nowhere. No, I'm afraid you'll have to spend the night at Marcombe Hall. It would be safer.'

'Oh, wonderful,' Kayla muttered. 'This just gets better and better.' She drew in a deep breath and closed her eyes, praying for strength and patience. Should she believe him? Could she afford not to? She decided she was too tired to argue and she couldn't face any more driving. 'Oh, very well. Thank you,' she finally ground out, and thought she saw the ghost of a smile on Sir Wesley's lips before he turned towards the Land Rover.

'Follow me,' was all he said.

CHAPTER 12

Eliza came running towards him, her face flushed and shining with happiness. Before he could utter a word she threw herself into his arms and hugged him fiercely, as if she would never let go.

'Jago, oh Jago, I have such wonderful news – I am with child!' There were tears running down her cheeks, but he could see they were tears of joy so he smiled and kissed her, despite the misgivings that immediately welled up inside him.

'Wonderful indeed,' he agreed, but his mind was working furiously, wondering whether John would suspect the child wasn't his. When had his half-brother last been at home?

Eliza put her cheek against his shoulder and to his surprise she began to sob in earnest. 'I thought I was barren. I thought I would never have a child of my own. I was so frightened. So afraid that John . . . and I didn't want to live my life all alone in that big house you know.' Her voice broke and he stroked her hair with soothing motions.

'Shhh, my love. Everything's all right now. There was never anything wrong with you. Why do you think John didn't have any children by his first wife? He probably can't sire any.' This was pure conjecture on Jago's part, although based on scurrilous gossip he'd overheard in the taproom of the inn, but it was the only thing he could think of to stop her tears. Unfortunately it had the opposite effect.

'Oh, no! What if he knows that?' Eliza's eyes opened wide in horror. 'He'll know the child isn't his. Dear God, what am I to do?'

'Eliza, listen to me.' Jago cupped her face in his big hands to try and calm her. 'If he's been trying to father a child ever since you two were married, he must still hope that he is able to. He'll be overjoyed to find that his suspicions were incorrect and as long as we are discreet, he'll never find out.' He bent to kiss away the tears. 'Now smile for me again. If there's a babe growing within you, you must be strong. For the child's sake you must pretend that everything is all right. And it will be, I promise.'

She leaned into him with a little sigh. 'You are right, as always, my love. You are so wise.'

Jago knew that wisdom definitely wasn't one of his virtues at the moment, but he prayed they could both stay strong now for the sake of their child. They had no choice.

The road inside the gates was flanked by tall hedges and trees, which protected them from the worst of the wind. When they finally pulled up in front of the house, Kayla only had a fleeting glimpse of a large, white-rendered building with a huge porch supported by Doric columns. She thought the house might have three storeys, but it was impossible to tell for sure in the darkness.

Sir Wesley was already out of his car by the time she parked.

'Do you have any luggage?' he asked curtly.

Kayla nodded. 'In the back seat.' She indicated a small suitcase. It was packed for a week, although she had only planned on staying for a couple of days, but she liked to cater for all eventualities.

He leaned into the car and picked up her case as if it weighed nothing at all, and she noticed for the first time how big he was, at least compared to her own measly five foot three inches. And he had broad shoulders that were straining against the wet, tight-fitting sweater he was wearing. Kayla slammed the door of the car shut with more force than necessary. Damn the man. What did she care how wide his shoulders were? He was extremely rude and he had obviously only invited her to stay because he had no choice.

Her train of thought came to an abrupt halt as they entered the house. It wasn't a house, she decided, it was a bloody castle. Well, a stately home at any rate. The entry was of immense proportions and Kayla stared in awe at her surroundings. The hall went all the way up to the full height of the building and was topped by a beautiful, intricately patterned glass dome, which no doubt would be breathtaking in daylight. A staircase rose majestically from the centre of the room up to the first floor, where it divided into two and continued upwards. Their footsteps echoed on a lovely black-and-white marble tiled floor and on either side of the staircase there were magnificent fireplaces. The whole room was decorated with ornate plasterwork, and Greek and Roman statues were placed at intervals in specially created niches.

Kayla didn't have much time to look around, however, as a short, round middle-aged woman came bustling towards them through a door at the rear of the hall, exclaiming at the sight of them.

'Oh dear, sir, you're absolutely drenched. And the young lady, too. Goodness, what weather, and so unexpected. Whatever next, eh?'

Kayla caught sight of herself in a tall mirror, which hung over an ornate hall table to the left of the front door. 'Good grief,' she muttered. She resembled nothing so much as a drowned waif, her hair protruding in spiky, wet clumps from the large clip with which she had put it up earlier in the day. Black rivers of mascara were making their way down her cheeks, and she swiped at them without any visible effect, thinking ruefully that Dracula himself probably looked better than this.

'I'm sorry, but I didn't catch your name?'

She realised Sir Wesley was talking to her and turned around. He was still wearing his sodden baseball cap, but although this shaded his eyes she could see the rest of his face clearly and she noticed he wasn't as forbidding as he had seemed outside in the dark. He might even be passably good-looking if he ever smiled. The sharp planes of his cheekbones framed faint laughter lines around a sensuous mouth, and his jaw line was covered in dark stubble. A fading tan indicated a recent spell abroad and Kayla envied him – she had to struggle to achieve even the tiniest amount of colour even after weeks in the sun. He cleared his throat and she became aware he was waiting for an answer.

'What? Oh, sorry, my name. It's Michaela Sinclair, Kayla for short.' She held out her hand, feeling awkward, and he shook it briefly. His felt warm to the touch, not wet and cold like her own, but she shivered nonetheless.

'Pleased to meet you,' he answered automatically, then turned to the other woman. 'Annie, Miss Sinclair will have to spend the night. The roads aren't safe at the moment. Can you see to a room for her, please?'

'Well, yes,' Annie hesitated, 'but all the guest rooms have been stripped for the restoration work this week, sir. Don't you remember?'

'Damn, I'd forgotten.' He thought for a moment. 'You'll have to put her in Caro's room then. There's nowhere else, is there?'

'No, sir. I'll see to it right away. If you'll come with me, young lady, I'll show you where you can dry yourself off a bit.'

'Thank you.' Kayla picked up her suitcase and followed Annie up the wide staircase to the first floor and along a corridor with gleaming wooden floorboards. A thick green Axminster carpet ran along the middle and muffled the sound of their footsteps.

Annie led the way into a huge bedroom with floor-to-ceiling windows flanked by dusky pink velvet curtains. An elegant four-poster bed stood in the centre of one wall, draped with hangings of the same material as the curtains and covered in a matching satin coverlet.

'Oh, this is lovely!' Kayla exclaimed. 'Are you sure this, er, Caro, won't need her room tonight?'

Annie smiled wryly. 'No, and I don't think she'll be needing it ever again, praise the Lord.'

Kayla raised her eyebrows at this strange comment but thought it best not to say anything. Had someone died here recently? She shuddered and wondered if she'd walked into a Gothic novel by mistake. After talking to paintings, anything might be possible after all. But hopefully she'd be too tired tonight to think about such things. Besides, she ought to be used to ghosts by now.

'There's a private bathroom through there,' Annie indicated a door on the left, 'and dinner will be served downstairs at six. If you want anything just ring that bell over there.' She pointed to a switch on the wall by the door.

'Thank you, but I'm sure I have everything I need.'

'Ring the bell?' she muttered, as Annie closed the door behind her. Now she definitely felt as if she had at least stepped back in time and with her wet clothes and bedraggled appearance, she certainly didn't fit into such grand surroundings. She ought to have been wearing a ball gown she thought with a wry smile, then shook her head.

It was just a room and it didn't matter what she looked like. Besides, she was only staying for one night. Not a moment longer.

After a long, warm shower and with her hair almost dry again, Kayla felt infinitely better. Perhaps everything had worked out for the best after all? It was a miracle that she'd ended up at Marcombe Hall despite all the wrong turns she had taken and with not a clue as to which direction she was travelling in. She decided fate was definitely taking an interest in her life at the moment, but she had yet to decide if this was a good thing or not.

Dressed warmly in a short, light blue, knitted skirt over leggings, and with a matching high-necked jumper, Kayla was ready to face her host again. She had applied fresh make-up and left her hair loose and the heavy tresses, which were now almost dry, swung behind her as she walked down the curved staircase. She ran a hand along the smooth banister and admired the hall once more. This really was a magnificent house. It would be the perfect setting for Jago's portrait, if only she could find Eliza for him.

First things first, however, where was the dining room?

'Bloody hell, Emma is enough to try the patience of a saint.' Wesley banged a fist on his desk in frustration and swivelled round on his chair to face the bookcase behind him in an effort to calm down. He had definitely never aspired to sainthood and felt entitled to let out a long string of expletives when confronted with his secretary's incompetence. Still, he knew it wouldn't change a thing, so instead he took some deep breaths and counted to ten.

He was interrupted by a soft knock on the door and then the hesitant voice of his guest, Miss Sinclair. 'Excuse me? Is anyone here?'

He turned back to face the room's entrance and saw her face peering in cautiously. 'Yes, I'm here, Miss Sinclair,' he said curtly. 'Come in.' He sighed and ran a hand through his dishevelled hair. He hadn't had a chance to change yet and although his clothes had started to dry out they were still clinging to him damply. He caught the sharp odour of wet wool from his sweater and wrinkled his nose. Hopefully his unexpected guest wouldn't get close enough to smell it as well.

Miss Sinclair entered the room, but stopped just

inside the threshold when she caught sight of the expression on his face. He realised he must look like thunder since she immediately took an involuntary step backwards and said, 'I didn't mean to disturb you, Sir Wesley, I was just looking for the dining room. Annie said to come down at six. Or perhaps I am to eat in the kitchen?' She checked the time on her watch in embarrassment, but he hardly noticed. He was too busy taking in the changes in her appearance.

Instead of the bedraggled creature he had brought in earlier, a very pretty woman was standing in front of him. Everything about her was tiny, but perfect. Well, everything, he amended silently, except her bosom, which was magnificent, emphasised as it was by the clinging jumper she wore. Wes swiftly directed his gaze elsewhere so she wouldn't catch him staring. The wet, straggly mop of hair had miraculously turned into a gleaming, ash-blonde mane, which hung in thick layers down to her shoulder blades. There were pale highlights that shone in the light from the chandelier overhead. Her face was dominated by a pair of huge eyes, which she had outlined by the skilful application of mascara, but she didn't wear any other make-up that he could see. Indeed, the slightly over-generous mouth didn't need additional colour, it was perfect the way it was, and he didn't think the slight flush on her high cheekbones was artificial either.

'Sir Wesley?'

Her voice recalled him to the present. 'What? Oh, I'm sorry.' He shook his head. 'I'm afraid you've caught me at a bad time. It would seem my secretary has walked out on me today and she claims not to be coming back, although I'm not sure if I believe it. She's said that before. Anyway, she's left everything in a bit of a mess and I don't know where to start or where to find anything. I suppose that explains why I didn't know you were coming.'

'Oh, right. Perhaps you'd rather have your dinner later, then? Should I leave you in peace?'

He shook his head. 'Oh, no, that would be more than my life's worth. If you're ever late for one of Annie's dinners you'll never hear the end of it, believe me. She's an absolute tyrant.' He got up and went round the desk towards her. He smiled to show that he was joking, but she didn't notice. She seemed to be busy studying his carpet and he guessed she felt awkward about having to stay the night. 'I hope you'll excuse me if I don't change for dinner?' he said, hoping to put her at ease.

'Yes, of course. I shouldn't even be here really, so please don't mind me.'

'It's not a problem. As you may have noticed, this is quite a large house and one more person under its roof won't make much difference.'

Wes tried not to stare at her, but it was difficult because she was even prettier up close. And she smelled divine – some sort of flowery perfume that made him think of making love in a garden on a soft carpet of grass and surrounded by honeysuckle and roses. He took a deep breath and brought his unruly thoughts under control. What was wrong with him? He'd only just met the woman and here he was fantasising about love-making. This wouldn't do.

He gestured for her to follow him and led the way to the back of the hall and into a smaller room. 'This is the breakfast room where we usually eat,' he explained. 'It's not as formal as the dining room, which we only use for entertaining on a big scale. It's been years since the last time. Must have been before my mother passed away.'

He went on chatting about this and that, but afterwards he could never remember exactly what he'd said, as he was too busy admiring his guest. She was lovely, to put it mildly, and he wondered what on earth had brought her to his house.

He couldn't wait to find out.

Sir Wesley seated her courteously, pulling out the chair for her, and Kayla again felt as if she had stumbled into a Regency novel by mistake. The impression was reinforced when Annie came into the room carrying a huge tray with two covered silver dishes, although at least the woman wasn't wearing a maid's uniform. Kayla almost giggled out loud. Maddie would have a field day when she told her about having dinner with a 'Sir' in a huge mansion, waited on by a servant.

'Thank you, Annie,' Sir Wesley said politely, and Kayla nodded her thanks as well.

'Bone *appetite*,' Annie replied cheerfully in mangled French, which made Kayla smile into her napkin.

Thankfully dinner didn't consist of umpteen different dishes as it would have done in Regency times; there was only a main course and dessert, and Kayla did justice to both. Now that she had relaxed a bit she found she was starving, and Annie seemed very pleased her efforts were appreciated.

Kayla tried to make small talk at first. 'So do you just run this estate then, with the help of your secretary?' she asked.

'Part of the time, but I'm also a corporate lawyer. I work freelance, specialising in helping companies with complicated contracts,' Sir Wesley told Kayla. 'I work mostly from home, but travel from time to time.'

'That sounds interesting.'

'Yes, I suppose it is.' He shrugged, as if he hadn't really thought about it.

'You have a beautiful home. Has it been in your family for generations?' Kayla already knew the answer, of course, but thought it might be a subject he'd be likely to want to talk about.

He wasn't very forthcoming, however, and appeared rather distracted, so after a short while Kayla concentrated on her food in silence. Sir Wesley ate with the scowl still in place, for the most part staring at his plate as if he would find the answer to his problems there, although from time to time she caught him gazing at her with a strange expression on his face. She judged it safer not to irritate him further by idle chatter. He didn't seem to notice until near the end of the meal, when he suddenly looked up.

'So what was it you wanted to see me about, Miss Sinclair?'

Kayla swallowed hard. He was putting her on the spot and it was time to test her acting abilities. She gathered her strength and rattled off the tale she had made up a few days earlier.

'I, uhm, understand that you own some paintings by Thomas Gainsborough and as I'm doing a paper on him for a course, I was wondering if you would let me have a look at them. Perhaps take a photograph or two, if you wouldn't mind?' Kayla felt very bad about lying to him, especially after he had so kindly invited her to stay and thereby saved her from getting lost in the storm. But her promise to Jago helped her to carry it off. 'I did tell your secretary,' she added defensively.

'Yes, I'm sure you did, although as I told you, that wasn't much use.' He smiled at last and Kayla drew in a sharp breath, nearly choking on her last spoonful of dessert. For a stunned moment it was as though she was looking at Jago. It was the same devil-may-care piratical grin which had so affected her in London, and come to think of it, there were other similarities, too. The straight dark hair – although Sir Wesley's wasn't black, but dark brown, and much shorter of course – the rough-hewn features, the mouth, the laughter lines running just so. Kayla dropped her gaze as she remembered thinking how big Jago was and that she'd had the same thought about Sir Wesley earlier.

Jesus, why didn't I notice all this before? It must have been because Sir Wesley had scowled practically since they'd met, she concluded. Now that his features had relaxed into a smile, he looked completely different.

Another thought intruded, puzzling her. Why should Sir Wesley look like Jago? Surely that was impossible? Jago had only been Eliza's lover, so he was no relation to Sir Wesley, although . . . It was Kayla's turn to frown. Had Jago planted a cuckoo in Sir John's nest? What was the baby's name again? Yes, it was even the same name – Wesley. She looked up and stared into a pair of very blue eyes with the beginnings of crow's feet at the corners. *Jago's colour!* That intense shade of blue had to be rare, especially when combined with such dark hair. Kayla swallowed hard. Yes, the cuckoo theory was a definite possibility, although they did also have a common ancestor in Jago's father. Kayla made a mental note to look for a portrait of Sir Philip.

The present day Sir Wesley interrupted her train of thought. 'That stupid girl wouldn't know a Gainsborough from the drawing of a six-year-old, so how she knew I owned any is beyond me. Anyway, I'll show them to you tomorrow. They have to be viewed in daylight to be appreciated properly.'

'Thank you, that would be very kind. I look forward to seeing them.'

And Eliza – how would she look in daylight?

CHAPTER 13

'I can feel him kicking. Can you? He's a lively one and no mistake.'

They were lying on Eliza's bed, the curtains around it half shut to keep out any draughts. Since the secret door route was no longer an option, Jago had found an easier way to get into the house. He'd simply asked Eliza to leave one of the downstairs windows unlocked on the nights when John was from home, and he'd had no trouble entering.

'I don't know why I didn't think of it before,' he'd laughed. 'Certainly would have made life easier.'

'But someone could still see you.' Eliza worried that the fierce butler, Armitage, would catch Jago in the act of what he'd see as breaking and entering.

'Don't worry, I'm very careful.' And so far all had been well.

He placed his hand on her stomach now, delighting in the butterfly movements of their child. 'How do you know it's a he?' he asked, smiling at her.

'Because he's never still, just like you.' Eliza pulled him towards her for a lingering kiss.

'I can be still. Especially if I have you sleeping in my arms.' He pushed her shift down her shoulder so he could kiss the soft skin without hindrance. 'After you've worn me out, of course.' He gave her a wicked grin.

'Not for long,' she laughed. 'But I like that about you. Your boundless energy, the way you're always achieving something.'

He made a face. 'I haven't achieved much. I just earn my daily bread like everyone else.'

'That's not what I hear.'

'Oh? Been listening to gossip, have you, my love?' He tried to distract her by moving his attentions downwards, since he didn't like being praised and he had an inkling of what was coming. But Eliza wasn't to be dissuaded.

'Yes, as a matter of fact, I have. And I hear a lot of good things about you. The poor people around here apparently never starve, thanks to you. Harriet told me that the free-traders of Marcombe share their gains equally and since I know you're the leader, that must be your doing.'

'It's only fair. We all need to eat,' Jago muttered.

'Maybe, but it's not how all gangs operate, is it? And as the one in charge, you could take a larger cut.'

'We all risk the same, so we all profit the same. Now can we please talk about something else?'

She took his face between her soft hands and

looked into his eyes, shaking her head at him. 'You just don't want to admit you're a good man, do you. But you can't fool me.'

'I wouldn't want to, but neither do I want you to raise me to sainthood. I'm not perfect, Eliza, and never will be.'

'You are to me, and that's all that counts.'

Kayla awoke heavy-eyed and with a dull headache throbbing behind her eyelids. Yawning, she looked over towards the window and realised that the wind and rain had finally stopped. All was blessedly quiet, at least outside.

A floorboard creaked and Kayla turned in the direction of the door. The room was still in semi-darkness and her bleary eyes couldn't make out any movement. She groped around on the night table for her watch. It was barely seven in the morning. She yawned again and stretched before rolling into a tight ball under the thick duvet. A further snooze was definitely called for.

She had gone to bed quite early since Sir Wesley needed to continue with his work, but despite her tiredness, she'd been unable to sleep. The thought that someone might have died in this very bed recently made her uneasy, and she jumped at every little sound. As the house was old, it was never quiet and there seemed to be constant movement in the joists and floorboards, which made little grating noises and creaks. These kept Kayla awake, even though she knew what they were. It must have been well past midnight by the time she finally fell asleep, only to dream of ghostly apparitions popping out of huge silver-covered dishes carried by a grinning Annie. She sighed.

'So you're finally awake.'

Kayla sat bolt upright with a gasp, clutching the covers to her chest, convinced the former owner of the bed had returned to reclaim it. However, she soon saw that the voice had come from a small face which was now peering at her from around the bed hangings. It belonged to a skinny little girl with dark hair who looked to be about seven or eight years old.

'God, you scared the life out of me! Who are you?' Kayla's heart settled into its normal rhythm and her breathing became slightly more even.

'I'm Eleanor, but everyone calls me Nell.' The smile which accompanied this statement was disarming and Kayla didn't have the heart to scold the little girl. She obviously hadn't meant any harm. 'I'm glad you're awake. I've been waiting for ages and ages and Annie said I wasn't allowed to wake you up, so I tried to be really quiet.'

Kayla smiled. 'Yes, well, I'm definitely awake now.' *And not likely to go back to sleep with you around*, she could have added. She patted the bed next to her invitingly and said, 'Why don't you come and sit here and tell me why you wanted to see me?'

Nell hopped onto the bed, bouncing up and down a few extra times for good measure. 'I told you, I was waiting for you 'cause I wanted to talk to you.'

'Oh, why? Did someone ask you to?'

'No, I was just curious. Annie told me Daddy had a guest and I wanted to see what you looked like. I wasn't here when you came yesterday.'

'Why not?'

'I was at a sleepover at my friend Olivia's, but I didn't like it so her mummy called Daddy in the middle of the night and he came and fetched me.' Nell made a face. 'Olivia was being horrid.'

'Oh dear. How nice of your dad to come and get you so late. And in torrential rain too! Good thing he has a Land Rover.'

'Yes, he's the best.' Nell peered at Kayla again. 'We don't have many guests. Are you going to stay? And what's your name?'

'My name is Kayla and I'm not going to stay for very long. I've just come to look at some of your dad's paintings. I take it Sir Wesley is your dad?' She remembered the entry in Debrett's now which had said Sir Wesley had 'issue', a daughter. It had slipped her mind the night before.

'Yes. I look like him, don't you think? I have dark hair and blue eyes just like him Annie says.' Nell fluffed up her hair in imitation of a grown-up woman and opened her eyes wide for inspection.

Kayla laughed. 'I'm sure you do. It's just that

the light in here isn't very good, so it was hard for me to see you properly.'

'Oh, I can fix that.' Nell jumped off the bed and before Kayla could protest the girl had pulled the heavy drapes open to let in the bright morning light. Kayla winced and blinked, trying to accustom herself to the glare. 'There, is that better?' the little girl asked cheerfully.

'Yes, er, thank you, just wonderful. So, tell me, how old are you, Nell?'

'I'm going to be eight in the summer. Daddy says that's very old and he can't believe it. I've already asked for a new bicycle for my birthday and maybe a Barbie house and a PlayStation, but I'm going to write a list soon so Daddy doesn't forget.'

'Is that all?' It seemed like quite an expensive list to Kayla and she wondered if Sir Wesley was really that indulgent a father, but she decided not to comment. It was none of her business, after all. 'So you're going to be eight, are you? Then, don't you have to get ready for school soon?'

Nell giggled. 'No, silly, it's the Easter holidays. I don't have to go back till next week.'

'Oh, I see,' Kayla managed faintly. 'Well, perhaps it's time I got up then and had a shower. Shall I see you later for breakfast?'

'Of course, but don't you want to come swimming first? Daddy says you should always swim before breakfast. It's good for you and makes you strong.'

Nell was now jumping up and down on one leg, unable to contain her energy it seemed. She followed the flowery pattern around the edge of the large carpet, hopping from bloom to bloom, switching legs occasionally.

'Swimming? In this weather? Surely the sea is still a bit too cold?'

Nell laughed uproariously and clutched her small tummy. 'No, no, not in the sea,' she gasped. 'I like you, you're funny, Kayla. I meant go swimming in the pool, of course, silly.'

Kayla reflected that 'silly' was obviously the word of the day. And she did feel rather silly, truth be told. She should have guessed a house this size would have facilities like that. She shook her head. 'Oh, of course. No, I'm afraid I can't, I didn't bring a swimsuit. I wasn't planning on staying anywhere where there was a pool. You go on though, I'll see you later.'

Nell didn't give up easily though. 'I'll get you one, you can borrow Mummy's old one.' And without waiting for an answer she sprinted to the door and left at a run, slamming it shut behind her. Kayla sank back under the cover. *Good Lord, what a way to start the day.*

Less than five minutes later Nell clattered into the room, triumphantly swinging a neon pink one-piece bathing suit in a circle over her head. 'See, I told you. Isn't this pretty? I'm going to buy one this colour next time. I love pink.'

Kayla, who had by this time resigned herself to her fate, regarded the brash colour with raised brows, but managed to lie convincingly. 'Yes, lovely.'

Wearing the bathing costume, which fit surprisingly well, and swathed in a thick white towelling robe with a towel tied round her waist for good measure, Kayla followed her tiny hostess down the back stairs to the basement level. Here they found double glass doors leading into a large structure that was partly under the ground floor of the house and partly sticking out into the garden in the form of a conservatory. Kayla gathered the house must have been built on a slope so that the front of the building was higher up the hill than the back.

Inside, there was a long, narrow pool with shallow steps at one end, and the room was much warmer than the rest of the house. Dotted around the perimeter of the pool were huge tropical plants in blue and white china pots, and at the bottom there was a mosaic in the shape of an indigo-coloured dolphin.

'I'm just going to put on my cozzie,' Nell announced and dashed off again into a small changing cubicle to the right. Kayla took off the bathrobe and towel and dangled her feet in the water. It was lovely and warm.

A huge splash made her shriek as she was drenched from head to toe, but she laughed and then jumped in quickly to catch the culprit. 'I'll get you for that, you little minx, just you wait.'

Nell screamed in delight as Kayla chased her, failing on purpose to catch the girl at the last minute. They both ended up on the shallow steps laughing and gasping for air.

'You're a very good swimmer, Nell.'

'I know. My daddy taught me when I was a baby. He just threw me in and I could swim already, he said.'

'Really? I've heard of that. It was very brave of him, though, I don't know if I could have done that with any baby of mine. What if you had sunk?'

Nell giggled. 'Then he would have rescued me, of course. Now it's my turn to chase you, okay?'

'All right, but I don't think you can catch me, I'm too fast.'

More laughter followed as Kayla let herself be caught time and again. She was just beginning to wonder if the little girl would ever tire of the game, when there was an even bigger splash next to them and they were joined by Sir Wesley.

'What on earth is all this noise down here?' He laughed and threw Nell high into the air. He caught her just before she landed in the water again and swung her around. 'I thought the house was falling down.'

'No, Daddy, Kayla and I were just playing.'

'That was very kind of Miss Sinclair. You didn't by any chance wake her up, did you, and force her to come down here?' He looked apologetically at Kayla, who shook her head slightly. For a moment, she was held spellbound by his gaze and she noticed his eyes seemed, if possible, even more blue this morning in the sunlight reflected off the water.

They were twinkling too, with amusement at his daughter's boldness she guessed, but she also caught a look of gratitude when she replied, 'No, I was already awake.' She glanced at Nell, who was doing her best to look angelically innocent. 'Well, at least almost,' she added. 'In fact, I was just getting up when Nell arrived, and now I think I'd better go and get dressed. I'll see you later, perhaps, Nell.'

She swam over to the steps and hurried to retrieve her towel, which she draped round her middle. Just before she left the room, Kayla saw Sir Wesley staring at her bathing costume with another of his frowns, and she realised that he'd probably recognised it as his wife's. Embarrassed to be caught using his pool and his wife's clothes without a proper invitation – Nell didn't really count, being so young – Kayla made her escape back to her room where she leaned against the door and closed her eyes. She really hoped he wouldn't be so angry that he decided not to show her any paintings at all.

'Oh, for heaven's sake,' she admonished herself out loud, 'stop worrying so much about what other people think all the time.' She had, after all, been rudely awakened by his daughter and had been kind enough to play with her instead of sending the child back to whoever was in charge of her. Surely that wasn't a crime? Well, if it was, then that was too bad.

Wes stared after his guest for a moment. He had, in turn, first been startled by the sight of her in his ex-wife's tight-fitting bathing suit and then bemused by his own reaction to her. He had wanted her. Instantly.

He was quite sure the little pink number had never looked that good on Caroline, but Miss Sinclair had filled it out very nicely. Well, more than nicely. The thought sent another shaft of desire through him, but he resolutely ignored it. He decided he must have been living the life of a monk for too long, but seducing young students who were guests in his house obviously wasn't an option.

'Daddy, I'm going to do a cannon ball. Daddy, look at me!'

Nell's insistence pulled Wes out of his thoughts and he ducked under the water in order to try and clear his mind. He came up and shook his head, then watched Nell's antics while he tried to block the images of Miss Sinclair which kept floating into his mind every time he so much as blinked. Her long, lithe legs, flat stomach, pert behind and curves. Luscious curves.

'Damn it,' he muttered. What was the matter with him? He hadn't reacted to a woman like this since, well, since he first met Caroline. And he'd been much younger then. Did prolonged abstinence make your hormones go crazy? It certainly felt like it.

He sighed. He wasn't looking forward to spending the morning in Miss Sinclair's company. It would be sheer hell. It had been bad enough before he had seen her in a bathing suit, but now . . .

Trying to think of other things, he turned back to his daughter.

'Come on, Nell, enough of this. Annie will be waiting for us.'

Breakfast was a meal that Kayla could usually do without, but after the early morning exercise she found that she was quite hungry. The kitchen, a cavernous white-painted room, was also situated in the basement, and Kayla made her way there by following the tempting smell of toast. It emanated from the back of the hall and seemed to permeate the entire house. Annie was busy cooking something, but turned to greet her.

'Good morning. You're up early.'

'Yes, I've been up for ages thanks to young Nell. She took me swimming.'

'Oh, no, is that where she disappeared off to? The little madam! And after I told her specifically not to disturb you. What am I to do with her, I ask you?' Annie shook her head.

'She did tell me you'd said that and she waited patiently until I was awake before saying anything, so don't worry.' Kayla smiled. 'I have to admit she startled me a bit though.'

'Well, I'm sorry about that. Now why don't you tell me what you want for breakfast and I'll cook you something.'

'Just some toast, please, but I can make it myself. There is no need for you to put yourself out on my account.'

'Nonsense, it's my job, isn't it. Just you sit yourself down and I'll see to it.'

Annie refused to listen to any protests and in the end Kayla was provided with tea, toast, jam and butter, and a few other things besides. She ate in silence, looking around at the bright, sunny room. It reminded her of the kitchens at the Brighton Pavilion, with copper saucepans hanging in rows along the walls, and several large, scrubbed pine tables to use as work surfaces. Annie was washing up in an old-fashioned white porcelain sink and there was also an ancient cast iron stove, which didn't look as if it was in use any longer. It was probably only kept for decorative purposes, Kayla thought, as the kitchen also boasted a large modern cooker and a shiny Aga set into a niche.

Halfway through her second piece of toast, Kayla ventured to ask a few questions.

'Nell let me borrow her mother's bathing suit. I hope Lady Marcombe won't mind?' She tried to make the query sound casual, but in actual fact she was consumed with curiosity about this woman whom she hadn't seen as yet. Last night, she hadn't just forgotten that Debrett's mentioned a daughter, but also the fact that Sir Wesley was married. So where was his wife?

'Goodness, no. Nell's mother doesn't live here anymore and if she didn't take it with her I'm sure she has no use for it. You go right ahead.'

'Are Nell's parents divorced then?' Kayla sipped her scalding hot tea carefully.

'Yes, about a year ago. She's only been back a few times since then and she never stays for more than a couple of hours.' Annie shook her head once more. 'I don't mind telling you, I find some people strange. Fought with Sir Wesley about custody something fierce, but once he'd won it was as if she didn't care. Just vanished. She's allowed to visit at any time, but doesn't seem to want to now.'

'How odd.' *Poor little Nell,* Kayla thought. The woman must be weird indeed. Kayla's curiosity was piqued even further, but she didn't dare to pry any more.

'Yes, but it doesn't seem to have done the little one too much harm. She's as cheerful as ever before. Never says a word about it and adores her father, she does,' Annie went on.

Kayla smiled again. 'Yes, I could see that. She, er, mentions him frequently.' She finished off her breakfast and stood up to put her plate and cup in the sink. 'Well, thank you, that was delicious. If you're sure I can't help you with anything, I'd better go and see if Sir Wesley has time to show me his paintings now. Perhaps I'll see you later?'

'Sure and you're welcome. And if you see the little minx, just send her along to me. You can tell her I said so.'

CHAPTER 14

Sir John Marcombe returned briefly to Devon after a long absence, only to inform his wife that he would soon be going back to London.

'There are certain matters which need my attention,' he explained, and to his great relief she didn't ask any awkward questions. She was a biddable little thing most of the time, and lovely to look at, but she had so far failed with the only thing he really required of her. There had been no child. This time, however, she surprised him.

'I have good news, John.' She smiled shyly and regarded him out of the corner of her eyes. 'I believe I am expecting at last.'

'You are?' He so far forgot himself as to embrace her, something he would never normally do. 'That is wonderful news! Wonderful, indeed. When precisely?'

'Well, I can't be certain, but I think the baby is due some time in March or early April, or so the midwife tells me.'

He frowned. 'You've seen the local woman?

174

Really, my dear, you must have better care than that.'

'What is wrong with her? I understand she supervises all the births for miles around. The housekeeper told me she is considered very good.'

'Yes, yes, but those are common people. You must have a proper physician, someone used to gently bred ladies such as yourself. I will find one in London and send him down here to attend you.'

Eliza smiled again, and he realised it wasn't often she did. Perhaps he had been hard on her? He should have invited more company down here for her. Well, time enough for that after she was safely delivered of his heir.

It was just as well he'd found himself a delightful little actress in London recently. He couldn't wait to return to her slightly overblown charms and infectious laughter and he had no doubt she would keep him occupied while Eliza was breeding. Then he'd do his duty by his wife again once she had recovered from the birth.

He drew a sigh of relief. The actress may not be as beautiful as his wife, but she was a damn sight more accommodating in bed.

'Sir Wesley?' After knocking, Kayla stuck her head round the door of his study, but there didn't seem to be anyone there, so she stepped inside and gazed around the room in admiration. It definitely wasn't your average boring office. It was more of an old-fashioned library. Mahogany bookcases, beautifully carved at the top, lined every wall and were filled with leather-bound volumes. Sir Wesley's desk, which was an enormous affair with large ball and claw feet, sat in the middle of the room facing a fireplace with a black marble chimneypiece and a huge gilt over-mantel mirror. The dark wooden floor was covered with deep-piled red Persian carpets.

As she was about to leave, Kayla saw a movement in the far corner of the room. She walked a bit further in and caught sight of Sir Wesley sitting at a smaller desk in an alcove made by a huge bay window. With a sinking heart she noticed that the angry expression was back in place. He was glaring at a computer screen and muttering to himself, while typing with two fingers, stabbing at the keyboard as if it offended him. He was also wearing headphones, which was obviously why he hadn't heard her. Cautiously she advanced into his line of vision and waved a hand at him.

'Oh, Miss Sinclair, I didn't hear you come in.' He lifted the headphones off and rubbed at his ears. 'God, but these blasted things are uncomfortable.'

'I'm sorry to disturb you yet again, but you said something about showing me the paintings in daylight. Or should I ask Annie perhaps?'

'Ah, yes. Er, well, the thing is, Emma has left me in a bit of a fix as I told you yesterday. I've tried to reason with her, but she refuses to come back this time. I don't know what's got into her. Problem is, I have to finish off this report before twelve and at the rate I'm typing it will probably take me at least that long, if not more. I never realised this audio business was so complicated. I keep having to go back and listen to what I've said several times. I'm really sorry, but would you mind awfully waiting until after lunch or are you in a hurry to be off?'

'Not at all.' How could she protest? She was a guest in his house, an unexpected one at that. Kayla was about to leave him when inspiration struck. 'Would it help if I typed your report for you? I'm . . . that is, I have been working part-time as a legal secretary to support my studies, so my typing speed might be a bit quicker than yours.' The faster his work was finished, the sooner Kayla would be able to find Eliza's portrait, she reasoned, and then she could leave this house, hopefully with mission accomplished.

Sir Wesley regarded her as if she was an angel come down from heaven to rescue him from the worst possible torture and his expression cleared. 'Would you really be willing to do that? Are you sure?'

'Yes, it shouldn't take too long if it's just one tape.'

'You have no idea how grateful I will be, Miss Sinclair. These things were driving me crazy.' He indicated the headset and she walked forward to take it from him with a smile.

'You get used to them, I promise.' He looked as if he didn't believe her, so she added, 'Well, after a few years anyway.'

He laughed, and she found that she liked the way his eyes crinkled up at the corners. They really were exceedingly like Jago's, and the contrast with his dark brown hair and tanned skin was startling. He may not be classically handsome, she thought, but he definitely wasn't hard on the eyes either. Again, like Jago.

'I'll take your word for it, Miss Sinclair, and will leave you to get on with it. Perhaps you'd better check what I have done so far. I haven't run the spellcheck on it yet.'

'Of course, and please call me Kayla if I'm going to be your secretary for the morning.'

'It's a deal if you'll call me Wes. I hate that "Sir" business unless I'm trying to impress some important client.' He returned happily to his own desk, and Kayla continued with his report after correcting a couple of misspellings.

In no time at all she had it ready, and after a few minor alterations Wes e-mailed it to his client, then sighed with satisfaction.

'I really can't thank you enough, Kayla.' He beamed at her. 'Will you let me pay you for a morning's work? It's the least I can do.'

'Oh, no, that's not necessary. You helped me out yesterday and if you'll just show me the paintings I'll be on my way. It was no trouble, honestly.'

'Well, thank you again. I have some bad news for you, though.' His expression grew serious. 'I was just talking to Ben, the gatekeeper, on the phone and I'm afraid you won't be leaving today.'

'What? Why ever not?'

'Some of the roads were flooded yesterday, as I thought they might be, and it will take at least another day before the water subsides enough for your little car to get through. And there's more rain on the way, I think. I'm sorry. I hope you don't mind putting up with us for another night? I'll try to be a bit more hospitable.' He smiled ruefully.

'Well, I . . . that is, of course not. I'm just sorry to have to inconvenience you again.' The sinking feeling in her stomach returned with a vengeance. Another evening spent in the company of this man was not a good idea. Definitely not. She was starting to like him, and the resemblance to Jago was becoming more pronounced by the minute. What if her strange infatuation with the painting spilled over onto Jago's descendant? She knew she hadn't acted rationally where Jago was concerned and it scared her.

'I told you already, it's no problem at all.' Wes hesitated before continuing, 'And if you could stand it, I'm sure Nell would love to spend a little more time with you. Her friends would have difficulty getting here on a day like this, so she's probably a bit bored.'

'Of course, I'd be happy to play with her for a while later on.'

'Great. Well, let's go up to the gallery then.'

'Here are the two seascapes which Gainsborough painted down by the coast nearby. I believe he visited Devon several times, but I'm not sure what year these were done.' Wes shrugged. 'Sorry I can't be more specific.'

They were standing in a beautiful long gallery at the back of the first floor of the house. Tall windows let in the light when their wooden shutters were opened, as now, and mirrors hung at intervals reflecting it back onto the artwork. Kayla concentrated on the paintings instead of the increasingly attractive man by her side and trawled through her memory for the necessary information from her hasty study of Gainsborough's life.

'It could have been in 1781 when he made a tour of the West Country with his nephew, Gainsborough Dupont. I think he came this way then. Or maybe they were painted two years before that when he was said to have spent some time near Teignmouth and Exeter.'

'I'm sure you're right. Or your guess is as good as mine. I'm afraid I don't know much about art. It's not really my thing.'

'Are these the only paintings you have by him?' Kayla tried not to hold her breath as she waited for Wes's answer. Although the seascapes were pretty enough they didn't interest her any more than they did their owner. But, of course, she couldn't tell him that and if she asked after Eliza's portrait outright she would have to explain how she knew about it.

'No, there are two landscapes over here as well.' Wes led the way to the next wall. 'We're very lucky to have them, or so I'm told.'

'Yes, indeed. So, two seascapes and two landscapes. I see.' Kayla felt the tension inside her slowly morph into cold disappointment when Wes didn't add the words she hoped to hear – that actually he had a rather spectacular portrait as well. She so wanted to be able to help Jago, but as Wes stayed quiet, she realised she'd obviously have to try some other way.

Had Jago been wrong and the portrait wasn't signed after all? If so, Wes obviously wouldn't know it was a Gainsborough. She'd have to surreptitiously check all the portraits in the gallery. After Jago's description she felt sure she'd recognise Eliza even without a signature.

It was also possible the painting of Eliza could have been inherited by any member of the family through the years. Then it would be a question of tracking down the various branches and checking who had it in their possession. There might be copies of old wills or something. She'd have to ask Jessie how to go about finding such things. Either way, she knew it would mean a lot of hard work. She swallowed a sigh and decided to try looking here first.

'Well, thank you for showing them to me. If you wouldn't mind, I'd like to make a few notes?' Kayla had brought a pad and a pen in order to seem more efficient and student-like. Wes spread his hands.

'Please, be my guest.'

'And would you mind if I took some photos?'

'No, as long as you don't publish details of the exact location of these paintings. We don't normally advertise the fact that they exist as we wouldn't want to attract art thieves. They're not precisely a secret, but still, if you're going to refer to them, perhaps you could just say something vague like "they're in the possession of a private owner"?'

'Yes, of course.'

'Great, thank you. I'll leave you to it then. See you at lunchtime.'

Just to make doubly sure, Kayla walked around the long gallery and checked each portrait in turn in case the one of Eliza had been overlooked and the Gainsborough signature lost. Most of them had the names of the ladies inscribed on the frame or in a corner, and there were no Elizabeth's that she could see. Of the ones that were unnamed, not a single one looked anything like the painting Jago had described. In fact, they weren't very life-like at all and Kayla didn't have that eerie feeling of being watched. None of the ladies were particularly beautiful, either, and Kayla remembered distinctly that Jago had said Eliza was lovely. Although, come to think of it, ideals of beauty were quite different in those days compared to those of the present time.

Jago's father was easy to spot, however, as the frame around his portrait had a huge brass plaque with 'Sir Philip Marcombe' and his dates. Kayla studied him for quite a while, but could see nothing of Jago in him at all apart from the eye colour, as he'd said. She concluded that Jago must resemble his Gypsy mother. Her theory about him planting a cuckoo in the Marcombe nest seemed very likely in the light of this, but she would have to ask him.

Kayla sat staring at the Gainsborough seascapes for a long time lost in thought. Her life had certainly changed considerably since Jago entered it. Was it really only a few weeks ago? He had turned everything upside down – her job, her marriage plans, even the way she acted. Three weeks ago she would never have considered lying to anyone deliberately, and yet here she was, pretending to be an art student when she couldn't draw to save her life. She shook her head.

'Oh, Jago, why did you have to pick me of all people? Surely there were other impressionable females at the auction rooms? You could have messed up their lives instead and left mine alone. I was quite happy the way I was.'

But the irritating little voice inside her head sniped, 'Were you really? Then how come you never once considered apologising to Mike to make up after your little row? Was it perhaps because you wanted a way out? Had you already regretted your decision to marry him?'

'Oh, shut up,' she muttered. It was all too much and she was too tired to deal with it right now. One thing at a time.

Wes tried to concentrate on his work, but somehow just knowing Kayla was somewhere in the house unsettled him. While they were looking at the paintings, he'd had a hard time not staring at her instead, and each time she'd turned those big moss-green eyes on him, he'd been mesmerised.

'This is ridiculous,' he muttered. 'She's a pretty girl, but too young for you.' An art student, for heaven's sake – she couldn't be more than nineteen or twenty and he was almost thirty-six. 'Get over it.' But time and again he found himself sitting staring out of the window instead of concentrating.

When Annie brought him some coffee and biscuits, he jumped a mile.

'Away with the fairies, were you?' Annie chuckled.

'Yes, didn't hear you come in,' Wes admitted.

'Finished showing our guest round then, have you?'

Wes felt as if Annie's knowing eyes saw way too much, but he managed to feign nonchalance. 'Yes, I left her to it. I'm not really into paintings, as you know.' He suddenly remembered the news he'd had earlier. 'Oh, by the way, Kayla will be staying at least another night. Ben rang to say the roads are flooded and he doesn't think her little car would get through. I told her and she didn't seem to mind too much.'

'And do you?' Annie asked.

Wes frowned. 'Do I what?'

'Mind her staying?'

There was amusement lurking in Annie's eyes and Wes wanted to tell the woman to mind her own business. At the same time he was aware that she was a treasure he couldn't do without, so he tried to answer her calmly. 'No, of course not. As I said to her, this house is big enough and one more night is neither here nor there.'

'Indeed. Well, I'd best see about some lunch then.' Annie turned away, but not before Wes had seen her hide a smile.

Damn it all! Am I that transparent? He hated the thought that he might be and very much hoped his guest wasn't able to read him as easily as his housekeeper seemed to.

CHAPTER 15

'**D**ear Lord, but he's as pleased as punch. Ye'd think he was the first man ever to have sired a child, so ye would!'

'Who?' Jago had been lost in thought, wiping tankards without really paying attention to what he was doing, but the words of Matty, the serving wench, brought him back down to earth.

'Why, his lordship, of course. Who else?'

Jago frowned. 'How do you know that?'

'My aunt told me. Works in the kitchens up at the hall, she does, and always brings uz the gossip of an evenin'.' Matty smirked. 'I hear a thing or two, I can tell ye.'

'So Lady Marcombe is expecting then?' Jago deemed it safest to pretend ignorance. It was women's matters after all. No one would expect him to have any interest in such things.

'Mr Kerswell, have ye not been listenin' to a word I've said these past weeks?'

'Not really, no.' He gave her a rueful smile. 'You do chatter a lot you know, so I don't pay much attention.'

'Well, honestly.' She put her hands on her hips,

186

which only made her look like a belligerent bull-finch, since she was as short as she was round. 'But yes, her ladyship's gettin' big with child and Sir John is walkin' around preenin' 'eself, as if it were all thanks to him.'

'Isn't it?' Jago teased.

Matty sent him a scowling look. 'Ye know as well as I do, Mr Kerswell, there'd be no babes wi'out uz women.'

He chuckled. 'I know, I know. But you couldn't do it without us either.' When Matty's fierce look deepened, he held up his hands in surrender. 'Either way, I wish the man well and hope her ladyship has a safe delivery.'

Of my child. But he didn't add that out loud.

And if Sir John was so pleased with the pregnancy, he could only pray the man never found out the truth. Jago was worried enough about Eliza without adding that to the equation.

His dark thoughts were interrupted by the entrance into the inn of a pale man in a threadbare coat. Jago smiled a greeting. 'Reuben, how are you? Feeling better? It's good to see you on your feet again.'

'Aye, but I'm still as weak as a kitten. It's makin' it hard fer me to find work.' Reuben coughed, his expression bleak as he battled to regain his breathing.

Jago nodded. 'Yes, that's understandable.' Reuben had been laid low with a chest infection and since he had a wife and five children to feed, going without income for any length of time was a potential disaster. 'But don't fret, I have your share of our latest "venture". Just hold on a moment.'

'But Mr Kerswell, sir . . .'

Jago pretended not to hear Reuben, and soon after he was back with a leather pouch hidden in his closed fist. He made sure the inn was still empty of customers, then passed the pouch to Reuben. 'There you are. Hopefully that should tide you all over.'

Reuben looked troubled and shook his head. 'It's not right, Mr Kerswell. I wasn't able to come on the . . . er, venture, so I'm not due any payment. If you could see your way to lendin' it to me though? I'll do my best to pay it back next time.'

'Nonsense. You're part of the gang and we look after our own. I know you'll do your share when you can. Just take it. You've earned it.' Jago tried to sound firm so Reuben wouldn't argue with him. He didn't want the man feeling he was being given charity, even though he was as Jago was in fact giving him his own share. He'd rather Reuben didn't find that out though, nor anyone else. It wouldn't do to be seen as soft or others might take advantage of him.

The man hesitated for a moment, then nodded, sense obviously winning out over pride. 'Thank ye. Ye're a good man an' I won't forget.'

When the door had shut behind him, Jago heard a sniffle behind him and turned to find Matty wiping a tear from the corner of her eye. 'What's the matter with you?' He frowned at her, but she just shook her head at him and gave him a watery smile.

'Reuben's right. Ye are a good man and the good Lord'll reward ye.'

Jago wasn't at all sure about that, but then Matty didn't know the half of it.

In the event, Kayla didn't encounter Wes until the evening meal. Instead she spent the afternoon trying to play a game with Nell on an old-fashioned Nintendo console. It was some sort of race where they each had a hand-held device to control the actions of a little figure who was driving a car on the screen. It proved surprisingly difficult, at least for Kayla who had never tried this particular game before.

During dinner, the little girl wasted no time in informing her father of their guest's lack of skill. 'Honestly, Daddy, Kayla came off the track every single time. Didn't you, Kayla?'

'Yes, I'm afraid that's true,' Kayla admitted. 'But you've had a lot more practice than me, you know. Just you wait until I get better at it, then I'll beat you for sure.'

'You're supposed to let guests win, Nell. Didn't I teach you that?' Wes winked at his daughter.

'Yes, but it was impossible. Even when I tried to lose, Kayla crashed before I had hardly got started.'

'Like I said, just you wait,' Kayla narrowed her

eyes at Nell in mock fierceness. 'I'll practise while you're asleep and I'll become an expert in no time, see if I don't.'

Nell just laughed. 'No way.'

'You have a lovely daughter,' Kayla told Wes after Nell, yawning hugely, had been led to her bed by Annie.

'Thank you. I think she's wonderful, but then I suppose most parents do.' Wes sipped his glass of wine and gazed into the distance. 'I take it Annie told you about my ex-wife, Caroline?'

'Only that you were divorced and Nell lives here with you.' Kayla squirmed slightly in her seat, feeling uncomfortable with this topic of conversation. She didn't want him to think she'd been gossiping about him, especially since she'd only been here a day.

'Yes, it was a shame, but these things happen. Caro had . . . some problems. Depression, that sort of thing. She became addicted to some of her medication, which makes her unpredictable and restless. She travels a lot in search of . . . well, I'm not sure what, to be honest. Whatever it is she wants out of life? She didn't find it here in any case and the judge thought it would be better for Nell to stay in her normal environment, that's why he awarded me custody. Although, of course, Caro can see her any time she wants.'

'That sounds sensible. Nell seems very happy and I can see that she adores you.'

He smiled. 'It's mutual. But I'm told little girls

often like their fathers best because they can wrap us round their little fingers. I'm pretty sure things will be different when she reaches her teenage years.' He sighed. 'I do try to make up for her not having a mother, but it's not easy. Annie helps too, of course. She's great with her.'

'Maybe you'll remarry before Nell hits her teens,' Kayla suggested, and was surprised to see a bleak look cross Wes's features.

'Not on your life. I'm afraid my one experience of the married state was enough to last me for a lifetime.' Kayla stared at him, surprised by his vehemence, but he didn't give her a chance to comment. Instead he changed the subject. 'But tell me, which firm do you work for in London? Perhaps I've heard of them? Before I started to work freelance I used to do a bit of everything.'

'It's called Martin, Bicknell and Taylor.' Kayla was on safer ground here, and the rest of the evening passed uneventfully.

The floorboards creaked and Kayla opened a sleepy eye, expecting to find Nell sneaking around again. Did the kid get up at the crack of dawn every day, she wondered?

The room was in complete darkness this time, however, and Kayla couldn't distinguish anything. She raised herself up on her elbows to peer into the gloom.

'Who's there?' Nothing moved, but Kayla thought she heard a noise as if someone had drawn in a sharp breath. She sat up properly, heart thumping faster now, and leaned over to turn on the bedside light. Before her hand could reach it, someone rushed past her bed at great speed and disappeared towards the far corner of the room. There was a scraping noise and Kayla gave a little shriek of fright and almost overbalanced. Her hand knocked over an old-fashioned alarm clock, which crashed to the floor, making an awful racket. Finally she managed to catch the light switch and the room was flooded with soft light.

Racing out of bed, Kayla stopped in the middle of the room and swivelled round, looking into every nook and cranny, but there was nobody there.

'Bloody hell,' she whispered. Had it been a ghost? Was she to be plagued with them for the rest of her life?

'I don't believe in ghosts,' Kayla mumbled to herself, then laughed somewhat hysterically. She hadn't believed in talking paintings either, but she did now. She groaned and put her head in her hands. Perhaps once you'd seen one ghost or spirit it opened some sort of floodgate for others to pester you. It was a scary thought, but a possibility she had to acknowledge.

There was loud knocking and someone called out her name. Kayla said, 'Come in,' without thinking and looked towards the door, but to her surprise it was a piece of the panelling of the wall which opened instead to admit Wes. 'Good grief,' she muttered. They had interconnecting bedrooms? She hadn't realised his room was so close.

'What's the matter? There was a noise and I heard you cry out.' He came striding towards her, a look of concern on his face. Kayla stifled a gasp at the sight of him wearing only tracksuit bottoms, his muscular chest and well-toned stomach in full view. She had been too embarrassed to notice his physique yesterday in the pool, but she could see now that he kept himself in shape. Very good shape. He obviously didn't spend all day, every day, behind his desk.

'I, er . . . th-there was s-somebody in here just now,' she stuttered, feeling her cheeks turn warm as his eyes rested briefly on her own nightdress. It hardly counted as such since it was a very old, worn and somewhat see-through T-shirt. It had once belonged to her younger brother and Kayla belatedly remembered that it proclaimed to the world in faded letters that 'Golfers did it to a tee'. She quickly crossed her arms in front of her chest.

'In here? You're sure?' He came to a halt in front of her and she took a step backwards as an insane desire to reach out and touch him flowed through her. She quenched it and gripped her own arms instead.

'Well, yes, quite sure, but whoever it was seems to have disappeared.' She felt idiotic now. Perhaps it had just been another stupid dream. Her imagination had certainly been working overtime lately. Damn Jago, it was all his fault.

'Which way did they go?' Wes began searching through the room methodically, and opened the door to the large wardrobe in the corner.

'To where you are now, I think, but it was dark. I didn't really see much.'

'Well, there's no one here now.' The familiar frown had returned and he flicked through the few items of clothing still hanging inside the armoire. 'I'll have someone come and check the security system tomorrow. We can't have strangers roaming about the house at night. But maybe it was just a dream?' he added, echoing her own thoughts. Kayla felt her cheeks flame again.

'Yeah, maybe or, uhm, do you have ghosts here? I mean, it's quite an old house after all and it wouldn't be surprising if some of your ancestors returned from time to time.'

Wes smiled and her stomach flipped over unexpectedly. He really had the most amazing smile and it lit up his blue eyes. 'Nope, sorry, I'm afraid there are no ghosts in this house that I know of. Don't mean to disappoint you. I know some people find it romantic and all that, but we don't have any headless spectres or even white ladies roaming the corridors.'

'Oh, no, I don't find it romantic. I mean, really, I'm quite happy about that. I don't particularly care for ghosts.'

'Okay, well good.' He came back to stand in

front of her, his nearness more disturbing than she cared to admit. 'Would you like to sleep somewhere else tonight, just in case?' He ran a hand over his chin and she heard the slight rasping noise made by the stubble and shivered. Was there anything sexier than stubble? Trailing your fingernails through it, then the slight friction against your skin when he kissed his way down to your shoulder and . . .

'Kayla?'

'What? Oh!' His words registered and Kayla stared at him, blinking with confusion. What was he suggesting?

He suddenly grinned in that pirate fashion as he caught sight of the look on her face. 'I only meant that we could swap beds if you like,' he said, and Kayla felt herself flush an even deeper red than before as she realised her mistake. 'Or perhaps you would prefer to share? I'd keep you safe from any passing ghost, I promise.' He was teasing her now, she could see that. His eyes were twinkling and he crossed smoothly muscled arms in front of his chest as he waited for her answer with a look that told her he was enjoying the conversation.

'Thank you, but that won't be necessary.' *And I'm sounding impossibly prim, argh!* Kayla wished she could have been the sort of woman who answered teasing with a flirtatious reply or at least a witticism. Instead she became tongue-tied and flustered. *Damn.*

'As you wish.' He was still grinning as he backed out of the room and returned to his own. 'Goodnight, then. Sweet dreams.'

'Thank you.' Kayla swished back to her bed in a huff. 'Fat chance of any sweet dreams now, you bloody pirate,' she muttered darkly. 'Well, don't think you can get round me with those flashing smiles of yours. I'm not falling for them, oh, no.' But the problem was that he probably could. His offer had been extremely tempting.

It was a long time before she slept and, to be on the safe side, she left the light on.

What the hell was that all about?

Wes put his arms behind his head and stared into the darkness, feeling more alive than he'd done for a long while now. Seeing Kayla in that ridiculous T-shirt, which didn't leave much to the imagination – more was the pity, or was it? – had left him wide awake. And horny as hell. No point not admitting it to himself. He sighed.

'And what exactly are you going to do about it?' he muttered. 'Nothing, that's what. Nothing at all.'

Was he having a mid-life crisis already? Was it possible to have one before you were even forty? If it meant lusting after young students, then he could only conclude that it was.

A thought hit him. What if she was a mature student? Maybe she'd worked for a while first and then gone back to do a degree. That would change things. He'd have to find out.

'But bloody hell, how do you ask a woman how old she is?' He'd been taught from an early age this was a subject that was definitely taboo. You just didn't mention it. End of.

He grinned to himself as his brain came up with another option – he'd get Nell to ask. Surely Kayla couldn't object to that? Nell was just a child so she wasn't constrained by grown-up rules, or not much. Wes felt vaguely ashamed to even contemplate using his daughter this way, but how else was he to obtain the information he needed so badly?

He just had to know, it was driving him crazy.

'Okay, so if she's younger than, say, twenty-five,' he told himself, 'I'll stay the hell away from her. But over that, she's fair game, surely?' Or would she think him too old?

Damn it all, why was life so complicated?

Just before sleep claimed him at last, one more question occurred to him. Why had she thought there was someone in her room?

CHAPTER 16

'Oh, Jago, I've longed for you so. I thought John would never leave, but he's gone at last. Left for London this morning.'

'And I you.' Jago felt the tension leave him as he smiled at Eliza and opened his arms to her, pulling her close. For days he'd been fretting, wondering if his half-brother would smell a rat once the initial euphoria about the pregnancy had abated. Although the rational part of his brain told him he couldn't protect her against her own husband, he'd still wanted to rush over to Marcombe Hall to make sure she was all right.

'Mmm, you smell like the wind and the sea.' Eliza buried her face in his shoulder and breathed in. 'Do you know, whenever we can't be together, I close my eyes and remember that. It sustains me until our next meeting.' She stroked his velvet jacket. 'In fact, I've memorised everything about you – the feel of your clothes when you hold me, the strength of your arms, the hardness of your chest against me.' She laughed self-consciously. 'It sounds ridiculous, doesn't it, but I love every-thing about you.'

He crushed her to him. 'No, I do the same. If I was blind I could still pick you out from among a thousand women.'

Eliza sighed. 'It's unbearable, this waiting, wanting. It gnaws at me constantly. Is there nothing we can do?'

'No, love, we must be patient.'

'I do not wish to be patient! I want to be with you, always. Oh, take me away, my darling, please take me away from here.'

'Where would we go? And you can't travel in your condition. Think of the babe.'

'I am thinking of it. I don't want it to grow up here, living a lie. We could go to the colonies, perhaps, or the continent? No one would find us there, surely?'

'It's too late, you are too far gone. You must be patient, sweetheart. I will think on what you have said and see what I can arrange, but we have to wait until you are strong and fit and the child also. We can't risk harming it.'

He bent to kiss her to stop her from arguing further, and as always the merest touch of their lips lit the fires within. They both knew it was wrong, they shouldn't want each other, but there was no way on earth they could stop themselves.

Not now, not ever.

'Kayla, I have a proposition for you.' Wes breezed into the kitchen the next morning, startling both his guest and his housekeeper. Kayla, who had been daydreaming about the joking offer he had made the night before, choked on a mouthful of tea when he said the word 'proposition'. He slapped her helpfully on the back.

'I'm sorry, what?' she managed finally.

Wes pulled out the chair on the opposite side of the table, turned it round and straddled it, leaning his arms on the back. He was wearing jeans and a T-shirt this morning and Kayla couldn't help a glance at his arms, slightly bronzed and dusted with fine dark hairs. There was something very attractive about a man's arms when they were just the right side of muscular, she thought. Not body-builder type, but still solid enough to give you the feeling they could protect you, keep you safe. She tore her gaze away and fiddled with her breakfast.

'Tell me, do you have to go back to your part-time job and your studies straight away or are you on holiday?' Wes asked.

'Er, I have the next couple of weeks off.' She wasn't about to tell him that thanks to an infatuation with a painting of his ancestor she wouldn't be returning to her previous job at all, but was in fact at a loose end.

'Excellent.'

'Is it?' Kayla was getting more confused by the minute.

'Yes, well it could be. For me. What I mean is, would you consider staying here for say, two weeks? To work that is. You did a great job yesterday, better than any other secretary I've ever had around here, and I'll make it worth your while, I promise.'

'What, as a temp you mean?'

'Precisely. Until I can replace Emma with someone like you who can spell more than her own name and possibly her boyfriend's. Not that there seem to be very many girls around here who can, but I live in hope. Anyway, I'll pay you double the going rate. So what do you say, will you do it? It would give you a chance to explore Devon a bit too, and I'm sure a lot of the stately homes around here have Gainsborough paintings for you to study. I could even find out for you. Or did you have other plans?' He was looking at her expectantly, if somewhat impatiently. He was obviously a man used to making decisions in an instant.

'Well, not exactly.' Kayla took a bite of toast and considered his proposal carefully. On the one hand, if he paid her well, it would give her longer to look around for a more suitable job back in London. Time as far away as possible from everything associated with Mike and the wedding was clearly also a good idea right now. Not to mention her disbelieving family, who had probably not yet forgiven her for ruining all the planning.

On the other hand, was it advisable to stay in this lovely house with its charismatic owner, to whom she was becoming more attracted by the minute, and his equally charming daughter?

Wouldn't she make more of a fool of herself than she already had?

In the end the lesser of two evils won.

'All right, I'll do it,' she decided.

'Brilliant! Could you start this morning? I have so much to do and I really could use some help.' He stood up and put the chair back under the table. Behind him Annie shook her head and muttered something about patience being a virtue.

'Sure.' Kayla laughed. 'Can I finish my breakfast first or do we eat on the job?'

He had the grace to look sheepish. 'No, no, please take your time. Sorry, didn't mean to hassle you. I'll be in the office.'

Kayla and Annie exchanged glances. 'Men,' they exclaimed in unison after he had left, and burst out laughing.

The two weeks flew by and Kayla enjoyed every minute. She wasn't sure if this was because she and Wes worked so well together, or just due to the attraction she felt for the man himself. She tried not to think about it, since she had no way of knowing whether that was part of Jago's magic. He had said she was under some sort of spell, but hadn't specified exactly what that entailed. She thought it would be logical to suppose it could include liking all Jago's descendants too. Not that she knew if it applied to Wes, but the more time Kayla spent with him, the more she became convinced her cuckoo theory was right. When she went back to London she was determined to find out.

On a beautiful, sunny Saturday in early May, Kayla had the morning off. She wandered into the garden behind the house, but for once she barely registered the lovely setting or the gorgeous weather. Almost by touch, she made her way to a stone bench without really seeing her surroundings. Everything was a blur because her eyes were filled with tears that refused to stop flowing. Kayla swiped at them angrily. She didn't want to cry, but somehow she couldn't help it. Today should have been her wedding day, the happiest day of her life. Instead she was sitting in somebody else's garden crying, wondering what went wrong and what she was going to do next.

If everything had gone as planned she would have been having her hair and make-up done by now, before putting on the exquisite dress which made her look so tall and elegant. The shoes that went with it had very high heels, but she had thought it worth the discomfort in order to feel really beautiful on her special day. And she'd wanted to look absolutely gorgeous for Mike.

Mike. It was strange, but she felt nothing at all when she thought of him now. She had no regrets, so she must have done the right thing after all. Thinking back she remembered that she hadn't even received a very romantic proposal. Out of the blue Mike had just asked her one day whether she thought it would be a good idea to get married since they made such a great couple.

'Are you serious?' she had asked suspiciously, thinking he was teasing her. He'd never before indicated that he was contemplating marriage, at least not for quite some time yet.

'Yes, perfectly. Actually, I heard old Mr Martin say the other day that men who are married climb to the top of their professions much faster than single ones. A wife is a real asset, he said.'

Kayla made a face at him. 'Well, if you think I'm marrying you for the sake of your career, you can think again, mister.'

'No, no, darling, of course I want you to marry me because I love you,' he protested, and somehow he'd persuaded her that he was sincere. Now she wasn't so sure. To Mike, his career was everything, and Kayla was certain she would have come a poor second, if not immediately, then definitely later on.

'So what are you crying for, idiot?' she asked herself. She should be thanking her lucky stars she had come to her senses before it was too late. Having to go through a divorce later on would have been infinitely worse.

Kayla closed her eyes and tried to redirect her thoughts. It was peaceful here in Devon. No traffic, no shrieking police sirens at all hours of the day and night, no tube trains rumbling under the buildings. Just birdsong, wind sighing in the trees and the distant sound of the sea. She let the tears flow down her cheeks silently. She wasn't sure why she was still crying, but it was cathartic. Perhaps she needed this cleansing of the past so she could move on, and she promised herself that after today, she wouldn't think of it again, ever. That part of her life was over. Maybe the tears were also partly from fear of the unknown. What was to become of her, what would she do with her life? She couldn't stay here forever. It was just a way of postponing the inevitable search for a new job.

She would miss Marcombe when she left. There was no doubt she had enjoyed her stay, despite the strange circumstances of her arrival, but now it was almost time to move on. Wes had been interviewing girls for the position of private secretary, although as far as she knew he hadn't made a decision yet. He would have to choose soon.

'Kayla? Why are you crying?'

A small clammy hand appeared out of nowhere and rested on her arm. Nell looked up at her in concern, her little face as serious as it could possibly become.

'Nell! You're always startling me.' Kayla tried to wipe her face with the sleeve of her T-shirt, and gathered the child close to her side with her other arm. 'I'm just a bit sad because I was supposed to be getting married today. But things didn't work out.'

'Why?'

'Er, well, my boyfriend and I had a fight and then we decided that maybe we didn't suit after all.'

'Why?'

'I don't know. I thought I loved him, but really I don't think I did.'

'Why?'

'Just because.'

'Because is not an answer. Annie says.'

Kayla couldn't help it, she had to smile. Nell was relentless in her questioning and completely logical in her thinking. She believed that every question had an answer and she would never stop asking until she was satisfied.

'Do you know what? I have no idea why I don't love him anymore. Sometimes you love someone and you don't know why, you can just feel it. But sometimes you discover that the person wasn't really worth your love, so you stop loving them.'

Nell frowned. 'My mummy and daddy stopped loving each other. At least, I think so. Otherwise, why did she go away?'

'I'm sure you're right. And now they are happier apart, don't you think?'

'I guess.' Nell looked up at Kayla, her eyes big and questioning. 'You wouldn't stop loving me, would you? Even if I was naughty?'

Kayla laughed. 'No, sweetheart. I'm talking about love between a man and a woman. The kind of love grown-ups feel for children is quite different and that never changes.'

'Oh, good.' Nell hugged her fiercely. 'Have you finished being sad now?'

Kayla held the tiny body close and returned the

embrace. Nell felt so small and fragile, her little chicken chest pressed hard against Kayla, but it was a wonderful sensation. A child's love was indeed different, trusting and unquestioning. If only she could find that kind of love with a man she would have no hesitation in marrying him. She sighed again.

'Yes, I think I've finished now. Shall we go and practise your skipping on the front drive?'

'Oh, yes, please. I did thirty-one in a row yesterday. I have to beat my own record now.' Nell chatted happily as they set off, small hand tucked into Kayla's larger one.

Kayla put the past resolutely behind her. It was time to move on.

'Psst. Nell.' Wes waylaid his daughter on her way back to her room to wash her hands before lunch.

'Daddy? What's the matter?'

'Shhh.' He put a finger over his mouth and pulled her into his office, closing the door behind her. 'Don't tell Kayla I asked you, but why was she crying? I saw you two in the garden earlier.'

'Oh, she and her boyfriend hit each other or something.'

'What?'

'She said they were going to get married today, but then they had a fight. So now she doesn't love him any more. I wouldn't love someone who hit me either.'

'Oh, I see. I don't think she meant fight as in

hitting, just arguing.' Wes didn't want to pry, but he often felt that Kayla was very reticent about her life in London, almost secretive in fact. He had wondered why; perhaps now he had his answer. 'She was getting married today, did you say?' Nell nodded. 'Hmm. Maybe we should distract her a bit then, so she doesn't think about it too much. Shall we take her down to the secret cove, do you think?'

'Oh, yes, Daddy. Let's!'

'Okay, you go and ask Annie to pack a picnic and I'll see if I can find Kayla.' For some reason he couldn't bear to think of her spending the day moping. Well, it wouldn't do to have a sad secretary about the place, now would it, he told himself.

Nell skipped towards the door, then stopped and spun around. 'Oh, and guess what? I finally remembered to ask her when her birthday is.'

'You did?'

'She said it's in August, the day before mine. Isn't that cool?'

'Oh, yes, very.' Wes hesitated, not sure if he should ask the question he'd really wanted an answer to. He'd told Nell to find out when Kayla's birthday was and how many candles would be needed for the cake. He figured that was better than Nell asking Kayla's age outright. Now he had half the information, but not the half he needed.

Before he could open his mouth, however, Nell added, 'And we'll need twenty-six candles, Daddy.

Do we have that many?' She looked awed and Wes almost burst out laughing.

'Er, we can always buy a few more. You're sure that's the right number?'

'Yep, she said.'

Wes felt relief flood him. Kayla wasn't too young and he was only ten years older than her. He could only hope she didn't think that was ancient.

CHAPTER 17

Sir John had been listening to his wife's screams and moaning for hours on end and was heartily sick of the whole business. Why did it have to take so long, for heaven's sake? It wasn't often he thought of God, but it occurred to him now to wonder why He had seen fit to make child-bearing such a difficult task. For everyone involved.

He slumped down into his chair once more and took a sip of brandy. He had already consumed half a decanter. At this rate he would be too drunk to see his heir properly by the time the wretched infant finally made it into the world. Angrily, he slammed the glass back onto the table, making half the contents slosh over the rim.

A short while later there was a knock on the door and at his curt, 'Enter', the fancy London midwife who had arrived with the physician he'd sent for came in holding a bundle. She curtsied.

'Now then, you have a fine and healthy son at last, sir,' she announced with a beaming smile and walked forward to place the bundle on his lap. He stared at the baby in stunned silence, but the child immediately decided to remedy this and began to scream. Loud, ear-splitting howls, proof that the infant had a good pair of lungs if nothing else. Sir John looked down on the red, screwed-up little face and the flailing fists, and felt a strange emotion flow through him. His son. His heir.

In an attempt to soothe the little mite he stroked the downy head, but as his hand dislodged the blanket he stopped and stared at the baby's hair in stunned horror. It was black. As black as the night outside. As black as Eliza's soul, damn her to hell. With a roar of anger he surged out of his chair, lifting the baby in the process and dumping the bundle unceremoniously back into the arms of the midwife, who gave a little shriek of protest and fright.

'But, sir, whatever is the matter?'

'That's not my child,' he declared in a voice quivering with fury. 'Neither my wife nor I have black hair.'

'Oh, sir, th-that will change,' the poor midwife stuttered. 'Most babies are born dark and the hair changes within the first few weeks. Same with the eyes, they'll change colour too,' she tried to reassure him.

He had turned his back on her, however, and wasn't listening. *The traitorous bitch!* He should have known. She'd looked so radiant recently and he had thought it was simply because she was expecting. All along there had been another man.

Well, he would have none of it. She could take her bastard and leave or better yet . . .

The midwife stood for a while waiting uncertainly, but in the end she tiptoed out of the room with the child clutched tightly to her. John watched her go, feeling curiously detached as sudden plans chased around inside his brain. No doubt the woman and the physician would scuttle back to London in the morning, as soon as they'd been paid. Good.

He wanted the house to himself when he visited his wife.

In the meantime, he'd finish that brandy.

They set off towards the coast, each one carrying something. Wes had a heavy cool bag filled with goodies from Annie's kitchen, Kayla was in charge of a large quilted blanket, and Nell led the way with a bucket and spade in one hand and a small fishing net in the other. They followed a well-worn path down to the cliffs and along the top. Kayla turned her face towards the sun and drew in deep salty breaths of air.

It really was a beautiful day with the sun shining onto a calm sea. Looking out over the water Kayla could see several boats, some with sails, some without, and further out a huge oil tanker. Sounds were strangely muted, as if her ears were stuffed full of cotton wool, and Kayla felt like she was in a different world. It was wonderful.

Ten minutes into their walk, however, Nell had

had enough. 'Daddy, my legs hurt. Aren't we there yet?'

'Not quite, sweetheart, but it's not much further. Remember?'

Twenty yards later Nell stopped again. 'I can't walk any more. Can't we have a picnic here?'

Wes glanced at Kayla and rolled his eyes. 'It's not much further, Nell. Come on, where's my strong little girl today?'

They managed another fifty yards before a plaintive, 'I want to be carried' was heard from the front. Kayla started to laugh.

'Give me the bag, Wes, and you can carry Nell for a little while.'

Wes looked grateful and apologetic at the same time. 'Are you sure you can manage? It's quite heavy.'

'Yes, I'll be fine. Don't worry. I'm stronger than I look.'

'Kayla is too nice to you,' Wes muttered as he lifted his daughter up for a piggyback ride. 'We'll have to toughen you up a bit, I think.'

The rough track down to the cove was extremely steep, but there were steps cut out of the rock in the worst places and they reached it at last. Kayla was enchanted. 'I can see why you call this a secret place,' she said to Nell. 'It feels like we're completely cut off from the rest of the world.' The tiny cove was surrounded on three sides by sheer cliffs and in front of them was the sea, shimmering in the bright light.

'It's even nicer in the summer,' Wes said behind her. 'It's so secluded you can even go skinny-dipping and no one will see you.' He said this in a perfectly normal voice, as if he was only giving her information about the cove and not actually thinking of skinny-dipping himself, but his eyes told a different story. Kayla felt a blush spreading over her face and down her neck. The thought of swimming naked with Wes was tantalising and one she'd do best not to dwell on.

The afternoon passed swiftly. They played games and paddled their feet in the ice-cold water, and after the generous picnic had been eaten, the two adults lay back on the blanket, replete and unable to move.

'Come and help me collect seashells, Kayla.'

'Let Kayla rest for a while, Nell. You go ahead by yourself,' Wes said.

'Okay, Daddy.' The little girl skipped off happily towards the water. 'But don't be too long.'

'No one tells you how much hard work children are before you have them,' Wes grumbled, but he didn't sound as if he really minded all that much.

'I'm sure it's worth it, at least most of the time.' Kayla had closed her eyes and allowed the noises of the seashore to wash over her, creating a sensation of relaxation and contentment. She breathed cool sea air in deeply and absently dug her fingers into the sand next to the blanket, sieving the soft mass through them, feeling its smooth texture.

'Yes, you're right.' Wes was silent for a while

before continuing. 'Kayla? I wanted to ask you something.'

'Oh, yes?' She turned her head and opened her eyes. He was much closer than she'd thought. His blue gaze was fastened on hers and for a long moment she felt breathless, wondering if he was thinking the same thing she was. The shushing of the waves and the whisper of the wind faded into the background and the only thing she was aware of was the man next to her. She wanted him to kiss her. Now. She inched closer, then saw him take a deep breath and turn away.

The spell was broken.

Wes cleared his throat. 'Well, actually, I was wondering if there was any way you could stay a bit longer? I can't seem to find any suitable girls who want to work in such an isolated place, and we work well together, don't we?'

Kayla swallowed. 'Er, yes. Yes, we do.' They had worked as a team, each complementing the other, and Kayla had been surprised at how quickly she'd adapted to Wes's methods. He was certainly a lot easier to deal with than Mike had ever been, although she'd tried not to make comparisons. Wes never ordered her to do anything or made her feel inferior. He always either asked her politely or sought her opinion as to the best way of doing something, then praised her efforts afterwards. It made her feel valued, even though she knew he was the boss.

She was surprised now by the sudden feeling of

joy which swept through her at the thought of possibly staying on. It also scared the hell out of her. She was beginning to care far too much about the occupants of Marcombe Hall, and not just in a professional capacity. And she still didn't know how much of it was Jago's fault.

'So will you stay? Please? You're by far the best secretary I've ever had. Everyone else will seem hopeless in comparison.' Wes tried out his most charming smile on her and Kayla felt herself weaken. Not that she was prepared to let him know he could influence her this way. That the mere sight of him made the blood in her veins fizz. He obviously didn't feel the same or he would surely have made a move on her by now?

'You think flattery will work, do you?' she challenged, trying to sound stern. But she knew she probably wasn't fooling anyone, least of all herself. The truth was she found it impossible to resist him. The rich timbre of his voice drew her in, mesmerising her, sapping her willpower, just like his rogue of an ancestor had done in the saleroom at Sotheby's without uttering a single word. She didn't have the strength to argue, so she capitulated with barely an inner struggle. 'Oh, all right, why not? I guess a few more weeks can't make much difference.'

With a supreme effort, Kayla managed a nonchalant tone, although how she did it she would never know. Then she remembered she was supposed to be employed part-time in London. 'Er, I'll just have to call my office in London to see if I can extend my leave of absence. And I'd better go back to my flat for a few days to collect some more clothes and things. Not to mention my course books.'

'Great.' Wes didn't seem to notice her slip. His smile turned into a grin of satisfaction, which was even more devastating than the purposely charming smile, and Kayla thanked her lucky stars that she was already lying down. 'Let's go help Nell find some seashells, she looks a bit lonely over there by herself.'

'Uhm, you go ahead, I'll be with you in a minute.' A normal activity was just what Kayla needed to take her mind off the man by her side and what his smiles did to her equilibrium, but she wanted some space to recover first. Thank goodness for Nell, she thought.

'There you are! I was beginning to think I'd have to send out a search party.'

The voice which greeted them as they stepped into the hall made Kayla jump, and for a crazy moment she thought Jago had come to join them at Marcombe Hall somehow. The inflection was exactly the same and the rich, deep nuances of it, although the West Country burr was less pronounced. She blinked to accustom herself to the gloom inside after the brilliance of the afternoon sun. Instead of Jago, she saw a younger version of Wes standing at the bottom of the stairs.

Her eyes widened. The resemblance to the man in her portrait was even stronger in this man and it gave her quite a turn.

'Oh hell,' she thought she heard Wes mutter from behind her. In a louder voice he said, 'Hey, Alex. What are you doing here?'

'Visiting, of course. What else would I be doing? Although naturally I didn't come to see you, but the little princess.' He held out his arms and Nell raced over to be caught and hoisted high into the air, shrieking with pleasure.

'Uncle Alex. Eeeehh, that tickles!'

'This is my brother,' Wes informed Kayla in a rather non-committal tone of voice. 'Alex, this is my temporary secretary, Kayla Sinclair.'

Alex put Nell down and came forward to shake hands. 'Nice to meet you.' He looked Kayla up and down and smiled in approval. Kayla noticed that Wes's brother had inherited the killer grin, but this time it had no effect on her. It wasn't as genuine and didn't reach Alex's eyes. She nodded curtly to show him she didn't appreciate being given the once-over in such a blatant fashion.

'I'd better go and wash some of the sand off before dinner,' she told them, and made a quick getaway up the stairs.

At least Alex had proved one thing – the Jago charm spell didn't work with all the males of the house. So did that mean only Wes was affecting her? Kayla wasn't sure what to think about that.

* * *

The atmosphere during dinner was strained and Kayla struggled to make conversation with Alex while Wes ate in silence, a closed expression on his face. Kayla wondered why the two were at odds, but put it down to sibling rivalry. She knew first-hand how annoying younger brothers could be when they chose to. She had one of her own.

'So what do you do, Mr Marcombe?' she asked politely, then wished she hadn't said something so trite.

'Oh, please, call me Alex, there's no need to be formal. As to what I do – I sell boats, yachts to be precise. A friend of mine is a boatbuilder and I help him to market them, show them off to wealthy clients, that sort of thing. With summer approaching, this is the perfect time of year to start touting for business around here. A lot of Londoners come down to the Devon coast during half-term and the holidays. I try to catch their interest with my friend's latest boat designs, taking them out for little jaunts, that sort of thing.'

'I see. I take it you're a keen sailor, then?'

'Definitely. I couldn't imagine life without a boat or at the very least being near the sea. It's in my blood I think. Seafaring ancestors, all that stuff.' He went on to describe his own craft, and some of the yachts designed by his friend. They sounded very luxurious, but since Kayla didn't know one end of a boat from the other, she just listened without venturing any opinions.

'And what brought you to this part of the

country, Kayla?' Perhaps Alex had noticed the bemused expression in her eyes, since he changed the subject so abruptly.

'Oh, uhm . . . I was studying art in London part-time and in particular paintings by Gainsborough. I was told Wes might have one or two in his possession, and I made an appointment to come and have a look.' Kayla found it hard to lie yet again, but Alex nodded, apparently finding nothing strange in her answer.

'And then he persuaded you to work for him instead?'

Kayla nodded. 'Yes, but only until he can find someone else. I've got to go back to London eventually.'

Alex smiled as if he didn't quite believe her, but said nothing more on the subject.

The rest of the meal passed quickly, although Wes's continued brooding silence was a bit unnerving. Kayla decided to ignore it. Whatever was going on between these two was their own business and nothing to do with her.

Kayla excused herself and left the dining room earlier than she normally would. Wes watched her go, but didn't ask her to linger. He knew he'd made her uncomfortable with his silence, but he'd be damned if he'd make small talk with his brother. Alex didn't deserve it. In fact, he shouldn't even be here.

'So what is it this time?' Wes asked, as soon as

he was sure Kayla was out of earshot. 'Short of money again? Someone chasing you for payments you can't cover?'

Alex scowled at him. 'No, I'm debt free. Well, as much as anyone ever is.'

'Why are you here then? I thought you said you were moving out for good last time you left. "I hate this fucking dump and you're welcome to it, you pretentious git", quote, unquote.'

Wes watched as Alex struggled visibly to keep his temper from erupting. 'I might have exaggerated a little,' he muttered.

Wes snorted. 'Yeah, I'd say. Well, just so you know, your pretentious git of a brother has bailed you out for the last time. If you've come here hoping for money, you can leave right now. I've given you more than your fair share and that's it. I don't owe you anything.'

Alex stood up and slapped his napkin onto the table. 'I don't want your damned money. You're welcome to it. But this is still my home, as far as I know, and I have a right to stay here whenever I want to. Wasn't that what Dad's will said? So if I feel like spending some time in Devon, I'll damn well sleep in my old room. And as I told Kayla, I've got to start touting for business. Dave's been after me to show off his latest yacht so I'll be staying for a while. *If* that's okay with you?' The final sentence was said in an overly sarcastic way, which grated on Wes.

'Fine. As long as all you want is room and board.'

As Alex stormed out of the room, Wes ran a hand across his forehead, trying to loosen the tight vice that seemed clamped around it. He didn't know why they found it so difficult to get on with each other, but he knew Alex resented the fact that Wes had inherited Marcombe Hall.

'The oldest son inheriting everything is a relic of times gone by,' he'd grumbled more than once. 'These days the property should be divided equally between any children.' But their father had disagreed.

'Don't be ridiculous, Alex. That would mean selling the place. Unthinkable! It's been in the family for generations and goes with the title. And you can't honestly expect Wesley to buy you out.'

The old man had tried to make it up to his younger son by leaving him a generous trust fund, but Alex never seemed to appreciate it. He always wanted more and was forever living beyond his means, buying expensive cars, boats and who knew what else. Wes suspected drugs were involved too, but there was no talking to him.

Well, enough was enough. It was time to let Alex sink or swim.

The final straw had come a few weeks previously when a mutual acquaintance had revealed that Alex had been seen cosying up to Caroline at a club in London.

'Very lovey-dovey, they were. But you don't mind, do you?' the friend had asked. 'Water under the bridge and all that, eh?'

'No, not at all. Why should I?' Wes had been forced to reply, but inside he was seething. He did mind. Not because he still wanted Caroline – he most certainly didn't – but because he suspected it was all an act.

Why the hell else would Alex want his brother's cast-offs? It had to be for the usual reason – Alex coveted everything Wes had. It infuriated him that this should include Caro though, especially as he suspected she'd only go along with it to irritate her ex-husband as well. And what could Alex possibly see in a woman ten years his senior when he had the pick of more or less every girl he ever met? They fell for him in droves.

Something wasn't right, but he figured if he refrained from mentioning it, perhaps the two of them would tire of the game. By not reacting, he would cheat them of their petty little revenge.

But damned if he'd play happy families.

CHAPTER 18

The house was silent, the midwife and physician had gone and the maids had cleared up the mess. Eliza was left alone to gaze adoringly at her son. He was so small, so vulnerable and so utterly beautiful. And so like his father. A stab of guilt sliced through her, but she was too exhausted to worry about it overmuch. Jago would find a way for them to be together. If anyone could arrange things, it would be him. She had absolute faith in him; it was only a question of patience, as he'd said. Now she must concentrate on regaining her strength and nurturing their child.

The baby was lying in a cradle next to her bed and she lay on her side staring at him, studying every tiny detail of his features, watching his little chest move up and down as he breathed. It was a miracle that she had given birth to this wonderful being and she didn't begrudge the seemingly endless pain she'd had to go through. Her son was worth it. She couldn't take her eyes off him even for a second. With a smile, she leaned over to kiss his soft cheek yet again. He sighed in his sleep, an adorable little noise.

A slight sound from the corridor made her turn her head towards the door and to her amazement Jago tiptoed into the room. He put a finger over his lips to stop her from saying anything, but she gasped nonetheless. In three strides he was by her side, pulling her close.

'Oh, Jago,' she whispered. 'Have you run mad?'

He smiled and pushed a tendril of her hair behind one ear before bending down to kiss her. 'Yes, probably, but I had to come. I needed to make sure you're all right and the child also. You are, aren't you?'

'Yes, we're both fine. Look, isn't he wonderful?'

Jago went round to kneel next to his son's cradle and touched the baby's soft cheek with reverence. 'He's perfect.' He looked up. 'As are you, my love.'

'John is downstairs.' Eliza felt anxiety churning her insides. 'You're sure he didn't hear you come in?'

'No, he's drunk. I heard him snoring fit to wake the dead.'

Jago's words reassured Eliza, but he didn't stay long in any case. 'I just had to see you,' he whispered, 'and now I know you're well, I can rest easy. Goodnight, my love.'

As Eliza drifted off to sleep, she felt as though she was floating on a cloud of happiness. Not long now, and her joy would be complete.

'So you've finally deigned to return to us lesser mortals, have you?' was Maddie's sarcastic comment on seeing her friend again, but as it was delivered with a huge grin and a hug, Kayla didn't take offence. 'I was beginning to think you were staying in Devon for good.'

'Well, to be perfectly honest, I didn't really want to come home.' Kayla grinned back. 'You see, there's this gorgeous man and his lovely daughter. Not to mention the grand mansion, the incredible scenery, the brilliant job and the top salary.'

'Uh-oh.' Maddie held up one hand and laughed. 'Don't tell me any more, I have a feeling I'm not going to like this.'

'Yes, you are. Just wait until I tell you everything that's happened.'

Later that evening Kayla collapsed on the sofa in her living room, having packed a large suitcase full of clothes and cleaned the flat from top to bottom. It was unbelievable the amount of dust which could accumulate in just a few short weeks, even when no one was living there. She felt exhaustion wash over her and closed her eyes.

'You certainly deserve a rest now,' a familiar voice commented, and Kayla nearly jumped out of her skin. She put a hand over her heart and sent a mock glare at Jago.

'You're determined to give me a heart attack, aren't you?' she accused. 'Honestly, I think you enjoy scaring me half to death.'

He chuckled. 'Not at all, my dear, but I have to confess I am dying of curiosity. If one can die of something when one is already dead that is.

Have you found Eliza for me yet? You have been gone an age, or is it simply my imagination? I'm never really clear about time passing.'

'No, I have been away a bit longer than I'd reckoned with, but unfortunately I haven't found Eliza. I've searched Marcombe Hall from top to bottom and there are no portraits like the one you described anywhere. I even tiptoed into the dusty attics one day when everyone was out, but there was nothing. I'm sorry,' she added when he stayed silent for a long time.

'Well, it was worth a try.' He sighed. 'I suppose I'm stuck here for all eternity then.'

'Oh, don't give up yet, Jago. I'm going to try and trace Eliza's descendants to see if any of them left the painting to some other branch of the family. Don't despair, we might still find it.'

'Do you think so? It is kind of you to put yourself out on my behalf.' He sounded downcast and Kayla had the urge to hug him, but she knew she never could.

'Not at all, I'm happy to do it. But don't you want to hear about her descendants? Or should I perhaps say *your* descendants, you wicked man?'

Jago chuckled. 'So I've been found out, have I? How?' Kayla heard the laughter in his voice and tried to look stern.

'You most certainly have, you old reprobate.' She wagged a finger at him. 'I couldn't help but notice a rather marked resemblance between you and Sir Wesley and his brother. You don't deny it?'

'What would be the point now, so long after the event?'

'I suppose you're right. But do they know?'

'Who, my great-great-something grandsons? No, shouldn't think so. A lot of people may have suspected it at the time and some knew for sure, but nothing was ever said openly. It wasn't the sort of thing you'd boast about.' He grinned, obviously unrepentant. 'Now do tell me how my descendants go on. And what about the house? Has it been much altered? Of course, it was never my property, but I remember it well.'

Kayla didn't feel at all strange about having a conversation with a man in a painting, which was weird, she reflected. It almost seemed normal now and she hardly gave it a thought once they started talking. She had accepted that this was happening and since he was such good company, she decided she might as well enjoy it while it lasted. The world was full of unexplained phenomena, why not talking portraits? She smiled to herself and started to tell Jago about Wes and his family.

'Maddie, I need Jessie's help again.' Kayla rang her friend first thing the following morning.

'Oh no, I'll be owing her favours until Doomsday.' Maddie sighed.

'Please, it's important.'

'Okay, fine. So what do you want her to do this time?'

'If it's not too much trouble, do you think she could put together some sort of family tree for Sir John's descendants please? I'll pay her for her trouble, of course.'

'Don't be silly, she wouldn't charge a friend. Besides, I'm sure she'll enjoy it, you know what she's like.'

'Yes. Well, can you get her to call me when I'm back in Devon, please? I need to ask her how to look for Marcombe wills which might mention the paintings as well. It may be that I have to search for that sort of thing locally. I seem to remember she told me wills were often kept at the nearest record office.'

'You're absolutely sure the painting of Eliza isn't at Marcombe Hall?'

'Positive, so someone else must have inherited it, unless her husband burned it in a fit of jealous rage or something. He did have cause, poor man.' Kayla giggled at the thought, although it hadn't been a laughing matter back then, she was sure.

Kayla told Maddie about Jago's 'cuckoo in the nest' and she chuckled. 'Yes, if he found out, that is. All right, I'll give Jessie the number so you can ask her what to do.'

'Thanks a lot, Maddie. I really appreciate it.'

'Oh, no! What in the name of all that's holy . . .?' Kayla stopped dead just inside the door to her room at Marcombe Hall and stared in horror at the dreadful mess. She couldn't believe her eyes. It looked as if a malignant whirlwind or poltergeist had swept through, leaving nothing untouched. Dropping the large suitcase where she stood, she turned on her heel and ran in search of Wes. As usual, she found him in the office.

'Hello, Wes.'

'Kayla, you're back!' His face lit up at the sight of her and she almost forgot her anger for a moment as warmth spread through her at his obvious pleasure in her return. 'Did you have a good journey this time or did you take any detours?' he teased.

Kayla managed a feeble smile. 'No, everything went well and I only got lost once. But Wes, can you come and have a look at my room for a minute, please?'

'Your room?' Wes looked puzzled. 'Why?'

'Something nasty seems to have happened to it while I was gone.' Without waiting to see if he followed, she went back upstairs, her heart thumping uncomfortably. As she opened the door she heard Wes gasp in surprise behind her.

'Jesus! What happened here?'

'Well, I was kind of hoping you could tell me that.' Kayla went over to the bed and lifted up one of her favourite sweaters, which had been virtually shredded. She looked at it forlornly. 'I guess the ghost that doesn't exist decided to return. Didn't you hear it?'

'Ghost? No way. This isn't the work of anything

supernatural.' Wes looked furious now. He walked around inspecting the damage with angry strides, lifting an item of clothing here, a book there. Every single one of Kayla's possessions had been either torn, cut or broken. A pair of scissors lay on the floor, open as if they'd been thrown away after the user had finished. 'Poltergeists wouldn't know how to use scissors, I'm pretty sure about that, but who the hell would do this sort of thing?'

'Somebody who hates me?' Kayla bit her bottom lip. The thought that anyone could dislike her this much was extremely unsettling.

'But why would anybody hate you? And anyway, you hardly know anyone around here yet. Unless you have some enemies from London who have tracked you down? You're not being stalked by your former fiancé or anything, are you?'

Kayla shook her head, then frowned. 'Hey, how did you know I had a former fiancé? I never told you that.'

'Just something Nell said.'

'Oh, right.' Kayla sighed. 'Sorry, didn't mean to snap at you. Guess I'm just a little bit paranoid right now.'

'Understandable. Don't worry about it, I shouldn't have mentioned it.' Wes stopped and stared out of the window, deep in thought. 'Hmm. It doesn't make sense though. I'll make some enquiries, perhaps someone has seen something. Leave it with me.' He walked over to where she stood next to the bed. 'I'm sorry, Kayla. I know some of these things probably can't be replaced, but I will try to give you compensation. Write me a list, please?' He slowly stroked her cheek, and she closed her eyes, savouring the comforting warmth of his large hand. She had missed him while she'd been away, more than she'd thought possible. When she looked up again he pulled her close and held her in a tight embrace. Neither of them spoke.

At length he let go of her, kissed her cheek and left. Kayla put up her hand to the spot his lips had touched and stood for a long time lost in thought. What had he meant by that? Was it just a comforting sort of hug and kiss, the kind you give a friend in need? Or did it have any deeper meaning? She wished she knew. But she couldn't read him and although he'd seemed so pleased to see her, he hadn't said he'd missed her. If he had, it was probably just in her capacity as secretary, but how she wished it was more than that.

With a sigh, she began the task of clearing up.

'You wanted to speak to me? Again?' Alex entered the office and closed the door behind him. Wes studied his brother's face carefully, but couldn't see anything that would indicate he was hiding something. Alex may be irritating as hell, not to mention lazy and with a devil-may-care attitude, but Wes had never known him to be deliberately cruel or vindictive. He was too easy-going for that.

'Yes. Take a seat.' Wes regarded his brother for another few minutes before coming straight to the point. 'Did you wreck all Kayla's things while she was gone?'

'Excuse me?' Alex looked genuinely surprised. If he was acting, Wes had to acknowledge he was damned good at it.

'While she was in London, someone entered her room and completely tore all her belongings to pieces – clothes, books, everything. Shredded. There wasn't a single item left untouched. Do you know anything about that?'

'No.' Alex had reverted to a sulky look. 'Why do you always assume that when something goes wrong around here it's my fault? And why on earth would I want to ruin Kayla's stuff? I like her, for Christ's sake.'

Wes ran a hand through his hair in a tired, defeated gesture. 'I'm sorry, Alex, but I couldn't think who else it could be. She doesn't know anyone here, except us and Annie, and I really don't think Nell would be capable of such malice. Besides, she likes Kayla too. So who would do such a thing?' A thought occurred to him. 'You wouldn't happen to have seen Caro around, have you? If she was in one of her weird moods, she might decide to smash the place up. Although why Kayla's room in particular, God knows.'

Alex shrugged and studied his fingernails. 'Beats me who could have done it, but if I hear anything I'll let you know.' His posture was slightly defensive, as if he wasn't telling the whole truth and Wes noticed he didn't reply to the question about Caro. Wes narrowed his eyes at his brother but decided not to push it. If Alex knew who the culprit was, perhaps he'd warn him or her off. He certainly hoped so.

'All right, thanks. Oh, by the way, are you staying long?'

Alex smirked. 'What, trying to get rid of me already, dear bro? Don't worry, I've nearly finished my business around here, so you won't have to put up with me for much longer. Another couple of weeks at the most.'

'That's not what I meant and you know it.'

'Don't pretend, Wes. I know you think I'm a waste of space.'

'Damn it, Alex, you're my brother and you're welcome here any time you want. It's your home too. I just wish you would take life a bit more seriously, that's all.'

'And I wish you'd lighten up a bit. You're not in your dotage yet after all, but I guess we'll never agree on that point, so I'll see you later.'

Wes stared after his brother who sauntered out of the room as if he hadn't a care in the world. Much as he hated to admit it, maybe Alex was right. Perhaps he did take life too seriously. Maybe it was time to live a little and let work take second place for a while. He'd been working far too hard of late and never did anything else. He rubbed his eyes with the heel of his hands.

He was just afraid he had forgotten how to have fun.

CHAPTER 19

John flung open the door to the bedroom so hard it ricocheted off the wall, making the furniture jump and sending an ornament crashing to the floor. His gaze fixed on Eliza, who'd turned around in fright, staring at him with huge eyes. The baby, startled out of his slumber, began to wail loudly, a piercing, terrified little sound. John ignored it and focused on his wife.

'Wh-what on earth is the matter?' she stammered. 'You're scaring the baby!'

'Bitch!' he ground out, his eyes boring into her, fury boiling his blood. His hatred must have been almost tangible, because Eliza began to tremble from head to toe.

'John?' she asked uncertainly, edging away from him under the covers.

She couldn't evade him, however, he saw to that. Quickly, he advanced on the bed and reached over to haul her out by a painful grip on her arm.

'No! John don't, I'm supposed to lie down,' she protested. 'The midwife said the bleeding won't stop otherwise. John, please!'

'So you thought you could cuckold me, did you?

236

Traitorous whore,' he spat and pulled her along towards the door. She tried to resist, holding onto the bedpost, but he backhanded her and she cried out and lost her grip. He grabbed her around the waist, making his way towards the door, while Eliza began to sob and stretched her hands out towards her screaming baby.

'No, John. My baby. He needs me, I must stay with him.'

'Shut up.'

He hit her, harder this time, and she fainted, crumpling into a deadweight. With the strength born of true rage, John hefted her up and slung her over his shoulder.

'Faint all you like,' he muttered. 'I'll not let you get away with this.'

She came to as he was staggering along a garden path, huffing and wheezing with the effort of carrying her. She weighed more than he'd thought.

'John, let me down, please. You're hurting my stomach and I feel nauseous and dizzy. Did you hear me? Any minute now, I'm going to be sick, I swear.'

He ignored her and kept going.

'Put me down,' she begged. 'Stop this, please. John, for the love of God!' Feebly she started to hit his back with her fists, but she was so weak it didn't have much impact. Still, he figured she might as well walk so he dropped her to the ground and she was momentarily winded.

'So you're awake again. Good. If you'd rather walk, so be it,' he said. He tugged her upright with a yank of her arm and began to stride along the path holding onto her with a death-grip. She protested again and tried to free herself, but without success. He was pleased to note that she had to follow him willy-nilly, and he paid her no heed when she complained that the cold, sharp stones on the gravel path were digging painfully into her bare feet. He could hear her teeth clattering together too, presumably both from the cold and the shock of being dragged outside. It made a glow of satisfaction spread inside him. It was justice, pure and simple.

'No, John! What are you doing? Have you gone insane?' She tried again to free herself.

'Hah, thought you could fool me, did you?' he muttered. 'Well, you should have found yourself a lover with blond hair then, shouldn't you? Stupid whore. Now you'll get your comeuppance. I'll see to it personally.'

'Don't be silly, of course the baby is yours. Not everyone in the family has blond hair, you know that. You're drunk, John. Can we not discuss this in the morning? Please! You don't know what you're saying.'

He wasn't listening. Nothing she could say would stop him now, he was determined about that. Relentless, he pulled her along towards the cliffs and although Eliza dug in her heels, bit him and tried anything else she could think of, he didn't let go of her. He knew full well she didn't have the strength to withstand him, drained as she was after her recent ordeal. Even her sobbing lessened after a while, obviously an effort when she needed the energy for walking and fighting him every step of the way.

Eventually they reached the cliffs and as he dragged her near the edge Eliza seemed to understand what he intended, for she started to fight him in earnest, hysteria lending her additional strength.

'No John, don't do this, I beg you. You really have run mad . . . Help me someone, HELP ME!'

She shouted and sobbed, flailed and kicked, but they both knew he was the stronger. And there was no one out in the middle of the night. There was only darkness.

Alex rapped smartly on the door to a cheap hotel room in nearby Kingsbridge. It was opened cautiously and the occupant peered out through the crack.

'Yes? Oh, it's you. Come in.'

He entered swiftly and shut the door so hard it vibrated for a moment. 'What the hell did you have to go and ruin Kayla's stuff for? Don't you have any sense?'

'Nice to see you too, Alex. And who's Kayla?'

'Don't play games with me, Caro. I'm warning you, I'm not in the mood. I've already had an earful from my sainted brother. That's enough.'

Caroline, a tall beauty in her mid-thirties with short, honey-coloured hair, fashionably cut, walked over to sit on the bed with her legs curled under her. She glared at Alex. 'What difference does it make to you what happens to that woman's things?'

Alex groaned. 'Don't you understand? You've made Wes wary now. He'll have his people on the look out for strangers and weird comings and goings. That's exactly what we don't want. I told you that we weren't supposed to arouse anyone's suspicions or attract any attention, for Christ's sake, that's why we came here and why you have to keep out of the way. No one would question my staying at the Hall – it's still my home after all – but you being there for several weeks would seem odd when you don't normally stay that long.'

'I have a right to visit my daughter.'

'Yes, but you don't, do you? When was the last time you spent more than a day with her? Never, that's when.'

'That's not to say I can't.'

'Well, bloody well do it in daylight, instead of creeping around the house wrecking stuff.'

Caroline opened a bedside drawer and took out a packet of pills. She extracted one and swallowed it down with angry movements.

'And *that's* not helping.' Alex nodded at the pills and scowled at her. 'You promised, no drugs while we're doing this job.'

'It's just diazepam, they calm me down. And it's no wonder I need them, with you storming in here in such a foul mood, shouting at me.'

Alex ground his teeth together, trying to keep his frustration bottled up. He took a deep breath before continuing in what he hoped was a more reasonable tone of voice. 'Look, all I'm saying is that you have to be a bit more circumspect. There's no point you hiding out here if you're going to do stupid things up at the Hall. Wes will smell a rat for sure.'

'The little bitch needed to be taught a lesson. She's living in *my* room and probably using all my things, so what does she need her own for? Nell told me she borrowed my swimsuit, can you believe it? The nerve.' Caroline's features, normally as lovely as any model's, took on an ugly expression.

'So you *have* seen Nell?'

'Yes. I popped in to say goodnight to her, as is my right. And don't worry, it's our little secret. I made her promise not to tell Wes.' Alex rolled his eyes, but she ignored him. 'Anyway, that's beside the point. That woman is trying to take my place, I just know it, ensnaring Wes and worming her way into Nell's affection. Nell does nothing but talk about her all the time and I'm sick to death of it. *I'm* the one who should be there, not living in this, this . . . well, look at it, for heaven's sake. I mean, I ask you – pink nylon sheets? It's disgusting. It's not what I'm used to, I can tell you.'

Alex sat down and sighed. He put his head in his hands. 'I thought you hated Wes, so what do you care whether he likes Kayla or not?' He ignored the rest of her outburst. Some things weren't worth fighting over. 'You said you were in love with me.' In his heart he had known all along that Caroline didn't really love him, but he hadn't cared. He just wanted her because she'd been Wes's and he'd known it would annoy his brother no end.

She was an incredibly attractive woman, with her lithe body and seductive ways, so being with her wasn't exactly a hardship. He had also thought they were kindred spirits as they both loved life in the fast lane and living in luxury without actually having to do much work in order to achieve this. Of late, however, the relationship had begun to pall on him. For that matter, so had the jet-set lifestyle and the things he had to do to stay afloat. He knew he was in too deep and he wanted out. But Caro had insisted they do this one last job together and he'd agreed. Then he'd finish with her.

She was right about one thing though. She did look incongruous sitting on the faded floral chintz bedspread, dressed only in a flimsy silk kimono. Like an exotic bird who had somehow ended up in the shabby nest of a sparrow. Caroline was the kind of woman who should be staying at The Ritz, or whatever the local equivalent was, and walk around wearing designer clothes and dripping with jewellery. But here she was, brought low by her own weaknesses. She was hooked on prescription drugs and alcohol. Just like he was. The only difference was that he admitted as much and wanted to do something about it. She didn't.

'Of course I don't love Wes,' she sneered in answer to his question. 'How could I, after what he's done to me? He's a complete bastard. But I wanted to be Lady Marcombe. He had no right to take that away from me. I'd earned it, providing him with a child and everything. Now I'm back to being a plain Ms. How boring is that?'

'You brought it all on yourself,' he muttered, but she pretended not to hear him.

'Anyway, that room is still mine. It was to be left intact for me to stay in whenever I visit Nell. That was the agreement, so why did he put her in there? So she could be conveniently close to his room, I bet. He'll have unlocked the interconnecting door first chance he got.'

'Look, the only reason she's in your room is because all the others are being redecorated, okay?' Alex tried to hang onto his patience, but it wasn't easy. 'Annie told me. And if Wes wanted to sleep with the woman, don't you think she would be sharing his own room? This isn't the Middle Ages.' Caroline started to say something, but he held up a hand to stop her. 'Enough, Caro. We have more important things to think about right now. We have to plan our next move carefully or we'll jeopardise the whole deal. If we don't succeed in our little venture, you'll be spending the rest of your life in hovels like this. Is that what you want? Now are you going to be sensible and help out, or should I take you back to London and manage it by myself?'

Caroline lit a cigarette and inhaled deeply before replying. 'Oh, very well. Let's finish playing your little games first. I'll deal with Wes and the bitch later.'

'They are not games,' he growled. 'This is dead serious, Caro, I wish you'd get it into that pretty little head of yours. And it was your idea in the first place, remember?'

She ignored his comments yet again and with an abrupt change of mood she stubbed out the cigarette and crooked a finger at him, smiling seductively. 'If you've finished being disagreeable, why don't you come and greet me properly? Haven't you missed me even a tiny bit, darling?'

Alex hesitated, then shook his head. For once he didn't feel any desire for her and if he was honest with himself, it was a relief. He tried to let her down gently though. 'Sorry, but I've got things to do. And I'm a bit tired. Couldn't sleep at the Hall last night. Wes always gets to me, you know how he is.'

Caroline didn't buy his excuses. She stared at him in disbelief before her lips tightened and fury made her eyes flash dangerously. 'I see. Well, perhaps I'll go and find someone else to play with then. I'm sure there are other little boys around here who wouldn't mind.' She flounced off towards the tiny bathroom and went inside, slamming the door behind her.

Alex sighed and cursed himself for a fool. He needed to keep Caro sweet until the deed was done. She knew too much. 'I am *not* a little boy,' he muttered, clenching his fists in frustration, 'so why won't anyone ever take me seriously?' But he knew it was partly his own fault.

He gritted his teeth and went to knock diffidently on the bathroom door. 'Caro, darling? I'm sorry, I didn't mean to offend you. It's just that I've had so much on my mind lately. Please, won't you come out and I'll make it up to you?'

He was kept waiting for a few minutes, then the door opened slowly.

'So what do you say we take the day off to do some touristy stuff, Kayla?'

Kayla looked up from the computer and found Wes standing very close. She breathed in his aftershave, which for some reason she found extra intoxicating today. It was a mixture of subtle spices with lemony overtones that made her want to pull him close. 'Er, sure, that would be nice.' She cleared her throat, trying to get her wayward thoughts under control. 'What's brought this on?'

He nodded towards the window. 'It's a beautiful day, too lovely to sit inside. And I've decided I need to live a little. I work too hard.' He grinned and shrugged. 'I'm turning into a boring old man, or so Alex says.'

'You're not old,' Kayla protested.

'You don't think?' He looked at her with a strange expression on his face that confused Kayla.

'Well, no,' she said, then added with a smile. 'You probably just feel that way because you're a dad. My sister told me she aged about ten years when she had her kids because she never got to sleep.'

'Very true. Speaking of which, I'd better go and tell Nell to get ready. You don't mind if we bring her?'

'No, of course not, why would I?'

Wes sent her a grateful glance and went off to round up his daughter.

An hour or so later they drove into the car park of one of Devon's many tourist attractions.

'"Canonteign Falls, England's highest water-fall",' Kayla read out loud from the little brochure Wes had handed her. 'Wow, sixty-seven metres, that's quite a drop.'

'It's actually man-made, you know,' he said, setting off towards the woodland trail that led to the waterfall.

'Yes, I know, but it's pretty impressive even so.' Kayla and Nell followed him eagerly, happy to be out of doors on such a sunny day.

They passed a small lake and entered a wooded area where the trail began. As they neared the first tiny cascades, Kayla could smell the damp air surrounding them and felt as if she had entered a greenhouse. She breathed in huge lungfuls of the healthy atmosphere. It was wonderful and she imagined the extra bursts of oxygen fizzing through her blood. There was moisture dripping down from all sides and moss and lichen covered the wet stones near the little brook. Further up the hill they encountered the lower waterfall, which the guidebook called Clampitt Falls. The roar of the water was incredible and the majestic cascade tumbled down the hill with surprising speed and force.

They stopped for a while to admire this sight before continuing upwards, climbing the steep path past huge tree roots covered in moss and ivy. The brook bubbling past them had lovely clear water and Nell and Kayla both bent down to test it to see how cold it was.

'That's quite warm actually,' Kayla said.

'Yes. Can I take my shoes off and paddle?' Nell asked with a hopeful look on her face.

'Not now. Come on, let's get to the top,' Wes replied. 'You haven't seen the best one yet.'

They all looked up in awe at the giant waterfall higher up the trail. The water came rushing over a sheer cliff face and fell straight down, making a terrible racket. It reminded Kayla of a huge, silver-coloured rippling ponytail and it was a lovely sight.

'This is beautiful!' Kayla exclaimed. 'Thank you for bringing us here, Wes.'

He smiled at her and sent her a teasing glance. 'You probably won't thank me after I make you walk to the top of the hill.'

'The top? You mean we're going further up?'

'Yep. Come on, this way.' He took Nell's hand and led the way up a narrow path. Kayla felt as if the forest was closing in on her as they followed the trail ever higher. They discovered there was a smaller fall behind the big one, but the path continued past this and upwards. They finally reached the so called 'Buzzard's View' at the top of the waterfall and stopped to look down, panting slightly from the steep climb.

'Oh, Daddy, everyone's really tiny down there, just like dolls.' Nell pointed to some people way below them on the path. Kayla had to agree they did seem quite far away, but she preferred not to look down for too long. Suddenly dizzy, she turned to continue along the path, anxious to get away from the drop. Little bubbles of panic rose up inside her, although she tried her best to stop them.

'Oh God, I can't look at that. I'll wait for you further down,' she called and stumbled away without waiting for an answer. She kept to the trail, which was rather dark in places under the dense foliage, and quite steep and slippery at times as well. Kayla had to concentrate very hard so as not to fall and soon stopped to catch her breath and wait for the others. She leaned against a trunk and closed her eyes for a moment. She hadn't realised the height would have such an effect on her.

'There you are, Kayla.' She opened her eyes and tried to muster a smile for Wes, who had caught up with her, but her smile turned to a frown at his next words. 'But where's Nell?'

'I thought she was with you. I left you at the top. I told you I couldn't stomach the height.'

'Yes, but she wanted to follow you, so I told her to stay close. In fact, I'm pretty sure she was right behind you.' Wes swore under his breath and Kayla felt her chest tightening with fear. 'Damn, I knew I should have kept hold of her hand.'

'Oh, no!' Kayla felt helpless and larger tentacles of panic groped at her insides. She swallowed hard and tried to think rationally. 'There are only two ways down from here – this way or the way we came. Let's go down one side each and meet at the bottom. One of us is bound to come across her. She can't have gone far.'

'Yes, you're right. And when I find her she's going to get a good talking to, I can tell you. She knows not to wander off on her own. I've told her a hundred times at least.' Kayla could hear the frustration and fear in his voice, but didn't comment. She felt the same and Nell wasn't even her child.

Wes stalked off in the direction from which they had come and Kayla continued along the trail she'd been following. The forest suddenly didn't seem as appealing as before – she found the darkness oppressive, the humidity unbearable and the path too muddy and slippery. It also felt as if it was never-ending and Kayla gritted her teeth in frustration. Every few yards she called Nell's name, but there was no reply. An icy lump settled in her stomach, making her feel nauseous. Where the hell could she be?

Visions of small bodies floating in water or lying lifeless at the bottom of a long hill started to torment her and she hurried on. She tripped over a tree root and hurt her ankle, but kept going all the same. There was no time to lose.

With a sigh of relief she finally emerged into the sunlight at the bottom of the hill, only to be met by a despondent-looking Wes. He shook his head at her unspoken question.

'Oh, Wes, what are we going to do?' She took his hand to comfort him and he squeezed it gratefully.

'I don't know. I suppose we'll have to alert the staff so they can organise a search party. Like you said, she can't have gone far. She's got to be here somewhere. Let's go over to the office.'

They headed for the buildings, which housed a café and gift shop, at a half-run, hoping to find the staff office nearby. In the courtyard next to the play area, however, Wes came to such an abrupt halt that Kayla bumped into him.

'Wes, what's the matter?' she said uncertainly.

'Nell!' he exclaimed and rushed forward. 'Nell, you're all right.'

Kayla stared in surprise as he ran over to hug his daughter who was sitting at a table eating ice cream next to an elegant woman with short, honey-coloured hair. 'God, you gave me such a fright. Where have you been?'

'Well, I was—' Nell started to say, but was cut short by the woman who fixed them all with an icy glare.

'Really, Wes, you should look after our daughter better. I found her wandering around all by herself in the forest without supervision. Honestly, it's enough to make me want to go back to court. I'm sure the judge would be interested in this little tale.' She smiled smugly and Kayla had a sudden urge to slap the woman's face. So this was Caroline, she thought.

Kayla put her hands in the pockets of her faded jeans and studied Wes's ex-wife. She had to admit the woman was beautiful, in the manner of a sleek, but lethal, cat. She had the most incredible complexion and enormous, almond-shaped brown eyes. Kayla thought Caroline looked completely out of place, however, since she was wearing a pale designer outfit, sandals and lots of chunky jewellery. Nearly everyone around them wore shorts or jeans and T-shirts, not to mention sensible walking shoes.

Wes scowled at Caroline and a muscle jumped in his cheek, making Kayla realise he was holding his temper in check, but only just. 'Well, what a coincidence that you should "happen" to walk by in the forest,' he retorted. 'That's got to be a first. I don't recall you ever wanting to trek through the woods before. I hope you didn't get your fancy clothes dirty or your shoes stuck in the mud.' He threw a scornful glance at her footwear, which on closer inspection did look rather muddy.

'Yes, isn't it a coincidence? I really felt I ought to take in a few of the tourist sights before I leave on my next trip. One can't possibly have lived in Devon without at least visiting Canonteign Falls, or so I've been told.'

Wes ignored his ex-wife and hugged Nell again, burying his face in her hair. 'I'm so glad you're safe, sweetie. It was lucky you found Mummy, eh?' Kayla admired the way he kept his tone even. It must have taken a lot of self-control.

'Yes, but—' Nell was cut short by her mother for a second time. Caroline didn't seem to want to hear her daughter's views on anything.

'Aren't you going to introduce me to your new, er, friend?' Caroline purred while looking Kayla up and down as if she were some kind of vermin. Kayla stared back defiantly. Caroline had no right to look so superior.

'This is Kayla Sinclair, my secretary. Kayla this is Caroline, Nell's mother.' Wes was very obviously reluctant to perform the introductions, as he did so in a wooden tone of voice. 'I think we'd better be going now though. It's getting late. If you'll excuse us, Caroline?'

'I suppose so, since I don't seem to have any rights any more.' Caroline glared at Wes a final time before standing up. She was almost as tall as her ex-husband and with a very slender figure. Kayla clenched her fists inside her pockets. The woman must be at least a head taller than herself and so elegant. It made her feel small and insignificant. Not to mention overweight, even though she knew well enough that she wasn't. In short, Caroline made her want to gnash her teeth. And she still had an urge to slap her.

After an exaggerated goodbye to her daughter, Caroline swept off towards the car park and the others followed more slowly. Kayla trailed behind Wes and his daughter despondently. All her joy in the outing had evaporated as fast as the water in the forest.

It occurred to her to wonder why Caroline should have annoyed her so much, since it was really none of her business. She knew that because she liked Wes, she had immediately taken his side, although unconsciously. But if she was perfectly honest, there was more to it than that. She sighed. Perhaps she ought to leave before her attraction to Wes got out of control? After all, he had stated categorically that he would never marry again, so there was no hope of him ever reciprocating any feelings she may have for him. He might want to have a fling, or relationship of some sort, but Kayla knew it would never be enough for her. No, it would surely be better to go away and try to make a new life for herself somewhere else. The only problem was, she didn't want to leave. With a heavy heart, she climbed into the car.

CHAPTER 20

The free-traders moved quietly and effi-
ciently, unloading the cargo onto the beach
in the dark. They were all sure-footed and
had no need for torches. They knew this stretch
of the coast like the back of their hands and each
man knew precisely what to do and carried out
his duties in silence.

Jago worked side by side with his men, doing
his fair share. It had been another good run, but
he was relieved it was nearly finished. Although
he knew Eliza had come through her ordeal, and
she and the baby were both fine, he couldn't stop
thinking about them. He ought to be concentrating on the smuggling operation, but found it
difficult. It required him to be alert for any possible
danger, and it was with a great deal of effort he
put Eliza out of his mind for long enough to do
what he had to. Since he would never willingly
jeopardise his men, somehow he managed it. The
operation was a success.

The sea was calm and the soft murmur of the
waves lapping gently onto the shore was the only
sound to be heard, apart from the occasional grunt

as one of the men hefted a particularly heavy burden onto his shoulders. The breeze was gentle, if somewhat cold, despite the fact that they were almost at the end of March. Even so, Jago felt the tension build up inside him. Something wasn't right. Everything was too quiet. He stopped to listen and scan the surrounding cliffs as best he could in the dark, but he couldn't see anything threatening.

He had just bent back to his task when suddenly he heard voices somewhere at the top of the cliffs. He couldn't make out any actual words, nor see anyone, but soon after, the air was rent by a scream of pure terror. A woman's scream which seemed to go on for a very long time, then was cut off abruptly.

All the men froze for an instant, before looking around frantically. A loud thump had been heard about twenty yards along the beach, and everyone ran for cover to hide wherever they could. A woman's scream usually meant that one of the look-outs had spotted the Excise men and was giving the free-traders warning. Many of the village women acted as look-outs while their menfolk were about their dangerous business. It gave them something to do while waiting.

Jago ran with the rest, leaving the cargo half unloaded on the beach and the boat unmanned. He threw himself down behind a boulder and waited for the thunder of hooves along the path up above, which would signal the arrival of the

Excise men. With a bit of luck they wouldn't see anything unusual and ride past as had happened on previous occasions. If not, well the free-traders would simply have to abandon the goods and run for their lives.

Time passed and nothing happened. Jago became more and more uneasy. He still had a niggling feeling that something was very wrong. If there had been Excise men they should have arrived by now. He remembered the strange thumping noise and decided to investigate. On all fours he crawled in that direction, slowly, inch by sandy inch, then stopped abruptly as his hands touched something soft. Something warm and human. A flowery fragrance rose to tease his nostrils, and he drew in a deep, shaky breath. He knew that scent all too well. Would know it anywhere. A vice clamped around his heart and he felt as if it stopped beating altogether.

'Oh, no,' he whispered hoarsely. 'Oh, dear God, no!' On legs which felt almost numb, he ran quickly to the little boat and fetched the lantern they had used for signalling earlier on. With trembling hands he managed to open its shutter, while his men came out of their hiding places one by one.

'What is it, Jago? What're you doing?' his best friend Matthew hissed, looking around anxiously. 'You're never using the lantern, man?'

'Follow me,' was all Jago managed to say, and the men trooped behind him over to the body lying so still on the sand. Jago directed the beam of light at the face and there was a collective gasp as they all realised who it was, staring with unseeing eyes into the black night sky. They looked at Jago, uncertain how he would react, but he had already known. It couldn't be anyone other than Eliza. And it was all his fault.

He knelt in the sand beside her body and leaned his forehead on her chest. Not a sound came out of his throat, although he wanted to scream and roar and shout his protests and apologies to the heavens. If only he'd resisted her, this would never have happened. If only he'd been stronger, she would still be alive. But she had been so beautiful, so exactly the kind of woman he wanted. And she had wanted him. Tempted him beyond reason.

'Dear God,' someone whispered. 'What'll we do?'

He suddenly remembered the baby and shone the beam of light round the surrounding area. To his relief there was nothing there. *Thank the Lord for small mercies!* He wondered what had become of the child, but for the moment there was no way of finding out. He prayed the little mite was safe with his nursemaid. Thinking back he knew he'd only heard one thump. He swallowed hard, clenching his fists around a handful of sand until he felt the grains hurting his palms.

'Jago.' Matthew touched his shoulder gently. 'Jago, we must get away from here. 'Tisn't safe. Shall we take her with us?'

Jago looked up at his friend and the rest of the men and saw that they shared his pain. They'd all known about Eliza and no one blamed him. But it was still his fault. With a heart as heavy as a boulder, he stood up. There were tears frozen inside him, but he couldn't allow them to surface now. Time for that later.

'Yes,' he whispered. 'Put her in the boat, please. Her murderer will pay for this, but first we must take care of the goods. Let's get to it, men.'

They continued with their tasks as swiftly as possible, and dispersed to hide the cargo in various places. Jago and Matthew stayed behind and pushed the big boat into the water. They began to row towards the village along the coast. If Sir John came to look for the body in the morning, he wouldn't find it.

Serve him right.

After dinner that evening Wes went off to have a long talk with Nell and Kayla settled down with a good book in the library-cum-office. There was a particularly comfortable sofa in there that felt as if it had been made for reading on. Soon Wes returned, however, and she looked up to try and judge his mood. He seemed subdued, but came to sit near her.

'Is she all right?' Kayla asked, putting her book down on the floor next to the sofa.

'Yes. Yes, she's okay.' Wes ran a hand through his dark hair, a gesture Kayla was becoming very familiar with. It made her want to push her own fingers through the shiny strands, but she resisted the impulse.

'That's good.'

'Mm-hm. I'm not sure I am though. Okay, I mean. Her disappearance scared the shit out of me, to be honest. Not quite the kind of outing I'd envisaged.'

'Scared me too. I kept imagining all sorts of horrible things, and all the time she was happily eating ice cream.'

Wes shook his head. 'Nell didn't just wander off, you know. She told me Caroline was standing behind a bush, beckoning to her and then she made her go down the hill with her without telling me. It was all done on purpose.'

Kayla frowned. 'I thought it was a strange coincidence that she should be there at the same time as us and just happen to find her own daughter in the forest.'

'Coincidence my foot. She somehow found out we were going and staged the whole thing. Or maybe she followed us and it was done on the spur of the moment. What I can't figure out though is why? Is she just trying to spite me? Get revenge of some sort? Or simply scare the living daylights out of me? If Caro is going to start doing stupid things like this, I'll have to have Nell watched twenty-four seven. I have no idea how I'm going to do that unless I hire a bodyguard or something. And that sounds ridiculous!'

Kayla took his hand and gave it a sympathetic squeeze. 'Maybe it was a one-off occurrence? Caroline has had her little joke at your expense now and the reaction she got must have been more than satisfactory. Let's hope that's enough. Surely she wouldn't want to hurt her own daughter?'

He laced his fingers with hers and held on briefly before letting go. 'No, I should hope not. But she's out of her mind on drugs half the time. God knows she shouldn't even be driving, let alone traipsing around the countryside. If only she'd get help, but she doesn't think she's addicted, won't acknowledge it. She keeps saying the medication is just to keep her on an even keel.'

'Isn't it?'

'Well, that's how it started out, but I'm pretty sure it's a lot more than that now. She may even be taking real drugs. Who knows? There's nothing I can do though. I have no legal right to interfere in her life.'

For a while they sat in silence, then Wes sighed deeply and stood up. 'I'm sorry, I'm not very good company tonight so I think I'll just go to bed. Thanks for your support anyway.'

'Any time,' Kayla mumbled after his retreating back and wished that she had the right to comfort him properly.

Wes stood looking down on his daughter, sleeping the heavy, innocent sleep that only children manage. He was swamped by the overwhelming

261

feelings of love for this tiny being. He didn't know how it was possible to care so much for someone and at the same time hate how scared it made him feel. The burden of responsibility was just too much sometimes.

Drawing in a deep breath he tried not to remember how close he'd come to losing Nell that afternoon. Even though it had been an illusion and she'd been safe the entire time, he knew now he could never let her go. If Caro thought she could manipulate him into having the custody order overturned, she was sorely mistaken.

Nell was staying right here.

Wes clenched his fists, then thrust his hands into his pockets. Caro. How had things gone so wrong between them? There had been a time when he'd looked at her with almost as much love as he did with Nell now. A different kind of love, but she'd been his world too. For a short while. But Caro wasn't the woman he'd thought she was. What you saw was only a façade.

He'd realised it after Nell was born. The birth had been difficult and for the first day or two Caroline had been in a state of shock and too much pain to take much notice of either her surroundings or her child. When at last he brought the baby to her, she looked massively disappointed and he remembered their subsequent conversation clearly.

'Oh, it's not a boy,' she said. 'Sorry.'

'Don't be silly.' He smiled at her and put their

child in her arms. 'Why wouldn't we want a girl? Look, she's beautiful.'

Caro gazed at the baby and Wes thought he saw an expression of distaste pass over her features. 'You wanted a boy,' she muttered, 'to inherit the title.'

Wes tried to keep a lid on the impatience rising inside him. Caro had been through an ordeal, he had to make allowances. 'It doesn't matter. The main thing is she's healthy. And she's adorable. See how she grips your finger if you put it in her hand?' He felt besotted himself and couldn't understand why Caro didn't immediately fall for the baby the same way he'd done. 'There's plenty of time for more children,' he added unwisely.

Caro started to sob. 'No! I knew it. You want me to go through all this agony again so you can have your Marcombe heir. I can't bear it.'

'Caro! I'm sorry, I didn't mean . . . Hey, don't cry. The midwife tells me all women feel that way at first, but it will pass. And if not, well, then we won't have any more kids. Honestly, it will be fine. There's always Alex.'

And Wes had believed it at the time. However, over the next few days he'd tried over and over again to make Caro take an interest in their little girl, but she never did. Instead she seemed to begrudge the time he spent with Nell, as if she was jealous of her own child. He almost thought she hated the little human scrap who had unwittingly come between them.

She tried to hide it at first, but in her weakened state she couldn't stop the querulous remarks that put Wes out of all patience with her. He spent more and more time with the baby, doing all the things she should have done. Caro accused him of usurping her role, of turning soft.

'Well, what am I supposed to do?' he shot back. 'You're not strong enough yet. Someone has to take care of her.'

But it was the beginning of the end. It wasn't long before their marriage began to disintegrate. For a few years they had managed to keep up the appearance of married life, although virtually living apart. Caro spent an increasing amount of time in London, where Wes later learned that she drowned her sorrows first with alcohol, then later with pills of varying kinds. When Wes found out about the drugs, however, he put his foot down. He told her to give it up or he'd divorce her. When she refused he began divorce proceedings. To her fury, everything had gone his way.

'I never wanted it to be like this,' Wes whispered into the darkness. But he would fight for Nell, no matter what.

And he wouldn't let Caro win because he knew she didn't love her own child.

Kayla was woken by a small sniffling noise and peered into the darkness, her heart beating a tattoo of fear until she guessed who it was.

'Nell, is that you?'

'Mm-hmm.'

'What's the matter? Come here and tell me what's wrong.'

Nell appeared by her bedside, a small dark shape in the faint moonlight, and sat down on the cover next to Kayla. 'Can I sleep in your bed for a while, please?' she asked.

'Well, yes, of course you can, if that's what you want, but shouldn't you go to your daddy? Isn't that what you'd normally do?'

'No, he's really hard to wake up and he doesn't like it when I cry at night.'

'Oh, I see. Scoot in here then.' Kayla made room for Nell next to her in the huge bed. She could have fitted four children in there with her with space left over, so it wasn't exactly a hardship. 'Now tell me why you're crying, please. Did you have a nightmare?'

'Yes. There was a ghost in my room, staring at me. It was very angry I think and it scared me.'

'How do you know it was angry?'

'I heard it swearing, like Daddy does sometimes, except I'm not supposed to say stuff like that.'

Kayla smiled into the dark. 'No, of course not, they're not very nice words are they. But you know what? I think it was just a bad dream. I had the same one a little while ago, or almost anyway. I thought there was someone in my room too, isn't that funny? Maybe our minds think the same way.'

'Were you scared?' Nell's voice still sounded

small, but she had stopped sniffling and instead snuggled up to Kayla, who put an arm round the little girl. It felt nice, holding a child like that, and Kayla realised she had come to like Nell as much as she liked the little girl's father.

'To be honest, I was a bit, but only because I was startled out of sleep. There wasn't really anyone here. I checked you know.'

'You're sure?'

'Absolutely. Now how about we try to sleep again? Otherwise we'll be awfully grumpy in the morning. I know I will, anyway.'

'Okay.'

As Nell snuggled deeper under the duvet and went to sleep almost instantly, Kayla was left to stare into the darkness, strangely unsettled. Something weird was going on in this house and she didn't like it, but perhaps it was just because it was an old house. There were bound to be ghosts here, despite what Wes said, and after her experiences with Jago, she no longer discounted any supernatural phenomena.

She would have to keep her eyes and ears open to see if she could solve the mystery.

Alex heard Caroline enter the room she called 'the hovel' without bothering to turn on the lights. There was no need since a harsh streetlight outside bathed the room in a strange, other-worldly glow. She was crying softly and bent down to take off her shoes with one hand, while the other groped around on the bedside table. He assumed she was trying to find the half empty bottle of wine she'd left there earlier, but it was gone. He had poured its contents down the sink.

He'd forgotten about her pills though and swore silently when he heard her rummaging in her bag, shaking something out of a container.

'Caro, where have you been?' he said, keeping his voice low but perfectly audible.

He startled her nonetheless and she dropped the shoe she'd just taken off, which fell to the floor with a clatter. 'Jesus, Alex, you scared the life out of me! What are you doing here? I thought you said you were meeting with someone.'

Alex switched on the bedside light. He was lying on top of the bed, fully dressed, and he turned on his side now to look at her. Caro shivered and turned away, swiping at the black mascara stains under her eyes surreptitiously.

'What's with the death glare?' she asked flippantly. 'You look just like your brother at his most pompous. Not a pretty sight, I can tell you.'

'Is that so.' Alex wasn't going to get drawn into yet another discussion about Wes. He'd had more than enough of those. 'My meeting finished early,' he told her, 'and I thought I would come and see you. I thought you'd be bored, but I guess I was wrong. Were the local boys to your taste, then?' He could feel his jaw clenching in anger, although if he was honest with himself, the thought of her with someone else didn't bother him at all now. He was more worried about her doing something stupid, which would draw attention to them. She must have seen that he was mad because she hurried to placate him.

'No, no, Alex, I didn't go out with anyone. I just went to . . .' She stopped abruptly and if she hadn't been wearing so much make-up, he was sure she would have been blushing.

'The Hall?' he finished for her. She turned away again. 'Please tell me you didn't go there again?' He didn't like that destination any more than the one he had imagined and she knew it. In fact, it was worse.

'So what if I did?' She tossed her head and sent him a defiant glance. 'I have a right to see my daughter. I gave birth to her, for heaven's sake. She doesn't belong to just Wesley, you know.'

'You have the right to see her in daylight, Caro,' Alex reminded her. 'Wes told me the agreement was that you can visit her at any time, as long as you don't take her away with you. There's no need to go creeping around at night. How do you get in anyway? I suppose you still have your key?'

'Uh-hmm.' She stared at the floor.

'Caro, I want you to promise me not to go there again until this business is finished. I really can't risk you getting caught at Marcombe late at night. Wes would be bound to get suspicious and then everything we have worked for would be ruined. No deal, no money, get it?'

'He won't catch me. He doesn't even know I go

there,' Caroline sneered. 'He's too wrapped up with that new woman of his, whatever her name is.'

Alex sighed. 'Her name is Kayla, and I told you she's only his secretary. I haven't seen any evidence that anything's going on between them.'

'Just shows how little you know about women. She'll get her claws into him soon enough. You wait and see. A man like that, with a huge house, a title and loads of money, she won't be able to resist. Filthy little gold-digger.'

'Oh, for Christ's sake, not every woman thinks that way, strange as it may seem to you. Could we concentrate on what we're supposed to be doing here? Wes and his secretary are not important at the moment.' Alex knew he was starting to sound almost desperate and tried to control his breathing. Normally he was very laid-back, but this latest venture was getting to him. There was too much riding on it and he just couldn't afford to fail. He'd really be up shit creek if he did and so would Caro. Not that she seemed to care, and as if to confirm this, she shrugged. Alex wanted to shake her, but he knew it wouldn't do any good.

'Fine,' she conceded at last. 'Let's get some sleep then. I sincerely hope this won't go on for much longer.'

'It won't, I promise. All is ready.'

At least, he hoped it was.

CHAPTER 21

The candles in the library at Marcombe Hall had burned low and Sir John sat staring morosely into the fire. Jago, entering soundlessly with his men, could see his half-brother had consumed copious amounts of brandy – the brandy they risked their lives to bring to gentry such as him – and it was obvious Sir John didn't hear the door close silently nor the key being turned in the lock, since he didn't stir.

'Good evening, Sir John.'

The man jumped and swivelled in his chair to stare with dawning terror at the group of thugs coming up to form a circle around him.

'Are you drowning your sorrows or celebrating the death of your wife?' Jago held his temper in check, but his voice came out hard and grim.

'What are you doing in my house? Out! Out I say. By what right do you invade my privacy in this manner?' Sir John spluttered, his face alternating between the paleness of fright and redness of anger.

Jago laughed mirthlessly. 'By what right did you murder your wife?' he countered.

'I've no idea of what you speak. As far as I know,

Eliza is upstairs resting. Now leave before I call my servants to have you evicted.' This time all the men guffawed and Sir John squirmed in his chair. Slowly he stood up to face them, swaying slightly from the effects of the brandy. 'Why have you come? What do you want?'

'We want you to write a little letter for us.' Jago walked over to the massive oak desk and opened several drawers until he found what he sought. He placed a clean sheet of paper, as well as a quill and ink bottle, on the desk. 'Bring him over here, men.'

Sir John was hauled over to his own desk and pushed into the chair unceremoniously. Jago watched as anger warred with defiance in his half-brother's eyes. For a moment the anger won and Sir John tried bravado. 'You want me to write you a letter? And here I thought my father had had you educated, Kerswell. Mind you, I always considered it a great waste of money. You obviously didn't learn anything. Told him so.'

He received a cuff on the ear for this piece of impertinence and Jago went around to lean on the desk opposite Sir John, his hands resting flat on the surface, his face too close for comfort.

'I'm a lot more learned than some people I could mention, and what's more, I know how to treat my womenfolk. Now write what I dictate, Sir John, or I will not be answerable for the consequences.' He emphasised his half-brother's title, making it clear it didn't weigh with him.

'And if I refuse?'

Jago grinned. 'I don't think you'd be that unwise, brother.'

'You're no kin of mine,' Sir John muttered, but he swallowed hard nonetheless and looked at the menacing leers on the faces of the other men. Without another word, he dipped his quill in the ink-bottle with shaking fingers and waited.

'Jessie, you're an absolute angel. You must have worked like a slave to produce a family tree so fast. And such a detailed one at that, I can't believe it. Thank you so much.'

Kayla had been astonished to receive a letter from Jessie after only a week and called immediately to say thank you. She'd thought it would take ages to put together a genealogy chart for Sir John, but Jessie had proved her wrong.

'No, no, it was really easy, you know,' Jessie protested. 'Marcombe is a very unusual name so it wasn't hard to follow Sir John's descendants, and they all pretty much stayed in that area, which helped too.'

'Well, I can't thank you enough. This was just what I needed. It should prove very interesting reading.'

'Any time, I'm happy to help. It's always fun when you find what you're looking for, so this family tree was very satisfying to draw up. Anyway, I circled all the people whose wills you should look for, did you see?'

'Yes, thanks. I'll go to Exeter Record Office and have a look, like you said.'

'Well, good luck. Let me know how you get on. You've made me curious now.'

Kayla decided she'd go the following day since Wes was out at meetings and had said she could have some time off. Exeter Record Office was situated in the city centre and she found it easily. She'd called up for directions and been told to use one of the park-and-ride facilities which stopped nearby. The staff proved to be very helpful, and she soon settled down to work her way through indexes of wills, some of which she checked more closely than others.

Sir John himself didn't seem to have left a will, but she found one for Sir Wesley, his son, who for some reason had left money to a group of Travellers, as well as the right for them to camp in one of his fields in perpetuity. Kayla smiled to herself – she detected Jago's hand here. He must have somehow informed the boy that his true grandmother was a Gypsy, perhaps even arranged for him to meet some of them. She must remember to ask him about it next time she went to London.

Disappointingly, there was no mention of any paintings in the will. The hall and all its contents had passed to his eldest son, another Wesley, with bequests to his other children. There were several items of furniture and jewellery, but no artwork of any kind so Kayla had to assume the paintings were included with the house and had passed to the heir.

She ploughed on, working her way through as many wills as she could find, including those of some of the daughters of the family who had married, and their husbands. By four o'clock she had to admit defeat. Just about every senior member of the Marcombe family had left a will, but not a single one of them had mentioned any large portraits or artwork of any kind. It was unbelievably frustrating.

'Oh, Jago, what are we going to do now?' she whispered, but nothing sprang to mind. She would have to think about it and perhaps confer with Jessie again. There must be something she had overlooked, some way of finding a clue to the portrait's whereabouts, but for the life of her she couldn't think of one.

She returned to Marcombe Hall in low spirits, but just as she reached her room her mobile shrilled.

'Kayla, I have some news for you.' It was Maddie, sounding excited and slightly breathless, as if she'd been running. 'Jessie asked me to give you a call because she's had to go away for the weekend and she tried to ring you this morning but you weren't there.'

'I was at Exeter Record Office with the phone on silent so I probably didn't hear. What did she want? She already sent me all the stuff she'd put together.'

'No, listen to this – she said to tell you she found one of those wills you were looking for here in

London. I guess the person must have died here or something, but that's not all. Just out of curiosity Jessie had a look through the Assize Records for your area, and guess what she found?'

'What?'

'Your Jago was put on trial for murder.'

'You're kidding! Who's he supposed to have murdered?'

'I'm not telling.' Maddie giggled. 'You'll just have to wait until you receive my letter with a copy of the records. See if you can figure it out in the meantime.'

'Maddie, that's not fair,' Kayla protested, consumed with curiosity now. 'Come on, tell me. I suppose it must have been Sir John. Jago can't have killed Eliza, he loved her.'

'I'm not saying a word. It'll do you good to have something to think about other than gorgeous men.' Maddie laughed again and hung up.

Kayla glared at her mobile. 'Well, really!' What on earth had got into Maddie?

And Jago a murderer? Somehow, she had trouble picturing it. Even though he certainly had a ruthless air about him, there also seemed to be a softer, inner core. And despite his affair with Eliza, Kayla felt he was an honourable man. So why would he have murdered someone?

She swore out loud in frustration. She would just have to wait until the wretched letter came to find out.

*　　*　　*

Her bad mood persisted throughout the day and increased the depression she already felt at having failed to find the painting so far. She started to wonder whether she shouldn't leave Marcombe Hall after all. Although she enjoyed working with Wes, their relationship had become a bit strained of late. After their excursion to Canonteign Falls he'd been taciturn and uncommunicative, and although Kayla understood his reasons for brooding, she didn't feel she had the right to interfere.

She wanted to help him, to comfort him, perhaps even to love him. The thought scared her, but she acknowledged to herself that she was extremely attracted to him. It was agony to watch him every night and not be able to put her arms around him. But would he welcome her love? She didn't think so. The harsh expression on his face during dinner that time when she'd asked him if he would remarry was etched into her memory. Wes had been badly burned and although he might want her in his bed, he would never contemplate marriage and commitment again. And that was what Kayla wanted. Not necessarily marriage, but definitely commitment.

The more she saw of Nell and Wes, the more she wanted to be part of their little family. She adored children and she wanted some of her own. It was one of the reasons why she had jumped at the chance to marry Mike, although he'd been rather lukewarm about the idea of starting a family straight away. She'd been confident she could persuade him, but she shuddered at the thought now. Mike would have made a terrible father, impatient and irritable, whereas Wes in contrast was great with Nell, very patient and loving.

'You're very restless this evening. What's the matter?'

Kayla came back to earth and noticed she had been pacing the library and that Wes must have been watching her for some time. 'Nothing. I was just thinking.'

'About your marriage?'

Kayla swivelled round and stared at him. Could he read her mind? 'Sorry?'

'Nell told me something about you getting married, remember? She said it all went wrong.'

'Oh, that.'

Wes smiled. 'She said you and your fiancé had hit each other and that was why the marriage was called off, but I'm afraid I didn't quite believe her. You don't look like you have violent tendencies.'

Kayla snorted. 'I don't, so just as well you didn't think that. But I don't remember telling Nell anything of the sort.' Kayla frowned and sat down on the sofa next to him, clasping her hands round her knees just to keep them still. 'I was supposed to have been married though, she got that part right. Only it didn't work out.'

'Do you want to talk about it?' Wes fixed his blue gaze on her and she had trouble focusing on her thoughts. She just wanted to drown in his eyes, to lean forward and . . . 'Kayla?'

'What? Oh, no. No, I really don't. There's nothing to say anyway. I realised I'd made a mistake and I'm just glad I found it out before the wedding went ahead. Although I'm afraid my family didn't quite see it that way. They thought four weeks before the ceremony was cutting things a bit too fine.' She made a small face and shrugged. 'I guess they were right, but I couldn't help it.'

Wes grinned. 'A bit upset were they? Well, they didn't have to marry the guy, you did, so I wouldn't pay any attention to them.'

Kayla smiled back. 'I didn't. I just avoided talking to them for a while.'

Wes stared at her mouth, as if he was mesmerised. 'Do you know, when you smile you have a tiny dimple just here.' He touched her cheek with one finger and Kayla drew in a sharp breath. That small contact sent a frisson through her and her nerve endings were suddenly on full alert, waiting to see what he'd do next.

'I'm glad you didn't marry someone you would have been miserable with,' he continued. 'Your mouth was made for smiling and maybe . . .' He bent his head forward and touched his lips to hers softly. A pleasurable warmth spread down to her stomach as if she was slowly melting inside. Kayla held her breath, not daring to make a sound or move so much as a muscle in case she scared him off, but to her great chagrin he pulled away. 'Sorry, I shouldn't have done that.'

The disappointment which flooded through her was so strong it was almost a physical pain. 'Why?' she whispered hoarsely. She couldn't help herself, she had to ask. Had to know why he'd turned away when she so desperately wanted him to continue.

He shrugged. 'You might take me to court for sexual harassment or something. You are my employee after all.' His flippant tone of voice suggested what had happened had meant nothing, was a temporary aberration. Kayla swallowed down a sob.

'Oh, no. No, I wouldn't do that. Goodnight, Wes.'

She stood up abruptly and stumbled from the room before the tears burning her eyelids had a chance to materialise.

'Well, damn, you handled that well, didn't you?'

Wes glared at himself in the mirror above the mantelpiece. Why had he kissed her like that and why on earth had he then tried to joke about it?

'Idiot,' he muttered.

He stared again at his face, wondering how Kayla saw him. He wasn't bad looking, but he didn't think he was special either. Caro had bragged to her friends that she'd caught a man who was both rich and handsome, but she stopped saying it after a while. Wes had a suspicion she'd only been in love with his title and the house, as well as her own social standing. So perhaps praising him had just been a way of obtaining this.

Besides, that was eight years ago, he was older now. He came back to the question he couldn't seem to find an answer to – was he too old for someone like Kayla? If he made a real pass at her would she think him a sad old git?

She hadn't run away screaming this evening. She'd just looked a bit stunned, then sad. And she hadn't kissed him back. Wes didn't know if his kiss had made her remember what she'd lost or if he'd confused her. *Did she like it?* It was hard to tell.

Maybe he'd lost the knack? It was ages since he'd kissed anyone after all. Just because he was still shaking with desire didn't mean he'd had the same effect on Kayla. He'd have to try harder.

He took a deep breath. Yes, that was it, the only way to find out, and he could deal with rejection, couldn't he? Nothing ventured, nothing gained.

CHAPTER 22

The walk down to the cliffs seemed to pass all too swiftly and John's few token attempts at resistance were met by guffaws from the men. He was almost paralysed with fear and had trouble making his legs move fast enough to keep up with the long strides of Jago and his helpers. The two brawniest of the men held his arms fast so that whenever he stumbled he still stayed upright. He didn't register pain, however, as his terror threatened to erupt into full-blown panic at any moment and blocked out any physical sensations.

The night was as black as the previous one, but the roar of the surf below the cliffs could be heard clearly. Louder and louder, the noise reverberated inside his head, making him want to scream. Why hadn't he realised how loud it was the night before? He suddenly understood how Eliza must have felt and bile rose in his throat.

Eliza. He now knew he'd been correct in his suspicions. She had indeed cuckolded him, and with his half-brother of all people, a common innkeeper despite the Marcombe blood which ran in his veins. The thought was unbearable, slicing through him like a sharpened scythe. Jago's son was lying in the Marcombe nursery, not his, never his. It was so unfair.

However, he wished he had taken less drastic measures to punish Eliza. He should have waited until morning, when the first heat of his anger would have subsided, as well as the effects of the brandy. A sound beating and divorce would have been enough. Then he could have kept the child, since he was never likely to have another. He could acknowledge it now, when it no longer mattered.

He wasn't able to have children.

When his first wife failed to produce any offspring he had blamed it on her and been relieved when she died of a fever. However, as the years passed and Eliza didn't become pregnant either, he started to suspect that the fault lay with him. None of his mistresses had ever come to him asking him to support any children, and he'd heard enough such tales from his friends to know this was common practice. What a fool he'd been. He should have taken what Eliza had offered him, and had his revenge later by depriving her of her son. It would have been just as satisfying. After all, he'd seen the way she was gazing at her child. But it was too late now. All too late.

The cliff edge came ever closer until finally he was so near he could have touched it with his foot. The two men released him and he turned to face his judge and jury.

'Have you brought me here to scare me into

confessing?' He still didn't want to believe they'd go through with this, despite what they'd made him write earlier.

Jago laughed, that cold mirthless laughter which so grated on John's ears. 'No, brother, we already know you're guilty. Now it's time to pay for your crime. It's your turn to die. As we can't trust the local judge to sentence you correctly we've decided to do it ourselves. Besides, dying the same way as your victim is much more fitting than a hangman's noose, don't you think? I'd call it poetic justice but what do I know? I'm but a poor innkeeper.'

The leering faces of the other men came closer and John began to shiver violently.

'Enough! You've had your fun and games, now let me go. I had nothing to do with Eliza's death. She was unhinged after the birthing and must have run out and thrown herself off the cliff.' John's teeth were chattering, but he managed what he hoped was a look of defiance.

Jago smiled. 'And how do you know that's the way she died? No one has found her body yet, have they? In fact, how do you even know she's dead? I saw no body lying in state up at the Hall. Didn't you claim she was upstairs, safe in her bed?'

John gulped for air. It was true. He had waited all day for news of his wife's death to reach the household, but there had been no word. Only the wet nurse had asked about Lady Marcombe's whereabouts, and John had fobbed her off with some lie about the lady resting. He opened his mouth to speak, but no sound emerged. He'd been caught out.

'Go on John, over the cliff, and all the way down to the beach. Just like Eliza. Only this time, no one is going to do any pushing. And I doubt if you'll end up in the same place afterwards. Your remains won't even lie in the churchyard with your ancestors – suicides aren't allowed that privilege.' More chuckles and some outright laughter greeted this sally.

Swivelling around frantically to find a way of escape, John nevertheless stood rooted to the spot. His legs wouldn't obey him.

'So what do you think men? Is he guilty?' Jago shouted.

'Guilty!' yelled the impromptu jury and the circle of men suddenly advanced on John with an almighty roar of rage. He took an involuntary step backwards out of sheer fright and his foot encountered nothing but air. In the next moment he was hurtling down towards the beach, down towards eternity, down towards what he knew was his rightful punishment . . . then darkness claimed him.

'We've got Gypsies camped in the top field,' Annie told Kayla the next morning, looking very cheerful about it. 'They have permission to be there, so it's nothing to worry about. Just thought I'd let you know in case you come across them, like. Wouldn't want you to be scared.'

'Right, thanks.' Kayla remembered the will she had found which had stated that the Travellers had the right to stay on Marcombe land whenever they wished. Naturally, she couldn't tell Annie she already knew about it, so she pretended as if it was news to her. 'Do they come every year, then?'

'Yes, sometimes more than once. It's not always the same group. There are several families who use that field.'

'I see.'

'You should go and see them. The women usually tell fortunes.' Annie laughed. 'Told me I'd win on the lottery, but it hasn't happened so far. I reckon that'll be in another life. And as for meeting someone tall, dark and handsome – fat chance. I think I'll just stick to my husband, thank you very much.'

'Actually I'd rather not know what the future will bring, especially not if it's something bad. I'm a bit superstitious that way.'

'Oh, it's all a load of rubbish and it's just a bit of fun really.'

Kayla wasn't as sure as she would have been a few months ago. Now that she knew there were such things as ghosts, or whatever one might call Jago, she couldn't see any reason why second sight shouldn't exist. Perhaps she should have her fortune told after all? It might help her to decide what to do with her life.

Wes kept her busy all morning and she forgot about the Gypsies for a while. The fact that Wes acted as if the previous evening's kiss had never happened exercised her mind to a far greater extent than the Travellers. She was typing on automatic, while her brain endlessly replayed the scene. He stroked her cheek, he told her she had a dimple when she smiled, he kissed her . . . and then he pulled back. She went over it again and again, her mind running around in circles. Where had she gone wrong? Should she have leaned forward more, thrown her arms around his neck and kissed him back with abandon, or said something? Was it just that he didn't find her attractive enough? *Why* didn't he find her attractive?

'Annoying man,' she muttered finally, trying to banish all thoughts of him for the moment. She was obviously wasting her time.

While she was having her lunch her thoughts returned to the Gypsies and she made up her mind to go and see them. What harm could it do after all? Annie was right, it was probably just a bit of fun and she could do with some cheering up, that was for sure.

Wes had gone out to a meeting, so Kayla made her way towards the collection of camper vans as soon as she'd finished eating. As she approached the site she heard the shrieks of children playing and voices raised in laughter. One of the Gypsies caught sight of her and the conversations stopped abruptly. After saying something to the others, the woman walked towards Kayla.

'Hello, can I help you?' She was young and

pretty in a sultry way with long, black hair hanging over one shoulder. Her colourful clothes became her well and she moved with confidence and grace. Kayla felt awkward by contrast.

'Uhm, yes, I was told you tell fortunes and I wondered if by any chance you would have the time to do mine?'

'Of course, follow me.'

Kayla trailed behind the woman, who led her over to an older lady seated at a table under a parasol. There was a second, empty chair and the women indicated that Kayla should take a seat.

'You have come for some answers, am I right?' the old lady said. She had eyes as dark as sloe berries, buried deeply among the tanned wrinkles. Kayla got the feeling those eyes had seen a lot and they blazed with intelligence and amusement.

'Well, yes, I suppose I have. Although you could say it was just curiosity that brought me. Annie told me you wouldn't mind.' She shrugged. 'How much do you charge?'

The woman smiled, a broad almost toothless grin. 'Friends of Jago don't have to pay. It'll be my pleasure to tell you what you want to know.'

Kayla gasped and felt the hairs on the back of her neck stand up. 'You, you . . . what? How do you know about Jago?' she stammered. She hadn't actually believed these people possessed the second sight until that moment, but how else could the old lady know such things? Kayla hadn't told a soul other than Maddie.

A cackling laugh greeted her words and the woman just tapped the side of her nose and nodded. 'Never you mind. That's my business. Now, what is it you wish?'

Kayla took a deep breath to steady herself. This wasn't turning out at all the way she'd expected. The light-hearted palm reading or gazing into a crystal ball she had imagined was far from the truth. The uncomfortable truth. Kayla almost changed her mind and had to force herself to stay seated. She took another steadying breath.

'Well, the thing is, recently I should have been . . . that is to say, I was going to get married but I broke off the engagement,' she said. 'I need to know – did I do the right thing or did I make a huge mistake? My family all seemed to think so, but it didn't feel like it to me, so I'm just confused. And, and . . . what do I do now?'

'Give me your hand.' The old lady grabbed Kayla's hand and turned it palm upwards before the latter had a chance to comply of her own accord. The Gypsy muttered something unintelligible, before saying, 'yes' emphatically.

'Yes?' Kayla tried to keep her hand steady, although she longed to snatch it away.

'You did right. He wasn't for you, the blond one. You were wise to back away. There would have been only heartbreak with that one.' The woman traced some of the lines on her hand with one finger. 'I see a dark man. He occupies your mind. You can't rid yourself of him until it's over.'

'Until what is over?'

The old one ignored her question and continued, 'There is danger here, you must beware. Dark places, enclosed spaces. Yes, darkness, keep away from the darkness and stairs.' She had her eyes closed now and her eyelids flickered slightly as she spoke as if she was seeing images.

'What do you mean? What sort of darkness?'

'Take care of the little one, she needs you. I see water and pain, a red stain spreading over white . . .' She was silent for a moment, then added, 'Jago will make it all right.' Then she opened her eyes and let go of Kayla's hand. 'That's all,' she said. 'I can't tell you any more.'

'But what . . .?'

'There's no point asking questions, I can't explain. It will all become clear eventually. Just follow your instincts and you'll be all right.'

'You think so?' Kayla gave a shaky laugh. 'But all that stuff about darkness and danger. I thought you were meant to tell me I'd be rich and famous and would marry a handsome stranger.'

The old lady gave her a shrewd look. 'You wouldn't be fooled by that, not like some. I told you the truth. I owe it to Jago.'

'I, I see. Well, thank you very much. Are you sure I can't pay you?'

'No. Friends of his are friends of mine. No payment necessary.'

Back in the office, Kayla sat and stared blankly at her computer screen for quite some time before she managed to get any work done. She still felt a bit shaky and wondered if she'd done the right thing in going to see the Gypsies. She was none the wiser after the woman's cryptic utterances, but at least she'd found out one thing – she'd been right not to marry Mike. But then she didn't need a Gypsy to tell her that. Deep down she had already known.

'Katerina, good to see you again! Are you well?'

Wes settled himself under the old Gypsy's parasol and smiled at her. They were old friends, since she and her fellow Travellers came every year. In fact, she was almost like an honorary grandmother to him, his own having died young. Katerina always made time for him and his brother when they were children, treating them as family, and a strong bond had formed between them. When he'd spotted the caravans on the way home from his meeting, he'd decided to make a detour.

'Never better, especially now I'm here again.' Katerina beamed back. 'And yourself?'

'Fine, fine.' Wes replied automatically, but something about the way Katerina looked at him made him take a deep breath and amend his answer. 'Well, a few problems, but nothing I can't handle. I think.'

She nodded and held out her hand. 'Want me to take a look?'

Reluctantly he placed his hand on hers, palm up. He'd never hesitated before, but this time, for some reason, he wasn't sure he wanted to hear what she had to say. Her pronouncements weren't always clear, but sooner or later they made sense and she was never wrong. That in itself was terrifying.

She was quiet for a while, then muttered something to herself before piercing him with her dark gaze. 'You have to be careful for a while, very careful, my boy.'

Wes pulled his hand back when she let go and drew in a shaky breath. He hadn't realised he'd been holding it. 'In what way?'

'In every way except one – love. Give that freely and you'll be happy.'

'Give it freely? I already do. I mean, I never stint when it comes to Nell. I try to show her how much she's loved in every way.'

Katerina shook her head. 'Not just the child. There are others who need your love too. And you're holding back.'

'Others, as in more than one?' Wes felt confused. If she'd said something along the lines of 'a petite, gorgeous blonde is waiting for you to make a move', he'd have understood. 'Not just a woman?'

The old lady cackled. 'No, not just that. Why, did you have someone in mind? Only I got the impression you weren't ready to settle down with anyone yet. Mind you, there was this lovely young woman who came to see me earlier and I told her a tall, dark and handsome man was in her future. Could be you, maybe? It was what she wanted to hear. They all do.'

'Now you're teasing me. You know I don't want to be trapped again. I told you all about it last time you came.'

Katerina wagged a finger at him. 'Ah, but there are ways of being trapped that don't feel so restrictive. Bonds you'd gladly be ensnared in. Allow yourself to experience this and all will be well.'

Wes smiled. 'Enough with the mumbo-jumbo, this is me you're talking to. I know you can see things, but there's no need for you to be so mysterious. If you're saying I should try falling in love, been there done that. It's highly over-rated.'

'I was being serious, but as always, it's up to you to decide if you want to listen. After all, I'm just an old woman, what do I know?' Katerina's smile was back to teasing, but Wes refused to play games.

'Don't give me that, you're a mere spring chicken. But if it makes you happy, I'll think about what you said, okay?'

'You do that and we'll see who's right, eh?'

We will indeed, Wes thought, but the gleam in Katerina's eyes made him wonder even so.

'Finally!' Kayla exclaimed when she came down to the entrance hall two days later to find that the postman had brought her a thick brown envelope from London. Despite several phone calls to Maddie, she'd been unable to make her friend reveal any further information.

'It's revenge for leaving me behind while you're

enjoying the good life at the manor house with his lordship,' Maddie had said and laughed.

'I am not doing anything with his lordship. If only!' Kayla hissed back, afraid of being overheard, but Maddie had hung up, still laughing. 'Annoying woman.'

Now she ran up the stairs two at a time and along the corridor to her room. Impatiently she tore open the envelope. Several large sheets of paper spilled onto her bed and she picked up the first one and began to read.

> *'A Calendar of the Prisoners in the County Gaol of Exeter for Trial at the Exeter Sessions, April 15, 1782 . . .'*

Kayla scanned the list and there he was, *'Kerswell, Jago, age 28'*. On the bottom of the next page it said:

> *'FELONY . . . Jago Kerswell. Brought in March 25, 1782, and committed by Thomas Paige, Esq, charged with having caused the death of Sir John Marcombe, Bt, late of Marcombe Hall . . .'*

Kayla began to read the Assize records and lost herself in the past.

CHAPTER 23

Jago stood impassive, gazing round the court-room from time to time, but mostly staring straight ahead lost in thought. Although he knew the charges against him were serious, he honestly didn't care what the outcome of the trial would be. Without Eliza, life wasn't worth living in any case, and he knew he'd as good as committed murder, however justified. If he was sentenced to hang, so be it.

'Jago Kerswell, you are accused of the murder of Sir John Marcombe of Marcombe Hall. How do you plead?'

'Not guilty.' Jago said the words automatically. Whether they were true or not, he reasoned there wouldn't be any point in having a trial if he said he was guilty. Let the man at least work for his verdict.

'Very well, let's proceed.'

He heard the judge say Jago had been brought to the Assizes because of the suspicions of the local magistrate. Sir John's body had been found on the beach and his valet, Thomas Binks, had run to the magistrate claiming his master had been pushed off the cliffs on the night of the twenty-fourth of March.

'And why would you suppose the defendant was the man who pushed your master, Mr Binks?' the judge asked.

'Well, there were these rumours goin' round, sir.'

'Rumours? About what?'

'Mr Kerswell bein' related to his lordship, on the wrong side o' the blanket, as it were, and them not gettin' on well.'

'I've already been told that this is true. That doesn't make Mr Kerswell a murderer. Was there a falling out between them? Did you actually see anything happen, Mr Binks?' The judge looked irritated.

'Well, no, sir,' the valet stammered, 'but why else would Sir John end up at the bottom of the cliff? He'd just become a father, to a son and heir no less. It don't make sense for a man like that to jump, now does it?'

'We're not dealing in suppositions here,' the judge told Mr Binks with a stern look. 'Only facts. Next witness, please.'

To Jago's surprise several people stepped forward, one after the other in quick succession, giving testimony in his favour. He listened with increasing amazement as they perjured themselves on his behalf, all sounding truthful and convincing. He hadn't realised he had so many allies and it went some way towards thawing his frozen insides. Many of them relied on him to lead the smuggling operations, to be sure, but quite a few seemed to be helping him simply because they held him in high regard. It wasn't something he'd expected.

Jeremiah Dunsmore, the village blacksmith, was one of them, looking like an upstanding member of society in his Sunday best. 'Aye, sir, I swear on oath the defendant was at his inn, the King's Head, within full sight of everyone the whole of the evening in question. I was there myself, sir, drinking cider, but not so much that I can't remember what was what. Only had the one pint, I did.'

Keziah Jones, the local whore, spoke up with a glint in her eye when it was her turn. 'I spent the rest o' the night wi' Ja- . . . er, Mr Kerswell, and 'e didn't leave my bed once. Now why would 'e? I wouldn't be doin' me job if 'e had.' Stifled laughter greeted this sally, making the proceedings seem less sombre for a while.

Harriet White, Eliza's maidservant, stepped forward, sobbing intermittently and clutching a handkerchief. 'It was so sad, your honour, an absolute t-tragedy. My mistress died in childbirth that night, and her so happy about her little boy. It-it's my honest belief her husband took his own life in sorrow. Who wouldn't? Adored her, he did. She was everything to him. Everything.' That was news to Jago, and probably most of the villagers, but the judge had no way of knowing this. He nodded and thanked Miss White.

Finally it was the turn of the local doctor, William Ward-Matthews, looking grave but composed and speaking in a sonorous voice. 'Yes, your honour, I attest to Lady Marcombe's death. I was called to the Hall in the morning, only to find that her ladyship must have died during the night. The body was already cold by the time I examined her. It's my considered opinion she'd died from loss of blood as a result of childbirth. Tragic, but all too common, I'm afraid.'

All these testimonials left the judge and jury with no option but to set Jago free because of lack of evidence. As he pronounced the verdict the judge glanced at Jago, a speculative look in his eyes, then nodded as if he was satisfied that justice had been done.

Jago nodded back, then walked out into the sunshine a free man.

When she'd finished reading, Kayla sighed with relief, her heart thumping loudly. Jago had been acquitted. *Thank God!* But she couldn't help the doubts from creeping into her mind. Had Jago somehow engineered Sir John's death so he could have Eliza all to himself? Was that why he couldn't rest now? She didn't want to believe it of him.

And if Eliza had died in childbirth, then what would have been the point? It didn't make sense. She needed to talk to Jago and until she had a chance to do that, she'd have to be patient.

After coming to this decision, Kayla picked up the next sheet of paper Jessie had sent. It was Sir John's will, dated March 24th 1782, which for some reason had been proved in London rather than Exeter.

'*This is the Last Will and Testament of me Sir John Marcombe of Marcombe Hall in the County of Devon, Baronet, being of sound mind and body. First I will and direct that all my just debts and funeral expenses be paid. I give and bequeath to my Dear Son, Wesley John Marcombe, all my worldly goods and possessions.*

I hereby make and appoint my sister-in-law Miss Sophie Wesley and my half-brother Jago Kerswell, innkeeper of the King's Head Inn at Marcombe, Guardians of my Son, until he shall attain the age of twenty-one, and I hereby make and appoint the aforesaid Sophie Wesley and Jago Kerswell Executors of this my Last Will and Testament.

In witness whereof I have hereunto set my hand and seal this Twenty-fourth day of March One Thousand Seven Hundred and Eighty Two.

Signed in the presence of . . .

There followed several names which Kayla could barely decipher, some of which had a cross next to them indicating the man in question had been illiterate and couldn't write his own name. She dropped the piece of paper onto the bed and stared out of the window for a moment, lost in thought. This didn't ring true. Why would Sir John appoint Jago the guardian of his son and call him half-brother in his will if he had never previously acknowledged the connection? Kayla was convinced now that Jago had engineered it all somehow and it was yet another thing she intended to ask him next time she saw him.

She sighed. At least he'd been able to see his son, even if he could never acknowledge him openly. Kayla shook her head and couldn't help but smile a little. 'Jago, you rogue,' she muttered. *Honestly the nerve of the man!* To force Sir John to make him guardian of little Wesley, it was the outside of enough. The man must have been livid. She chuckled at the thought.

'Oh, Jago,' she whispered. 'I wish I'd known you back then.'

Kayla spent the next few days calling all Sir John's living descendants whenever she was alone in the office. It was her last hope. She had to make sure the painting hadn't passed to one of them unofficially by way of a gift, which was possible. Wes had several meetings in London, which was a relief to her since she didn't want him to find out her real reason for coming to Marcombe.

After ten such phone calls, however, Kayla slumped over her desk defeated. Not a single one of the people she'd contacted had ever heard of a painting of their ancestress, and almost to a man they referred her to Wes. She felt extremely guilty when several of them kindly offered to contact Wes on her behalf and she had to decline. It wasn't in her nature to tell even white lies and she found the whole process very difficult.

In order to cheer herself up she rang Maddie for a good moan and told her all about her unsuccessful quest.

'. . . so you see, no one has the painting. It must have been destroyed long ago. Oh, how am I going to tell Jago? He'll be so disappointed.'

'Don't give up yet, it might just have been sold. There's no reason why anyone should destroy a Gainsborough for goodness sake.'

'I suppose not, but how am I ever going to find out?'

'Hmm. Well, maybe you'll have to hire an art expert or something. They might know what to do.'

It was the only suggestion they could come up with and they agreed Kayla would come up to London the following weekend to try and find someone who could help her. She hung up feeling depressed and more or less defeated.

'Why does everything have to be so difficult?' she muttered.

★　　★　　★

'So you've not found her yet?' Jago's voice, echoing her own despondency, didn't make Kayla feel any better.

She shook her head. 'I'm sorry, Jago. Our last chance is this art expert I spoke to today at Sotheby's. He's agreed to do some research for me. At huge expense, I might add.'

'I really appreciate your efforts, you know that, don't you?'

'Yes, Jago, I know. Let's talk about something else for while.' She chuckled suddenly, as she remembered all he had to answer for. 'Such as your misdeeds perhaps?'

She could almost hear the piratical grin in his voice. 'To which of my many heinous crimes might you be referring?'

Kayla began to tick them off on her hand. 'Well, shall we start with murder? Smuggling? Or perhaps blackmailing?'

'I have no idea what you mean.' He lifted his chin, looking very haughty, but Kayla knew it was an act.

'Oh, come on.' She gave him a severe look and tapped her foot impatiently. 'I wasn't born yesterday and I'll have you know I've read an account of your trial, as well as a copy of Sir John's will. I refuse to believe that man wrote a single word of it without, shall we say, some slight coercion?'

'Oh, very well, I'll start from the beginning shall I?' Jago gave her a lopsided grin that had her shaking her head at him.

'Good idea. I can't wait to hear this. Bet it'll be a good story.'

She wasn't disappointed.

'So, your little girlfriend's left you, has she? Is it permanent? Maybe she couldn't stand to live in such a boring place either.'

Wes was standing on the drive, ostensibly watching Nell as she skipped her way round the oval bit of gravel outside the front of Marcombe Hall. In reality, his thoughts had kept straying to Kayla, wondering how soon she'd be back and why it should matter so much. He hadn't heard Caro coming round the back of the house.

'Where did you spring from?' he asked, frowning at her.

'Been for a walk. Just passing by.'

Yeah, right. Caro didn't do country walking, as he knew well enough. 'I mean, where are you staying? I didn't know you were still in the neighbourhood.'

'Nearby.' She smirked. 'Annie told me you'd given *my* room to the ditzy blonde, so I didn't have much choice.'

'She's not ditzy,' Wes started to say, then realised he didn't want to be drawn into an argument about Kayla. 'And the guest rooms are all decorated now so you're welcome any time.'

'You'll move your girlfriend out of the adjoining room for me? How sweet of you.'

'That's not what I mean at all and you know it.

I could ask Kayla to move, but I don't see why it matters where you sleep. And she's not my girlfriend.'

'I see. Lover then, if that's what you prefer. Or friend with benefits? I hear you've sworn off serious relationships.' She laughed. 'Nice to know I had such influence on your life.'

Wes clenched his jaw and tried to breathe slowly so as not to rise to her bait. She was an expert at needling him and he wasn't surprised by the fact that he wanted to refute her allegation. What she'd said suddenly made him think though – was he really going to let his experiences with this infuriating woman dictate what he did for the rest of his life? Just because he'd fallen in love with the wrong person, was he right to shun relationships forever?

That would mean she'd won.

This epiphany hit him right between the eyes and he almost reeled. He turned to look at Caro, really look at her. He saw a beautiful woman, but an embittered, dissatisfied, mentally unstable one who would never be happy unless she was the centre of attention. His love, his wealth, his title, none of it had been enough once she had to share it with their child. And that wasn't his fault. He'd tried his best, done everything in his power, and failed, but only because it wasn't in Caro's nature to compromise. Not all women were like that. Kayla wasn't like that. So why should he judge them all by Caro's standards?

Relief flooded through him and he felt as if a

weight had suddenly been lifted from his shoulders. He beamed at her and said, 'Thanks, Caro. You've no idea how helpful you've just been.'

'What?' The smug expression faded and was replaced with one of confusion. 'What are you talking about?'

'Nothing important. Now did you want to spend some time with Nell or did you just come to annoy me? I'm sure our daughter would love some quality time with you. How are you at skipping rope?'

'I . . . skipping? I don't do skipping.'

'Ah, no, I forgot, it will probably ruin your manicure, right? Or your hairdo.' Wes laughed. 'But you know what? My friend-with-benefits-I-haven't-yet-sampled is great at skipping, so you might want to practise a bit. You wouldn't want to be outdone, would you?' He beckoned to his daughter. 'Hey, Nell, come over here and lend Mummy your skipping rope. And give her a few pointers while you're at it.' He turned back to Caro, who was staring at him as if he'd lost his mind. 'I'll be in my office. Call me when you're done.'

He strode back into the house whistling something he couldn't identify himself, but it didn't matter as long as it was a cheerful tune. 'Nope, haven't lost my mind,' he muttered. 'I think I just found it.'

Back in Devon once again, Kayla was preoccupied, thoughts of Jago and the horrible deaths suffered by Eliza and Sir John constantly on her mind. She understood why he had acted the way he did, and he'd sworn to her he hadn't actually pushed the man, but with hindsight she could also see things from Sir John's point of view. The fact of the matter was that his wife had been unfaithful with his own half-brother and it was no wonder he had become unhinged with grief and fury. The whole story was a tragedy for everyone involved, not least little baby Wesley.

She also waited anxiously for news from the art expert, but when he finally did contact her it was to dash her last hope into the ground.

'I'm sorry, Miss Sinclair, but I've been unable to find out anything about the supposed painting of Lady Marcombe. No one has ever heard of it and as far as my colleagues and I are concerned, no record of such a portrait has ever been found. I wish I could help you, but as you said the story must have been made up, perhaps by someone wishing to sell a fake Gainsborough.'

Kayla thanked him and posted off the requested cheque, and that, she thought, was that. She had tried her best and failed.

The following afternoon Kayla and Wes were going through a particularly tricky contract line by line, when there was a knock on the office door. Annie stuck her head round the frame, looking slightly worried.

'I'm sorry to bother you, but have either of you seen Nell recently?'

Wes and Kayla looked at each other and Kayla felt her stomach muscles contract involuntarily.

'Not since lunchtime, no,' Wes said. 'I thought she was with you.'

'Well, she was, but then her ma turned up and they went out into the garden for a while. I was watching them from the window, only they've disappeared now and I just wondered if they'd come inside. I know as how you said they weren't to leave the grounds, so they must be somewhere about.'

Wes stood up and Kayla saw a muscle flicker in his jaw. 'When did Caroline arrive, Annie?'

'Oh, must have been a couple hours ago now. Yes, just after lunch as I recall.'

'And when did you last see them from the kitchen window?'

'Maybe an hour after that? I'm sorry, but I'm not sure. The garden's so big, I didn't think nothing of it at first. And to begin with I heard little Nell laughing. You know how loud she can be.'

'I'd better go and look for them,' Wes said.

'I'll come with you,' Kayla offered. She indicated the contract they'd been working on. 'I can't finish this on my own anyway.'

'Okay, let's go then.'

Once outside the back door they went in separate directions in order to speed up the search, but when they converged some time later neither had seen any sign of Nell or her mother. Wes was looking grim and Kayla felt very anxious herself.

'Bloody woman,' Wes muttered. 'What on earth is she up to now? She knows she's not supposed to take Nell anywhere, not without my permission. I know it sounds harsh, but there were reasons.' He shrugged.

'Well, what do we do now? Can you call her mobile?' Kayla was racking her brain trying to come up with some ideas, but her mind was blank.

'Tried that, went to voicemail.' Wes suddenly hit himself on the forehead. 'Wait a minute, Caro's car! We haven't checked if it's still here.' He set off at a half-run towards the front of the house, where he came to a halt. 'It's gone. She must have taken Nell with her.'

'I don't remember hearing a car,' Kayla said. 'Are you sure she didn't come on foot?'

'Well, maybe, but we were so wrapped up in that damned contract, I don't suppose we were paying attention.' Wes sighed. 'I'll have to go and report this to the police in Kingsbridge. I know Caro's licence number, so perhaps they can help me find her. There's nothing much else I can do.'

'What about me? Do you want me to continue to look around here?'

'If you wouldn't mind, although I doubt you'll find her. No, Caro's up to her tricks again. Honestly, it's enough to try the patience of a saint.'

He stalked off to find his own car and went

roaring down the drive a few moments later. Kayla followed the Land Rover with her gaze for as long as she could, then turned to continue the search, although without much hope.

CHAPTER 24

After thanking everyone who had testified on his behalf, Jago headed straight back to Marcombe. Nice though it was to be surrounded by well-wishers and supporters, he needed to be alone for a while. Before and during the trial, he'd tried not to dwell on the fact that Eliza was gone, but now he knew he had to face the future without her. He felt mostly numb, as if an icy chill had spread from his gut and into his every vein. It would have been so easy to sink into misery and either drown his sorrows with brandy or find some way of joining her in the afterlife. But there was a compelling reason for him to stay alive.

He had a son.

Officially the boy may not be his, but Jago had no intention of letting anyone else bring him up. The will he'd forced John to sign had been taken to a lawyer to be proved. The doctor, who'd turned out to be a stalwart ally, had added his signature as a witness, and no one doubted his word. He'd come to see Jago in prison to tell him all was proceeding smoothly.

'I can't thank you enough, Mr Ward-Matthews,' Jago murmured through the bars, keeping his voice down so no one would hear them. 'Although, if this trial ends the way the judge would no doubt like, your efforts will have been in vain.' It wasn't something he wanted to think about at that point.

'We'll see, we'll see,' the doctor had replied. 'The Lord and the law work in mysterious ways.' And he'd been right.

Out of habit, Jago entered the Hall via the kitchen and found the servants seated around the big scrubbed pine table eating their midday meal. They all looked up and an expectant hush fell over the room. The butler, Armitage, stood up, an expression of relief spreading over his features.

'Mr Kerswell,' he said. 'I take it all went well?'

'If by that you mean I'm a free man, then yes. I rode ahead of the others, but they'll be back soon. I just . . .' He suddenly came to a halt, not sure how to proceed. He had the official right of guardianship over his son, but to all intents and purposes the child was now the owner of this house. The boy was also master of the people in front of Jago, who in turn was nothing but an innkeeper. It was an awkward situation, not to say impossible.

To his surprise, Armitage came to his rescue. 'You've come to make sure the little one is safe, I presume? I'll take you up to see him now. He's as right as rain and the wet nurse is a dependable woman, clean and healthy. Lady Marcombe chose her herself before the birth.' At the mention of his late mistress, the butler's expression turned bleak, but he quickly regained his usual equilibrium.

As Jago followed the man upstairs, he couldn't help but ask, 'So it's common knowledge then?'

'That you're the boy's guardian, yes.'

It wasn't what Jago had meant, and he was sure the butler was well aware they were speaking of the child's parentage too. 'You don't mind?' The question encompassed both subjects.

Armitage stopped outside the nursery and turned to Jago, his gaze frank and open. 'Her ladyship was well liked by the staff and we all want what's best for her child. As long as you perform your duties towards him in a fitting manner, you'll have our support.'

Jago knew the butler had said as much as he was ever going to say on the subject and it was enough. He nodded. 'Thank you, Mr Armitage, I appreciate it and I promise you I'll do my best.'

Armitage put out his hand and they shook on it.

When Wes returned, Kayla could see immediately that he was in a foul mood.

'What happened? Were the police not helpful?'

'I'm sure they would have been, only I never got that far.'

'What do you mean?' Kayla frowned at him in confusion. 'Did you change your mind?'

'No, but there was no need to ask them for

assistance. I found the stupid woman myself. She was sitting at that outside café down by the harbour having coffee. I saw her when I drove past.'

Kayla let out a sigh of relief. 'Oh, thank God. So Nell is still with her mother then?'

'No,' Wes growled. 'And Caro claims she left her here, playing quietly in her room.'

'What? Oh, no . . . But I've looked everywhere, even in the attic.'

'Well, we'll just have to look again. Caro was so smug, I'm sure she's hidden her somewhere, just to give me another fright, but I'm damned if I know where that could be. I swear the woman should be locked up.' He paced the hall, and Kayla could see he was trying to think where to look next. 'Let's start at the beginning, in the garden. If we call out perhaps Nell will hear us and be able to reply. You go and make a start and I'll get Annie and Ben from the gatehouse to help out as well.'

'Okay.' Kayla set off for the garden, but she knew in her heart that Nell wasn't there. So where was she?

An hour later Nell still hadn't been found and Kayla was sitting on a bench in the garden resting her head in her hands. She could hear Wes calling for his daughter, but she was sure it was no use. There had to be another way.

Suddenly inspiration struck and she almost gasped out loud. 'Of course, why didn't I think of it before,' she muttered. Standing up so abruptly her head swam for a moment, she set off at a run towards the field that contained the Gypsies, praying they hadn't packed up and left. If anyone could help them find Nell, it was the old lady. This was her chance to prove she really did have the second sight.

Panting heavily from her sprint, she came to a halt at the edge of the field. At first it looked empty, but then she spotted the ancient caravan partly obscured by a tree and quickly set off towards it. As she rounded the corner she saw the old lady sitting on the top step in the open door, smiling her toothless grin in welcome.

'There you are, young lady. I've been expecting you.'

Kayla was trying to get her breath back and couldn't reply straight away. She swallowed hard and blinked away tears of relief that threatened to fall. 'Thank God you're still here,' she panted. 'I was afraid you'd be gone.'

The old woman smiled again. 'The others left, but I told them to come back for me in a week as there was something I had to do first. Now ask me your question.'

'Nell . . . the little girl . . . do you know where she is? Is she safe? Please, I'd be so grateful if you could help me. We've looked everywhere and Wes, that's her father, is so scared. Me too.'

The woman nodded. 'I know Wes and little Nell. It's as I thought. Well, I can't tell you exactly, but

I can say this – she's waiting on the sand and she's starting to feel cold and frightened. You must find her quickly. She wants to go home.'

'The sand?' Kayla scowled, not satisfied with such measly information at first, but then understanding dawned. 'The sand! You mean she's at the cove? The one she and Wes took me to a couple of weeks ago?'

'Aye, that might be the one. As I said, I can't tell you for certain. All I see is sand and the little 'un sitting there forlornly. Go now. Your instinct will guide you.'

'Thank you.' On impulse Kayla bent down to hug the old woman and heard a chuckle behind her as she began to run back down the path to the house. At the edge of the field she paused and turned to wave at the Gypsy lady, who returned the salute, then she ran as fast as she could to find Wes.

'Down in the cove? Why on earth would she be there?' Wes looked at her in disbelief when she came hurtling into the kitchen, babbling about Gypsies and fortune telling.

'You don't actually believe Gypsies can foretell the future, do you?' Annie said, looking as though she felt sorry for Kayla. 'It's just a bit of fun, you know.'

'No, I mean yes, I mean, I don't know, but we have to at least look. What have we got to lose?'

Wes was still frowning and Kayla felt like

314

stamping her foot and screaming in frustration. She didn't have time to explain to him now just why she knew the old lady might genuinely have the sight. He'd never believe her anyway.

To her surprise he nodded and said, 'You're right, come on.'

'You believe me?'

He gave her a distracted smile. 'I believe Katerina. I've known her all my life. If she says Nell's in the cove I'd bet anything on that.'

'Well, really,' Annie muttered, shaking her head at the pair of them, but Wes ignored the house-keeper for once and took Kayla's elbow to steer her out of the kitchen.

'Let's go. We have to hurry. It'll be getting dark soon.'

They took the car as far as the top of the cliff, then set off down the path, trying to keep their balance while walking as fast as they could. Wes went first, so he could block her fall if Kayla should trip or slide on the loose gravel, and consequently he was the first to spot his daughter.

'Oh, sweetheart, there you are!' Kayla heard him cry out, before he took off at a run.

'Be careful,' she called after him, but he paid her no heed.

Nell was sitting on the sandy beach, her thin arms wrapped around her legs and her head bent over her knees while she rocked back and forth. As Kayla came running down the last part of the path, slipping and sliding dangerously, she could hear Nell crying and it was a heart-wrenching sound.

'Nell, honey, we're here. Everything's going to be okay,' Wes called out and sprinted across to his daughter. He picked her up and hugged her fiercely, as if he'd never let her go again.

'Daddy, where have you been? Mummy said you'd come soon, but it's been ages and it's almost dark and I was so scared.'

'Shh, it's all right. I'm sorry, but Mummy must have forgotten to tell me to come because I didn't know you were waiting. Look, Kayla's here too, she didn't know either.'

Wes sent Kayla a look over Nell's head and in it she saw despair at the stupid trick Caroline had played on him, but also enormous relief that Nell was safe. She felt the same way herself, so she went over and put her arms round both of them and it felt so right.

'Yes, I'm here. Everything is fine now.'

They stood like that for what seemed like ages, then Wes said, 'Come on, we'd better get you home, sweetie. You must be starving. I know I am.'

'Oh, yes, can I have Marmite sandwiches?'

Wes laughed. 'You can have anything you want. Anything at all.'

He looked at Kayla again and they smiled at each other. Nell was safe and it was all that mattered. From now on they wouldn't let her out of their sight and they knew Annie wouldn't either.

Caroline would have no more opportunities for foul play.

'Kayla, would you like to go to a dinner party with me tomorrow night?'

Lost in unhappy thoughts about her failure to find the picture of Eliza, the question took Kayla completely by surprise. She looked up from her computer screen and blinked at Wes. Things had calmed down in the Marcombe household and were back to normal, with the exception that Nell was kept under constant supervision. Wes had been taking his turn at playing with his daughter after school and Kayla hadn't expected him back so soon.

'Sorry? A dinner party? Where?'

'One of my oldest friends lives not too far from here and he and his wife are having a little get-together. They rang just now and they've asked me to bring someone.' Wes smiled ruefully. 'They've been saying that since Caro and I got divorced and I always come alone, so I thought it would be nice to surprise them this time.' He shrugged. 'If you'd rather not, I understand.'

Kayla pulled herself together and pushed Jago to the back of her mind for the moment. 'No, no, I would love to. I mean, it would be great to meet some new people.'

Wes chuckled. 'Yes, you must be sick and tired of us here at Marcombe. You never see anyone else.'

'No, of course I'm not tired of you. I like it

here.' *I could stay here forever,* she could have added. It was heaven on earth and the longer she stayed, the more she enjoyed it.

'You're sure you want to come?'

'Yes, thank you. I look forward to it. Is it a formal do? Just asking so I know what I should wear.'

'Nothing formal I don't think. Actually, I never pay attention to what females wear, so I couldn't tell you. But I'm going in dark chinos and a casual blazer if that's any help? No tie.'

'Oh, very helpful,' Kayla answered sarcastically. 'I wear that all the time.'

Wes laughed and shrugged. 'Well, you look good in everything, so don't worry too much about it.'

Kayla felt a blush spreading over her cheeks, then told herself not to be so silly. Sure, he'd given her a compliment, but he hadn't sounded serious. She mustn't read anything into it. He was just being polite.

But he had asked her to a dinner party and she was determined to look her best.

Kayla made him eat his words since he certainly seemed to pay a lot of attention to the outfit she finally chose to wear. A minuscule black silk skirt showed off her legs in sheer black tights. This was worn with an extremely tight sky-blue top which had Wes's eyes glued to her for a full five seconds before he recovered, making Kayla smile inwardly. High heels made her about four inches taller and

318

she had finished her outfit off by adding a long string of pearls. They were a twenty-first birthday present from her parents and she wore them tied in a loose knot at the bottom, with a pair of matching dangling pearl earrings.

'Wow!' he finally breathed. 'You look far too nice to go to a mere dinner party. I should be taking you to some fancy restaurant instead.'

Kayla punched him playfully on the arm. 'Don't be silly. This is nothing special.'

'You could have fooled me.'

'You don't think my skirt is too short?' Kayla asked, remembering Mike's horrified look when she'd arrived at his parents' party. She didn't want to embarrass Wes in front of his friends.

'Are you kidding? Definitely not. With legs like that how could it possibly be too short?'

Kayla felt her cheeks heat up again. 'Why, thank you.'

To Kayla's great relief Wes's friends turned out to live in what she would term a far more normal house than Marcombe Hall. It was a large Victorian terraced house on the outskirts of Totnes and Kayla thought it was lovely. She told their hostess, Sarah, as much.

'Thank you. Peter and I are very pleased with it now that all the builders have finally finished. But don't they take an age! I honestly thought they'd moved in here with us.' Sarah laughed and led the way into the sitting room where Kayla was introduced to several other people, all equally charming and all very pleased to see Wes with a woman by the look of things.

'It's about time he came out of his shell,' one older woman whispered in Kayla's ear. 'Do him a world of good to forget about the divorce.' Kayla didn't want to spoil their pleasure by telling them she and Wes weren't a couple. It was easier just to smile and nod.

Dinner was excellent and the wine flowed freely. Kayla relaxed and for the first time in weeks she felt truly alive again. She joined in the conversation and was accepted into Wes's circle of friends without hesitation. Her neighbours at the table vied with one another to tell her stories about him, and she laughed at youthful follies and mishaps. From time to time she glanced across to where he sat, and more often than not she found him looking at her, a strange expression in his eyes. It made her warm all over and she squirmed in her seat.

Wes couldn't take his eyes off Kayla. From the moment she'd swept down the grand stairs into the hall at Marcombe he'd been in a daze. She looked absolutely stunning, her outfit sexy and sophisticated all at once. The only problem was he'd have liked to rip it off her then and there.

Peter and the others ribbed him about his new 'conquest' and he went along with their joshing, taking it in his stride. Underneath, however, he found himself wishing they were right. He'd be proud to call Kayla his and he was sure now that she'd never behave the way Caro had. If Kayla had a child she would love both the baby and its father. She had a big heart with room to spare. There was no selfishness, no petty jealousy, no attention seeking.

She was beautiful outside and in.

He caught her eyes across the table and thought he saw an answering gleam. Could she tell how much he wanted her? Did it scare her? Or did she want him too?

He needed to find out, but not here, not now. He'd have to be patient.

It was the longest dinner party he'd ever attended.

They took a taxi back to Marcombe as they'd both had too much wine. In the darkness of the back seat Wes took her hand and twined his fingers with hers. Kayla didn't resist. It felt right, safe and exciting at the same time and sent little sparks shooting up her arm. They didn't speak, but the simple enjoyment of holding hands was enough for the moment.

'Would you like a drink?' Wes asked her when they were safely back at the Hall. 'I've had such a good time, I don't really want the evening to end yet.'

'Me neither. A drink would be nice, thank you.' She followed him into a small sitting room at the back of the hall and he produced two glasses of amber liquid.

'Do you like brandy? I'm told my ancestors always bought the very best, the smuggled stuff.'

Kayla tried not to smile. Jago's cargo, of course. 'It's not really my thing, but right now I'll drink anything.' She leaned on the fireplace and took a sip. The warm liquor burned all the way down, but a pleasant feeling spread rapidly through her veins. 'It's not bad actually. I can see why it was so sought after.' She held it up to the light to study the rich colour.

'It's wonderful. Just like you were this evening.' Kayla looked at him, startled. 'My friends all liked you.' Wes smiled. 'You have no idea how many times I was told what a lucky dog I was to have such a date.'

'Well, I'm glad you didn't have to be ashamed of me.'

'I could never be that.' Wes put his glass down and came to stand in front of her. 'Kayla, I've tried to fight it for weeks, but I have to admit I'm incredibly attracted to you. I know it's wrong since I'm your boss and I'm probably too old for you, but . . . it's driving me crazy, so I have to ask. Do you think you could ever feel the same way about me?'

Kayla felt her eyes grow huge with wonder. *At last!* For an answer she put her arms around his neck and pulled him close. 'Definitely,' she murmured.

It was Wes's turn to look surprised, but he quickly recovered and put his arms round her, tightening the embrace. The pirate grin appeared in response to the smile she gave him, sending a shock wave through her. How she loved it when he looked like that. She'd never tire of it. He stared into her eyes, as if he was giving her one last chance to run away, but she knew she didn't want to. No way. Right here was where she wished to be.

Wes bent to kiss her. Softly at first, asking permission with actions, not words. When she didn't protest, his kisses soon grew more demanding and Kayla responded in equal measure, seizing her chance this time. She wasn't about to throw it away again that was for sure. They kissed for what seemed a very long time and desire built up inside her, making her legs shaky and her whole body fizz with awareness of him. She craved more of his touch and when his hands began to stroke her back, then move lower down, she sighed with satisfaction. He cupped her bottom with both hands and pushed her closer, which made her wriggle slightly, and she heard him groan.

'Oh God, Kayla, I want you so much,' he whispered between kisses, 'have wanted you for ages. Ever since I saw you in that ugly pink bathing suit, in fact.' She clung to him as delicious sensations assailed her from every part of her body.

'Take me upstairs, Wes,' she whispered back in a husky voice she hardly recognised as her own, and he didn't need to be asked twice. With seemingly no effort at all, he lifted her into his arms and headed for the door. She bent to open it with a giggle, and turned out the light as they passed through on their way into the hall. Up the stairs he carried her, despite her protests that she was quite capable of walking.

'I can't wait that long,' he answered, striding down the corridor in a tearing hurry. They passed her door and entered his bedroom, and within minutes they had shed their clothing without even bothering to turn the lights on. Wes backed her up towards the bed, kissing her like there was no tomorrow, and then they fell onto the soft mattress.

Kayla had never wanted anyone with such fierce passion. It was almost frightening in its intensity, but it felt right. And so did Wes. Although they were both impatient and almost shaking with desire, he took his time and made love to her tantalisingly slowly, making sure she was with him all the way. Kayla had never experienced anything like it. She never wanted it to stop.

She told him so afterwards, when her breathing was returning to normal and her pulse rate had calmed down slightly. He chuckled and pulled her into his arms, enclosing them both in a cocoon of duvets. 'It doesn't have to stop, you know. We have all night,' he whispered.

Kayla smiled into the dark. He was right. And she was going to enjoy every minute of it.

CHAPTER 25

The door to the nursery at Marcombe Hall opened silently on well-oiled hinges and a woman stepped inside and looked around. Jago had been pacing back and forth, rocking his small son in his arms and crooning to him softly. Now he stopped his perambulations and bowed to the lady.

'You must be Lady Marcombe's sister,' he said, speaking in a near whisper so as not to wake the little boy.

'Yes, I'm Sophie Wesley. And you are . . .?'

'Jago Kerswell.' He bowed once more. 'I assume the lawyer told you who I am?'

She inclined her head in acknowledgement and he noticed she had the same ash-blonde hair as her late sister, but there the resemblance ended. Sophie had none of Eliza's beauty, not even the hazel-green eyes. She looked just what Jago knew her to be, a plain spinster in her early thirties. There was intelligence lurking in her eyes, however, and something else, humour perhaps. She didn't look down her nose at him and he warmed to her immediately. Eliza had spoken highly of her, telling him Sophie had a kind heart and the patience of a saint. She would need both now, he thought.

Jago held out the sleeping baby to her. 'Here is your nephew, ma'am. And mine, as the lawyer may have mentioned,' he added.

She took the bundle from him and gazed at the tiny scrap of humanity nestled within. 'Oh, he's adorable,' she sighed. 'You have no idea how I've longed for—' She stopped abruptly and, to hide the blush spreading over her features, buried her face near the baby's. His heart went out to her, a woman so suited to being a mother, yet she'd never been given the chance.

'You will take care of him? And make your home here?' Jago couldn't quite keep the anxiety out of his voice. He had wondered if he'd done the right thing in making this woman little Wesley's joint guardian, but he'd been unable to think of anyone else suitable. And Eliza had told him how Sophie was used to caring for her nephews and nieces since she herself was never expected to marry. Without either beauty or a dowry poor Sophie had had no hope of that.

Sophie looked up. 'Oh, yes. I will look after him as if he were my own, I promise you. And living here will be heaven after . . . well, after going from place to place in a never-ending round of visits to my siblings. At last I can settle down.'

'Good. He will need love having lost both parents.'

She gave him a searching look. 'Both parents? If I don't miss my guess he still has one left.'

'Miss Wesley, I—'

'Sophie, please, since we're in this together. And there's no need to explain anything to me. I may be plain, Mr Kerswell, but I have never been dim-witted and Eliza's letters were rather transparent. As long as you help me raise this child, I shall never ask any questions nor give away your secret.'

'Thank you. You're very understanding.' He reached out to caress the downy head of his son. 'And my name is Jago.'

'Jago,' she repeated with a nod. 'We'll do our best for this little one. And it will be enough.'

Late morning sunlight was pouring in through half-open curtains when Kayla finally surfaced the next day and she found herself alone in a huge sleigh bed. Wes was nowhere to be seen and she wondered if he already regretted last night. She had thought he might have changed his mind and would be open to the possibility of a permanent relationship. But perhaps it meant nothing more to him than a one-night stand?

No, that wasn't the impression he'd given her at all.

Suddenly restless, Kayla opened her eyes fully and checked the time. 'Jesus!' Half past eleven. How was that possible? She never slept that late normally.

She sat up in bed, absently combing out her hair with her fingers . . . and came face to face with Eliza.

The enormous portrait hung over the fireplace directly opposite Wes's bed and Kayla recognised her immediately, both from the style of painting and from Jago's description. It had to be her. It couldn't be anyone else. Shock and elation washed over her, making her gasp and draw in a deep breath, then slowly she smiled.

'Well, I'll be damned.'

Intrigued she swung her legs over the side of the bed and padded over to peer at Eliza more closely. 'So that's where you were hiding,' she whispered. 'No wonder I couldn't find you, I never thought to look in here. Wes must like you too since he hung your portrait in his bedroom.' But why hadn't he mentioned this painting when she asked him if he had other Gainsboroughs? Maybe it wasn't signed? She looked in the corner of the canvas expecting it to be blank, but there was a clear signature just as Jago had told her. So Wes must have known. Kayla frowned.

Near the signature the artist had painted one half of an open book with part of a verse from a Shakespeare sonnet printed on it: *'Shall I compare thee to a summer's day? . . .'* Kayla whistled softly. So that's what Jago had meant – the other half of the same book was in the corner of his portrait. She remembered it clearly and if the two were put next to each other they would fit together perfectly. He'd been right, she was the owner of a genuine Gainsborough.

He had also been right about something else – Eliza was indeed absolutely lovely. Her simple green dress blended in with her surroundings to the point that it was difficult to make out where the gown ended and nature began, but it didn't matter because the viewer's gaze was immediately drawn to Eliza's face, which was quite simply radiant.

'I see what you mean, Jago,' Kayla whispered. And no doubt that look of supreme happiness was because Jago had been nearby when the painting was done. For a short period of her life Eliza had been happy.

Kayla felt sadness well up inside her for the way the poor woman's life had ended. Thrown off a cliff, never to see her newborn son or the love of her life again. And yet, if Jago was right, she, Kayla, had the power to reunite them and now that she'd found Eliza the time had come to put this to the test. It was an awe-inspiring thought and Kayla needed to think how best to broach the subject with Wes.

First things first, however. She couldn't speak to him about anything until she found him and there was also the small matter of last night. Would he still want her this morning? There was only one way to find out. Either way, she needed a shower. Not to mention some breakfast, or should that be brunch? A loud rumbling noise from her stomach made her opt for the latter first. She picked up one of Wes's large T-shirts and pulled it on, together with her pants, then headed for the kitchens.

'You've been keeping secrets from me, haven't you?'

A soft pair of arms sneaked round Wes's middle from behind and he almost dropped the piece of toast he was just fishing out of the toaster.

'Kayla! I was going to bring you breakfast in bed.' He turned and hugged her back, shivering with desire when he noticed that she wasn't wearing anything under the T-shirt she'd appropriated. He only had on a pair of tracksuit bottoms himself so her breasts pressed against his naked chest, the thin material between them just adding an extra frisson when they moved. He kissed her, but although she returned his kiss with enthusiasm, she soon pulled away and wagged a finger at him.

'No more until you tell me the truth. Why do you have a Gainsborough in your bedroom? And why on earth didn't you tell me about it?'

'Oh, that.' Wes had forgotten about her quest and right now he'd rather concentrate on other, more pleasurable pursuits. But he could see she was determined to have an answer and the sooner he gave her one, the faster he could get back to ravishing her. Perhaps right here in the kitchen? The thought made him smile.

'Wes!' She prodded him. 'Spill.'

He shrugged. 'It's been a family secret for ages. I'm not sure who started it, but it was decided we wouldn't tell anyone the portrait existed. That way thieves wouldn't be tempted to steal it and our insurance premiums could be kept to a minimum. As far as I know, it's always hung in the master bedroom – hardly anyone ever goes in there except for trusted staff. I'm sorry, I couldn't tell you when you first came and later on I forgot you were even interested, to be honest.' He kissed her throat and nibbled at her shoulder, pushing the overlarge T-shirt out of the way. 'I kind of had other things on my mind, you know.'

'Hmm. Well, I guess I'll forgive you then, but are you sure you want to . . .?'

The rest of what she'd been going to say was lost as he put his mouth on hers, silencing her. Talking could wait until later as far as he was concerned and she soon agreed.

They made love on the kitchen table, of all places, something Kayla had never done before. None of her previous partners had ever been that adventurous, but Wes seemed to want her anywhere, any time, which was a heady feeling and increased her own enjoyment no end.

'What about Nell?' she managed to ask, before surrendering totally to the swirls of desire surging through her.

'I found a note from Annie saying she'd taken

Nell down to her cottage,' Wes murmured between kisses and Kayla gave herself up to the sensations that were building up inside her yet again. She couldn't seem to get enough of this man and his every touch excited her. It was sheer bliss.

After a leisurely brunch and some time spent reading the Sunday papers in companionable silence, Wes wanted to go for a swim, but Kayla was too exhausted for that.

'Haven't you had enough exercise for one day?' she teased.

'There are different kinds,' he'd countered. 'And I can see I'm going to have to stay in shape now.'

'Well, I'm having a shower. See you in a while?'

'Absolutely.' The smile he gave her almost made her relent and go with him, but she desperately wanted to shower and change, so she headed upstairs.

She went into Wes's room first and stared at the portrait for a while. 'I'm so glad you're not lost,' she whispered, wondering whether Eliza would start talking to her as well. The woman in the painting remained immobile, however, and with a sigh, Kayla began to pick up bits of her clothing, which seemed to have ended up all over the room. The tights were missing, but as they had been ripped anyway, she decided to forget about them.

On close inspection of the panelling, she found the connecting door to her bedroom and unlocked it. Kayla went through into her room, leaving the little door slightly ajar in case Wes should come back, and went to the bathroom. She emerged a short while later after a refreshingly hot shower and walked over towards the huge wardrobe to find some clean clothes.

There she came to an abrupt halt and frowned. The door to the wardrobe stood open, but she could clearly remember closing it the night before. Someone had been in her room again. Her heart made a somersault and she hurried to check what had been shredded this time.

Nothing was torn or even out of place, but there was a strange smell coming from the depths of the wardrobe. Kayla stuck her head in and wrinkled her nose. 'Phew, what's that?' She took a cautious step inside and trod on something soft. It was Nell's favourite teddy bear, Alfie.

Kayla bent to pick it up, then went further into the wardrobe. The back panel wasn't quite in place and there was a musty smelling draft coming from that direction. On closer inspection it proved to be a door. A cleverly concealed one. At last she understood.

'Of course,' she muttered to herself. 'A secret entrance.' For the smugglers perhaps? Or just the inhabitants of the house? No wonder people could come in and out of her room without being seen. But who? And what was Nell's teddy bear doing here? Unless . . . 'Oh, no!' Panic-stricken, Kayla rushed out of the wardrobe and started to throw on clothes willy-nilly – some pants and socks, a pair of old jeans and a T-shirt, then a sweater.

Nell had gone through the panel, whether alone or not she had no idea, and her only thought was that she had to go after her. Nell might be in danger and maybe it wasn't too late.

Hastily sticking her feet into a pair of trainers, Kayla pushed open the back panel door fully and found a set of stairs leading downwards. She didn't hesitate, but went down into the dark. When she reached the bottom, she could see the vague outline of another door and felt along the wall for a handle of some sort. It took a while, but her fingers eventually encountered an old-fashioned latch, which she lifted. The door opened on what must be newly oiled hinges, as it didn't make a sound, and Kayla found herself outside the house. Looking back she could see why no one had noticed the opening. It blended in perfectly with the stonework around it. She pushed it to, but didn't close it completely, just in case she'd need to get back in again.

She looked around and noticed a trail in the wet grass. It had rained during the night and it was clear that someone had walked away from this door in one direction only. She hesitated. Should she go and get Wes? But he might still be in the pool and then it would be ages before they could leave. Something told her time was of the essence and she decided to go with her gut instinct. She set off, following the trail towards the coast.

Where was Nell? And why would she have gone this way? She had to find her. It was the only thing she could think of. Everything else faded into insignificance.

It wasn't until much later that she remembered the Gypsy's warning. '*Beware dark places and stairs. Keep away from the darkness.*'

'Oh hell,' she muttered, but there was no turning back now.

The sound of the sea had been steadily growing in strength for quite a while when Kayla finally came round a large clump of gorse bushes and spotted an old, crumbling building. It looked like some kind of large gazebo, with windows towards the sea and a little verandah facing inland. Could it be Jago's trysting place? He'd told her he often met up with Eliza in a summer house by the coast. This must be it. The thought made Kayla swallow hard as she remembered how their love ended, but then she pulled herself together. She had more important things to think about right now.

She stopped and crouched behind the bushes for a moment, just to be on the safe side. There were no sounds and nobody in sight. After scanning the surrounding area one more time, Kayla sprinted across to the summer house and peered inside. It was fairly dim in there and it took a while before her eyes adjusted to the darkness, but then she gasped. The small, pathetic figure of Nell was sitting slumped against an old bench, wrapped in her blanket and with her eyes closed. For a heart-stopping moment Kayla thought she was hurt, or even worse, but then she saw the child was just asleep.

She tiptoed over and knelt next to her on the rotting floor planks. She put the teddy bear, which she was still carrying, down and felt inside the blanket to make sure the little girl was breathing. The small chest rose and fell with comforting regularity.

'Oh, sweetheart,' Kayla murmured and caressed Nell's hair. 'What are you doing here?' Nell stirred and opened sleepy eyes that seemed unfocused.

She'd been drugged, Kayla realised. Sleeping pills perhaps? She hoped it wasn't anything worse.

'Kayla.'

'Sshhh.' Kayla put a finger over her lips and looked around. There were boxes and bags stacked around the walls and on top of some of the benches. This meant there must be people nearby. People who were presumably up to no good and might hurt Nell. But who? Surely all this stuff couldn't belong to Caroline?

Nell muttered something unintelligible and Kayla shushed her again and whispered, 'You have to be quiet so I can get you out of here.' To distract the little girl she held up her teddy bear. 'Look, I've brought you Alfie. You must have dropped him and he didn't want to be left behind.' Nell took the bear with a sleepy smile and Kayla bent towards her and held out a hand to help her to her feet.

'Can you stand up? Walk? Or do you want me to carry you?'

Suddenly Nell's eyes became more focused. She blinked and then cried out, 'No, Mummy. Noooo!'

Kayla looked up in surprise, but before she could turn around something hard struck the back of her head and the world disappeared in a flash of stars.

Wes went for a leisurely swim, enjoying the gentle exercise. Kayla was right, he didn't really need it right now, but it was relaxing. And he hadn't entirely been joking – he'd need to stay in shape if he was going to keep up with a girlfriend – partner? – who was ten years younger. He smiled to himself. He'd managed to tire her out completely last night though, but he wanted to be able do it all over again come evening. He still couldn't quite believe that she was finally his, but he'd make damn sure she never wanted to leave now.

With a sigh he pulled himself out of the pool and stretched, before making his way up the stairs to his room. He wondered idly what Nell and Annie were doing. It had been kind of the house-keeper to take care of his little girl. Annie would normally always ask before doing anything like that. In fact, he couldn't recall her ever writing him a note before, but she knew Wes and Kayla had been to a party, so she must have figured out that they would sleep late and tried not to disturb them. Just as well. He wanted to spend what was left of today only with Kayla.

He entered his room and found all Kayla's

clothes gone. He noticed the connecting door standing open, and walked over to it calling her name, while listening for sounds of the shower. Was she still washing her hair or something?

'Kayla? Kayla, are you there?'

There was no reply and he strolled into her room and looked around. A faint smell of shampoo mixed with perfume came from the direction of the bathroom, but when Wes peered in there, it too was empty. He turned around and saw the clothes she had worn the night before lying in a pile on the floor next to the wardrobe, and its door standing ajar. He figured she must have dressed and left already, and he had just missed her. But where had she gone?

'Damn,' he muttered. He had hoped to catch her still in a state of undress, but she must have headed downstairs again via a different staircase.

On his way out of the room he passed the wardrobe and became aware of a cold draught snaking its way up his naked chest. That was odd. He stopped and looked around again. The window was closed, so where was the air coming from? Another draught slithered round his ankles and it seemed to be coming from the wardrobe, so he stuck his head inside it and drew in a sharp breath when he found the cause. The back panel was wide open and he could see a flight of stairs leading downwards.

'Jesus,' he breathed. 'Bloody hell!' He hadn't really believed Kayla's stories of a nightly intruder, but now . . . 'Oh, Kayla, I shouldn't have doubted you.'

He'd also never believed the tales of a secret entrance or priest's hole somewhere in the house. His father had told him there was supposed to be one, but knowledge of its exact location had been lost when a previous Marcombe died rather suddenly before passing on the information. It would seem that someone had found it. Who?

A terrible fear gripped him, but he managed to stop himself from rushing down those stairs. 'Think,' he told himself. What could have happened? Had Kayla just found the door and decided to investigate on the spur of the moment, or had someone forced her to go through it? No, she would have come to tell him about it unless she'd had a very good reason not to. Such as being coerced. But why would anyone want to harm Kayla? It didn't make sense, but a picture of her room with its contents shredded rose up in his mind.

'Think rationally, man.' He closed his eyes and concentrated. What did he need? Hurrying back to his own room, he pulled on a T-shirt and a pair of trainers. He was already wearing tracksuit bottoms. Then he grabbed a torch from his bedside table and a baseball bat, which he kept handy in case of intruders. Not that he'd ever needed it before. It had only been a precaution.

He switched on the torch and took the stairs behind the wardrobe at a run, but when he reached the bottom he found that he had two choices – either continue down another set of stairs, which presumably led to the cellars, or go out via a door set into the thick wall. He touched the door and noticed it wasn't quite closed, so he surmised it had been used very recently. Therefore Kayla must have gone that way.

He forced himself to stop and think again. He needed to be careful. If something terrible had happened to Kayla he had to make sure he didn't make the same mistake or fall into a trap of some sort. Wes shook his head. He would be on his guard, but he had to follow. What other option did he have? Giving up further speculation he pushed open the door and peered at the grass. The path made by several sets of feet was clear to see and as the footsteps went only one way, Wes followed.

A short while later he knew where he was heading. Or he could guess, at least. The old summer house hadn't been used for years but he and Alex had spent a lot of time playing there as children. Who was using it now though?

A few minutes later he heard voices, and he crawled forward to hide behind some bushes and listen without being seen.

What was going on?

CHAPTER 26

The note arrived out of the blue one afternoon and froze Jago's insides with sudden terror.

Please come immediately. S.

Had something happened to little Wesley? That didn't bear thinking about.

Jago left what he was doing and set off at a run, not stopping until he'd barged in through the kitchen door of the Hall and was standing there panting, trying to catch his breath. One of the maids gave a little shriek of fright at his abrupt entry, but he ignored her and fixed his gaze on the cook.

'What's happened?' he demanded. 'Is the boy ill?'

Wesley was a sturdy six-year-old who'd so far breezed through life in rude health, but Jago knew children caught illnesses easily. It was his greatest fear because it was the one thing he knew he couldn't protect him against.

The cook shook her head. 'The little 'un is fine, don't you fret, my lovely. No, it's Miss Sophie as needs assistance, I'd say.'

Jago frowned. 'In what way?'

'We 'ave a visitor, so we do, and although Miss Sophie's tried to speak to 'im, 'e won't listen. 'Igh an' mighty so-and-so.' Cook pursed her lips. 'You'd best go see. They be in the salon, I reckon.'

His breathing under control, Jago went upstairs and knocked on the door to the finest room in the house. It was never normally used and most of the furniture was under Holland covers. As he entered he could see these had been removed however, and he wondered what the occasion was.

'Ah, Mr Kerswell, there you are.' Sophie stood up and curtseyed politely, her eyes sending him unmistakeable distress signals. 'This is Mr Henry Marcombe, cousin of my late brother-in-law.' Turning back to her guest she finished the introduction. 'And this is Mr Kerswell, little Wesley's other guardian, as I was telling you earlier.'

Jago bowed to the gentleman, who gave him the merest nod and looked him up and down with an expression of distaste. Jago knew he probably didn't show to advantage in his everyday working clothes, but he hadn't thought to change. He ignored the man's rudeness and took a seat next to Sophie.

'Are you visiting these parts then, Mr Marcombe?' he enquired.

'No, I've come to take charge of young Wesley, as I've been telling Miss . . . er, Wesley.' He clearly found it irritating that the child had her surname as his Christian name. 'It's time he was sent to school and he needs his male relatives to see to his education.'

'We have already applied for a place,' Jago informed the man tersely. 'He'll be going when he's ten. He's to have a tutor until then.'

'Preposterous! Boys need to start no later than seven. Mollycoddling by females won't do him any good. I've obtained him a place from September onwards and I've just been informing Miss Wesley of the arrangements.'

'I'm sorry to have to disappoint you, Mr Marcombe, but young Wesley isn't going anywhere without my agreement. I'm his legal guardian and so is Miss Wesley.'

'If I understand correctly, you're but an innkeeper, and why my late cousin should see fit to name you in his will is a mystery. I'm sure you'll appreciate that those of us who are actually related to the boy and move in the same circles as he will be expected to do, know what's best for him.'

'No, I don't.'

'As I said, that's because you're a—'

'I know what I am, Mr Marcombe, but it doesn't make me a fool. Besides, you'd need Miss Wesley's permission as well and I doubt she'll give it.' He raised his eyebrows at Sophie, who seemed to take courage from his presence.

'Certainly not,' she said.

'Well now, that's another thing.' Mr Marcombe scowled at her. 'It's not seemly, you bringing up a boy on your own and living here alone when you're not even married.'

Sophie raised her chin. 'There are servants aplenty and besides I . . . I'm betrothed,' she stammered, a blush stealing up her throat when Jago flickered a gaze at her, trying to hide his surprise.

'To whom?' Mr Marcombe asked rudely, as if no one in their right mind would offer for her.

Her blush deepened. 'That is none of your business, sir.'

'Of course it is. I demand to know since it'll affect the boy's future.'

Sophie sent Jago a panicked glance that told him she'd been prevaricating. He stood up and went to lean nonchalantly on the mantelpiece. 'She's engaged to me, Mr Marcombe,' he lied. 'And if you're now satisfied that all the proprieties have been observed, I would suggest you take your leave. It's at least an hour to the nearest town and it will be dark soon.'

Mr Marcombe's florid cheeks turned dark red at this none too subtle hint and he got to his feet. 'Now see here, Mr Kerswell, you can't—'

Jago was taller and he took a step forward in his most intimidating manner. 'No, you see here, Mr Marcombe. The late Sir John's will was legal in every way and has been proved according to law, which means you have no say in anything. There isn't a thing you can do about it, is that clear? Now my future wife and I would appreciate it if you'd be on your way.'

Marcombe opened and closed his mouth several times, then thought better of it and stomped out of the room. Jago heard Armitage bidding the man goodbye out in the hall, before slamming the front door shut. He looked at Sophie, whose shoulders seemed to slump, while she closed her eyes and exhaled.

'Thank you,' she whispered. 'I'm sorry, but I couldn't deal with him on my own.' Tears spilled over and rolled down her cheeks. 'He's not the first, you know. There have been other relatives, but I was able to handle them. They all seem to think I shouldn't be here.'

Jago went over to her and pulled her close, cradling her head so that she'd lean it against his shoulder. 'Shh, you did the right thing. And you should have told me about the others. You know I'm here to help.'

She was stiff in his arms at first, but when he didn't let go she relaxed against him for a moment. 'Thank you, but you don't need to—'

'I think I do.' He looked down at her. 'Will you do me the honour of marrying me, Sophie? It would probably be the best thing for all of us, if you can bear it. And it might stop any other relatives from visiting unexpectedly.'

He knew it wasn't the most romantic of proposals, but he could never promise a woman his heart because he'd already given it away. And Sophie was nothing if not practical, as she'd proved over the years.

Sophie looked into his eyes and frowned. 'It's not necessary. I'm aware of how you felt about Eliza. Although perhaps a marriage of convenience, a business arrangement on paper only . . .'

He kissed her cheek. 'Oh, I think we can do a bit better than a business arrangement. It's possible to like someone a lot without being head over heels in love, you know. I like you, respect you and I promise to always treat you well. What do you say? Shall we give it a try? It would make life a bit less lonely for both of us.'

She wiped her cheeks and gave him a watery smile. 'Very well, let's. And a pox on Mr Marcombe and his ilk.'

Jago laughed and hugged her tight. 'That's my girl.'

'For Christ's sake, Caro, what are you going to do next? Honestly, you're nothing but trouble.' Alex was, if possible, even more furious this time. Did the stupid woman not have an iota of sense?

'That's not what you say when we're in bed, darling,' Caroline purred, and stroked his arm, but he shook her off impatiently.

'This isn't the time for your little games, Caro. Not only are we stuck with Nell now, if you won't take her back, but you've gone and landed us with Kayla. What the hell am I supposed to do with her? Don't you think she'll tell the police what she's seen?'

'Well, throw her overboard then. We can take

346

the two of them on the boat with us, and you can let me and Nell off in France. As for her,' Caroline prodded the lifeless form of Kayla with the toe of her boot, 'just dump her somewhere. Wes can find himself another bimbo.'

Alex opened his mouth to speak, but closed it again. There was no point arguing with Caroline, she obviously wasn't sane at the moment. Her eyes were glassy, the pupils dilated. She'd probably taken some drug or other. Perhaps she'd sampled the goods they were smuggling? If so, she wouldn't listen to anything he said. Instead he bent to pick up the sobbing little bundle that was his niece.

'She hit Kayla, Unc-uncle Alex. D-don't let Mummy do that again, p-please. Now she's dead. I don't want her to be dead.' Nell was inconsolable.

'No, of course not, princess. Nobody is going to hit anyone again. And Kayla isn't dead, I promise you. She's just resting. She'll be fine. Shhh now, why don't you sleep for a while too? Then when you wake up, you and Mummy can do something nice together in France.'

'I don't want to go to F-france. I want to go home to Daddy,' the little girl wailed, becoming more and more hysterical by the minute.

'That's just great. Now see what you've done.' Alex glared at Caroline, but she held out her arms and took the child from him.

'Here, let me deal with her. She is my child after all, and I'll make sure she stays quiet. You go and finish off whatever it was you were doing.' She turned to Nell. 'Here, darling, why don't you have some of that nice drink Mummy gave you earlier? You liked that, didn't you? And you must be thirsty after all that crying.'

Alex stomped off, swearing foully under his breath. As he reached the verandah Nell's wails stopped. 'Good. At least the stupid woman can be of some use then,' he muttered. But when this was over he never wanted to see her again.

Wes remained motionless listening to this exchange. Neither Caro nor Alex were bothering to keep their voices down, so they obviously didn't think anyone would find their hiding place.

He ducked down as Alex came storming out of the summer house and set off towards the Hall. It looked as though he was checking whether Kayla had acted alone so at least he had his wits about him. He soon came back, however, and Wes thanked his lucky stars he'd shut the secret entrance carefully. Alex must have thought Wes was still in the house and in the dark as to Kayla's whereabouts. This was to Wes's advantage, as otherwise Alex might be spooked into doing something drastic.

He debated what to do next. On the one hand he had a burning need to rescue his daughter and Kayla, both of whom were obviously being held against their will. He wasn't even sure if Kayla was all right, but he assumed his brother would have protested more strongly if there had been anything seriously wrong with her. Alex may be irresponsible, but he wasn't a murderer. And as for throwing her overboard – no, Wes refused to believe Alex could do any such thing.

On the other hand, if Wes attempted a rescue on his own he might be taken captive himself, and then he would just have made matters worse. There must be others involved in this operation who could turn up at any time, and all he had was a baseball bat, which seemed pretty ridiculous in the circumstances. Could he risk leaving Kayla and Nell with their captors for a while and go for help? Almost against his will he decided this would have to be his course of action. He had no idea how many people were helping Caro and Alex with whatever illegal business they were conducting, but they might be dangerous. Therefore, he needed backup.

Reluctantly leaving his loved ones in the summer house, Wes went back the way he had come even more cautiously than before. He entered the house via a back door, the key for which he always kept hidden in a safe place outside. Back in Kayla's room he made sure the secret panel in the ward-robe was closed in case his brother or ex-wife decided to come back again for some reason. He didn't want them to suspect he was onto them.

Then he called the police, went and got himself dressed warmly and went down to the jetty further along the coast where he kept his own small boat.

It was a sailing boat, but with an outboard motor, and he intended to watch the proceedings from a distance in case his help was needed. He had a feeling he would have a long wait, however, as whatever Alex was up to would most certainly take place in the dark. He sat down and tried not to think of Kayla and Nell.

Consciousness and light beckoned but Kayla resisted. Instinctively she knew that going there meant pain and she held out for as long as possible. A tiny voice called out to her, however, and she couldn't withstand it.

'Mmm. Mmhmm!'

Kayla's eyes fluttered open and she immediately shut them again as a knife-edge of pain sliced through her skull. 'Ouch,' she mumbled. Whatever she was lying on was rocking and nausea rose up in her throat. With her eyes closed she listened for a moment and realised that she could hear waves slapping against a hull, so she must be on a boat. She swallowed resolutely to rid herself of the queasiness, then took a deep breath and tried to open her eyelids again.

This time the pain didn't hit her with quite such force and she managed to bear it for long enough to see who was making a noise next to her. There was a light, although only a very faint one, which showed Kayla that she was on the floor of a small wood-panelled cabin. Without moving her head too much she peered around and caught sight of

Nell. The little girl was leaning against the wall, her hands behind her back, and she had been gagged.

'Oh, sweetheart, what have they done to you?' Kayla struggled into a sitting position, ignoring the thousand hammers that started to beat on an anvil somewhere inside her brain. She shuffled closer to Nell. The child was crying, large tears streaming down her cheeks, her nose was partly blocked with mucus and her face was mottled red. Kayla could see that she needed to take off the gag quickly or Nell might be in danger of suffocating. The girl looked to be on the verge of panic, which could be fatal. Kayla set about calming her down as rapidly as possible, speaking in whispers in case their captors were nearby.

'Please, Nell, don't cry. I'm awake now and I will help you, I promise. But you have to be brave for a little longer. I'm going to get that thing off your mouth, but it's going to take a while because my hands are tied behind my back. Are yours?' Nell nodded. 'Okay, but please, no more crying, understand? There's a good girl. If you stop crying you can help me and together we'll get it off much faster, do you see?' With relief she noticed that Nell's hiccoughing sobs lessened, and the little girl nodded her head again to show she had understood.

'All right, here's what we'll do. I'm going to turn around and I want you to lie down behind me with the back of your head near my hands so I can reach the knot. Do you think you can do that?'

'Uh-hmm.'

'Good. My hands are only tied at the wrist, so I can still use my fingers. Let's try it then, shall we?'

Shuffling on her bottom, Kayla turned around and she heard Nell do the same. She stretched out her fingers as far as possible, and shortly afterwards she could feel Nell's hair.

'Great, Nell. I can almost reach. I've got the top of your head. Can you come a little bit closer, sweetie?'

Nell scooted round some more, and Kayla's fingers finally encountered the gag and the knot that tied it. It took her a few minutes to undo it, as it had been tied quite hard. She murmured encouragement to Nell all the while to stop her from panicking.

'It's getting looser now, I can feel it. Almost there. Almost . . . Yes!' At last the knot slipped open and she pulled the gag off. She turned her head to see Nell taking deep breaths, before bursting into tears again. 'Shhhh, it's okay now,' she soothed. 'You're all right. Just take a few more deep breaths, that's it.'

'Oh Kayla, I c-couldn't breathe,' Nell hiccoughed, leaning her head against Kayla's shoulder. 'I was sleeping and when I woke up that thing was tied on me.'

'That sounds horrid, but it's gone now and if

we can keep quiet, hopefully no one will come back and put it on again. Lucky I woke up, isn't it?'

'Yes. I-I thought you were d-dead, but Uncle Alex promised Mummy wouldn't hit you again.'

'Uncle Alex? Is he here too?' Nell nodded. 'I see.'

Kayla mulled this over for a moment. She wondered if Wes knew his brother was involved in something illegal, but she didn't think so, although he might have had his suspicions judging by the hostility she'd sensed between the brothers.

She turned back to Nell. 'You know, my head is very hard. A little knock on the back isn't going to kill me.' Even if it felt like it at the moment, Kayla added silently to herself. 'I tell you what, if we sit with our backs to each other we should be able to undo the ropes at our wrists too. What do you think? Do you want to have first go?'

'Oh, yes. Let's try.'

Ten minutes later they were both free and Kayla hugged Nell for a while until the child had stopped crying. Then she set her down next to her.

'Listen to me. We have to be clever now, Nell. We don't want anyone to know that we're free, so if you hear someone coming you have to put your hands behind your back again. Then wind the rope around your wrists and pretend it's still tied. Do you see what I mean?'

'Yes, I can do that. I'm good at pretending.' Nell's eyes were huge in her little face, and

Kayla's heart went out to her. *Oh God,* she prayed, *please don't let anything happen to her. She's so small, please protect her.* If only she knew what their captors meant to do with them. Surely Caroline wouldn't harm her own daughter though? It was only Kayla who was in real danger.

'Okay. I'm going to tie the gag around your neck so it looks like you managed to spit it out, then maybe they won't get suspicious.'

Not long afterwards someone came down the steps and switched on an overhead light. Kayla and Nell blinked and huddled together, their hands behind their backs.

'So you're awake finally. Well, thank God for that at least.' It was Alex, wearing an almost identical scowl to that of his big brother. 'I thought for a while the stupid woman had killed you.'

'Not yet, although she was probably hoping she had.' Kayla glared at him defiantly. 'But you almost killed your niece here. Honestly, gagging a child is a dangerous thing to do. She nearly choked to death, you know.'

'Gagging? I didn't gag her.'

'Well someone did. I managed to get it off her just in time. See, there it is.' Kayla nodded at the bright pink scarf around Nell's neck.

Alex clenched his fists and looked, if possible, even more furious. 'I swear to God, I'm going to wring her neck. Of all the idiotic, hare-brained . . .' Words failed him.

Nell began to cry again. 'No, Uncle Alex. P-please don't kill Kayla. I-I love her.'

'What? Oh no, princess, I'm not going to hurt Kayla. I was talking about someone else and it was just a figure of speech. I promise.'

The boat shuddered as if it was coming to a halt, and soon after it bumped into something. Kayla held her breath, wondering whether they had arrived at their destination, but Alex sat down on his haunches in front of his niece and said, 'Are you all right there for a little while longer? You have to stay down here while I finish some business and then I promise I'll take you back home.'

Nell nodded. 'And Kayla too?'

Alex stood up and glanced at Kayla, indecision clearly written on his face. 'Of course, princess,' he finally said. 'I'll do what I can.' He looked tired and weary and Kayla almost felt sorry for him. Almost, but not quite. This was partly his fault and he was obviously up to no good.

He turned to climb back up on deck and disappeared through the hatch. All was quiet, and there was no sound other than the waves swishing gently round the hull. Kayla could still feel the rocking motion, but tried to ignore it. She didn't want to be sick on top of everything else. She wondered how far out to sea they were and whether it would be possible to swim to safety, but decided it would be too risky with Nell in tow.

She was just wondering what else she could do when suddenly a commotion broke out on deck.

They heard someone say something through a loudspeaker, then voices shouting and footsteps running in all directions. The shrill voice of a woman – Caroline? – mixed with the deeper tones of several men. What was happening? Had someone come to rescue them? A faint hope stirred inside Kayla, but then she realised whoever it was might not know they were on board. She was pretty sure they had stopped the boat for some other reason.

Kayla had just decided to make their presence known when someone came hurtling down the steps. This time it was Caroline and she rushed over and grabbed up Nell in a single fluid motion. Before Kayla had time to even blink, the woman was halfway up the steps again, carrying the struggling, screaming child. Kayla sat frozen to the spot and Caroline disappeared through the hatch.

'Shit.' What was the crazy woman up to now? Kayla had to find out. Her recalcitrant legs finally obeyed her and she staggered to her feet. Cautiously she climbed the steps and peered out onto the deck, where a strange scene was being played out in the floodlight from two police or coastguard boats. Kayla shielded her eyes with one hand to see better.

'I know my ex-husband is behind this,' shrieked Caroline, holding on to Nell with the strength born of desperation. 'You can tell him if he doesn't call you off, I'll drop his precious daughter into the sea and he'll never see her again.'

'Caroline, for Christ's sake, what's got into you?'

Alex came rushing along the deck, an even deeper frown settled on his features.

'Don't come any closer, Alex, or I'll kill you.' Caroline pulled out a knife from somewhere and brandished it in front of her. Nell screamed, then went still. Kayla thought the poor child must be in a state of shock from the recent events. She felt decidedly shaky herself, so God only knew how this would affect a seven-year-old.

Alex stared at the knife in disbelief. It was long and sharp, and quite lethal. 'Where the hell did you get that?' He shook his head. 'Caro, be reasonable,' he tried, speaking in a cajoling voice. 'Come on, darling, don't do anything silly now. This is your daughter we're talking about. You know you'll regret it.'

'The only thing I regret is not hurting Wes when I had the chance. I could have killed him in his sleep so many times, or set his precious house alight, but I didn't. I was a fool,' Caroline hissed. 'Wes!' she hollered. 'Are you out there?'

'Yes, Caroline, I'm here,' came a voice from across the water, just out of range of the lights.

'Hah! I knew it. You couldn't resist gloating, could you? Well, this time I'll have the final word. That damned judge can't help you now.' She inched towards the railing and Kayla readied herself for a sprint across the deck. If the madwoman was going to throw her own daughter overboard, Kayla would dive in after her. She had to save Wes's child. She just had to. Unless

Wes got to her first – she was sure he'd dive in as well.

For a long while everyone just stared at each other, weighing up their options. It was a stand-off and no one could win without Nell getting hurt in the process. Kayla could see that Caroline was off her head on some substance or other. She had that wild look in her eyes that showed she was high as a kite and not in possession of her usual faculties. This made her doubly dangerous, of course, and totally unpredictable.

But she couldn't look everywhere at once.

Kayla saw Alex glance in the direction from which his brother's voice had come and then further along the railing. When she followed his gaze, she noticed a shadowy figure pulling himself up onto the deck. *Wes, thank goodness!* Alex made a sudden move, presumably in order to divert Caroline and stop her looking towards Wes. Then he stopped, keeping a wary eye on the sharp knife in Caroline's hand. He took another look around and must have noticed Kayla before she could duck down, but he didn't say anything. Instead he nodded ever so slightly in Caroline's direction and Kayla nodded back. He was going to try something and she'd be ready to help. As was Wes, who had moved to crouch behind a large pile of boxes that were stacked on deck.

'Are you going to call them off, Wes?' Caroline was shouting into the darkness, her voice shaking now.

There was no reply. Obviously he couldn't answer or he'd give his position away. Kayla wondered if Caroline would suspect something, but apparently not as her next words proved.

'Wes? Oh, I get it. You're sulking now.' With a hysterical laugh Caroline went closer to the railing anyway. Kayla thought for a horrible moment that Nell's mother was going to throw her terrified child into the water no matter what happened, and she had to stifle a cry of anguish.

With perfect timing, Alex and Wes chose that moment to make their move. They rushed forward, one from either side.

'Caro!' they both called out. She swivelled towards Wes first and Alex took the chance to snatch his niece from Caroline's death-grip, then jumped to the side when Caroline realised what he was doing and slashed at him with the knife. It caught him on the upper arm, but he only let out a grunt of pain and continued towards the railing, still holding Nell. With the child in his arms, he jumped into the water.

Kayla saw him surface a few yards away and, with Nell in tow, he swam into the darkness. She registered the fact that he was swimming towards the coastguard and breathed a sigh of relief. Nell would be safe.

Meanwhile, Caroline was trying to stick the knife into Wes, who unfortunately hadn't been able to grab hold of her. The woman was screeching at the top of her voice the foulest of curses, railing against Wes in particular and fate in general. The two of them jumped around in a macabre dance, with Wes keeping just out of range as the knife, gleaming in the light, came down again and again. There seemed to be no way he could get hold of her without being hurt and Caroline was working herself into a murderous frenzy. She was like a one-woman dervish, at one with the lethal weapon in her hand. Kayla felt rage boiling up inside her against this woman who seemed about to seriously hurt the man Kayla loved. It was an anger so pure, so hot, so overwhelming, she had never experienced anything like it. There was only one way to assuage it and she acted without thought.

She surged out of the hatch and ran towards Caroline, throwing herself at the other woman from behind and hitting her with her fists. 'Shut up! For God's sake, shut up.'

'Kayla, no!' She vaguely registered Wes's voice, but she was too furious to stop now. She forgot about the knife, forgot about the fact that Caroline was much bigger than herself, and more importantly, forgot they were on a boat. The deck rolled suddenly and the three of them lurched sideways. Kayla lost her footing and grabbed at Caroline to stop from falling, but it was too late.

They all went sprawling onto the deck and Kayla quickly rolled out of reach, looking to see if Wes was hurt. He too had moved out of the way, but in the event, it proved unnecessary. Caroline only made a strange gurgling sound and then she went limp. Her eyes stared up into the sky, but she didn't blink. Kayla looked down and saw the red stain spreading rapidly across the shiny white deck. Caroline had fallen onto her knife.

'Oh my God. What have I done?' Numb with shock, Kayla sat stock still and just stared at the expression of surprise on Caroline's face. She was incapable of moving. Once more the Gypsy's words echoed round her brain. *'I see water and pain, a red stain spreading over white . . .'* She had been right. Kayla tried to remember the rest of what the woman had said, but the effort was beyond her.

'Kayla? Are you okay?' Wes crawled over to put a hand on her shoulder, shaking it slightly. She managed to nod, but closed her eyes. She couldn't bear to look at him. He must be so angry at her for not listening to him. And now she'd caused Caroline's death . . .

'Kayla, I've got to go and see to Nell, but I'll be back, all right? Just stay here.'

She nodded again and then he was gone. Soon after there were voices, and hands helping her to her feet, but she was oblivious to them. Someone draped a blanket over her shoulders. And then she started to cry. Huge, hiccoughing sobs racked her body, and she couldn't control them.

'There, there, miss, it's over now. Everything's going to be all right. The little girl will be fine and you too. There now.' The kind voice went on and on, but Kayla paid no attention. How could everything possibly be fine? After what Caroline had done, Wes would definitely never want to marry again. And Nell would hate Kayla for causing her mother's death. Kayla might even be put on trial for manslaughter. There was no future for her here now. None at all.

CHAPTER 27

'Father? Father, please don't leave me yet.'
Jago cracked open first one eyelid and then the other, his vision swimming for a moment before he was able to focus on the young man sitting on a chair next to his bed. 'Water,' he croaked, his voice rasping. It was no wonder, he thought, since it felt as though his throat had been scored by nails, leaving it burning and sore.

'Here, let me help you.'
Jago's head was lifted and a cup held to his lips. He drank half the contents, the liquid blessedly cool even though it hurt to swallow. He blinked and looked at Wesley again.

'You shouldn't be in here. Might be catching,' he said.

Wesley shook his head. 'No, the physician said you brought this on yourself by going out in the boat on such a freezing night. What were you thinking? You should have left it to others. Now you have bronchitis or maybe even congestion of the lungs.'

Wesley knew what Jago and the others did, but had learned to turn a blind eye ever since Jago

363

had pointed out how his clandestine outings helped the poorer members of the community. The boy had grown up a caring landowner, but even his best efforts weren't always enough. The smuggling was still a necessary evil.

'I'm not too old yet,' Jago protested. 'They needed me. Oversee things.'

'You were already ill, Aunt Sophie told me.' Wesley stood up abruptly and started pacing by the bed. 'I thought you were dying last night.'

Jago heard the anguish in his son's voice and it sent a warm glow through him to know the boy cared. He and Sophie had two other sons now, but this one was special, even though he'd never openly show any preference. He frowned as something niggled at the back of his mind, then it came to him and he turned startled eyes on Wesley.

'What did you call me before?'

Wesley stopped and flung himself onto the chair again. 'Father,' he said, sending Jago a challenging look. 'I called you Father.' When Jago didn't reply, he added defiantly, 'Well, I'm not blind, you know. I do own a mirror.'

Jago had to smile at that, but soon grew serious again. 'I told you your grandfather was Sir Philip Marcombe, the man who sired me,' he said, but Wesley glared at him.

'I've seen his portrait and all the others. No one in the family has ever been this dark. Only you. I thought perhaps if you were dying, you'd admit the truth.'

Jago closed his eyes, drawing in a deep breath. 'Stop telling me I'm dying because I'm not.' He opened his eyes and looked at Wesley. 'And I would gladly admit the truth, so long as it stays between you and me.'

'Why the secrecy? Are you ashamed of me? You're a bastard yourself, why should it matter to you?' Now that he'd been reassured Jago wasn't in imminent danger of dying, Wesley seemed to feel free to give vent to his anger.

'Come now, boy, haven't I taught you to use your brain? Think about it. What would have happened if I'd told the world? You'd have lost Marcombe Hall to that toad Henry and you'd have been nothing but the son of an innkeeper.'

'I wouldn't have cared. I'd never have known, would I?' Wesley was still scowling.

'Ah, but you're forgetting one thing. Your mother would have been branded a whore, albeit she wasn't around to hear it. Would you have wanted that?' Wesley looked like he was about to say something he might regret and Jago held up a hand. 'No, she didn't deserve it. And I'll tell you why.'

Despite the burning in his throat he told Wesley the truth about his mother and the husband who had ill-treated her. The boy was nearly eighteen, old enough to know about the murder, even though Jago could see it shocked him. When he'd finished his tale, he lay back against the pillows and fought for breath.

'Now do you see? I couldn't let my brother win, even in death. If I'd acknowledged you, it would have been a victory of sorts for John.' He put a hand on Wesley's arm. 'But you must never think for a moment that I'd have been ashamed to own you as my son. And if it had ever been necessary, I would have done it.'

Wesley nodded and put his own hand over Jago's, gripping it tightly. 'I understand, Father. Thank you for telling me.'

'I always intended to, but I thought to wait. I see now I was wrong.'

'No, you're almost always right.' Wesley smiled. 'You'd just better be right about recovering too, because I'm not letting you leave me yet, do you hear?'

'Never fear, son. I'll be with you for a while yet.'

The lighting on the ward was subdued when Kayla woke up and she gathered it must be late at night. Her head felt woolly now, rather than painful. They must have given her a sleeping pill or strong painkillers. Perhaps it had been for the best. The worst of the shock had worn off and she could think rationally again. She knew that technically she wasn't responsible for Caroline's death, the woman had brought it on herself and it had been an accident, but she still felt terrible about the whole event. She should have left it to the professionals, or Wes, who would have known how to deal with Caroline. Instead, she had let her anger rule and her attack had been the catalyst for disaster. Would Nell ever forgive her for causing her mother's death?

She sighed and turned her head on the pillow. Her gaze encountered a pair of very blue eyes and for a moment her heart gave a leap, but then she saw that it wasn't Wes or Jago. It was Alex.

'Shhh,' he whispered. 'There's someone keeping guard outside.'

'What? Why?' For a split second she wondered if she would be charged with manslaughter after all, but Alex soon put her right.

He managed a small smile. 'I'm a prisoner, remember? They fished me and Nell out of the water, but because of the knife wound they had to bring me here before taking me into custody. I guess these were the only two beds available tonight, or they would never have put me next to you, I'm sure.'

'What were you doing, Alex? Was it drugs? Smuggling?'

'Yes.' He sighed and stared at the ceiling. 'I don't know how I could have been so stupid, but someone persuaded me it would be easy money. A friend of Caro's, who made it all seem like a doddle. She'd helped him before and they'd never got caught. They told me all I had to do was go out with my yacht, rendezvous with another boat and give them the stuff which was delivered to us here earlier in the week. Then everything else would be taken care of and I would get a cut. It seemed a piece of cake. And I desperately needed to pay off some debts. Caro and I had been living way beyond our means for quite some time.'

'Well, you probably would have pulled it off if it hadn't been for Wes. He must have come after me through the secret entrance and heard you and Caroline.'

'Secret entrance? So that's how she got in and out. I did wonder . . .'

'You didn't know about it?'

'No, I never went with her at night. I knew she sometimes went to the Hall, but I thought she just stood outside or something. She wasn't always . . . rational.'

'You mean she was off her head?'

He gave her a rueful smile. 'Yes, most of the time and it was getting worse. I think she'd gone onto the serious drugs rather than just antidepressants or whatever, but I only did a bit of cocaine myself.' He shuddered. 'No more though. Never again.' He shook his head. 'So she found the secret entrance, huh? I'll be damned. Wes and I looked for that when we were kids. Never found it.'

'It's at the back of the wardrobe in my room, or what used to be Caroline's room.'

'That explains it. I thought she still had a key to the house. In fact, she told me she did.' He rubbed his face as if it was all too much to take in.

'Lucky for me that Wes went for help instead of trying to rescue us on his own as I did.' Kayla gave him a considering look. 'Are you angry with

Wes for calling the police or coastguard or whatever they were?'

'Hell, no! I would've done the same thing. He
was only thinking of Nell and you, I'm sure. He
usually doesn't care less what I'm up to. My
biggest mistake was to get involved with Caro. I
just wanted to get back at Wes somehow, thought
it would annoy him, and she could be quite . . .
uhm, tantalising when she wanted to be. Guess I
was flattered she wanted me rather than my
brother. Hah! What a moron. I'm afraid she had
me under her spell for a while, and I didn't see
her bad traits until it was too late.'

'You'd never hurt Nell, would you?'

'No way! I love her so much myself, it never
occurred to me her own mother could ill-treat her.
I never quite believed Wes's stories, but I should
have listened to him.'

'Yes, it was strange. I wonder why she was like
that?'

'Jealousy, pure and simple. Caro couldn't stand
not to be the centre of attention. She'd been
Wes's world, but when Nell came along she had
to share his affections. Caro didn't do sharing.
Never had – she was a pampered only daughter
and all that. And, of course, drugs played a big
part. She was definitely on something tonight, I
saw it in her eyes. Nell's better off with Wes, I'm
sure of that.' He turned to her again. 'I would
have taken you both back, you know. Especially
after that gagging business. I'd never have sailed

to France or done anything else Caro wanted. Do you believe me?'

'Yes.' Kayla closed her eyes. She felt completely drained of energy. 'So what will happen to you now?'

'Oh, I'll go to prison, I expect. But it's what I deserve, so I'm not complaining.'

Kayla smiled. 'That's an unusual attitude. Most criminals wouldn't agree with you.'

'No, I suppose not. I think I've just finally grown up and now I'm going to take my punishment and go on from there. You can be damned sure I'll never do anything this stupid again.'

'I'm glad to hear it. Let's get some sleep now, Alex. My head is starting to hurt again. I promise to come and visit you if I can.'

'Thanks. Sleep well, then.'

When Kayla woke the following morning Alex was gone and so was the guard. She was glad they'd had their nightly conversation though. It made her see him in a whole new light. And despite everything, she had a feeling he'd be all right now, no matter what sentence he had to serve first.

She asked the doctor how Nell was doing, and was assured the little girl would be fine. 'She's had a shock, to be sure, but children are remarkably resilient, you know. Her father is with her now.'

'Right. I'd better not disturb them then.'

She waited all morning, but Wes didn't come

to see her and her spirits plummeted ever further. Maybe he couldn't bear to be near her after what had happened. The thought depressed her no end. After a final check-up she was discharged in the afternoon and took a taxi back to Marcombe Hall. A distraught Annie was waiting for her, and it took quite a while to calm the woman down and explain everything that had happened.

'Oh, goodness, to think it would come to this,' Annie wailed. 'I always knew there was rivalry between the brothers, but not to this extent. And that Caroline! Oh, poor, poor little Nell . . .'

In the end Kayla pleaded a headache and went to her room, unable to cope with any more wailing, and she was still there in the early evening when Wes returned from the hospital. He knocked on her door and tiptoed in when she called, 'Come in.'

'Kayla. How are you?' He sat down on the side of her bed. She thought he looked pale and drawn, which was of course natural in the circumstances. Kayla wanted to pull him close and comfort him, but held back. She was still unsure what he thought of her part in the drama.

'I'm fine thanks. Just a headache, but the doctor said it would probably hurt for a few days and then disappear.' She looked away. 'Is Nell okay?'

'Yes, thank God. She's still a bit shocked, but they keep her sedated most of the time and whenever she wakes up she seems better each time.' He ran a hand through his hair in a tired gesture.

'I'm glad. I'm sorry to have caused her pain, but it was an accident, I swear.'

'Oh, it wasn't your fault. I'm sure Nell will understand. It will just take time for her to come to terms with all this. And me. To think that Alex, my own brother . . . He should have come to me for help. I can't believe he didn't. Although to be fair, I did tell him I'd bailed him out for the last time.'

Kayla desperately wanted him to take her in his arms and hold her, but he sat unmoving and gazed into space. The silence stretched between them.

'Maybe you'd better get some sleep,' she finally suggested, and he nodded and stood up as if in a trance.

'Yes, I have to admit I'm a bit tired. We'll talk more later.' And without a backward glance he left the room. Not through their private connecting door, but through the one which led to the corridor. Kayla took this to mean that their intimacy was at an end, and as soon as the door closed behind him she rolled into a tight ball of misery and let the tears flow. How long she cried for she had no idea.

Wes stumbled towards his own room, too weary to be able to think straight. He'd been awake all night and all day, keeping watch by his daughter's bedside until he knew for sure she was going to be all right, and it had taken its toll on him. He was completely drained, both physically and mentally.

As he undressed and fell onto his bed there was a thought nagging at the back of his mind, something to do with Kayla. But he was too tired to reason it out at the moment, too tired to do anything except sink into blessed oblivion.

When at last he woke up the following day, Kayla was gone, together with all her belongings. He remembered then what it was that had been bothering him. He should have stayed with Kayla, slept in her bed or brought her to his room, but he was so used to going to his own room alone that in his befuddled state it hadn't occurred to him until afterwards. And now, it seemed, everything was too late.

'Where did Kayla go?' he asked a silently weeping Annie, who was busy in the kitchen as usual, although not working at her normal speed.

'To London. Said she didn't want to intrude at this sad time.' Annie turned anguished eyes towards him. 'I tried to make her stay, honest I did, but she was determined. Said it was best she left, that Nell would hate her for causing her mother's death, and . . . oh, I don't know what else. There was no reasoning with her.'

'I see.' Clenching his teeth tightly together, Wes made his way back to his office. First things first. The most important thing was to see to his daughter, then he would let himself think about Kayla.

CHAPTER 28

The Gypsy camp was set up in a small clearing next to a stream, the wagons drawn into a semi-circle for protection. Approaching it on horseback, Jago drew a sigh of relief. It had taken him weeks to track them down and he was weary beyond words. The light from several campfires beckoned, and the soft strains of music could be heard floating through the still night air.

He hadn't come for the entertainment, however, and upon his arrival made straight for the oldest caravan without speaking to anyone. Painted in bright colours and decorated with exquisite fretwork, he knew that despite its age it was nevertheless the best one of them all. And it housed the woman he had come to see.

She was waiting for him on the tiny back porch, sitting on the step gazing into the distance as if she had all the time in the world. When he came closer, she looked up briefly and smiled.

'Hello, boy, I've been expecting you.'

He bent to kiss her leathery cheek, criss-crossed with wrinkles, but still soft and smooth. 'Hello,

Granny Tess,' he replied calmly, used to her uncanny ability to foretell events. 'And do you also know why I have come?' He tethered his tired horse to a nearby bush.

'Not this time, young 'un, but I expect you'll tell me soon enough. Come and have a bite to eat first, you must be famished.'

He smiled at being called 'boy' and 'young', since he was definitely getting old now, but then his gran was so ancient herself, perhaps he seemed a mere youngster to her. He nodded and followed her over to a small open fire not far from her wagon, where he sank down onto the dry ground next to her. The plate of food she handed him was devoured quickly, then he gave it back to her with a smile and a thank you. They sat in amicable silence for a while and he studied her out of the corner of his eyes. Granny Tess was the closest thing he'd ever had to a mother since she had raised him after his own mother died birthing him, and he loved her. Amazingly wise, she had inherited more than her fair share of mystical gifts from her ancestors, and he had never made the mistake of underestimating her abilities. The matter he needed assistance with this time, however, was different. He tried to find the right words, but found it difficult.

'I need your help, Granny Tess,' he finally said. She nodded as if this was a foregone conclusion, and he continued. 'It concerns the next life, not this one. Do your powers reach that far?'

'That depends, boy.' She frowned, putting him in mind of a crinkled old prune. 'I can't wake the dead, if that's what you're after, although I might be able to communicate with one or two of them. Nor can I change someone's fate once they are set on their course, only give warning beforehand. What is it you want me to do?'

He hesitated for a moment. Perhaps he was asking the impossible, but it was worth a try. 'There is someone with whom I wish to be reunited one day, Granny Tess. A woman. She loved me in return, but she's long gone now. Is there any way . . .?'

The old Gypsy woman turned his face gently towards the fire and held it still while she peered deep into his eyes. For a long time they sat like that, motionless, while she probed his mind. He didn't flinch, nor even blink, he was used to her ways and accepted them completely. He even tried to help her by concentrating on her penetrating gaze, as she had taught him when he was a child. Finally, she released him and sighed deeply.

'You have acted unwisely, but you were guided by love and therefore there is hope. You did right, Jago, to come to me. I think I can help you, but it won't be easy and there will be certain conditions attached. Are you willing to be patient?'

'I would wait for all eternity, if necessary.'

She gave a short cackle of laughter. 'Well, it may not be quite as long as that, but you're not far off. It's how it will seem to you. You're sure this is what you want?'

'Yes.' He'd never been more sure of anything in his life, except his love for Eliza. Sophie was gone too now, and Wesley and his half-brothers were all grown men, who no longer needed him. He knew his life was almost at an end and this was all he had left to do.

Granny Tess smiled at him. 'Very well then, let us begin . . .'

'So you're back at last, but you don't look very happy. Do I assume you have bad news for me?'

'No, Jago. No, as a matter of fact I have excellent news for you. I found her, your Eliza. She was in Wes's room all the time, would you believe it? It was the only place I never thought to look.'

'Wonderful! And it was as I said? Did you see the proof?'

'The Shakespeare sonnet you mean? Yes, I saw it.'

'Excellent. So now you can sell me to Eliza's owner at enormous profit and everyone will be happy. Why the long face?'

Kayla sighed. 'It's a long story, Jago, but don't worry, I'll make sure you're reunited with Eliza. Only, I don't want any payment. In fact, I want to forget you ever existed.'

'I don't understand.'

'Listen, and I'll tell you the whole sorry tale.'

⋆　⋆　⋆

A week later Annie came rushing into Wes's office.

'There's an enormous parcel arrived for you. You'd best come and see this for yourself.'

'A parcel? I haven't ordered anything.' Puzzled, Wes followed her into the hall.

'Took two big men to carry it in, so it did,' Annie told him.

'I can see why, but what is it?'

Wes went in search of a crowbar since the so-called parcel wasn't wrapped in paper, but boxed in wood. It had 'Fragile' and 'Handle With Care' stamped all over it, so it took him ages to carefully open it. When he finally managed to extricate it from all the bubble wrap inside, Wes whistled softly. He was staring at a huge portrait of a striking man who looked very familiar. He tore open the envelope that was taped to the frame and read the accompanying letter.

Dear Wes,
Please accept this painting as a gift to thank you for my time in Devon, which I enjoyed immensely. The man in the portrait is, I believe, your five times great-grandfather, Jago Kerswell. He had an illicit affair with your ancestor's wife, Eliza, whose portrait you already own. (She's the one in your bedroom.) Since they were deeply in love, I think they deserve to be together now, as they never could

be in real life. Don't ask me how I know this, but it's the truth, and I hope you're not offended to learn that your lineage is not quite as perfect as the first Sir John would have liked everyone to believe. I enclose a family tree and some other information on your ancestors which you might find interesting. Please, hang the two portraits side by side – that is all I ask.

Give my love to Nell, I miss her terribly. Tell her again how sorry I am for what happened. I hope she can forgive me in time.

Best wishes,
Kayla

Wes studied the portrait of his ancestor and smiled for the first time in days. The resemblance between them was there for anyone to see, and even more so to Alex. He didn't doubt the truth of Kayla's claim. He had often looked at the portraits upstairs in the gallery, wondering why they all suddenly became dark and swarthy after a certain date, where before they had all looked pale and blond. He had attributed it to some dark-haired lady, but now he knew the real reason.

'Why you old devil. So it was all your fault, huh?' He stared at Jago. 'Well, thank you. Now I can finally see the light at the end of the tunnel.'

As he turned to go in search of Nell, he thought for a fleeting moment that he saw an answering grin on Jago's face, but when he stopped to look again the man was as serious as before. It had only been an illusion, of course. Whistling, he set off down the hall.

CHAPTER 29

Kayla smoothed out an imaginary crease in her formal skirt and made sure the buttons of the matching jacket were all done up properly. When she couldn't procrastinate any longer, she lifted her hand to ring the bell of Marcombe Hall. She heard it pealing somewhere in the nether regions of the house and suppressed a shiver of apprehension. She probably shouldn't have come.

But how could she have stayed away?

She glanced a final time at the gilt-edged card in her hand and swallowed down her anxiety. The message was clear and definitely entitled her to be here.

Miss Michaela Sinclair
You are hereby invited to
A RECEPTION WITH DRINKS AND CANAPÉS
In honour of the official unveiling of a new portrait by Thomas Gainsborough, a recent addition to the Marcombe Hall collection.
July 15th at 3.00 p.m., First Floor Gallery,

Marcombe Hall
RSVP

Kayla was so pleased for Jago as this must mean his portrait had finally been hung next to Eliza's. She just had to see him there, one last time, before she closed this chapter of her life. Then she could move on. Or at least, she hoped so.

The door opened and a young man in smart livery bowed to her and took the invitation card she proffered. She'd never met him before and assumed he must have been hired for the occasion. It was obviously going to be a big do, perhaps even with the local mayor present or some other dignitaries. The flutter of nerves in her stomach subsided a little. She could hide in a crowd. Good.

'Please follow me,' the young man said, and led the way up the staircase. He pointed towards the long gallery. 'The reception is in there, madam.'

'Thank you.'

Kayla heard the soft strains of classical music and was impressed. It would seem Wes had pulled out all the stops for the occasion, even going so far as to hire musicians. There would probably be caterers and formal waiters too, if the young man in the hall was anything to go by. She was glad he was going to so much trouble on Jago's behalf. If he was still listening, the old reprobate should be pleased to be causing such a stir.

When she entered the long gallery, however, she came to a halt. She could still hear music playing from somewhere, but there were no musicians in the room. Nor were there any waiting staff, only a couple of tables covered with white cloths and with champagne in buckets, crystal glasses and trays of canapés set out. And worst of all, there wasn't a soul in there apart from her.

Kayla did a three sixty degree turn. No one at all.

Her eyes were drawn to the two huge portraits that now hung side by side on one wall. 'Hello,' she whispered, but felt silly talking to a painting here. Jago's enigmatic smile was in place and she thought she saw his mouth twitch, but he didn't reply. She hadn't expected him to. Not in public. Although there was no public right now, which was very odd.

'Where is everyone?'

Again, no reply, and Kayla was beginning to feel uncomfortable. Surely she couldn't be the first guest to arrive? She checked her watch. It was ten past three – she'd arrived fashionably late on purpose, in order to blend in with the crowd.

She frowned. What the hell was going on?

Just then someone entered from a side door and walked towards her. 'Kayla. You came.'

The familiar voice set Kayla's heart thumping so hard she could barely reply. Wes. She'd missed him. Oh, how she'd missed him and seeing him now, at last, was making her feel breathless. Just the sight of him melted her insides and the composure she'd been so sure she'd be able to hang onto flew out the window. *Damn.*

'Uhm, yes. Yes, of course I came. I wanted to see Jago and Eliza . . . I mean, hanging together.' The swirling in her stomach was making her incoherent so she stopped talking and just watched Wes.

Why hadn't he called her? Texted? Or something. She hadn't heard a word for two whole weeks, apart from a short note thanking her for the painting and saying he'd 'be in touch shortly'. Then the formal invite.

He came to a stop in front of her and shoved his hands into his trouser pockets as if he wasn't quite sure what to do with them. He looked amazing in a charcoal grey suit – designer if she wasn't mistaken – and matching shirt and tie. The stubble on the lower half of his face – also designer? – made Kayla want to reach out and touch him, but she put her hands behind her back to resist the temptation. His eyes were a vibrant blue, as always, but with a slightly guarded expression. She swallowed hard and looked away. So he was dressed for the occasion. But what occasion? They were still the only people here.

'You look lovely,' he said. 'Formal clothes suit you.'

'Thank you, but I'm beginning to wonder if I should have bothered. What's going on, Wes? Is this some kind of joke?'

He shook his head. 'No, not a joke. It seemed

the only way to get you to come back though. You appeared determined to stay in London. You didn't so much as call to see how Nell was, but I figured you might come and check on your painting.' He frowned slightly.

'Me? But I was waiting for you to call,' Kayla blurted out. 'I thought you'd let me know if she could bear to see me. And I didn't want to intrude. She'd had a shock after all and these things can take time.'

'Really?' Wes's expression cleared and he smiled at last. 'Thank God for that.'

'What do you mean? I caused Caro's death. I deprived Nell of a mother. Have you told her? I should have listened to you, but I—'

Wes held up a hand to stop her torrent of words. 'None of it was your fault. I thought I made that clear? Nell doesn't blame you and neither do I. Caro brought it on herself. Nell is a little too young to understand right now, but when she's older I will explain about the drugs and everything. At the moment she's absolutely fine and waiting to see you. If that's what you want too?'

'Of course I do. I've missed her.' She didn't add, 'and you'.

Wes turned and called out, 'Nell! It's okay, you can come out now.'

The little girl came rushing out of door at the far end of the gallery and ran towards them. She threw her arms round Kayla's legs until Kayla hunkered down to hug her properly.

'Kayla, Kayla, I've missed you so much! Why didn't you say you were leaving?'

Kayla blinked to stop from crying. 'I've missed you too, sweetheart, and, er, I was called away suddenly. There was something I had to do.' She looked up at the little girl's father, who nodded as if he approved of this white lie.

'Have you finished doing that now then?' Nell wanted to know. 'So you can stay here?'

'Er, well . . .' Kayla was floundering, not sure what to say next, but Wes came to her rescue.

'Let Kayla stand up, Nell. Remember what I told you?'

Nell's eyes twinkled with mischief and she giggled. 'Yes, Daddy.'

'Okay then, are you ready?' Wes looked at his daughter and held out one hand to her. 'On the count of three, right?'

Nell nodded. 'One, two, *three*.'

The two of them dropped down on one knee in front of Kayla and said, in unison, *'Please will you marry us? We love you!'*

Wes withdrew his other hand from his trouser pocket and held out an old-fashioned jeweller's box. Inside, nestled on white velvet, was an exquisite antique ring, made up of a thick band of gold set with a dark purple amethyst surrounded by diamonds in the shape of two hearts. It was the most beautiful thing Kayla had ever seen and she gasped.

She stared into Wes's eyes and saw the love

shining in their blue depths. It made her want to cry with happiness, but she realised that he – and Nell – were still waiting for an answer. 'Yes, please,' she whispered, her voice a mere thread because her throat was so clogged with emotion. 'If you're both sure?'

Wes stood up. 'We've never been more sure of anything, isn't that right, Nell?'

Nell was by now dancing around them, jumping from one foot to the other with excitement. 'Mm-hmm, that's right, Daddy. Come on, do the ring thing like they do in Disney movies.'

Wes laughed and took the ring out of its box, slipping it onto the fourth finger of Kayla's left hand. It was a snug fit, as if it had always belonged there.

'It's perfect,' she whispered. 'Thank you so much.'

'Are *you* absolutely sure?' he asked. 'You can see what you're letting yourself in for.' He nodded in Nell's direction. 'It won't exactly be a bed of roses.'

Kayla smiled mistily. 'I wouldn't miss it for the world,' she told him. 'I love you. Both of you,' she amended and laughed at Nell's antics.

'I, or should I say we, love you too.' He kissed her as if he would never let her go, but his daughter had other ideas. She tugged at his jacket.

'Now that's sorted, can we eat? I'm hungry. Please, Daddy? Please? You promised.'

Wes reluctantly stopped kissing Kayla. 'There's

no peace for the wicked,' he sighed, 'as I'm sure my ancestor Jago found out.'

Kayla laughed. 'Oh, believe you me, he may have been wicked, but he is at peace now. Truly at peace.'

She glanced over Wes's shoulder, up at the two portraits, and saw Jago's smile broaden in agreement. He winked at her and nodded towards Eliza. When Kayla looked at her she saw the woman's lips move and a faint whisper reached her. 'Thank you, we'll be eternally grateful.'

'What was that? Did you say something?' Wes had been concentrating on trying to calm Nell down and turned to look at Kayla.

'Just that I can't believe I can be this lucky.'

He kissed her again and pulled her close. 'I'm the lucky one and I'm not letting you go, ever. We'll be together for all eternity.'

Just like Eliza and Jago, at last.